Totally Bound Publishing books by Ellen Mint

Happily Ever Austen
Pride and Pancakes
Rash and Rationality
Madeline's Park

Coven of Desire
Retail Hell
Claw
Snow Print
Fang
Whisper
Badge
Wings
Scales
Thorns

Collections
Some Like it Haunted: Ink
My Bloody Valentine: Love's Curse

Coven of Desire

THORNS

ELLEN MINT

Thorns
ISBN # 978-1-80250-554-2
©Copyright Ellen Mint 2023
Cover Art by Kelly Martin ©Copyright August 2023
Interior text design by Claire Siemaszkiewicz
Totally Bound Publishing

Published in 2023 by Totally Bound Publishing, United Kingdom.

THORNS

Dedication

Yes, it is green.

Chapter One

Stone

None of this is right.

No matter how hard I stared at the data, none of it made sense. Conquest arriving here was an ill omen, but unsurprising. He'd been believed to have resumed his activities to a world-encompassing crescendo thirty years prior. What had me snapping pencils at my desk were his known accomplices. He'd only worked with humans before. Now there were demons, werewolves and sins approaching his marked residences at all hours.

Why?

"You're gonna give yourself eye cancer."

I didn't jerk at Detective River's booming shout.

"That's a myth," I said, sitting back in the office's ergonomic chair and closing my pile of notes.

River picked up one of my pens and gnawed on the end. "Maybe that's just what they want you to think."

We'd worked together for nearly ten years, and I had yet to learn his first name. It was easier that way. Besides, I didn't need a name to know the make of a man. He was infuriating with his conspiracy theories, but solid in the field. I could deal with a laugh about the earth being pomegranate shaped as long as he had my back.

"Wha' ya working on?" he asked, his drawl slipping out. Those years of training to suppress any hint of our individual history had never seemed to take with him. "Conquest? Really?"

"He is a being of unimaginable power. I am keeping tabs," I said, locking down my computer to the best of my ability while being aware of the IT djinn that watched over everything.

"And Zimmerman told you to cut it out."

Even if other agents were trailing Mr. White, there was no reason not to have all hands on deck. Besides, the distraction kept me too busy to deal with other matters. As I gathered up the broken pencil bits, I noticed the middle folder in my stack. In the day's shuffling, a bikini picture had fallen out.

"Who's this?" A hand lashed out from behind and snatched up the image. I spun in my chair to find Drake leering at the image of a potential witch in a very form-fitting bathing suit.

On the back of the cheap printing was an old form for a ghost exorcism. We tried to recycle even while keeping everything as physical as possible. I focused on the line about telling the homeowner to leave a salt circle outside the door instead of Drake's sharpening eyes. "They let you keep naughty pictures around, Stone? That's not fair."

"It is not—" I ripped the image from his hand, tearing it at her neck in the process. "It's for the job."

Returning it to the pile, I slammed the folder to the back of my in-pile, which I should have done earlier.

"You telling me that's a green skin?"

"Potential," I said.

He whistled without a care, setting off the werewolves in the maul tank. "If she turns out to be a wicked witch, I call dibs."

My hand found its way into my pocket. I didn't realize until my palm clenched around the familiar curves of the scuffed-up keychain. No one else remembered her. Perhaps an occasional flash of familiarity would appear in their eyes, but no one knew her name. No one knew she'd escaped from our labyrinthian jail and fled into the night. No one but me.

"You can't call dibs," River argued back.

Drake glared at him. "What? You think you got a shot? She looked pretty young. Gonna need someone to fill her up soon."

"You cannot stake a claim when the Council will decide where to use her." River set down his chewed-up pen and turned from Drake.

Drake pried at my folders, hunting for the photo. "I wouldn't need long to get the job done."

He jerked when I slapped my hand down on his. "That's a boast certain to send all the girls running," I countered. "If you will excuse me, I have work to get to."

River nodded, then told me that, should we need to head out, he'd be ready. Drake pouted. "We need to fill you with tequila and set you loose. Work that two-by-four out of your ass."

Pinche mamón.

As I turned my back on the idiot, both he and River stood at attention.

"Gentlemen."

The voice caused me to leap to my feet without question, slamming the pull-out keyboard into my thigh. I ignored the pain with a smile and faced Director Zimmerman as he hustled through the open office. An unknown woman in the same black suit and skinny tie walked just behind him. He slapped Drake on the back and pointed a finger to his office suite. "We've got a meeting. Spur of the moment. Just bring your ass…and a pen."

Drake nodded, took the director's hand in his and shook it. Zimmerman stared with a laugh perched on his lips. He didn't let it go, but he looked over the brown-nosing man to me. "Stone? You made any progress on that witch?"

"Ah…not yet, sir."

"It's been a month."

I frowned deeper. This farce couldn't go on much longer. I'd either have to pull her in for a second time and do an encore to our song and dance, or dispose of her on my own. "I'd prefer to be thorough and slow, than quick and fail," I said.

Zimmerman smiled and slapped me on the back. "Good man. Come on. We've got a lot to talk about."

As I tugged open my drawer for my notebook, my gun rattled to the front. For a brief flash, I almost reached for it. My heart pounded in my ears as I stared at the cold steel, but I wouldn't need a gun for a meeting. We were Animal Control, not the NRA. Closing the drawer and leaving my piece behind, I followed Drake and River into the chief's office.

The last time I'd been here, we had been fighting off a complete containment disaster. One we still hadn't determined the cause of. My gaze darted to the secret escape hatch behind the director's desk when the mystery woman stepped in front of it. She folded her arms and tipped her head low enough that the plain sunglasses slid down her nose. Eyes of purple burned at me.

Strange. Not without precedent for the AC to work with creatures in disguise. But it was also highly rare.

"A-hem," Zimmerman coughed. The woman shoved her glasses up with her middle finger and fell back into place.

"Please, take a seat," the director said, waving a hand to the two chairs. There were three of us, but River slipped in beside the woman without pause. Almost as if he had known this meeting was going to happen.

And he didn't think to tell me? Rude.

"Sir, if this is about the incident in the break room, I can assure you that rusalka came on—"

Zimmerman raised a hand to silence Drake. "This is a matter of utmost secrecy. What I am about to reveal cannot leave this room. Understand?"

I flipped to the level-five-clearance pages of my notebook. They were charmed so only my eyes could read them. Jerking my head, I held my pen poised above the pages. "Ready, sir."

He did not launch into his laundry list of requests. Instead, he gazed down at me with an expression I'd never seen on his weathered face. For as long as I'd known him, he'd had enough wrinkles to put a bulldog to shame. But they had always lifted with a warmth and lightness, reminding me more of a grandfather than my *abuelo* did.

"Stone? Catch this."

I barely had a chance to drop my pen before he flipped a flat coin my way. It landed in the middle of my palm and a flush of pain burst up my arm. I kept my face neutral, using every second of training to hide the agony. Revealing the pain was an opening for most monsters, and some grew stronger from it.

"Sir?" I asked, my voice level even as my skin began to blister. Whatever charm this was, it was powerful.

Zimmerman reached over and plucked the coin from my palm. On instinct, I slammed it shut, but not before we both caught the oblong redness burned into my skin. He stared into my eyes and sighed. For a flash, his lips opened as if to speak, but the director pulled it back and pocketed the coin. He looked to the woman, who nodded.

I prepared myself to learn what was so dire. No doubt this had to do with Conquest and whatever he was planning. I held my pen above my notebook, ready for the answers.

In one fluid motion, Zimmerman extracted a silenced gun, held it to Drake's head and pulled the trigger.

"What!" I jumped, uncertain who to protect in that moment. Drake's brains splattered against River's suit, the man staring down at the gray matter staining his shirt. Before I could even pivot out of the chair, the muzzle turned on me.

It took all my focus to look up from the deadly metal pressed against my heart and into the eyes of the man holding it. "I'm sorry," Zimmerman said. The pressure struck first, then the sound. I collapsed backward, my body and the chair slamming to the carpeted floor. Pain spidered across my chest, my lungs filling with my blood.

No! Drake dead. River... Numbness leadened my limbs, but I could still dig my fingers into the ground. Tugging, I tried to pull myself as if I could protect him.

My partner of ten years wiped off the brains of one of our fellow agents and nodded. The director, the man that'd saved me from murderous creatures in my youth, pocketed his gun as if nothing had happened. Cold seeped into my chest, the pain unbearable. I'd faced down the worst monsters the realms could throw at us, but I'd never known this agony that was ripping my lungs to wet tissue. Each breath filled them with more of my blood. And with every heartbeat, a small slug pressed tighter and tighter against the only organ keeping me alive.

Zimmerman scooped up my notebook, now stained with my blood and Drake's brains. He flipped through before pocketing it. With a jerk of his head, he led the two remaining people out of the door. Before walking away, he said, "Tell Mr. White," and slammed the locked door.

No one would come in, not even if I screamed, but my voice was drowning in blood. I reached into my pocket, trying to find any salve to slap on the gunshot wound in my chest. My numb finger snagged on a ring, and I wrenched out that cat keychain. It flew out and landed in a puddle of my blood.

Chapter Two

Layla

"Well…" I wafted my extended toes back and forth, barely kicking up a breeze in this stifling attic. A bead of sweat dripped down my ankle and circumvented my waving calf before a wide palm caught it.

Garavel kneaded my muscles, weary after hours doing every odd Gopher job on the app. His once-hard fingers softened to butter as he caressed his hand down my naked leg and up my barely clothed ass. He chastely landed on the top of my panties, not even letting a finger dip under the seam.

I lifted my cheek off of his vast chest, Garavel not even flinching as I put more weight on his pecs. His eyes glowed with a golden sheen as he stared down at me pressed across his body like a blanket. "Aren't you going to teach me how to use your sword?" I teased.

He darted his gaze from my face to the bare breasts I happened to be unsticking from his skin. Just before I leaned up high enough to reveal both nipples, I slipped my arms under them and circled my pointed foot, waiting for an answer.

Instead of the quick dart down my bared cleavage, Garavel took his time. Sweat beaded across his bald head, causing his glorious ebony skin to shine. I decided to pretend it was my ample rack doing it instead of the sweltering summer heat and lack of air conditioning up here. He drew his hands up the small of my back, pressing me tighter to his little white loincloth that hid absolutely nothing. It was a wonder Ink didn't wolf-whistle at him when they'd pass in the hall.

"The question is..." Garavel leaned up higher, taking me with him like I was a feather. He bent lower and whispered in my ear, "...can you handle it?"

A burn hotter than the summer sun burst on my cheeks. I gulped and tried to not stammer even as I slid my hips to brush my panties against his rising sword. "I mean...I have before."

He blinked and smiled. "You have? Excellent." Garavel fully sat up with one arm draped around my back to take me with him. My ass, the only clothed part left, slid off of his thighs and landed on the unforgiving wood.

Why'd he sound so surprised? He'd been there, usually crying out compliments in the midst of his coming. Despite Ink's persistence, we'd kept it to just the two of us. No reason to go cliff diving when he hadn't even dipped his toe in until a month ago.

Garavel shifted his long legs and stood. Okay, he hobbled. The attic came to a sharp V at the top but only reached six feet. The seven-foot-something angel had no choice but to bend. It left me lying at his feet, tugging on a curl while staring up his mountainous body.

Strong didn't begin to describe it. He looked like he could hold both the world and Atlas.

With a smile, he shook those wide, formidable shoulders back. In a flash, his wings erupted. They scraped against the far edges of the house, dusting off the cobwebs before he bent them back. I watched his face for a grimace, but none came.

"How's it doing?" I asked, glancing to the wing that'd had a brace on it until a couple of days back.

Garavel looked too. He folded the once broken wing, then took a knee. The floor shuddered below me. For a brief moment I feared what would happen if it gave out. And how Ink would crack jokes for months after. Garavel inched closer. He drew his wing tight, then flourished it out. The tips of the feathers danced across my skin, causing me to gasp.

"Your hands are without fault, lady witch."

I smirked. "My mouth's pretty talented too."

Garavel didn't gulp. He didn't look away or furrow his brow in confusion. "I know," he said with a sly smile, though a hint of redness still burned on his cheeks. "Ah, but you wished to know my sword."

My smirk spread into a ravenous smile when Garavel reached behind his back. From some pocket dimension, he yanked out his massive literal sword. It was so huge, he had to duck down just to get the tip out. As it swung through the air, a sound like the ringing of a bell whipped off the edge. The blade stopped right at the side of my head and I couldn't stop the yelp of surprise.

I caught my reflection in the blade polished to a mirror shine. Hair in desperate need of a professional touch, eyes red from the ragweed kicked up by the mower, skin ashy after sweating out a bucket and a half. I didn't know how any man could look at me without screaming, never mind the four who adored me. Absently, I tried to at least shape my mess of knotted twists and wished for a jar of Vaseline to appear.

"I'm uncertain how much I can show you in this tight space, but not for want of trying," Garavel said so damn earnestly my heart snuggled under a blanket of aw.

Pushing the tip of the blade to the side, I looked away from my mess of a face to focus on him. "When I said I wanted to use your sword, I didn't mean the one you keep on your back."

He frowned. "No? But I don't have any…"

I drew the side of my ankle against his blazing inner thigh. As I went, I lowered my eyelids while gazing up at Garavel. He wrapped both his hands around the hilt of the metal sword and began to tremble. When my toe brushed against his balls, he gasped and dropped his sword. It landed with a loud clang, but Garavel didn't even notice. I'd managed to stretch enough to trace my big toe up the winding vein in his real arsenal.

"You…you meant for us to… Ah…that explains the shedding of… I thought it was only for the…"

"Garavel?" I dropped my foot to sit up. Even with him on his knees, my head barely made it past his nipples. I had to strain to catch the back of his neck and pull him down. "Stop talking."

He smiled and bent lower, leaning me onto my back as he perched above me. "As you wish," he whispered before kissing me. If there were a god, it'd be like kissing him. Ink was sin incarnate, a burn so hot it was liable to go nuclear. Cal was both feral and sweet, laying claim to my heart and refusing to let go. Daniel was…I didn't know yet. But Garavel… One touch of his lips and my skin hummed. Maybe literally—I couldn't tell as my ears clogged with a heavenly choir. A glow of peace and prosperity radiated off of him and around me, making my body both go numb and hyper-reactive at the same time.

"Fuck!" I groaned, incapable of telling him in words what his touch meant. My head flopped back, straining my neck. He curved his arms under my shoulders and proceeded to kiss down my exposed throat. The humming in my blood grew to a Gregorian chant. I dug my hands around his bald head, drawing my nails into his impenetrable skin.

"Yes. Bite me!" I cried out.

Garavel paused. He didn't drop me, but he leaned back, his lips pressed tightly together. "I'm sorry, my lady," he whispered. Worried, I tried to sit up as he turned his head. "I don't think I can."

Damn it. I was too used to my up-for-anything demon and my orally fixated werewolf.

"The idea of doing anything that could cause you harm, even if you ask for it…"

I brushed my palm over his trembling cheek. "It's okay. You did nothing wrong." *Me, on the other hand…*

He didn't turn to face me. But he placed his lips against my open palm and kissed it. "If I may, I'd like to try something with you I've been thinking of."

"Why, Garavel…" I laughed and guided him closer to my lips. "Have you been entertaining naughty thoughts?"

"Perhaps. On occasion. All the time," he confessed against my mouth.

"Ink would be proud," I said, then kissed him.

Garavel guided me to my back as he pressed his lips against mine. A soft flush thrummed from the top of my collarbone across my breast. It wasn't until the waning sunlight cast feathery shadows over my chest that I realized he'd used his wing to touch me. He extended it high and bent the second wing so the whole of his downy soft feathers brushed over my skin.

As he shimmied them upward, Garavel smiled at me. The touch was so light I barely felt it at first, but each one increased the sensitivity of my skin. I found myself panting as he glided the last of his wing away.

"How does that feel?" he asked with a curious quirk.

My breath caught and I mashed the heel of my palm to my forehead. A heat burned between my thighs that had nothing to do with summer. "A...mazing," I gasped out.

"During the war, we'd dance to the amusement of our angels," Garavel mused. He shifted his wing so it rolled inward, forming a circle of feathers that he rubbed back and forth across my nipple. The touch bordered on a tickle, applying no pressure but building through my body straight to my core.

"It required control of every feather or else you could plow into a mountain."

Shifting, he thrilled my other breast with his left wing while he circled the tip of his pinkie over my throbbing nipple. One touch, a little flick of his short nail, and I cried out. Pleasure zapped through my brain like a sweater in a high-heat dryer. Garavel pulled back, putting his focus on teasing my left breast. I'd swear my skin was pulsing after each feather's caress. Even the tumbling dust motes in the sunlight sent ripples through me when he'd finished.

This time, Garavel traced his pinkie down my breast, following the inner path before sweeping under. The sensitivity caused me to curl my toes, my thighs parting on their own. Everything from the waist down wanted release, now, while my brain hung on his every touch.

"Every movement, no matter how tiny…mattered." He slipped his right wing down my spreading cleavage then kept going. Past my belly button, he swerved, then drew his feathers against my inner thigh.

"Oh, fuck!" I moaned, grinding against the whisper-soft touch.

Garavel grinned at my reaction. Suddenly, he snapped his wings together, flattening them just above me so all I could see was a forest of white. They curled to my sides in one fluid movement, revealing the man behind it all. His head was bowed as he gazed at my skin, red with a sex flush. He dropped his feathers until just the tips brushed against my flesh. First he circled them around, then under my breasts. Each touch set off a heavenly choir in my head.

With a stern grunt, Garavel barely shifted but his wings flipped, shivering the feathers' quills up the sides of my throbbing nipples. I grabbed for the only sense in this glowing sea of pleasure and dug my nails into his warm back. My solitary lifeboat drew his wings down until the tip, the softest part, shivered against my nipples.

One touch. That was all it took and I'd either orgasm or explode, or both. But Garavel didn't follow it up with his pinkies, not even his lips. I groaned in agony as he swept both wings down my waist and spread out my thighs.

"Holy…guacamole!" My brain was swiss cheese, spitting out nonsense as I hung on. The summer heat met my soaked vulva and the humidity shot up.

"Your garden is well watered," Garavel whispered in awe.

"My…what?" Every brain cell had popped. All I could do was whimper and pray for that thin loincloth to stop messing around and let the cock come out to play.

Chuckling, Garavel strung his wings back, guiding my legs up with the force of his downy feathers. He pressed his laughing lips to my belly and left a kiss of joy. As he pulled his wings behind him, my legs settled around him. Garavel reached under his loin cloth and clung tight to the shaft below. The fabric hid nothing, his dark cock a shadow ready for a hard fuck.

Garavel kissed higher. My breasts pooled across the top of his bald head as he crawled closer on his knees. I slipped my legs down, trying to use my heels to force off the loincloth. There was some damn clasp but it was made out of gold and a pain in the...

"Oops." I winced at the tear and tried to drop my leg. Garavel caught it, and pressed me back.

He undid the catch himself and let his ripped loincloth drift to the ground. "Patience is a virtue...I've never had much truck with."

I began to laugh just as Garavel thrust inside of me. There was no bearing down and praying for lube as with Cal. He slipped in without pause, but he didn't need the girth or the length. A warmth that felt like a hug for my heart radiated off of him. As it shivered through me, from my famished vagina up to my chest, bliss overcame me. It was like the post-orgasm floating sensation had come before the fireworks.

Which was when Garavel began to thrust. Hard. Without end. Each pound of his cock burst through the calm, sending my pleasure skyrocketing. But as he pulled back, the bliss took over, leaving me gasping and ever tumbling in this void. I could barely speak. I just wrapped my hands around his head and pulled him to me. He muttered with his pillowy lips, prayers falling as he screwed his eyes shut tight.

I kissed him with each thrust, my lips, my throat, my entire chest tingling as the orgasm rose in him. We were both close. Golden specks rose off his ebony flesh, growing brighter by the second. He'd radiate like the sun when he came, and I felt as if I'd walked through its corona every time.

"Layla. My lady. My—"

"Looks like the..." The attic door flung open just behind my head. The second I heard it, I tried to tip back and my heart sank at the flash of blond. "Oh, shit!" Cal spun around, but I could see the back of his neck turning beet red. "Sorry, I thought you were..."

"Are werewolves taught no manners?" Garavel thundered. Unsurprising, as he was on the cusp and he hated Cal.

"Well, I was born in a barn. Okay, the generator shack." Cal waved a hand as if he didn't want to get into this. "Uh, babe, when you're finished." He shivered at the word but kept plowing forward. "We just got our clinical assignments. Okay. I am leaving and closing the door. Bye."

Clinicals? Already? I shook the thought of what my life was about to become away and focused on Garavel and coming instead.

"Has he no shame?" the angel thundered.

"It's not like he knew." I'd told him I'd be up here practicing, and I guess the euphemism had flown over his head, too.

Growling, Garavel bent over me and his wings flared back, framing his face like an old hellfire painting. I shivered in both striking fear and bottomless horniness. Garavel wrenched my thighs tighter and he thrust faster than before, staking a claim he knew would only last for an afternoon. "I adore you. I would die for you. I shall kill for you."

Each declaration was answered with a deep pounding, his cock ripping away the bliss. I scraped my nails into his hardening skin, the soft flesh replaced by impenetrable ebony. Garavel began to lift me off the floor, his hands clasped behind the curve of my spine. My head lolled back as I was helpless in his grip, riding along on this path to damnation.

"You are my lady. My witch. My —" Garavel's creed stopped cold. His wings began to flap and he pulled me so my clit landed right on the base of his cock.

The fuse caught, a single spark racing from my vagina up my chest. When it hit the powder keg in my brain, I knew nothing but pleasure. Every pain vanished from my body, every worry and fear. I both floated in bliss and trembled from the depths of debauchery.

As the sparkling lights faded from my eyes, I found cool relief in my black angel. His smiling face came into focus and I wrapped my hands around his cheeks. He caught one and kissed the knuckle. "You are mine," Garavel declared.

Except I'm also an incubus's, a werewolf's and a ghost's. When did this all get so complicated? Oh right, the second a sex demon showed up in my living room.

Unable to tell him what he wanted to hear, I pulled Garavel to me and drank deep of his holy spirit with a kiss.

Chapter Three

Cal

Damn.

Haphazardly, I shoved the ladder back up while trying to shake away the image of Layla on her back with white wings above her. She'd been damn near glowing, her lips flushed and open wide as if she were waiting for another cock to join in on the fun. And the image was now embedded deep into my brain.

I let go of the bottom of the ladder and realized at the last second that the latch hadn't caught. It flew downward and nearly sliced into the back of my heels. Just as I reached to catch it, another hand did so first. I figured out who it was even before noticing the crimson sleeve.

Without a care, Ink hurled the fallen ladder up. It was lucky it didn't impale through the roof. Ah shit, I knew that smirk. "I can..."

Suddenly, he thrust a long strip of Pantone colors beside my face. Ink scrutinized them carefully, adjusting the reds up and down before he smiled. "Yes, I believe that's the one. I shall call it 'Peeping Pervert' red."

If anyone was a pervert in this house, it was him, always butting in and watching the second one of us had Layla alone. He'd been less careful than ever with his human disguise, often letting his tail sweep across tables and tug books off shelves. The horns were making a regular appearance whenever we were with...

I had imagined that gasp of pleasure. At least I convinced myself of it until I heard her crying out a mix of incoherent cursing and Latin spells. Grabbing Ink by the arm, I wrenched the sex demon out of the spare bedroom and into the hallway. He gladly followed behind, offering no resistance as he kept flipping through his stacks of colors and swatches of fabric.

I could argue with him, tell him I'd had no intention of walking in on Layla with the angel. But there was no point. He either wouldn't care, or wouldn't believe me.

"Why do you have those?" I asked instead, fighting to take some control in my own house. It was such a circus, I kept waiting for the elephants to arrive.

He didn't even look up, just kept pawing through his colors. "Did you catch a glimpse of our winged friend's flaming sword?"

"His...?" I sneered and shook my head. "No. Nor do I want to."

"Pity." He finally put away whatever he was messing with to stare at me. "I have a bet with the ghost I have no intention of losing."

"What? That I'll be the first she'll ask along for the feathered threesome?"

The incubus laughed and patted me on the shoulder. "How delightfully deluded your ego is. If any is to accompany them on this sojourn into the debased, it shall be I."

"And why haven't you already?" I'd barely rolled off Layla the first time together before Ink shoved his nose in and insisted he tag in.

"He is a fledgling, fresh from the nest and uncertain of his wings. Best to give him time to plow his once virginal fields before moving to higher difficulties."

"So for me or Daniel…?"

Ink brayed. "The ghost is little more than a marital aid, used to watching and of little concern."

"And me?"

His smile turned devious. "It's not as if you weren't as curious as her."

My throat constricted and a ringing pounded in my ears. It wasn't that he was wrong… It was that I'd never faced that truth. Layla at the mercy of another man was something I shouldn't get hard over. That wasn't what good, loyal boyfriends did. But the way her lips opened as another cock pounded her to pieces…

A cold breath sputtered against the back of my ear. "I won't tell if you don't." Ink glanced down to my cock, which I knew wanted out. I didn't even bother to hide it away, but as I slipped a hand into my pocket, I brushed the fabric against the crown.

Fuck. The jolt shot through me, almost sending me tracing down the thick head like I was a pimply teenager learning what that thing in my pants could do. Jacking off through my pants was not acceptable once I'd gotten wet dreams under control. With all the strength in my body, I reached lower, willing my erection to calm down. Mentally, I tried to run through the last round of boils and sores from an old textbook Daniel had found.

"Looking for this?" Ink asked.

As I glanced over my shoulder, he opened his palm to reveal a small black—

"What the shit!" I slammed my hands over the ring box and yanked it away. "Don't go waving this around. Why do you have it?"

I took only a quick peek, spotting a glint of silver. Whew. At least he hadn't pawned it for fabric scraps.

"You left it in your trousers for the last wash. I did not think you wanted a symbol of your love to suffer the spin cycle."

Oh. I shoved the ring box deep into my pocket. I'd only had it in my possession for four days, but the stress had made that feel like an eternity.

"Though next time I shall leave it to the wilds of the dryer."

"There isn't gonna be a next time."

Ink stared me dead in the eye like he wanted to call me a liar, but I meant it. All the stars had finally aligned. We were both off for the night, it was a new moon, I'd bought the best steaks and even hung up a curtain of fairy lights. It was perfect.

"And the others are all on board with your intention to ask for the legal hand of our beloved?"

Damn it.

* * * *

Layla

I stuffed my hair back behind my ears and ran for the front door. As I went, the shadow of a man with massive wings drew over me.

"Your bottom looks spectacular from this angle!" Garavel called out before he swooped into the air. My cheeks burned at the compliment and I absently twisted the fallen hair around my finger, knotting it more. For a brief moment, I paused and stared between the two entranceway pillars. They framed the orange and pink sun as it tumbled through the trees and the man flying in the center of it. An entire two months and I still got butterflies watching him do that.

"Where's your spell book?"

I yelped at the unexpected voice and head shoved through the door. Daniel blinked disconcertedly, his features lit by the harsh fluorescents of the library where he had died instead of the golden light of sunset. He stared past my shoulder to Garavel and snorted. "So that's why you didn't come down the stairs. Looks like his wing's back to normal. Guess I won't need all those veterinary med books after all."

Gliding past him, I pushed open the door he'd ghosted between. The wood shoved through him, Daniel showing no signs of being able to stop it. That was good. As much as it hurt him to not touch it, it'd hurt worse if he could.

He blinked harder, then focused on me. I pressed my lips together, feeling self-conscious as he took a languid stroll down my curves. The camisole stuck to me like a second skin. I feared I wasn't getting it off without a pry bar or a talented incubus. Daniel took his time staring over my dotted shoulders bared to the summer heat. As he boldly focused on my chest, he swallowed and crossed his arms.

A low growl rumbled from him and I shivered. "You know you don't have a bra on?"

"I don't?" On instinct, I reached down to cover myself. Cold hands slipped over, then inside of mine. Daniel took control, keeping my palms from shielding my nipples away from growing longer in the chill.

He paced closer, using my hands to rub over the top of my breasts, barely concealed behind a scrap of polyester. His moan grew deeper, with a gravel that'd weaken any knee. Daniel dipped my fingers into my cleavage, tugging the neckline lower as he watched.

"You did that on purpose. To torture me."

"Ah." I laughed at the idea that my scattershot brain had the mental capacity to handle how a spoon worked, never mind leaving my underwear behind just to tease my guys.

My arms jerked down. Daniel took control up to the elbow as he whispered almost against my lips. "Because you want me to torture you." He pressed my arms together, tightening them around my breasts. "Even if I can't touch you…" He reached my right hand under the waistband of my shorts, a tight squeeze.

I braced my quivering thighs as he strained my finger for my soaked panties. Daniel's brown eyes blazed with a spine-quaking certainty. He brushed his cool lips to my ear as he dove a finger in. "I know exactly how to drive you mad."

"Babe? Did he drop you off outside again?"

The second interruption by Cal killed the festivities in an instant. Daniel slipped away from me and kept walking to the other side of the room as Cal came in from the hallway. He spotted me standing next to the open door and smiled.

"Thank the moon," Cal muttered like a prayer. With a quick jog, he ran over and scooped me in his arms. I expected a peck, but he kissed me hard with his palms clamped to my hips. I draped my arms around the back of his neck, my libido in a spin cycle as it bounced from one man to the next. As Cal pulled back, he nipped my lip and I yelped before shivering.

"I hate when he does that. What if he drops you?"

"He's not going to drop me. He's built like a..." Okay, that might not be the best thing to tell Cal. *Don't worry about my other boyfriend, he's stronger than all of you combined.* They'd been on cool acquaintance behavior lately, which was better than I could have hoped. I was trying to think of a response that wouldn't restart the Cold War, when I noticed Cal's eyes had found far better distractions.

His stance opened wide and I didn't need to rub against his jeans to guess why. He ran a palm over the scruff of his chin and a growl far more feral than Daniel's rumbled in his chest. *Oh shit.* I looked over to my poor ghost who was partially phasing through the wall as if about to run from Cal tossing me onto the couch for some wolfy fun.

"The clinicals. Email. You said we got our first assignments?"

He paused in running his stubble over the side of my neck, his lips landing on the hollow below my ear. "Right. Yes. We should go and look at those. And celebrate. Lots to celebrate tonight."

It was one step closer to being a nurse, but I wouldn't call it champagne popping. But as Cal smiled down at me, I'd have agreed to a diamond gala. Taking my hand, he led me to the dining room, which served as our intelligence operation now. Cheap bookcases filled the once regal room, all of them stuffed to the brim for Daniel's work. On the middle of the table was Cal's laptop and my phone charging beside it. I reached for that and frowned at the screen darkening at the edges.

Didn't matter. I could still use it, and Ink hadn't complained enough to get me to buy him a new one. Maybe if I donated a kidney I could afford it. "What'd you get?" I asked while opening my email.

"I didn't look. Just saw what it was and came to…went to get you." He blushed all the way to the tips of his ears. It was so damn adorable how red his pale ass turned. "I wanted to do it together."

"That's so sweet," I said, opening Pandora's box only for my phone to glitch. "Damn it."

"Huh. Guess I'm gonna spend the next six months in pediatrics," Cal said with the biggest grin.

"You tending to a bunch of sick kids, making them feel better, holding their hands when they're scared and…" The idea sounded funny in my head until I said it out loud. It was perfect for him. A knot formed in my stomach as he read through the email. We couldn't have kids — not together, anyway. And I wasn't stupid enough to not see how Cal lit up when he saw one. Would make stupid faces at babies just to entertain them in stores.

If I couldn't give him a baby, then what…

My phone screen finally brightened. Maybe we'd be in pediatrics together. Maybe we'd have a chance to talk about what me not giving him a kid would mean for —

"ICU? Damn it!" I clenched my hand around my phone, wanting to shake it until another answer rolled out like a Magic 8 Ball.

"That should be a challenge."

"I don't want a challenge. I see enough blood and guts in my personal life. Which makes me sound like a serial killer." Some days it felt like it. *Hey, because of your DNA or the whims of angels from the dawn of time, you have to protect the entire world from monsters. Have fun with that.*

As my head slumped to my chest, a calming hand rubbed my shoulder. "You'll do amazing. It's hands-on stuff, which you're wonderful at. And think of how many desperate people you can save with your magic."

Casting spells without anyone catching on would be a challenge, but… He kept massaging away the knot, pulling my forehead to bounce against his. With each second, more of my stress melted away and I found myself smiling. Saving people. Being an angel of life on a ward where seconds counted. Yeah. I might be the best damn nursing student they'd ever had.

"I love that," Cal whispered.

Blinking, I stared up to find his ice-blue eyes gazing at me in wonder. Before I could ask what he meant, he pulled me close and kissed me. This wasn't the bursting-panties kiss of before. It caressed my lips with a promise that this could last for a lifetime. I clung tighter to him, pleading for more.

"Dinner is served."

I jerked at the hand that planted on my ass and found Ink bowing deeply with a dish towel dangling off his other forearm. As he rose up, he put on the airs of a snooty waiter, but his eyes still blazed as he stared at me. He'd noticed the lack of bra faster than anyone else.

"All right." Cal pumped his fist with more exuberance than taco night might deserve. "Thanks."

"You let him cook?" I gasped.

"Um…he helped," Cal said, before whispering in my ear, "Mostly with set-up. So, no intestinal distress tonight for either of us."

"Yes, it shall be a night to remember." Ink sighed as if he were already bored. That was weird. Dinner was his favorite time as he created abominations the world had never seen and would never see again. What was going on?

Ellen Mint

Cal extended an arm to me and he bowed his head. Ink's hand slipped off my ass and he walked away. Growing more wary with every second, I took Cal's hand. He placed his other over top of mine and patted it. "It's so nice out, why don't we dine in the garden?"

"Okay," I agreed, fully lost.

He guided me out of the dining room and toward the kitchen and the backyard door. I'd almost kicked it down in order to break into his house what felt like years ago. Strangely simpler times when I just thought he was involved in a murder and not a werewolf. Cal began to explain all that he had planned for dinner. I nodded along to most of it, growing more confused.

A single, sharp knock broke through his menu. We all paused and looked back.

"And the green beans are fresh from the market with a simple—"

Another two knocks slammed into the door, then the sound of something hitting it hard.

"Ink? You wanna…?" Cal prompted.

"Continue acting as your manservant for the eve? Why not?" Exasperated, he took a step. Before he could teleport, I grabbed his cuff.

"Wait. That might be Dana coming over to celebrate. I'll let her in." I slipped out of Cal's grip and left the two of them standing by the kitchen. He pulled his hand out of his pocket and called to me, but I'd already reached the door.

"Perfect timing," I said, pulling on the latch. "We were just—"

"Good evening, Miss Leeland."

Stone! He looked rough, his hair tugged from a low knot and wet. His clothing was torn and he smelled like fireworks and sewage. I took a step back, ready to slam the door in his face and run.

He threw himself forward, slamming one hand to the door to keep it open. As he did, his other hand fell from his chest, revealing a stain of crimson. Stone stared at the wound then he caught my eyes. Without the sunglasses, the green irises burned as he said, "I need your…" His body crumpled to the ground.

Chapter Four

Layla

Is he dead?

I raced to catch him, time stilling. My arms slipped under his jacket, straining the blood-stained shirt across his chest. He fell against me, almost sending me to my ass. The chest pressed to mine didn't rise, nor did the heart beat. *Oh, god.*

"Allow me." Hands tugged Stone from my grip and I tightened my fingers.

Ink stared down at me as if I'd disappointed him. *What is going on?*

"He's hurt," I muttered, struggling to understand. Last time I had seen him, I'd had a siren wipe my existence from his memory. Had it not taken? Had he come to finish the job? Then why was he bleeding from a chest wound?

With no struggle, Ink hefted Stone's limp form off of the ground and dropped the man on his shoulder. "He is deceased. Allow me to —"

Stone's head shot up and he gasped in air. For a brief second, his bright green eyes homed in on me, then he groaned and crumpled against Ink. "Still unpleasant."

"What the… Is that a witch hunter?" Cal jogged over and glared at Stone, whose blood dripped down Ink's shoulder. "Oh shit, he saw her!" He leaped over as if to protect me from a man who seemed unable to move.

"He knew where to find her. And you, and I. Think on that threat," Ink said, "while I dispose of the body."

"He's not dead." But he had been, at least for a second or two. He looked like it again, his arms dangling helplessly. He'd almost killed me. If I hadn't found Valerie in time, he would have, even if it hadn't been his end goal.

A little whine roared in the back of my head. His sleeves were tugged up, revealing the line of scars circling up his arms. The feel of his skin on mine, ripping my clothing, spreading my thighs came back in a flash. No, that was the siren's doing. Not real. I'd never…

Ink jerked, causing Stone to moan hard. "He will be soon enough. Give me but a moment."

"Wait." It was Cal who grabbed him before he zipped off to some torture dungeon. "You don't find it strange that a dying witch hunter shows up at the door of a witch and werewolf?"

"What I find strange is your lack of claws." Ink glared at him before he stared at me. My first instinct hadn't been to hurl spells at Stone, but to catch him. I braced myself for the incubus pointing it out. Instead, he turned away. "He threatened your mate, nearly killed her. Had I not been there to properly thrash him, you would have little need for the crystal champagne flutes."

Another gasp broke from Stone. This time he slammed two hands to Ink's back and sat up. As he did, a wave shuddered down Ink, ripping away his human façade and revealing the demon below. "Please, we can help each other," Stone gasped.

"How?" Cal pressed.

"Save me, and I'll give you whatever you want." He looked past both men about to tear him to shreds to focus on me.

"Do not even contemplate his double-edged promise. I know djinn with better outcomes to their deals."

"Babe?"

I wrung the locket hanging off my neck, listening to the chink of each tiny chain through the loop. My eyes skipped off the about-to-be-bloody tableau to Daniel standing beside the door. We had the feather, the demon's blood, I wore his bone around my neck. All we needed was...

"Unicorn skin."

Ink groaned, tossed his head back, and in one fell move hurled Stone off his shoulder. Snarling, he stomped away as I raced to the dying man. Before I could even test his pulse, Cal ensnared me. I stood above as Stone struggled to look up.

"Unicorn skin for your life."

* * * *

Stone

The werewolf deposited me on the couch. A stale pizza box served as a pillow, but it could have gone worse. Cold blood dribbled from the hole that wouldn't heal. Each drop burned like acid, yet I didn't make a sound. Instead, I cupped my palm over the wound and waited as a round table argument broke out.

"Can you do it? Get me some unicorn skin?"

"That depends," I said before gasping. The numbness was returning, which meant another round of my heart stopping then jolting back to life was on the horizon. I'd shattered the last bottle of my healing draught in the tunnels. This pain was at full force.

"On?" the witch prompted, her arms crossed below her chest. Even with my blood burning and draining from my body, it was impossible to not notice just how fucking tight her shirt was. My imagination was quick to fill in what little I couldn't discern. An image of her, naked and stern, burned in my head. "Ah, *puta*!" What little blood I had served no purpose *there*.

To my surprise, her rigid lip and boiling glare softened. "Here..." She waved her fingers and whispered a spell under her breath I could recite along with her. I breathed deep, anticipating the proper healing of a witch, when the under-demon snatched at her hand.

"Why are you wasting your energy on that? We are better off waiting five minutes, then burying the witch hunter under Calvin's begonias."

The wolf flinched at the idea. "Could we *not* start a mass grave in my garden? I just got it weeded."

This was getting me nowhere, and it seemed obvious the incubus had only grown more protective over time. "I've already died, numerous times," I interjected. That caused him to smile, a most nefarious grin, though it seemed to surprise the others.

"How are you still breathing?" the wolf asked.

I shook my head. This was getting us off track. "A blessing."

"You mean a spell you forced a slave witch to cast."

Was that how they spun it outside of the covens we controlled? They probably all talked while gathered around their cauldrons about how witch hunters would drink blood and eat babies. A scoff broke at the ludicrous idea and I caught a flash of claws from both men. Coughing instead, I stared up at her. "I should be healed and on my feet, but I'm beginning to suspect the bullet inside of me is cursed. I cannot die, and I cannot heal."

"Good," the incubus snarled. He slammed a hand to my chest, then placed a claw right over the bullet wound. As he shoved in through the freezing hole, I couldn't shake off the pain and cried out.

"Ink! Stop!" She tugged him back.

Fury burned on the incubus's face, a fury aimed only at the witch. "No. I know what you have rattling in your mind. You think you can save the whisper by saving the monster. But I will not allow it."

"That isn't your call," she argued back.

"He, and all of his kind, tried to kill you." The incubus jabbed at me, then snarled. "And if you save him, he'll do it again. Won't you, witch hunter?"

Magic must be contained. That was the core tenet I had lived by for the past twenty years of my life. Even bleeding at the doorstep of a free witch, I couldn't deny it. Instead, I kept my mouth shut.

"I'm with the demon." The air shifted and a hazy outline of a young man appeared. That must be the ghost that'd tried to interfere during our job offer.

"Daniel…" She reached out for him, despite being unable to touch him. He stormed past and leered at me from above.

"As long as he lives, he's a threat to your life, Layla. Can't you see that? He has to die."

"Hell take me, the ghost is making sense," the incubus said, feigning a swoon.

Leeland glared at the assembled monsters. "You think, if he's here, that he's the only one who knows I'm a witch? That the entire Animal Control agency isn't sitting outside waiting to pounce the second you hurt him?"

That would be a wonderful twist. I groaned and stretched out, death nipping at my heels and rising.

"Why here?" the wolf asked. He took a knee beside the couch and stared me in the eye. "Why Layla? There's tons of other witches, magic you could have called on. But you came here instead. Why?"

"Because…oh, fuck that burns! I was shot by…" The muzzle flashed in my memory, his eyes staring not at me but through me. He hadn't even looked at my prostrate form, just walked away as if I meant nothing. "My director."

The demon laughed uproariously. "The chickens are pecking themselves to death. I say let them."

"Don't you want to know why?"

Leaning down, the demon hooked his claws around my collar and yanked me to his face. "I couldn't give a shit if it's because you saved too many puppies from drowning. You hurt Layla and for that you'll suffer a thousand deaths at my hands."

"Is that why or is it because you faced a moment of humanity in rescuing her?"

The demon snarled and flung me back to the couch. My head struck the armrest, sending sparks across my eyes. Stomping away, he kept his back to me. "We leave him to die. Agreed?"

"Yes," the ghost said.

"What? No. We're not..." The witch's defense ended as the door blew farther back.

A booming voice called out, "I did not expect the entrance to be open for me."

"Then you'd have smashed into it like a pigeon," the werewolf muttered.

He clasped an arm around Layla and I caught a flurry of white wings obscured behind his back. So this was the demi-angel we'd been hiding sightings of. And he had found the wayward witch, who'd taken him in, of course. "Heaven's gift, what happened to this man? How do we help him?"

"We don't, big guy," the demon said. "He dies, we get on with our lives. The bottle of champagne would be perfect to christen the death of the witch hunter."

"I don't understand. We save people. We save hurt people, right?"

The witch nodded and bit her lip.

"So we save him. Glad that's decided. What can I do to help?"

"We are not..." The ghost leaped closer and stared the large man in the eye. "He is a liability. A danger to everyone here, especially Layla."

"But he can't even move."

The incubus and ghost stood on one side, the angel on the other. To my surprise, it was the werewolf who rose to his feet. "I'm saving him."

"What?"

"Calvin, are you suffering from moon madness? Do you not remember what this man tried to do—"

"It doesn't matter." He shook his head and stared down at me. "I can't let him die. Not if I'm ever gonna be able to look myself in the eye again."

The demon, fearing the democratic process, threw both his hands into the air and groaned. "Every one of you except for the ghost is suffering from early-onset dementia. He is a threat, a danger. Layla. My bond, you of all people know that he is crafty. This could be a trap." He took her hand and tenderly brushed it "Put aside your weeping heart for once."

She wrenched her hand out of his and stared him in the eye. "My heart is just fine, thank you. Besides, we don't have to help him, just call an ambulance. Let the hospital—"

"Stop!" I managed to sit up and clasp my hand around hers before she even reached for a phone. Her eyes opened wide, and I became acutely aware of every blade and claw reaching for my throat. "You cannot dump me in a hospital. They will find me and finish the job."

"I approve of this hospital idea. Let his fellow witch hunters off him. All our consciences are clean. His death was his own doing."

I snickered at the certainty in the demon's words. He'd condemn me in a second, as if he didn't have a trail of corpses that could circle the earth in his past. "You don't understand. It isn't the hunters that are behind this."

"Then who is?" the witch pressed, her fingers folding around mine.

For a moment, I gazed at where I held her and a half dream bubbled in my mind. I'd almost swear that palm had once ripped open my pants. Shaking it away, I stared her in the eye. "Conquest."

Chapter Five

Cal

I shoved the ring box deep into my jeans pocket. There was no hope of popping the question while a man potentially died on my couch. The introduction of our personal bogeyman only clinched the deal.

At the single word, Layla gasped. I wrapped my arms around her and rubbed up and down her sides, but she'd gone pale. Ink laughed. "And what pray tell would a Horseman have to care about your ten-penny operation?"

He clutched his palms together, the claws lengthening, as he stared down the witch hunter guy. I'd seen the incubus annoyed, exhausted and even perturbed. But this was a level I hadn't even thought possible—pure hatred. Hatred required caring, and I never knew he was capable of caring about anything beyond himself.

The detective shifted, shoving the old Gio's pizza box deeper into the couch. "You have no idea the powers at our disposal."

"Due to the magic you siphon and steal from tortured witches," Ink damn near spat at him, a hiss boiling in his tone.

"Are you really one to talk, demon?"

Ink shifted his foot, ready to launch onto the guy. Even if Stone wasn't near death, he didn't stand a chance against a pissed-off demon. I clamped a hand hard to Ink's shoulder and pushed with all my strength. His body shivered, threatening to break the hold with a brush of his hand, so I said, "Save the fight for later. It's not honorable to kick a man when he's down."

"You presume I care for honor or the state of his manhood." Ink huffed, though he relaxed his back leg and I let go.

"We gotta figure out how to fix him. Get that bullet out. Any ideas?"

The demon narrowed his eyes at me. "I refuse to participate in this farce that will only get you killed. Until you need me to gut him, I'm done."

"Wait, you—" The pain in the ass vanished in a hurt huff. "You could pluck it out. Dan...iel?" I smiled painfully from remembering too late. The ghost stared at me as if he wanted to start a fight too. "Any chance you could reach into his chest and do a ghost grab around the bullet?"

"No."

"I mean you carry books and—"

"I said no!" He flared a dangerous blue, then backed off. With his shoulders high, he glared at the detective, then said to Layla, "This is dangerous. You're gonna get hurt. You can't trust men behind badges."

She snorted and rolled her eyes, but they landed on the pale face bleeding out on the couch.

Brushing up against her, Daniel whispered in her ear. She closed her eyes and clenched her hand around the locket, then reached for him, only for the ghost to leave, the same as the demon. It left me standing on the side with Garavel, a very strange place to be.

He'd pulled out his cat, who was already as long as my forearm, and scratched her black chin. "Why cannot the lady witch use her magic to dislodge the wayward arrow?"

"It's cursed. You missed that bit while..." *Flying around my neighborhood drawing the eyes of witch hunters right to us.* I bit down the thought that'd only make the situation worse, but filed it away for a frank discussion later. An angel in the attic was one thing, but letting him have free rein could have gotten her kidnapped or worse. That wasn't happening.

Garavel's eyes widened. "Ah, yes. Best to remove it with care. Bouncing a spell off a cursed object can only make it worse."

"Brilliant." I reached for Layla. She didn't react as I drew my hand down her arm. It wasn't until I whispered, "Babe," that she jumped and stared at me. "I don't think we've got a choice. We're gonna have to pull that thing out ourselves."

"What? But we're not...we're not even nurses. We're students. I don't like digging out splinters. Where would we even do open thoracic surgery? The kitchen? He'll die from one of Ink's deep-fried meatloaf ice cream sandwiches falling inside."

Oh, I knew that voice. Pitching her tone higher, her lips pulled back, she was nearing a breaking point. I caught her chin and turned her eyes away from the dying man. "You've got your magic. You can use that to keep him alive."

"That's not enough." She waved her fingers and I frowned. That spell of hers had yanked me from the jaws of death. I'd been beaten to a pulp and she had gotten me back on my feet in minutes.

"You have no idea how strong you are," I whispered. Her cheeks pinked and she dipped into her shoulders as if I was blowing smoke up her ass, but it was true. In a year's time, Layla had grown to a power that could rip open hell and she didn't realize.

"Look. I don't think we'll have to cut him up. Just get in through a small hole and yank it out. Then you blast him with all your healing spells, and…"

"And if it doesn't work?" Her cute nose crinkled at the top. I leaned forward to kiss it and the dread in her dropped into me. The chances of him surviving this seemed nonexistent despite what I'd said. But what could we do? Leave him here to suffer for days or weeks as he kept snapping back to life?

Give Stone to Ink to do whatever he wanted with him?

No. We needed him alive. He was the only way to get back into Animal Control and erase any mention of Layla. *This has to work. This will work.*

"It's gonna," I said, kissing her burning forehead. "Trust me." I leaned back, when Layla wrapped herself tighter and nuzzled against my chest.

"How do you do that? Make everything feel okay?"

It was what I did. Take every whipping, every beating, every break and punch, put them in a box and smile. My lips tugged out of habit, wanting to pretend everything was fine. But that instinct was what had sent me down a dark path. Instead, I focused on her steady heartbeat, her gentle breathing and her scent of jasmine and lightning that meant home.

"I'm going to get some tools to help," I said. The detective groaned, his tan skin pale as a sheet and covered in sweat. "And I'm gonna go fast. There's a table in the closet. Maybe put down some tarps."

I reached for my keys when I caught sight of the clock. Rush hour. It'd be bumper to bumper down the whole highway and into downtown. "Garavel? I can't believe I'm asking this, but you think you can give me a lift?"

He blinked in concern and glanced at Layla. She placed a hand on his exposed arm. "Please?"

That was all it took. "Very well. But I will require directions." When two massive hands landed on my waist, I leaped into the air.

"We can save that for outside. I'll direct you."

He tucked Fiona back onto his shoulders. Rather than dip into her magical space, the cat perched there to survey the proceedings.

I scratched her head, causing her to purr while I watched Layla. "Babe?"

She glanced over at me.

I was leaving her alone with a witch hunter. I was the worst boyfriend in the world. "Stay safe."

* * * *

Layla

So help me, if this is all some trick to... Stone moaned, his once pink lips as pale as uncooked fish. I picked a blanket up off of the floor and wiped at his clammy forehead. He groaned again but turned his head, pressing his skin against the yarn as I tried to wick away his sweat. I really shouldn't have been using a blanket Cal's mother had knitted to clean up a witch hunter. But the agonized groaning stilled and I kept going, clearing off the top of his chest.

There was no escaping the hole. It looked odd. I'd seen far too many bullet wounds for my liking before my nursing career had even started. Those had burns to the tattered skin, and usually pieces of muscle and bone gushed out with the blood. This was a perfectly round hole, almost as if everything on him had healed up to the point of the slug in his chest.

The blanket slipped and my finger glanced against his skin. It was freezing. "Are you cold?"

He could only offer a micro-nod. I tucked the blanket around his legs and feet. That once imposing suit looked ludicrous under a green and blue afghan. Out of habit, I reached for his shoes and Stone shifted. "Please. That's... I'd rather you not touch my feet."

"Embarrassed by them?" I asked, trying to lighten his deathbed.

"Beautiful women touching my feet has a tendency to cause my blood to flow where it is unwanted at the moment."

Oh! I turned my back to him to disguise my blush. *I shouldn't be feeling awkward about that. I should only be feeling rage. He's my enemy. He tried to kill me, like Ink said. Though, he also saved me, tended to my wounds. Rubbed salve all over my shredded feet.*

Does he remember that?

"How many?"

Stone raised an eyebrow. It was strange to see his eyes without the inhuman glasses in the way.

"How many of your men are waiting outside this house?"

He shook his head. "None."

"Don't lie to me. I'm not an…" Daniel's cutting word snapped back at me and tears burned in my eyes. "I'm *not* stupid."

"If there were any witch hunters outside your door, we'd both be captured and dead by now."

"But you know what I am. You've remembered, somehow."

Stone chuckled and rustled in his pocket. "It took some time to piece it together. Whatever spell you used was powerful and thorough. Nearly thorough."

It hadn't been me but a siren I'd set loose — another stone of guilt to add to the mountain.

His hand slipped out from under the blanket and he opened his palm. "This gave you away."

I stared down at the witch kitty keychain Cal had given me for Christmas. It was banged up, the acrylic cut, but a flood of gratefulness and protectiveness sent me reaching for it. Stone nearly closed his fist until he let me take it out. Just wrapping my hand around it brought back memories of the New Year's road trip to hell. Of hunting for Daniel's body. Of losing the last connection I had to Cal before the water pulled me under.

"That must mean something to you," Stone said.

It was a silly little gift. Something he had bought because it had reminded him of me. And that was why it meant the world to me. All I could do was nod and carefully place it in my pocket. Cal was gonna be so happy when… Were any of them going to be happy with me after this?

"It does. Thank you. I mean, you stole it after kidnapping and torturing me. So maybe I shouldn't be saying thank you."

"You expect an apology."

"For the torture? The kidnapping? The theft? The stalking of me and my guys? No. Why would anyone want an apology for that?"

Stone chuckled. The man with a gaping chest wound weeping blood was laughing at me. "Out of everything, it was that acerbic tongue that stuck to my memory the strongest."

"If you like that, you're going to love this part. I'm not saving you out of some sense of duty or my bleeding heart. You're going to live, then you're going to get me unicorn skin. And after that, delete any mention of me, Ink, Cal or Garavel from the witch hunter database. Understand?"

He stared up at me towering above him. "That's a tall order."

Tremors ran up his arms. He bit down on his lip, no doubt trying to silence another groan of agony as his body began to slip back to death. I could heal him, probably take away a lot of the pain, but I wasn't budging.

"It's your only option."

"So saving the world and stop...gah! Stopping Mr. White doesn't figure into your demands?"

I didn't blink. I couldn't. Mr. White was coming for me. He'd told me as such. And he'd said other things that still had me reeling...like claiming that he had created me. I shook it all away and glared at him.

"Is it a deal?"

He groaned and jerked his head. "Very well. Though the unicorn sk..." He cursed sharply and I dropped to my knees. Running my hands over his body, I whispered the healing spell.

Magic seeped from my palms through him. As it took hold, he jerked once then collapsed back with a sigh of relief. I knew that one too well. I was getting tired of knowing it.

"You didn't have to do that," he said as if he was annoyed at me helping him.

"Would you rather I let you suffer?"

He didn't answer and stared at the old fireplace. When we had run out of space, we'd started stuffing boxes of books inside. One on top was about the four horsemen during the Middle Ages. As Stone didn't seem to be in a talking mood anymore, I staggered up. Rather than check my phone just to worry about Cal, Garavel, Ink and Daniel, I picked up the book on Conquest and fell into the armchair.

"No one knows about you."

I dropped the book and stared at Stone, but he'd turned to face the couch. "I made certain of that."

Chapter Six

Layla

The card table nearly buckled as Stone's weight flopped onto it. I lashed a foot under and caught it, my arms straining as I glanced over to find Ink lingering in the hallway. "Little help?" I called.

He drew a claw down his chin. "Let it fall."

Damn it, Ink. The pressure shifted, and the table rose. As the latch clinked into the proper position I should have put it in, I rubbed Garavel's back in gratitude. He gave me a quick thumbs-up, then wandered to the side to watch. Stone's legs dangled off the edge. One shoe fell, striking the plastic paint tarps I'd found in the garage. Cal tugged over the torch lamp and tried to tip it on the couch to cast a surgery light across Stone's bare chest.

"I'm gonna try to clean the area, but it'll hurt."

Stone chuckled. "I've had...holy!"

Cal scrubbed a wad of cotton loaded in iodine across the wound. It seeped into Stone's scars, turning them a dark umber until his skin glowed around them. My eyes kept trailing away. I couldn't understand how someone would have caused so much pain to a child.

Stone sweated bullets, though sadly not the one in his chest. I dabbed at his forehead with a clean cloth and he wrapped his hand around mine. He dug his fingers into my skin and clung as tight as possible. His whispered cursing stopped and he flopped back, but his grip didn't let up.

"There. I think that's good enough." Cal wiped at his forehead with his elbow and tossed the wad of iodine into the trashcan. "That was the easy part."

He reached for the autoclaved packs on the little nightstand that had to serve as our workstation. After prying off the tape, he unrolled the blue fabric to reveal a handful of scalpel handles, a pair of forceps and clamps.

"Did you steal those from a hospital?"

"Steal? No. I *borrowed* them from a vet who helps with werewolf issues."

"Angering your flea collar supplier seems an unwise move," Ink unhelpfully added.

"Are you going to stand there this whole time?" I shouted at him. My face heated below the mask from my manic breathing, but also against my forehead. It wasn't just Ink—Daniel was floating around on the edge of the living room.

The incubus folded his arms and stood in the doorway. "When he inevitably betrays you, I'd prefer to be present to cut down on injuries."

"Great. What about you? Are you going to help?" I less than nicely sniped at Daniel.

He could at least read through a textbook, keep watch over Stone's vitals or something. Daniel stared at a man with a bullet in the same place he'd caught one and shook his head. "No."

This is insane. No heart monitor and our antiseptic is a handful of bottles of iodine and alcohol.

I gulped at the tight squeeze and looked at Cal holding a scalpel blade just above Stone's skin. "What about anesthetic? He can't be awake for this."

"Babe..." Cal had stripped off to his waist and doused his skin in alcohol. The stench radiated off him, but it wasn't enough to knock Stone out. "I can't nick that stuff. They'd trace it back."

"But—"

"It would not work regardless." Stone's words were soft and crackled, as if he were hanging on by a thread. "Part of Hunter training so we can't be bamboozled by sleep spells."

I frowned. Mine had worked on them. But this wasn't the time to mention that.

"Well, then...this is gonna hurt like shit. Ready?" Cal glanced over, the plastic goggles refracting the lamp's light across his eyes.

No. Fuck, I don't want to do this. It's insane. It's going to kill him.

But as Stone moaned and his grip slackened on my hand, I tightened my hold. We didn't have a choice. "Do it," I said, and amplified my magic. Instead of casting a normal spell to heal any wounds, I directed the magic to act like an IV drip. Slowly, it worked into his system, unknotting the wound muscles spasming from pain.

"Making the first incision—" Blood welled up and Stone tossed his head back to scream. I reached to clamp a hand over it, when an angel appeared.

"Here," he said, pushing a leather strap into Stone's gaping mouth. "This should help."

Stone bit down on it, his eyes blazing. He nodded to Garavel, then looked at me. I was supposed to keep it going.

"Layla?"

I can't do this. It's insane. It's torture. It's…

"Babe? Should I…?"

Clenching my hand tighter around Stone's, I leaned close to him and opened up my magic. "Keep going."

* * * *

If the sun had risen and set again, I wouldn't have noticed. All my attention was on Stone, his vitals, his eyes, the color of his lips. It wasn't until I heard a clink and Cal stepped back that I realized it was over. He waved the forceps, clenching a copper mushroomed slug. "It's out," he said and moved to drop the cursed object onto the nightstand.

Ink swooped in and plucked it up.

"Careful." I called while casting a real healing spell over Stone's open wound. "That thing's…"

Ink twisted it between his claws, then flicked it into the air. As he caught it, he smiled. "Iron. Interesting." Without explaining more, he pocketed the bullet and vanished.

Why would I expect any help from my damn incubus? I closed my eyes, directing my magic to fill Stone's body. It'd been a mess of tissue, muscle and bone while we tried to save him. But as he breathed deep, his heart growing steadier, I couldn't help but notice he didn't have an ounce of fat on him. His lithe body was more cut than Garavel's, who had literally been carved from rock.

The slit skin began to flatten and knit together. And, as I risked a peek, the burrowed hole to his heart filled in. He was going to make it. Even still, I made certain to add more of my magic, terrified that after all of this he could die the next day.

"Cal, that was…" I raised my head and smiled as he unmasked. It was so stupidly unfair how hot he was. I reached a hand for him, and my body gave out. I tipped to the side, about to send my chin slamming to the card table. Cal caught me in time, and he held me tight to his chest.

"Are you okay?" he asked.

I barely nodded, my neck too exhausted to try. My forehead crashed against his pec and I wanted to snuggle with him for days.

He ran a hand over my hair and swayed with me. "It was the blood, wasn't it? Makes you swoon into my arms."

What? I looked up to find him smiling. Oh, a joke. Pretending to be normal. "Yes, and I need my big strong boyfriend to protect me from it." I'd hollowed myself out, a feeling I was coming to know better than I should. The first time, Stone had done it to me, taking away my magic until I had nearly died. The second, I had done it to myself to save a demon I'd known for a day.

It wasn't just painful—it wasn't just exhausting. I feared I was walking a line that if I wavered on for even a moment, I'd fall and never rise again.

"Babe, I would give anything to take you up to bed right now." Cal opened his arms and passed me to Garavel. The angel scooped me up like I was a doll. "But I've got to clean up and get him somewhere. Can you take care of her?"

"Gladly." Garavel bowed his head and took a step back. Garavel's heat and the rumbling inside of him lulled me deeper to sleep. I began to snuggle against him, when Cal caught my hand.

He held it, even with the strain, and ran his fingertip against the back of my ring finger. Even on the verge of collapse, I sensed mysteries hiding in his blue eyes. I tried to sit up to ask, but he smiled and let go. "Sleep well. Okay. I love you."

"I lo—" A massive yawn broke up my sentiment. " —ove you too."

All I heard was a single groan from the man we'd saved before I blacked out in Garavel's arms.

* * * *

Cal

Absently, I flicked the ring box open. This was not how I had wanted tonight to go.

I slammed the lid shut.

The steaks were charred briquettes after a dangerous dying man had stumbled through my door. The raccoons had torn down the lights while lumbering across the branches, leaving them in a tangled mess. And the romantic playlist I had on my phone was cycling through a low frequency to keep me awake as I watched the hopefully-not-dying man.

I opened the box again.

She had been supposed to freak out as I got down on one knee. Stare around as if it was all a game, then — as she realized what was happening — tear up and cry out yes so loud the neighbors shouted at us. Then we'd dance, she'd stare at her ring in awe and I'd take her upstairs.

I looked up to the dark second floor. At least she was getting some rest. I knew better than to say it, but she'd looked rough after that. The damn fool had no idea how close he'd been to dying on my old card table. And he had her to thank for it.

Now we have a witch hunter to deal with. Oh, and if he wasn't lying, Conquest's palling around with the rest of them. Is Eric involved too?

Knowing my luck, yeah. This wasn't the time to go asking any life-changing questions. I closed the ring box and slipped it into my pocket. Rising, I inspected Stone's bandages. He wasn't bleeding much, not after Layla's spells. But after all that, I didn't want to risk sepsis, so I changed them out.

"Your touch is surprisingly gentle."

I didn't pause, only dumped the wadded bandages into the trash can to burn later. "What do you want, Ink?"

"For the world to make sense."

"You're gonna be waiting a long time for that."

"Indeed. Perhaps you can illuminate the part you play in this nonsense. He tried to kill her. He could yet kill her."

I finished placing the tape on Stone's skin. It dipped into the strange markings all across his flesh. If the witch hunters made them go without anesthesia, it didn't seem so surprising that they'd carve them up with ritualistic scars either. "I know," I said to the probing incubus.

"Are you also aware of the flush to her cheeks whenever she thinks of this one?"

What? I craned my head back to stare at him and he snickered. "Apparently not. Is it a secret? Oh, perhaps I should not have mentioned."

"Maybe you just don't know what you're talking about. Layla…she cares, maybe more than she should."

"Very much so more than she should. It's a wonder her caring heart hasn't reduced us all to dust."

I dropped the scissors to the coffee table harder than I'd meant to. Stone shifted but didn't wake. He'd been out cold since we had removed the bullet. "Curse her heart all you want, but it's what I love about her."

"Then you're both fools." He snorted.

"Fools in love."

Ink groaned. "If I wished to hear the rambling poetry from a man suffering late-stage syphilis, I'd speak with the ghost."

"Where is Daniel?"

"Heaven if I know." Ink shrugged and stared at his nails, the claws long gone. But he kept darting an eye over at Stone as if prepared to finish the job. Would he kill Stone against Layla's explicit wish because he hated the man so much? Or was he just as bound up in her caring heart as the rest of us?

"I'm getting a drink. After tonight, I need two. You want anything? Pop-Tart? Oreo? Oreo between two Pop-Tarts?"

Ink didn't respond, his focus on Stone. In this state, the man was as helpless as a newborn kitten. Maybe more so. At least the newborn kitten had cuteness on its side. Rather than listen to more morbid pouting, I pushed off for the kitchen, fairly certain he wouldn't do anything.

A hand snagged my arm, pinning me in place. "Your attempted proposal has failed because of him. Are you not enraged by it?"

"That's the thing about marriage — it's for life."

He audibly groaned but I shook him off.

"I've got time to try again." Smiling at Ink's deep scowl, I took a step for the kitchen.

"What proposal?"

"Holy moon!" I leaped out of my socks. As I came down, I realized I'd accidentally sliced my claws through the wall's sheetrock. *Damn it.*

Daniel only glanced at the damage before focusing on me. "What's the demon talking about?"

"Chosen to grace us with your presence, oh ghost of the loins. You're just in time to watch our failed vote snore."

Was Ink trying to distract him? If so, it didn't work. The ghost who was nothing more than a cold spot in the house began to harden. He refused to move and, as I tried to push past him, my hand slowed in the heavy air.

I didn't want to do it this way, but I was out of options. "May as well get everyone. Where's Garavel?"

"I'll fetch him," Ink said and vanished.

Heavy footsteps clunked overhead and I pretended not to hear them coming out of my bedroom. We weren't trying to rip each other to pieces, but we weren't at the sleeping-in-the-other-man's-bed level yet.

"Hello, fellow warriors," Garavel boomed at the top of the stairs. I winced at the sound and pointed to the sick man. He raised a hand, pulled a face and carefully tiptoed down the stairs. It'd be comical on a man so huge if he wasn't disturbingly graceful as well, like an elephant that did ballet. "Sorry. Ink said I was needed."

"This is all Calvin's show. I hope you can wow them."

Both ghost and angel stared at me, one with venom, the other more happy distraction. I'd spent the past month painstakingly planning every word I'd say to Layla, and hadn't spent a second deciding what I'd tell them. "Well, the thing is—"

"He's proposing to Layla," Daniel interrupted.

"Wonderful," Garavel shouted before dropping his voice. "What's the proposal? Is this about battle tactics?"

"In a way," Ink said, slapping his wide shoulders in a brotherly hug. "Think of it as the joining of one army with another."

"That doesn't seem wise. With no clear chain of command, it would be a volatile situation that'll lead to many deaths."

"That is matrimony at its heart." Ink smirked.

"It is not… I'm asking Layla to marry me," I tried to explain to Garavel, but he seemed as confused by that as Ink's metaphor. "We'll be—"

"Why now? Why not wait until I have my body back?" Daniel interjected.

"Didn't seem like you were in a hurry for that earlier." I folded my arms tight and stared at him.

His snarl increased. "That was to protect her. I will not risk her life for my gain."

"Should we review the evidence to the contrary? Let us see, there's the angel feather that nearly burned her face off."

"All right, Ink," I said.

"The demon blood that almost sucked her to hell."

"Will you stop prattling?"

"And now we have the unicorn skin in theory provided by a—"

"Knock it off!" I shouted at him, causing a flare of surprise in his smug eyes. My cry echoed off the silent house, pinging from every beam back to me. It was a minute before anyone spoke again.

"Why would the ghost being solid matter in joining forces?" Garavel asked. "He serves the lady witch far better in this state."

Peals of laughter broke from Ink to the point he doubled over and wiped at his dry eyes. I turned my back on the two of them and focused on Daniel.

"I know why you're doing this," he said before I could explain. "Before I'm whole again, you're gonna lock her down."

I snorted. "You make her sound like a bicycle."

"A married woman won't have time for an incubus, an angel and a highly talented punk musician."

"When you were trapped in that library, you should have read up on women's lib. They aren't chained to stoves anymore." I shifted on my feet, growing uncomfortable with Daniel's accusations. They were too much like the shit my bastard sperm donor would pull.

"You expect me to believe this will be some, what, utopian polyamory wedding?"

"Well, I don't care much what you do. If you all want to marry Layla…"

"No, thank you. Matrimony is only useful for exploiting grudges…and occasionally good wine," Ink said.

Garavel leaned closer and whispered, "Is this that army thing? Because I still don't believe that's a wise tactic."

"The angel's with me. Bachelors for life!"

Methinks the demon doth protest too much. I saw the way he stared at her, especially when Layla wasn't looking back. "Two down, what about you?"

"I'm dead. They don't let dead people get married."

This was going nowhere fast. How in the hell did she put up with all of this? With all of us? It must be that damn caring heart Ink kept cursing.

"Why now? You haven't been together for a year, yet. Why are you proposing? Why not wait?"

"Because..." My hand wormed its way into my pocket. It plucked at the box, prying it open. I slipped the tip of my pinkie through the little ring, finding comfort in the cool band.

Because facing off against the queen of sex demons and not even batting an eye made me realize what I always knew. Because having Layla sleeping beside me every night isn't a temporary thing. Because I love her and I want the whole damn world to know it.

"Because she keeps getting into dangerous situations. One day she's going to wind up in the hospital. Without a husband, or even a fiancé, the one making the decisions will be her mother. Do you want that?"

Daniel shivered, his gaze darting over to Ink who nodded slightly and turned away. "While I do support her demon-banishing policy...I don't think that woman has Layla's best interests at heart. Is that really why? The practical filing taxes together reason?"

"I love her too."

He snorted. "We all love her. Well, aside from the demon."

Ink strangely kept his mouth zipped.

"Fine. I guess… I guess I can't stop you."

"A glowing endorsement," I muttered to myself.

Daniel nodded, then suddenly shot forward. A knee-quaking voice cursed in my ear, "But if you try to get rid of me, I will make your life a living hell." Before I could respond, he faded away, either back to the library or Layla's bedside. I'd been doing my best to pretend he wasn't watching her sleep in the middle of the night. She probably wouldn't want to hear that.

"Congratulations." Ink slapped my shoulder, hard. "I usually need a good afternoon to enrage the ghost to the point he's making blood oaths. Take a bow."

"Yeah." I pulled my hand out of my pocket, leaving the ring in its box. "Lucky me."

Would Daniel try to stop it? Would he ruin the romantic surprise? Or was he plotting how to get rid of me before I could ask her?

Stone groaned and I put all of that in a box to focus on my patient.

Chapter Seven

Layla

As I stumbled down the stairs, I came upon a sight that'd melt any heart. A giant wolf had curled up on the couch and a tiny black kitten nestled on top of his warm fur. Poor Cal must have just passed out after transforming. The angel who acted as his guardian sat in the chair with his mouth open, snoring away. I reached out to rub my hand over Cal's head and he shifted in his sleep. It wasn't enough to wake him, but Fiona stood on all four paws. She beamed her green eyes at me, then leaped onto the empty table behind the couch.

The empty...

Where's Stone?

A crash broke in the kitchen and I jerked. If Cal was transformed and Garavel asleep, that left...

He wouldn't.

He would. Oh, Ink might show a second of remorse. Who am I kidding? He'd be a smug asshole about it while burying the body.

Hoping to stave off a major disaster, I ran for the kitchen while lacing fire up my arms. The magic came without question, my sleep having refilled me. Without thought, I kicked in the door. It slammed back on its hinges to reveal a half-naked Stone leaning by the stove. He kept shaking a pot back and forth while stirring.

"You're...not dead?" I stuttered, looking around.

"If you're fishing for praise, he seems incapable." Perched on the counter like a cat angered at a trespasser, Ink glared at Stone and looked about to swipe at him.

"From what I can recall, you did very little to help," Stone said.

"You shouldn't be up. You just about...we did surgery on you." I didn't shake off the fire, which had reached the tips of my fingers, leaving them sparking like birthday candles.

Casting a slow look over his shoulder, Stone leaned over and blew on my hands. The fire snuffed out. "Careful. Old houses like these can be quite flammable."

Ink leaped to his feet. "As you see, he's hale enough. Allow me to toss this cretin out on his buttocks."

"And if I resist?" Stone argued back.

Ink's demonic grin shook me but Stone only licked batter off his finger. "I hope you do. It'll be more fun that way."

"Ink, stop." I slipped in between both men. Ink wrapped a hand around my waist as if to protect me. Or perhaps it was to give him an easier way to swipe at

Stone. Showing how little he cared, Stone kept his back to both of us as he continued his cooking.

"Last night you talked about Conquest. What do you know about him?"

Stone glanced over his shoulder. "Plenty. Alias Mr. White, he's been forming inroads with the most unlikely of allies. I've tracked his movements for the past three months, built up quite the dossier."

"Then you must have some plan to stop him," I said. Ink groaned and slumped back, though he kept his hand on my hip.

Watching the sulking demon a moment, Stone said, "First I have to find out what he's planning. Then I stop him and save my...peers."

"You don't...know?" I blinked and glanced at Ink. His smile was back and growing. He looked about to break into laughter, and I almost wanted to join in. The witch hunters acted like they controlled every level of society, that they could ambush and kidnap anyone at a moment's notice. But I knew something they didn't.

"And you do?" Stone asked.

"Yeah."

He chuckled and stirred his pot some more. "Forgive my surprise, but you expect me to believe that Conquest shared his secret agenda with a random witch and her pet demon."

"Pet incubus, thank you very much," Ink said.

"He didn't so much share as shout it at us when we crashed his party."

The spoon clattered from Stone's hand and hit the floor. "You...you broke into a Horseman's party? And survived? How? Why? I..."

His flabbergasted face only made me smile and stick out my chin. "Maybe you could learn a thing or two from a random witch. I didn't just escape him once, either."

"Yes, it's become an obsession with you," Ink growled. He tightened his hand, pulling my ass flush with his hips. Instead of the seductive press of his cock, I only found a protective palm ready to swat Stone away.

"You know why Conquest has taken over the minds of Director Zimmerman and more?" Stone said as if he couldn't believe it. He turned and brandished a spatula at me. "Explain. Tell me now."

I didn't even see the hand swipe, only heard the clink as the metal head of the spatula hit the ground. Ink held his claws out, ready for a second attack. "Threaten her again and that will be your little partner next."

Stone took the threat of castration rather well. He placed the broken handle on the counter and stared at me. "Please."

"He's going to rip apart every barrier between the realms."

A cascade of high-pitched giggles broke from Stone. I'd expected him to be the type who'd laugh with a single gruff bark, but he kept shaking as more peals burst. "That's what he thinks? It'd destroy this world. It'd..." Suddenly, he went stone silent, his lips flattening and his face paling.

"It'd give him the entire universe to conquer," I said.

"This explains..." He turned his back on us again and muttered to himself in Spanish. I caught 'mundo' and 'apocalypse.'

"If you'd be so kind as to provide the payment you promised, you can move on to stopping a Horseman from bringing about the end of the world." Ink grinned at him.

Stone wiped at his forehead, pressing back his thick, deep brown hair. "That will...not be an easy get."

"He intends to renege on the deal. Allow me to return the bullet to his chest." Ink fished the bullet out of his pocket and walked closer. Stone's eyes widened and he held a hand up to stop him.

"I did not say I couldn't. Only that... Do you mean you want the skin of a unicorn or unicorn skin?"

I clung to Ink's arm to get him to stop. His feet froze but he leaned closer, almost pressing the bullet against Stone's bare flesh. "There's a difference?"

"Unicorn skin is a rare gem that can aid in solidifying spells. It turns prismatic in the presence of magic, but to human eyes is a dull rock. The skin of a unicorn is exactly what it sounds like."

A shudder climbed up me at the thought of needing the hide of a unicorn even if the last one I'd seen had stabbed a woman in front of me. "The first one, I'm pretty sure."

"Only pretty sure? It's a hard ask either way. You'd better be certain."

"I am!" I shouted, tired of being questioned every second.

"Then once I have saved my people from the clutches of Conquest, I'll get you your unicorn skin."

The memory of Daniel ripping their giant demon-slaying gun to shreds stampeded through my mind. If I didn't cast this spell soon, I could lose him forever. "Not good enough. I saved your life. You owe me."

"Hm, in a hurry. Now I'm wondering—"

"You don't need to know." *God! Why does he make my blood boil every damn time I have to talk to him?* I wanted to grab the bullet from Ink's fingers and shove it into Stone's eye. My hackles rose and Ink shifted behind me. It almost sent me to twist around and shout at him, but he calmly extended the cast iron at Stone.

"Why don't you cook in this, promise-breaker?"

Stone barely looked at it before turning away. "I'm nearly finished. Thank you."

Ink smirked and hefted the pot back, though he kept it in his hand. What the hell was that all about? My phone trilled at me and I checked. Dana. She wanted to meet up about the... Oh god, clinicals. It was going to start next Monday. I wasn't ready for this. I didn't know anything. I...

Maram's coming too

I glared at Dana's text. She might have been chill about Fariah dating a djinn—disturbingly cool about it after the shit I'd gotten for being a witch—but I wasn't convinced. Pretending to help before sticking in the knife was what djinn were known for. Forgetting everything else, I texted back that I was coming and would be there soon.

"Morning. What smells like...high school lunch?" Cal walked in completely naked, his nose wrinkled and mouth wide for a second yawn. I only glanced up a second, but it was enough to send my heart pounding into the stratosphere. All those shifts had left him looking like a body builder at peak condition. His mountain needed to be conquered. Cal must have caught on as he smirked, glanced his hand to his thigh and drifted his gaze down me.

My phone blared again, Dana texting that she had saved me a seat at Grizzly's. I didn't have time to take a Cal ride. "I have to go."

"What?" Cal gasped, before another yawn broke out. "Where?"

"Dana, and Fariah, and…" I swallowed my worries about Maram. "And they want to talk about clinicals. Figure out a schedule. I shouldn't keep them waiting."

"Uh?" Cal drew his gaze from me to the silent Stone who'd fully turned away from the naked werewolf. Though, I couldn't help but notice the blush running down the side of his neck. "What about him?"

"Keep him *company*, at least until he provides the unicorn skin," I said while running for the door.

"As I said, I won't…" Stone looked to me, but the naked werewolf got in the way. Cal crossed his arms.

"We're quite polite to guests here, as long as they're polite back. Right, Ink?"

"There's none more hospitable than an unscrupulous demon."

There wasn't time to worry about my boys. Cal could keep Ink in line. At least I doubted they'd do anything to harm Stone. Drive him crazy, on the other hand… Torture by naked hot men — it was a shame I couldn't sit back and watch.

* * * *

I weighed the rising July heat against the fact my car was running on fumes and decided to walk. There was a noticeable lack of extra kidneys I could sell to fill the tank. At least a steady breeze blew back my cotton sundress and with it my beading sweat. Children chased each other with hoses and robins fluttered in their wake trying to dig for worms. The normalcy of it unnerved me. I clutched my purse tighter to my side, tempted to reach in for my spell book when an ice cream truck rolled past.

Anybody could be with Animal Control. Anyone could be on White's payroll. He swore he was going to use me, that he'd need me for his plan. So why wasn't he coming for me? *What are you waiting for?*

A hand wrapped around my arm. I dropped a foot and spun around. My hands dug for my spell book, ready to smash whoever was grabbing me, while I raised my knee to kick them in the crotch.

"Excellent reflexes." Ink caught my foot and held me so I had to hobble to keep my balance. "Though I'm afraid it would not do much to harm me."

"I didn't think I was swinging at you," I said, stuffing my book away. In my flustered, amateur pirouette, half of my limp twists had gotten stuck to my forehead and mouth. Dragging lip gloss across my cheeks, I pried my hair out while maintaining a modicum of dignity. All the while, the drop-dead gorgeous incubus watched with a wry little smile.

"Why are you…?" I began, before sighing. "Cal." It wasn't surprising he'd tell Ink to follow me. It was, however, that Ink had done so.

"He believes you require an escort." Ink extended his elbow as if he was taking his job seriously. I wanted to toss it off because I didn't need him, but my heart was still pounding from his unexpected appearance. Wrapping my hand around his biceps, I let Ink lead down the sidewalk.

"Though my absence does leave the wolf and bird alone with the enemy," he said with a clench in his jaw. Everything else in this world was a lark to the nearly immortal demon. Everything except witch hunters… and I'd let one stay at our house.

"How much do you hate me right now?" There was no point in dancing around it. Ink could promenade for weeks without end.

He snickered and cocked an eyebrow as if in surprise. "Do you believe me to be infested with fleas and wear a tag around my throat? I am not as soft-skinned as your baying wolf."

"Right. Like you're not mad about what happened with…"

A trio of kids no older than twelve rode past. But I couldn't stop my voice from dropping, as if White or the hunters would employ pre-teens. "Stone."

"Me? Upset that you allowed an enemy not only entrance but knowledge of our lair and let him remain there still? Why ever would I feel annoyance at such a maneuver?"

"Sarcasm doesn't become you."

Ink snickered. He pulled back my hair and whispered in my ear, "Everything comes from me."

"That's not what I…"

He winked and I accepted the loss of wits. It was probably best to let him have one anyway. No doubt he thought the same as Daniel. We walked in silence as I stewed in my mind. At the end of Cal's street, I turned us right where the houses opened up onto a busy road filled with random businesses.

"Go on. Say it. Tell me I'm stupid. That I'm an idiot for trusting Stone. For thinking that he might actually…help." Why did I? There was no reason, but watching him bleed out and beg for my help, I couldn't turn away. I honestly thought he'd at least hold up his end of the bargain. For me.

Ink fell silent. He ran his palm over the back of my hand where I still clung to his arm. The muscle slackened below my grip before tightening tenfold.

"You are often brash, leaping before the land has even had a chance to render."

"God, you've played too many games on my phone."

"And you put far too much faith in the goodness of others, whether they have shown reason to deserve it or no."

I bit my lip, trying to fight off the tears wobbling in my eyes. I hated that the word hurt, that it still stung after all these years. Taunts from high school shouldn't mean anything ten years on. I was an adult, studying not just medicine but magic. So why did the word I'd heard countless times from teachers and counselors cut me to the quick even now?

Warm fingers brushed my cheek and I realized I'd closed my eyes tight. Opening them, I caught a soft amber glow in Ink's eyes. "Your heart bleeds for creatures both great and small, and bastards from the depths of an underworld never before imagined." Ink spat at the ground as if cursing Stone to damnation. "That does not make you stupid. Foolish, perhaps. But they say that about every great hero. Only a fool would rise against an army they could not hope to defeat, the reason meaning little with death at the door."

I collapsed into his arms, my tears falling freely. Hiding my face against his chest, I tried to get control of my internal rollercoaster. "Why are you being so nice?"

"If you desire me to be naughty, I believe there is a leather belt in Calvin's trunk."

The flush didn't deter me. "I mean, you hate Stone. I'm the reason you're stuck with him. You should hate me too."

"My bond." Ink caught a big fat tear on the edge of his claws. He balanced it like a raindrop and gazed down at me. "I can be annoyed, exhausted, concerned and weary of you. But I cannot hate you."

Because demons weren't built for hate or…? I stared at him, the why perched on my lips.

Ink had to feel the question in my heart as he took a deep breath. "The reason is fairly pedestrian. I am in—"

The air thickened to gray fog. Ink's once solid body began to melt from my fingers. I swiped at the air, hoping to strike him, but my hands passed through nothing. "Ink? Ink!" All the world vanished, leaving only the rolling clouds. Oh god, had White pulled me back into the in-between?

Short heels clopped on the sidewalk. I reached into my bag and spun around, prepared to launch a thousand spells at once.

"Laylee." My mother tipped her head to me and folded her arms. A thousand bangles caught as she did, the noise of rain on the roof echoing through our cloudy bubble.

"Mom? What the shit is all of this?"

"You are forever surrounded by…them." She sneered at the idea of my guys, which was the most motherly thing she'd done since her death. "This seemed the easiest."

"I haven't seen you since the beach. You could have at least called." I held up my phone which was losing battery at a rapid pace in here. *What is this thing?*

To my surprise, my mother paled and she nodded. "I suppose I could have. If you'd give me your number."

"You never even asked. I... What do you want?"

Did she know about Stone? Should I tell her that White had control of the witch hunters? Of course, Stone could be lying and I might lead my mother into the same trap I was walking into. Better to keep quiet and see.

My mom reached over and patted both my shoulders. "I wanted to see you."

"Uh huh. Then you invite me to brunch, or we get our hair done." I frowned, remembering the mess I had on my head. "You don't banish my boyfriend..."

"He's a demon."

"Incubus."

"Let's not split hairs. Sex pest then. One you need to stop wasting your time with. You're nearly twenty-six."

Well, at least she remembered my birthday. Kind of. "Not for another three months."

"That isn't enough time. Your fertile year is nearly up."

My eyebrows shot clear up into my hairline. They became a permeant fixture with my baby hairs as I stared at her. "Excuse me? Women can have babies into their forties. Or fifties." I wasn't even sure I wanted to pop one out, certainly not while the world could end and everyone and their uncle was trying to kill me.

"Witches are not women."

"We're what? Rocks? Fungi?"

"Fine, we are women, but not like mortal women. Once your magic takes hold, you become insanely fertile."

My heart jerked. I hadn't seen any mention of that in my spell book. Preferably in huge red letters with a skull and cross bones. All I could manage was a small "eep." What did insanely fertile mean?

"More fertile than a cat in heat. One time is all it takes. It is your duty to protect the line. But you've been carrying on with men who can't do anything."

"Hey!" They could do lots of things, especially two or more at the same time.

"You need to get pregnant. Now."

I flung her hands off and nearly leaped out of my cute wedges. "Holy shit, Mom. You come back from the dead just to demand grandkids?"

Clasping her hands to her forehead, my mother muttered, "Didi was supposed to explain all of this. She…" Her low growl dropped to grief in an instant. Didi's death was fourteen years ago for me, but a month to my mom. I wanted to comfort her, before I remembered her demand to cram my uterus with a witchling.

My mother suddenly reached into my bag and yanked out my book. "This. You see this." She flipped the pages that to her were blank. Anger boiled through me at anyone else touching my book. I sprang for it and my mom let go.

As I clutched the tome safe to my heart, she sighed. "All of those spells are from your ancestors. A line of witches dating back centuries, maybe even a millennium. Magic built upon magic. If you do not have a daughter, all of that will be lost forever."

She couldn't be serious. My entire reason for existing was to keep some medieval witch's spell for dowsing from vanishing into the ether? I flipped through the pages, watching each life's work written down before it was snatched away. Hundreds of women put in the same spot as me. How many hated what they were forced to do? How many didn't want to?

I gasped and slapped my hand to my locket. "Did you want me?"

"What?" My mother stepped back like I'd slapped her.

Auntie Didi had been less a second mother to me and more the first. She had taken care of my skinned knees, had played with me for hours when I was trapped inside. My mom had only gone through the motions because she had to. So when it came time for her to fake her death, she hadn't batted an eye at abandoning the daughter she never wanted.

"Layla..."

"No. I'm not ten. You can't just send me to bed. Or make Didi fix it. Did you only have me because of this stupid lineage bullshit?" Conquest's final taunt came back to me. "Did you sleep with the Horseman to make me?"

"What? Gross. Layla, where do you get these infernal ideas? No. I assume he's as sterile as your incubus, but I don't want to know."

Then what the shit was he talking about? "He told me he made me. What if he...? I don't know. What if he infested my father? They call him Pestilence too, after all."

"Your father..." My mother's suddenly heartfelt plea clanged shut. "He's a good man."

"That's all you ever say. Who is he? Why him? Why make me?"

"That's enough!" she shrieked at me. *If I'm not the daughter of some harbinger of the apocalypse, then who am I? What am I?* "You are here because I chose you. Yes, I wanted you. Yes, it is my duty, as it is yours. So…do what you were created to do. Guard the realm by protecting the line. And stop asking about your father."

My mother took a step back and the clouds seeped in around her. I reached a hand out to grab her, but caught only thin air. While I swiped my palms back and forth, the dark fog churned, but as the light pierced through, I realized the truth. She was gone.

Tipping my head back, I screamed in frustration. All she'd left me with were a million questions. Suddenly, arms wrapped around me from behind. Before I could react, I was yanked down into a crouching ball.

"I've got you."

Cal. Exhausted and grateful, I bent my forehead to the sidewalk.

"Where is he? It? Them?" He waved an arm around before returning it to me.

"There was an impenetrable barrier here. Whoever cast it must have lost a fight with our beloved," Ink declared proudly.

I moaned. "It was my mother. She…she wanted to talk."

Cal let me go, but I didn't want to get out of my turtle shell. He rubbed a reassuring hand over my back and I risked peeking back into the world. As I looked up, I was shocked to find not only Ink behind him but Garavel and Daniel. They were ready for war, Garavel extending his sword and Daniel… When he caught my eye, I looked away, my heart churning with too many unhealed scars.

"What the hell about?" Cal asked holding a hand out to me.

As I took it, I stared up into the eyes of my sweet, hot werewolf who could only make babies with other werewolves. There was no way I could tell him. "Who knows. She's cryptic as always."

He helped me up, then crushed me in a hug. Just as I thought to return it, Garavel hefted both of us and kissed me on the forehead. "We were concerned that the Horseman had made his move."

"Or Animal Control," Cal added.

"Let us face facts, when it comes to our beloved, there is a myriad of options." Ink's words cut but his tone soothed. He caught my dangling hand and pressed my knuckles to his lips. The only odd man out was Daniel, incapable of holding me. And at that minute, I didn't want him to.

"Sorry for scaring you all. I wish she'd just text."

Cal sighed. "My mom texts just to tell me to call her."

We fell into a moment of lightness, the ice cream jingle in the air, the sun beating down. I wanted it to last for another year, or five. Adding a child into this mess... No. I couldn't do it.

Wiping away the thoughts of duty and motherhood, I stared at all my men. "If you're here, who's guarding Stone?"

Chapter Eight

Stone

The rented bed stank of moldy potatoes and toe fungus, but I had no intention of sleeping anywhere near it. It had confused the man out front when I'd asked for the room alone.

After locking the door and slipping in the chain, I yanked out the cardboard drawers in the nightstand. They practically crumbled to pieces as they hit the floor. When I yanked open the third one, the Gideon's Bible fell out. A moment of Catholic guilt hit me as I stared at the worn gold lettering. No doubt that good book had been used in every sinful way possible.

She could have asked for anything. Power was always preferable. Money. The Almighty knew the agency had it in spades. But a single ingredient a well-connected witch could get her?

I placed the Bible on the bed with reverence and movement caught my eye. My heart stilled, but it was only my reflection in the mirror above the bed. Of course there was a mirror up there. My hair was scattered across my shoulders, partially obscuring a hot-dog-eating contest T-shirt I had 'borrowed' from the werewolf. It hung off me in every wrong way, but I couldn't stop staring at the stranger in the mirror. Without the uniform, I looked like a no one, a scraggly man in need of a shower or a fix. Certainly not the last line of defense between existence and oblivion.

My fingers moved on their own, touching my forehead, then my sternum. In doing so, I pressed the still tender flesh of my wound and I shook off the last of the sign of the cross.

"It's the glasses," I said. They helped to hide my unnerving eyes. Everyone else in my family had normal brown eyes, except for me. *Chaneque*-touched, my *abuelita* would say, though usually after she'd made off with the boxed wine.

I focused on the emptied dresser. Knocking against the sides, I listened intently until I heard a thud. A smile rose for the first time since I'd belly-crawled out of the sewers. I slammed my fist through the thin plywood. It crumpled inward to reveal a safe. After entering the code, I had to rip away the rest of the back of the dresser. Water damage had sealed it against the door. Here was hoping the contents hadn't been destroyed as well.

Pulling the safe open revealed a medium-sized black box. To the untrained eye, it looked as if it was solid with no way to break in. I placed the box onto the bed and ran both my fingers around the invisible seam. When I struck the latch, my ramping heart calmed. I flipped both clasps.

"Thank god," I gasped. The cache was full and undamaged. I loaded the baggy jeans with data drives, a burner phone to read them and a handful of blank documents should I need to forge an identity. Instead of an untraceable debit card, the currency pocket held an envelope stuffed with cash. How old was this one?

It wasn't much to live on, but if I worked fast, it wouldn't need to be. As I shoved the money into my back pocket, the cache shifted. The replacement suit that'd need a good pressing slipped down to reveal a photograph.

My heart dropped. It was tradition for the agent to leave a memento of themselves whenever they replaced a cache. I used to put a proper Mexican Coke in each one. But this…

The Polaroid was fading to an ocher, but Zimmerman stared back at me through time, not with stern grit as he fired into my heart. Nor with a steady hand as he'd guided my ascendency through the agency. This version wore the same fatherly smile he'd used on me when my life had been shattered and reborn.

I pinched both my fingers at the top of the picture, prepared to rip it to pieces. A rage I was trained to corral boiled. *He shot me. He left me for dead. I had to crawl through raw sewage and beg for a witch's help.*

But he saved my life.

My will broke. I slipped the picture into the envelope with the money. Weary of the façade of normalcy, I yanked the stained hot dog shirt off. The dingy, pitted mirror above the dresser revealed the truth. Absently, I traced along the scars. They swooped in curved lines across my whole chest and clear down to my thighs. Dots and whorls filled in the gaps. It'd be appealing if they hadn't been done against my will.

A scream bubbled up from the depths of my memory. I couldn't remember what had happened, only the pain in my heart and the searing on my skin. But I didn't have to know. It was obvious from the evidence etched into my flesh. At thirteen I'd cried out in agony, and the only one to come to my rescue had been the man who had shot me.

My wandering hand found its way over the new wound. The flesh was knitting so fast, it was almost like the bullet had never happened. The old scars filled in, returning to what they'd once been. It didn't matter how many cuts and bruises I took, they always bounced back.

I raised my shoulders, watching the muscle flex beneath baby-soft skin. The healing draughts were powerful, a lifesaver in battle. But nothing beat good old-fashioned rest and time. At least, I hadn't thought so, until her...

The tip of her tooth pressing deeper where her light brown lip became pink. A lingering scent not just of magic but jasmine as her hair brushed against my cheek. Her graceful fingers prying off my shoes and holding my ankle.

I blinked, the haunting green of an impenetrable forest staring back at me. The witch could have asked for anything. Money, fame, power. Freedom. But she had chosen a rock instead.

Unfurling the suit and groaning at the wrinkles, I risked the roach-infested bathroom and turned on the shower, praying it could get hot. As steam rose, I hung the suit off the shower rod and stepped inside. The last twenty-four hours washed down the drain, taking with them any regrets lingering in my heart.

Oh, I'll give the witch her unicorn skin. An agent always repays his debts. Then I'll take her into custody, banish her sex demon, collar her werewolf and chain down her angel.

The fate of humanity always comes first.

* * * *

Layla

The throbbing in my head barely vanished as I stepped out of the confusing shadow world. Three of my men looked up with expectation, but I shook my head. "Too many people —"

A jogger ran past us, smudging my ward and wiping away the shadow memories I'd tried to explore. It'd been working at first. I had been able to track Stone out of the back door, through the neighbors' yards and into a side street before he had cut across a busy park. After that, it was pure chaos.

"You are aware the danger a witch hunter knowing your location poses?" Ink asked, loud enough to draw curious eyes. "Why not just build a pyre right now?"

I snapped my book shut and walked away without answering. Cal caught up. At first he followed a step behind, probably waiting to tell me I was going the wrong way. Then a hand slipped under my bunched fist. I opened my fingers and lay them on top of his. "Whatever he's planning, whatever they're going to do..." He clenched his fingers around mine. "I'll protect you."

"That was hardly in question," Ink said, popping up beside me. "We shall all protect you, without pause or reason. Though it would be preferable to have a plan. Unless the plan is to wing it as always."

"I don't understand this threat." Garavel stopped enjoying the flight of a moth and joined us. "Don't they hunt with witches?"

"Wrong way around, my feathered chap. They hunt witches, and have taken to using them for their means."

"Yeah, they're as bad as those mages you fought," Cal added.

That received a frosty reception. Garavel slammed a foot into the ground and glared at him. "No one is as depraved or vile as the mages of old."

"Says the guy that didn't see their lair."

"Retorts the wolf unaware of the atrocities his creators committed."

I was about to step in, not needing this, when Cal dropped his gaze. "Fair enough. I don't know how bad it was. Just like I have no idea what Stone and the rest of his hunters will do."

I tugged on the chain of my necklace, pulling the heart higher up my chest until it fell. My skin broke out in goosebumps. From the corner of my eye, I caught the ghost haunting me both literally and figuratively. Daniel hadn't offered to help hunt down Stone. I'd assumed he'd gone back to the library, but instead he drifted on the outskirts, watching.

"No one else knows."

"Babe?"

Cal's pet name jolted me. I hadn't realized I'd said that out loud. "Stone told me that...that he'd been keeping my existence a secret. The spell only wore off on him."

"You'd sooner get the truth from a preacher in a bordello than a witch hunter." Ink laughed at the idea, and he could have been right. There was no reason for

Stone to protect me, and a dozen reasons for him to lie. But my gut told me he was telling the truth.

"There's also the White problem. If Conquest really has taken —"

"Another lie from a man so crammed full of them his eyes turned green."

Cal scratched his chin. "I think you mean brown, not... Never mind."

"We should focus on Conquest. He's dangerous." Garavel got to the heart of the matter.

"Which is a good reason to get that unicorn skin. Bring Daniel back, Layla does her memory woo thing and we know White's big secret. Boom. All the problems solved." Cal made it sound so easy.

I pressed the heart locket tight to my palm and watched Daniel. He couldn't interact with the world, no chasing after the ball, feeding the ducks, not even batting the branch falling through his head out of the way. Trapped in this purgatory until it became too late. Even Ink didn't know where ghosts went, but it couldn't be anywhere pleasant.

We needed him back.

In the distance, he raised his head, his eyes wide and mouth partially open. Maybe he had an apology all ready to go. Maybe he wanted to explain himself.

I turned away. We might need him, the world might need him, but I couldn't talk to him. Not yet, anyway.

"That's why you did it. Saved Stone. Right?"

After a second, Cal's words reached me. I stared up into his trusting eyes. I had saved my enemy because... I couldn't let him die. Even if he'd refused to help me, even if he told me a hundred hunters were waiting for the signal, I'd still have tried. Ink was right — my damn heart would do me in.

"Ah, Calvin, if that is what you believe, I have a palace on the banks of the Nile to sell you."

Cal stared long at Ink, digesting his comment, before he groaned. "Let me guess, you think it's about sex."

"All of history is about sex. Either the conquering or refusing of."

"Sounds more like a hungry incubus putting shit in Layla's head again. She's not gonna fall for a man that tried to kill her."

Right. I had almost died by his hand. There were nights I woke in a cold sweat fearing that void growing inside my body. I could never want to have anything to do with that tortured, scarred... A flash shivered down my spine. Of Stone's lips pressed to mine, his hands kneading my ass and his knees spreading my thighs. It was the siren. That thing put it all in my head. Not...

My cheeks burned and, as I tried to disguise the blush by batting at an invisible bug, I caught Ink watching. He knew. Any depraved thought that passed through my head was his for the cultivating. It didn't matter as long as it made me horny. But this time, he scowled.

Maybe Stone wasn't a threat. Maybe everything he had said was a lie. All I knew was that I had to get that stone before the world lost Daniel and our only hope of stopping Conquest's apocalypse. I fell to silence while the guys kept bickering. Most of it was background, good-natured ribbing, even Garavel getting a comment here and there. But the absence of Daniel grew into a looming void.

By the time we all stumbled back to the house, my body drenched in sweat, I fell into Ink's arms. "I want to crawl into a bathtub filled with ice." I groaned.

He drew his chin against the side of my neck and whispered in my ear. "Shall I watch as the heat of your body melts the ice into beads of water glistening across your golden skin?"

That was not helping my overheating problem. Whatever argument we had seemed to have vanished as he slipped a hand down my waist and pulled my chest to his. His cock rose, wiggling its prehensile way between my thighs even as they pressed together. "Or would you rather I join you?"

Cal groaned and hefted a bag of trash from the can in the living room. "We should burn this. If my garbage man sees this much blood, they're gonna ask questions."

Blood? "Wait!" I wiggled out of Ink's impatient arms and grabbed the bowing trash bag. Stone's blood. Of course! Wads of bandages were covered in it. "This has to be enough."

Looking first to Ink, who sighed dramatically, then me digging for blank paper, Cal asked, "Enough for what?"

I slammed a piece of construction paper to the floor and smiled. "I know how to track Stone."

Chapter Nine

Cal

With my ass, I slammed the fridge closed and walked the rest of the used dishes to the sink. As I dove elbow-deep into suds, Ink appeared and yanked open the door.

"What are you doing?" I scolded. "We just ate."

He paused, half an uncooked sausage dangling from his mouth. Tugging it out, he waggled the limp wiener at me while talking. "You ate a bland concoction of casein and gluten."

"It was mac and cheese, dude."

"Precisely." He squirted a huge glob of horseradish into his palm, rolled the sausage in it and ate the whole thing. I couldn't tell if he was trying to be disgusting on purpose or accident.

Then he darted an eye up at me as he licked the last of the white goo off his palm. Incendiary, of course. If he wasn't causing shit, he was stirring the pot.

I ignored any attempt by the horny incubus to rile me up and returned to the cold dishwater. "How's she doing out there?"

"Pacing. And avoiding the ever-watchful eye of the ghost. Has she decided the gifts of creation and destruction would be put to a more useful task than bringing back a single human?"

I had a pretty good idea why Layla was mad at Daniel, but I wasn't gonna tell Ink. Mostly because he'd just make it worse to piss Daniel off, even if it'd hurt her too. "I dunno," I said with a vague shrug.

"Calvin, your attempts at lying are as pathetic as your culinary creations."

"Says the demon…" I snatched the full packet of protein bars out of his hand. "Who's eating me out of house and home."

"There are plenty of foodstuffs in the larder. And if not, you can always take down a deer or two."

A lone wolf hunting a deer… I shook my head at the idea. I hadn't even attempted any hunting, in fur or otherwise, since I was a teenager. Not a lot of people liked to hire a single mother with three always hungry kids. I wasn't even the one who'd take it down. That was Mark's job. I frowned, wiped off my hand and pulled out my phone.

Nothing. Not even a text from him in nearly six months. I knew his opinion of Layla, witches in general, but I still wanted to tell him. We were all we had left.

"Are you certain this is the correct size?"

I caught a flash of silver and spun around. Pinched between Ink's fingers was the ring, which he kept twisting to catch the weak light in my kitchen. Even seeing it, I slapped my pocket and yanked out the empty box. How in the hell did he...? "Don't wave that around!" I shouted, jabbing the box at him.

He raised an eyebrow and sighed. With the slowest movement possible, he placed the ring back where it belonged. "You are aware once you have made the bargain, that ring shall decorate her finger. Many shall see it and judge you accordingly."

"That's not why..." I paused in stowing it away and took a peek. "What do you mean judge? What's wrong with it?"

The second I'd spotted it in an old antique shop, I had known it was perfect for her. At least, I thought I had. If anyone knew Layla's deepest desires, it was the demon with a direct line to them. "Do you think she'll hate it?"

He flattened his lips and shrugged. "Who's to say?"

"You. Just now." *He's fucking with me because Layla's distracted and he's angry at her but would rather take it out on the rest of us. The ring's beautiful. Not as beautiful as her, but good enough to sit on her hand. Hopefully.*

Secure enough to not fall into a flustered panic, I put it back in my pocket and focused on the dishes. Sadly, the demon wasn't done torturing me. Ink settled in next to me, watching as I rinsed. "Have you decided upon the setting of this grand exchange of property arrangements?"

I wasn't rising to his anti-marriage bait. Taking a breath, I stared at the plate. The tiny soap bubbles sparkled as they caught the yellow chandelier light, almost like a bottle of champagne. "No. The backyard's too...pedestrian, isn't it? Maybe I should go for something bigger. Like a fancy restaurant?"

Ink raised a single shoulder.

"Or I could take Layla to a baseball game. Have them put it on the jumbo screen." That was a terrible idea the second it left my mouth.

The slow look from the incubus only cinched it. "And you believe our beloved to enjoy the doldrums of leather hitting wood? Outside of the bedroom, mind."

Yeah, fair point. I drew my palm across my throat, thinking of the last time she'd placed the black leather collar there. No Ink, no Daniel, certainly no Garavel. Just her in a pair of peek-a-boo panties and me strung up at the end of the tether at her command.

"Ah, there is an idea. You should propose mid-coitus," Ink declared with a smirk, his gaze directed at my crotch.

I didn't even bother to hide my erection and laughed at his idea. "What every girl wants."

"Is there a time when the head is more clear than after the expulsion of seed?"

A shudder climbed up my spine. "Don't call it seed ever again."

"Man jelly? Seaman's chowder?"

"Do you have a book of these?" I put the last of the plates on the drying rack then pulled the plug. Ink watched me dry off my hands and push on the kitchen door with far too much curiosity. Through the gap, I caught Layla pacing all the way down the hall in the living room. She held the map in her hands, the tattered goose feather drawing quickly. A heavenly light glowed behind her. My brain knew it was the lamp but my heart was dead certain it was her angelic halo.

"I assume you are prepared for the possibility of her saying no."

Sure. I could run off into the woods and never come back. Throw myself into a pit of spikes. Maybe set myself on fire.

"Is there anything you don't try to ruin?" I asked instead of answering him.

"Hm... Bacchanalias, assuming the olives are pitted." The demon scratched his bare chin and accompanied me by the door.

The beauty pacing in the living room stopped. She quirked her head to the side, causing her hair to fall against her neck. Closing her eyes, she rubbed one hand into her weary neck and her lips parted in a silent moan that fed me soul and body. I could watch her read her spell book for hours. I wanted to do that forever.

"Do you think she's going to turn me down?"

"I am not privy to foretelling the future. You shall have to ask an oracle for that information."

"So you have no idea what she'd do, just wanted to make me feel like shit for the fun of it. Right." Why wasn't I used to his tricks by now? How long until his random cutthroat comments slid off of me like water?

The demon watched Layla the way I had. Not with lascivious intent, not even with a wanton hunger. He stared as if entranced by her mere existence. When he caught me catching him, Ink dropped his gaze. "There are myriad ways your proposal could go wrong. I imagine most of them are in your head right now. But..."

He sighed and took a step back. "She is bound to agree."

"What does that...?" I glanced over my shoulder to find Ink gone. One second he was all 'You must be devoted to her if my fellow incubus powers don't work on you' and the next he was 'marriage is a fool's errand

and she'll cut out your heart and roast it in her hand.' Whatever the hell was eating him up, it'd be nice if he'd come to grips with it before driving the rest of us mad.

I tugged the ring out for a quick look. Not the jumbotron. Not a fancy restaurant. No, it needed to be for Layla, every part of her.

"Guys?" Her voice rose from the living room, beckoning all of us. I secured the ring and joined them. Ink popped in, landing on the couch. Garavel stood by the front door and Daniel hovered next to the TV. In the spotlight, she held up not just the magical map, but an old print one from a gas station. "We've found him."

Chapter Ten

Stone

The nondescript truck used to haul ancient artifacts turned down a maintenance road into a wooded area. I left my car parked far from any perimeter checks. While it wasn't strange for Animal Control to have business in forests, often having to trap gnomes, sprites and foul-mouthed brownies, it was odd for Conquest. He preferred to do his work in C-suites or grand halls.

I slotted the bandolier of potions around my chest and reached into the backseat for my weapons bag. Vibrations rattled up my leg. Instinctively, I almost collapsed to my stomach and prepared to scope out the threat. I caught myself just in time. If I had, I'd have broken a dozen bottles and unleashed hell on earth on myself. When I took a breath, the lurching fear cleared enough for my mind to realize I was alone and my phone was ringing.

No one had access to the burner phone's number. No one except...

"*Mamá!*"

"*Mijo*. When are you coming to Selena's birthday? We need you to pick up a cookie tray from Ralphs."

Selena? A vague face rolled in my brain with brown hair and freckles. She couldn't be a niece as I had no siblings, but probably a cousin. There were a multitude of those.

"I can't. I have to work."

Even though I was a grown man in my thirties and halfway across the country, my mother sundered my soul with the use of my full name. "You have skipped the last two Christmases, your father's bowling championship, three *quinceñeras* and I have yet to see you on the day I pushed you out of my body in nearly five years. This is unacceptable."

"*Mamá*, I can't drop what I'm doing and fly out to see you. My work is vital."

A truck roared and I dove into the brush.

"All I hear is excuses. That will not... Raul, are you listening to me?"

"*Si*," I whispered with the phone pressed tight to my head. It wasn't a truck that drove past, but a BMW with blackened windows. Was Mr. White risking his sterling clothing for a trek through grass stains?

"Why are you so quiet? Speak up."

"This isn't a good time. I'll...talk to you later."

"Do not try to brush me off. I am your mother. I gave birth to—"

My entire body puckered in shame as I hung up on my mother. It wasn't that I didn't want to see her. I loved her. My whole family were exhausting but supportive in their own way. The only way I could keep them safe was by doing my job. If Conquest got his way, if he kept controlling Zimmerman and the rest of Animal Control, then there would be no more birthday parties to get drunk and slip and slide at for anyone.

I stood up and my pants leg vibrated. Oh, my mother was angry. No doubt she was muttering every curse word I got my mouth washed out for while my father sat in his chair pretending he was deaf. I couldn't risk discovery or distraction, so I shut off the phone.

I'll be getting a slipper in the mail.

That's a problem I can solve later. This one can't wait.

Most of the trees around here were thin, modest wind breaks for farms, or small copses planted by Scouts looking for a badge, but this area held ones older than the country. I didn't risk the road and took the path less traveled. Frost was out of his mind for suggesting that one. Branches and wild sawgrass sliced through my suit. I had enough lingering health draught that it tackled the worst injuries, but it would wear off quickly.

The moment I heard voices, I veered away to trek up a rising hill. Based upon the sounds of construction and orders, they were setting up in a small valley ringed by trees. The higher I traveled, the shorter the foliage became until I was nearly bent in half to keep my head from poking out. The suit and tie seemed glamorous. Saving the world from monsters, knowing how to exorcise demons and weave spells all sounded cool. They had rarely mentioned how often I'd be crawling on my belly through every disgusting liquid just to get to point B.

It's no wonder I haven't had a girlfriend in… My brain less than helpfully provided the number, but I ignored it. "Mom's gonna start in on grandkids again," I muttered to myself as I assembled my scope while lying flat in the wet mud. It was easier to let her think that was impossible because I was a busy bachelor instead of the truth. I wouldn't be walking away from that fight.

I eyed up the distance, guessing they looked about three hundred feet away, then adjusted the focus. "Holy..." The lens bounced and I zeroed in. Twelve massive standing stones formed a circle around a granite altar. The brainwashed agents weren't putting the stones up. They were painting runes on each one.

Time of year, darkness of the brush, they had to be using minotaur hair to draw... I focused, expecting to find glittering iridescence. But no, the runes were done in streaky crimson. Blood. At a guess, human.

I'd broken up many sacrifices. Sometimes from witches, sometimes from demons, though just as often from sycophants who had found the wrong book at the used bookstore. Eyes in Crockpots, spleens crammed into Tupperware, once tongues in tongue-depressor jars — it was part of the job that I shrugged off every night. But watching men and women I'd worked beside, CCed memos to, exchanged shitty Christmas gifts with chilled me to my marrow. How deep had Conquest worked his vile fingers?

I cupped the bottles I'd placed beside me. *I swear, I'll free you all.* After that, Mr. White's free ride would end. I adjusted the scope, trying to spot Director Zimmerman. There was no sign of a man with his sleeves rolled up or the sun glinting off his bald spot. But as I checked the nondescript faces of every man and woman above a suit and tie, I landed on the last one I'd hoped to find.

River. My partner of ten years had a finger to his ear as he listened to orders to paint standing stones with human blood. When he'd scraped off Drake's brains, I had told myself he was pretending. He was faking to get close to Zimmerman in order to infiltrate. But the longer I watched him carry out every minute order with the excruciating detail I'd seen each day, the more my heart sank. He wasn't pretending—he was as brainwashed as everyone else.

I had to get to him first.

Picking up a vial and rag, I rose to my haunches and waddled down the hill. Hard to be a cool badass when dressed and moving like a penguin, but it'd keep my head from getting blown off. As I drew closer, I picked up the inane chatter of a construction crew.

"Watch your six."

"Back up before I hit you."

"What's that?"

I dropped to the ground and covered the back of my head with my hands. Holding my breath, I prayed for the quivering grass to be dismissed as the wind or a rabbit.

"Eh, just a squirrel. Damn it, you missed a spot on the connecting stone!"

How am I going to get River away from them?

"I'm checking the perimeter. We need this place secure before his arrival," my partner declared. He wiped the blood from his hands and strode away. Perfect.

Everyone else leaped into work, paying no attention to the shadow lurking just outside their sacrificial altar. River moved as if without purpose. To the inexperienced eye, it'd seem like he was wandering, keeping any potential onlookers completely off balance. But I'd worked with him for nearly a decade. I knew every trick.

He wove his way out of the line of sight and into the heavier brush. *Here's where he'll stir it with his foot, scattering any wildlife.* I watched, my thighs clenched to leap up and take him out. River walked over, stopped and leaned back on the ball of his foot. Then he strained his foot out.

Now! I slammed a palm to the ground to shove myself up. A horn blared from the road and River spun his head around to find it. *Shit!* I dropped as fast as possible, but it left my cover shaking. That caught his eye.

"Hello? Any cute fluffy bunnies who shouldn't be here?"

His voice burned through my clenched jaw like a broken tooth. Not because it was unsettling, but because it was so normal. That voice had told me about how he hated mustard, how he had lost his front tooth from a baseball to the face. The day he was gonna propose.

River abandoned the taller grass to walk closer to me. I tensed. He reached a hand behind himself, grabbing for the holster hanging off his back. River began to tap his tongue against his teeth, a sound I'd had to suffer relentlessly on stakeouts. I dug my fingers into the wet mud to keep from screaming.

I couldn't risk looking. I had to trust my instincts. Dropping my face, I waited. The shadows shifted across the ground. River's lanky form stepped closer. His foot lifted from the ground. I raised my hands, but no, it was a feint. He pulled back, then rammed it forward.

Blind, I slapped my hands together and caught the surprised ankle of my ex-partner. With all my strength, I yanked him off his feet. "What the...?" was as far as River got before his back slammed to the ground. I scrambled, crawling over top of his wriggling body.

Pinning back his armed hand, I slammed it to the ground. But even with the force, he clutched tight to the gun. That was our training. My only hope was surprise, and boy, did my appearance shock him.

"Stone?" He blinked, forgetting all we'd been taught. Was it guilt? Or did he think a ghost had just laid him out?

Either way, I wasted no time. Folding my fist tight, I pinned my knee to his chest, and punched him in the head. It caused his neck to snap back, getting him twice. Not enough to knock him out, but it'd leave him woozy. Working fast, I uncorked the vial with my teeth and drenched the rag.

Hands clamped to my knee, trying to shove me off, but he was too late. Just as he reached back to punch, I collapsed the rag over his nose and mouth. River held his breath. He tried to fling me off, one hand digging into my wrist. I couldn't pull him off either, as I had to keep the gun pinned.

Breathe. Breathe it, you son of a...

I raised my knee and slammed it into his chest. River gasped and, as nature intended, he pulled in a strong dose of oxygen tinged with a geas-erasing potion. He got one more punch to my exposed wrist before his eyes rolled back and he fell to the ground like a ragdoll.

After waiting another thirty seconds to make certain he wasn't faking, I grabbed River's feet and pulled him into the trees. He could sleep it off without anyone the wiser and wake up the man he used to be. Far from the road, I left River snoring. Poor Wanda. At least she'd be getting him back tonight.

I picked through his pockets, taking anything of interest. As I pulled the earpiece out, a voice said, "He's here."

I turned to face the road just as a stretch limo rolled down the dirt road. "Mr. White's arrived."

Chapter Eleven

Layla

I steeled my spine and nodded. One by one, each of my men stood. Cal roughed a palm over his scruff. Ink smirked and unfurled his wings right into Cal's mouth. After spitting out the feathery shadows, he sighed and leaned to the side to see me. Garavel gave Fiona one last scratch then placed her on her cardboard kitty castle. With our little mascot secure, he pulled out his sword and gave it a twist. Massive barbed spikes formed on the ends of the hilt. Finally, Daniel...

"First we help him, now we hunt him?"

"It is a rather delightful irony the witch hunters of old would be proud of. Or douse in holy water while they recited an apocryphal Nicene creed. Six of one."

Daniel waved a hand over the paperback copy of the *Malleus Maleficarum*. Whenever I'd looked up from the map, he'd read a section of the manual for the old witch hunters. Or, as Ink had explained, "A sexually frustrated priest who needed to accept his passion for hot rods thrust up his backside."

I could explain that I was doing it to help him. That we needed the unicorn skin to bring him back before it was too late. But at Daniel's focused look, I dropped my head. Shame boiled in my belly. If I wasn't so stupid, I never would have lost Stone in the first place. Or trusted that he'd honor his word.

Instead, I tucked my spell book inside my purse. As it settled in, the leather straps on my bag tightened. The spell I had cobbled together seemed to be working. No hand but mine could pull out my book or remove the bag as long as it rested inside. I had no intention of going mad tonight. "Are we ready?" I asked, offering cursory glances.

Stone was a wily pain in the ass who'd been trained to combat people like us. But he was also one man and, for all his crafty tricks, he couldn't dodge forever. I caught the flipping pages of the first witch hunting manual. It landed on a woodcut image of a woman screaming her head off while cheering assholes burned her. Maybe Stone and all the rest deserved worse than a heavenly demonic magical werewolf team-up. History certainly wasn't on their side.

"My bond…" Ink sidled up beside me. "If you will indulge me."

I puckered my lips, but instead of savoring one last drink of my magic, he swung a long piece of velvet around my shoulders. As the violet radiated silver runes when I shifted, Ink clasped a plain silver brooch against my neck. "What is this?"

"Protection."

"Ink, it's like nine thousand degrees out. I'm not wearing it." I reached up to take it off, when his hand caught mine. To my surprise, Cal cupped my shoulder and he aimed his puppy eyes at me. I didn't need this damn thing. It weighed me down, and I already felt like I was burning up. But I couldn't say no either.

I dropped my hand and nodded, only for the cloak to tug on the brooch, embedding it into my throat. *The second we're done, this thing is getting stuffed behind the dryer. Not even Ink would look there.*

"Ah, and one more little surprise should the witch hunter decide to be the conniving bastard we all know he is." Ink snaked his hand into my bag and let go. Something heavy pulled on my shoulder like he'd dropped a five-pound weight in there. I reached in to see what it was, but he scooped me up into his arms.

"I shall take Layla near the site of the infernal hunter."

"Wouldn't it be smarter if we all went together?" Cal asked. He patted his pocket to jangle his keys.

"Ah yes, give the men with spyglasses and attack bees time to spot us in your rattling truck."

Attack bees? Cal mouthed at me, but I shrugged. "Then how am I going to get there?"

Ink jerked his head and Garavel bent down. "Holy…!" was as far as Cal got before the giant angel scooped him into his arms. He wiggled as if to leap out, before catching me in the same position. "This should probably bother me more than it does."

"Accept your lot in life, wolf. It'll make the rest of your days pass in ease," Ink said. He was about to take a step and yank me to the old woods where Stone was hiding, but I stopped him.

"Garavel?"

He didn't look pleased to be holding Cal, both of them wearing the expression of a wet cat, but as he looked down at me, he risked a soft smile.

"Be careful. Both of you. Who knows what they have for aerial support?"

"I shall cleave the head off this dangerous Aerial and any other creature in their employ!" Garavel boomed.

I opened my mouth to explain, but Cal caught my cheek. "I'll explain, and watch out for potential missiles. Moon take me, my life is weird. Ink? For fuck's sake, keep her safe."

"Every endeavor of mine is for the sake of fucks." Ink damn near beamed as if he'd been waiting to use that line. Then his gaze drifted down to me, and the proud, mischievous smile melted. "As long as I stand, no harm will come to her."

Because if I die, he dies. I had to remind myself of that, otherwise my heart might start thinking he cared for a reason he kept insisting was impossible. A twinge of concern clotted my incubus' dangerously handsome brow. I reached up to kiss it away, and the cloak snagged, choking me.

"Get us out of here so I can take this thing off!"

"You heard our beloved," Ink said. Garavel's wings erupted, knocking against every picture frame in the living room. Cal didn't even wince, only held a hand out to wave to me. The angel ducked and took off through the front door. I watched the fading sun catch on his bright white feathers before the world jumped.

The living room stacked with too many books and plates became an oppressively hot forest. Cicadas wheezed louder than a motorcycle, momentarily blocking my hearing as I stared around the thick trees and wild grass. "Oh fuck, why didn't I put on bug spray?" This place had to be loaded with ticks and mosquitoes.

A hand clamped over my mouth. Panic burbled in my blood even though I knew who it belonged to. Ink sank to his knees, carrying me with him. When we struck the ground, he let go of my mouth and pointed. We were supposed to land far from Stone, then Ink would scope out the situation.

But as I traced Ink's finger past the shifting grass and through a copse of trees, my stomach flipped. Twelve stones stood in a disquieting circle, each radiating an unholy glow around the red paint. Queasiness bubbled up to my throat the longer I stared at the runes. It felt...oh, god. It felt like every time Conquest had hurled me into the in-between.

"Ink..." I whispered, barely above a breath, trying to tug him to me. If Conquest was here, we had to abort. Stone, sure, maybe even a couple of extra witch hunters for good measure. But taking on the Horseman was so far above our pay grade. He could obliterate us with a sneeze.

We had to leave, warn Garavel and Cal. I yanked on Ink's opened shirt, nearly snapping a button off, but he wouldn't look my way. Slowly, he raised his finger to point out the shifting tall grass. A brown head with hair tucked into a low ponytail poked up from the dying grass. Stone didn't see us, all of his attention on the unnerving circle powering up for a very bad night.

Ink raised his head and smiled. "The snake has revealed itself."

"No—" He dropped me and vanished, appearing right behind Stone. The witch hunter didn't see the demon latching onto the back of his suit and hurling him ten feet to the ground. I had taken a step, weaving a spell to keep Stone pinned, when the glow of the circles hardened to a blue light and sealed off the stones. Ink noticed just as the setting sun crashed into utter darkness.

* * * *

Stone

Where's the bastard?

The stones were spitting errant magic into the world. Through the lenses of my special glasses, I was able to see what no human could. Tendrils of blue stretched from the vibrating runes up into the sky and down into the ground. Whatever Conquest was up to, it was tampering with the bones of the earth.

A sound I didn't notice shifted, a soft tone growing louder and faster. One by one, the brainwashed agents dropped their brushes and gathered around the altar. They clasped hands and chanted, the words shivering in my ear. I slammed my shoulder to the side of my head. One of the agents stepped away, leaving a gap. His hood slipped off, and my stomach sank.

Director Zimmerman gazed at the sacrificial circle with pride. Magic seeped from him, spells I'd never seen shielding him. They were so powerful, they could have only come from the puppet master. Zimmerman gave one last nod before approaching the limo. It stood out like an excavated femur in the forest.

As he wrapped his hands around the handle and pulled, I steadied myself. Rising, I placed the rifle on the balance block and lifted my sunglasses. The director shifted into view down the scope, then he moved and blinding whiteness stepped out of the limo.

"Ah ha!" A hand dug into the back of my shirt. The claws flayed my skin as they went, nearly causing me to scream. Before I could even reach for it, the monster flung me back. Rocks tore at my flesh and pounded into my lungs. I fought to keep from exhaling, knowing I needed all my oxygen for what was coming.

The second I hit, I tried to rebound, prepared to attack. From out of the sudden darkness, the hand clamped to the front of my shirt. Its owner hauled me up like I was a ragdoll. I kept rising, my feet kicking thin air. In shaking to find the assailant, my glasses fell down my nose and I stared into the demonic fire of the incubus's eyes.

"What are you doing, you fool?" I dug into my pocket, blindly bypassing the dozens of capsules for the one I needed.

The creature laughed. Not the cute smirk he used on her. This came from the bowels of hell. He shifted his grip, impaling his thumb claw into the base of my throat. I gulped, wet blood dripping down my chest as he shook me. With a great heave, he yanked me closer.

Brimstone and death burst from his lips, blanketing my nose. "Honoring a debt."

"Is this about the damn unicorn skin?" Seriously? They'd attack now for a simple ingredient?

The demon drew his fingers up, releasing my shirt but holding me by my chin. He raised his lips in a snarl, revealing every jagged tooth for shredding flesh. "No, witch hunter. It's about you paying in blood."

He reared back with his other arm, the claws pinched together and aimed to pierce through to my heart. I flicked my thumb, hoping I'd guessed right. If not, it wouldn't much matter. The demon watched my eyes, savoring the fear I couldn't shake. My about-to-be-flayed heart pounded faster, and every vein under my scars was about to explode.

"But she wanted me—"

"She'll get over it," the demon interrupted. He thrust.

I slammed my palm into his arm. The magic took hold in an instant, freezing every denizen of hell in place. His claws sliced through my jacket and shirt. Just the tips scraped over my skin. I breathed, but a very shallow one.

"You're trapped, demon."

"So are you," he said. His hand was still clamped to my chin, keeping me hoisted in the air. "Shall we stay like this until the end of time? I'd quite enjoy the up close view of your body wasting away to dust."

I tried to wiggle my way out, but his grip was iron. I shouldn't have waited so long. In my flailing, my glasses tumbled off into the grass. Without them, I wouldn't be able to predict the magic lines. No matter. First, I needed to get free, then resume...

When did it get so dark?

Despite sunset being hours away, the sky was churning with black clouds. Green lightning splintered through the sky, whipping it into a vortex before spiking off. If I could see that with my naked eyes, then what was really happening in the circle?

I needed to break free, and fast. With my free hand, I dug for the only blade that could pierce demon flesh. Quenched in the blood of angels from before the realms existed, it could destroy Lucifer itself if anyone cared enough to bother.

"Why are you laughing, demon?"

"I'm picturing a raven squatting on your skull while it devours your eyeball. Just the one though, so you can watch every peck."

And she brought *that* to bed? Witches.

Cold that bit deeper than a Siberian winter radiated up my finger. I'd found it. Clasping my hand to the hilt, I yanked the blade out. He watched, unable to defend himself, and showing no concern. No matter the sin, they shared one commonality—an ego the size of the *Titanic*.

"Ink?"

I jerked, nearly dropping the blade at her voice. *He brought her here? Is he mad?*

Damn it. Forget the witch. Twisting my arm until the wrist popped, I rammed for the immobile demon. At the last second, he jerked back and the deadly blade sailed on past. His arms dropped and I plummeted with him. Rather than fall, I landed on the balls of my feet and readied myself for a witch attack.

Her body glowed with a striking mix of greens and purples, the jagged lines splintering off her raised hands. One she held out to me, the other cupped her precious book. The power coming off of her was breathtaking. I'd only ever seen such a force once before, when she thought no one was looking.

"If you intend to kill me, do your worst."

"I'm not trying to..." She glared at her incubus. "Ink? What did you say to him?"

The snarling pit bull became an unimpressed poodle at her ire. He folded his arms as if he wasn't about to gut me and shrugged. "The usual biting remarks between best enemies. 'I'll disembowel you.' 'No, I shall.'" He dropped his arms and said in a cold tone. "Turn your back. You need take no part in this. I'll end it, and all our troubles will be over."

"You damn... Look at the sky!" She pointed behind us toward the standing stones. The demon took his time twisting his head in the direction. Just as he turned, I slashed with the blade. He raised a hand and clamped onto my wrist.

"Naughty, naugh—ah!"

I nicked the back of his hand and, as ichor welled up from the unsealing wound, he let go. The demon clutched his bleeding paw in shock. "This hurts? You hurt me, you insignificant—"

He was fighting stupid. I twisted the blade around, prepared to strike up through his chest. The demon roared, claws and fangs out. His human illusion vanished, the shadow wings blending in with the darkening sky. I wove on my knees, dodging the first attack. His chest was wide open. I shoved the blade up.

A force slammed through my body. It sent me flying ass over end into the air. Rocks and saw grass tore apart my hands and face before slamming into my spine. I tried to bolt up, but the pressure didn't vanish. Instead, it increased, shoving me deeper into the wet dirt.

"What. Did you do. To Ink?" Fire blazed in her eyes, her hand outstretched as she walked to my vulnerable body.

"I…"

My body slammed another inch into the ground, bedrock cracking into my bones. I'd known this witch was strong, her book's size revealing a long line. But this power was beyond belief. It was as if the earth itself was digesting me.

"Tell me. Now!"

"He's been—"

Ropes erupted from the ground, wrapping around the witch's arms. They yanked her hands, cutting off the flow of force, before pulling her to her knees. She cried out, enraged. Had River already woken? I took a breath, testing to see there were no broken ribs, and sat up.

Or I tried to. Ropes formed of the earth erupted around me, pinning me back. Everywhere they touched burned, the stench of copper and blood baking into my flesh. I gasped in agony when the rope pulled my head back. My heart sank as Director Zimmerman walked closer, flanked by two badged witches.

"So here's where you've been hiding, my boy."

Chapter Twelve

Stone

Hard, cracking ground slammed into my knees. I flexed my bound hands, testing the tensile strength. The movement must have caught Zimmerman's eye as he stopped propping the once-again frozen demon up by the altar. He waved a finger and ordered, "Keep an eye on him."

"What about the witch?"

"That one's mine."

An inhuman chill swirled through the stone circle. With each click of his cane against the dirt, a vibration radiated outward, causing me to clench my teeth. Mr. White paused next to the faceless robes and calmly adjusted his lapel. To my rising bile, the director of witch hunters bowed to the Horseman. "Shall I leave her for you?"

Layla'd been bound and gagged beside me, her hands zip-tied to her ankles. She should have been drowning in inescapable dread. But above the white rag, her eyes blazed with fury.

Conquest finished his preening and loomed taller. Not by rising on his tiptoes. No, his body stretched, sending his head into the towering clouds. "Don't worry. I'll collect my property in due time."

I'd swear I could feel her white-hot cursing. The words were muffled from the rag, but the sentiment was inescapable. Too bad four-letter words couldn't stop the apocalypse.

"If you'd please finish the arrangement. I have pressing matters to attend." Conquest sounded bored and looked to his limo. Someone was still inside. His champion? I had yet to find that name.

Zimmerman smiled and headed for the altar. "Of course. Do you mind?"

The strange woman who'd been beside him when he'd shot me grunted. She turned to the stand of badged witches dutifully casting spells. Without pause, she wrenched one off the ground and threw her onto the stone altar.

Are they going to…?

A blade swept fast, glinting from the woman's hand as she sliced open the witch's throat. Blood sprayed against the executioner's face. My stomach knotted at the long, white tongue that licked her cheek clean. Cold seeped up my hands and I clenched them tight.

"Layla? What the fuck is going on?"

The harried voice caused me to risk turning away. A man who'd died thirty years ago stood behind me, his ethereal body eclipsed just by Layla. The rest of the agents were too enthralled gathering the witch's blood and smearing more runes over the altar to notice his arrival.

"Please talk to —"

"Do not move," I snarled. To my surprise, he did as I said. Here I'd assumed they were allergic to orders and common sense.

"Fuck you," he cursed and took another step.

"You are currently hidden from their sight and our only hope. If you move, they will catch and banish you. Or worse."

The ghost laughed. "They can't see me."

I raised an eyebrow and looked back. The leather jacket and fading blue streak spoke of a young man trying to rebel again a society he barely understood. If I was lucky, there might be some wisdom in his old eyes. "I can."

The ghost jerked as if he finally realized I'd been talking to him. Even if the agents weren't wearing their special glasses, Conquest would see him for certain.

"I'm not leaving."

"I had no intention of getting rid of you."

"Unlike last time."

Mother Mary, did these people let anything go? I struggled to look past the rising sphere of magic coated in spilled blood. They'd left the demon propped up on the other side of the circle, his claws extended while ichor dripped off his wounded hand. That might be our only answer, assuming he didn't kill me first.

"I'll free you, Layla," the ghost whispered in her ear. She jerked and shook her head.

"She's right. Don't waste your limited strength with that. Get to the demon and break the ward keeping him pinned."

"Help Ink before Layla?" He sounded like he wanted to vomit at the idea.

"I mean, if you can..." I said, setting off the chain reaction I wanted. The ghost vibrated with barely suppressed rage, a fury only known by those who'd seen the other side of the grave. Though, instead of conquering the demon, he waggled a finger at me.

"When this is over, I'll gut you myself."

"We'll see," I said, smirking.

"Stone?"

Damn it. The ghost had enough sense to vanish. I didn't look at the demon, but dropped my head. Tensing my forearms, I slipped the zip-ties higher without moving a muscle.

"What are you up to?" The director left the un-sacrificed witches to tend to the rolling blood orb. He took a step closer to me and the winds shifted. I risked looking past him to find the ghost standing behind the frozen demon. *Oh great, he can't find the ward. It's on the...no, not the ground. The tree. They painted it on the... Pay attention!*

The ghostly flailing caught their attention. I needed a distraction. "Why?" I screamed from the depths of my soul. It'd be acting if I hadn't been suppressing the question for the past two days. "Why are you doing this? Why did you shoot me?"

"The better question is why is it still alive?" Conquest suddenly showed an interest in me and not the ghost struggling to scratch a line through the solid ward. Just a minor crack, that was all it needed. "You told me you'd ended it. I don't take kindly to lies."

"I did. I put a bullet in his chest. He shouldn't have been able to shrug off solid iron." In all my years serving beside him, facing off against nightmares from the dawn of time, I'd never heard a wobble in my director's voice. Not until now.

"Is it because I was getting close? Because I know your secret?" I shouted at Conquest.

For a moment, the Horseman glanced down at me. A storm rolled in his eyes but he sighed and looked away. "You? It's not what you know, it's what you are. Though, perhaps you could be useful in the end. Drain him."

"What?" Zimmerman jerked.

Conquest sighed. "Use him or the witches. But leave that one be. She's for later." He pointed a finger at Layla and walked back to his limo. "I expect results. There's no reason to voice the 'or else.'"

The door slammed, momentarily cutting through the rabid chanting and crackle of thunder above. Zimmerman stared down at me, one hand loosely wrapped around the same gun he'd used to shoot me. "You…you fool. Do you have any idea what breaking your seal has done?"

He lifted the barrel. No quick shot without tears this time. His cheeks were drenched as he struggled to aim first for my heart, then my head.

What seal? What the hell is he talking about?

"I have served you and the agency loyally since I was seventeen years old!" I shouted. My skin bulged as the ties lodged tightly below my elbows. Gritting my teeth to hide the pain, I jammed a foot to the ground and rose. "Every mission, every order, I followed. I've done everything you asked of me from the moment we met. Everything."

His gun rattled as we both glared at each other. The troubled child who'd steal rosaries to drop into toilets had become the loyalist agent. And it was all because of him.

"Director Zimmerman. Matthew?"

He gulped and cupped a hand under the butt of his gun. "You should have stayed asleep," he said, and placed his finger against the trigger.

The air shifted and a man's ass slammed into my stomach. I stumbled back, struggling to keep from falling as the demon took every bullet meant for me. He stared down at the damage and laughed. "I've had quite enough of you." The incubus lashed out with his claws to gut the director, but when he bounced against Zimmerman's chest fire burst up his arm.

"Holy armor won't protect you from me." The demon lashed out with all his furor despite his claws puffing up in smoke.

I wrenched my arms apart as fast as I could. The zip-tie shattered, freeing me. I dove for the witch and yanked off her gag. Even knotted in a sneer, her lips formed a spell and an invisible force shoved off of her. It somehow clipped through the demon, but hurled Zimmerman and every agent back against the stones. The body of the dead witch flopped to the ground, the last of her blood staining the ground.

Dipping my head down in prayer, I realized I had forgotten to untie Leeland. I reached for my knife when her bonds exploded. Pieces of flaming hot plastic nicked my cheek and ear.

She stood up.

"You sons of bitches!" She raised her hand with a rotating ball of fire. The witch strode for the center of the sacrifice with her hair whipping about. Hot winds met the cold, forming a vortex swirling around her. She stretched both hands out, both palms holding fire. "This is for fucking kidnapping me," she shouted and hurled the first one.

It struck the rock just above the stunned Zimmerman. At the last second, he dodged the flames. The rampaging witch didn't even blink, but hurled her second fireball at the same rock. The stone cracked, and the top half tumbled to the ground.

"Damn it," Zimmerman cursed, before he turned to the mysterious woman. "Ello?"

Rising to her feet, the mystery woman Ello dug her nails into her suit and ripped it off. Massive wings burst from her back. Feathers coated her legs, ending in talons that stepped out of the tattered pants. As she raised her head, horns of feathers sprouted and she flung her wings back.

A harpy!

Her shriek shredded through my marrow like nails on a chalkboard. The witch dropped her spells to cover her ears, which was when the harpy took flight. Rocketing off her talons, she slammed straight into Leeland and hefted the witch into the air.

"No!" I reached for one of the scattered weapons and tried to take aim. The harpy bobbed on the wind, her wings tucked in tight for a bank while the talons dug into Layla's shoulders. The witch wasn't giving up without a fight, but there was little she could do as the creature turned to follow the escaping limo. She was being taken to Conquest.

It wouldn't be long before the harpy shot clean over us and for the road. I had one chance. Leveling my aim, I tried to compensate while the witch wove back and forth into the scope. If I wasn't careful, I'd hit her instead. Not yet. Not yet. Not...

The brown feathers burst into view, and I reached for the trigger. Blinding white streaked across the scope's lens. I ripped my sight from it and stared in shock at the giant black angel plowing into the harpy. An aerial battle broke out, the angel swinging a massive sword while the shrieking harpy dodged. As the blade came for her throat, the harpy opened a talon to catch it. One foot wasn't enough to keep Layla airborne.

"She's falling!" I shouted. The dark shadow beside me vanished. Helpless, I trailed the witch plummeting two hundred feet out of the sky. Not to her death, but certain to be a broken femur or two. Red streaked across the horizon toward me and Layla vanished.

"Stone. What have you done?" The irate voice of the director pulled me from the witch's disappearance. No doubt the incubus had caught her and carried her off. Fine. I didn't need her help anyway.

Zimmerman wiped at his mouth and winced. He stared at a line of blood, for once his, spilled on the ground. Hobbled, he stood along with the other agents.

"You're working for the enemy," I shouted. With one hand I aimed the gun, the other I dug through my pocket.

The man who'd given me my first job, had written the letter that got me into college, had sat by my hospital bedside after the wight attack, raised his gun. "You're lacking vital information, Agent."

"Or you've been compromised, Director."

He snickered and ran a finger over his mustache. "Your hair's grown again. It's nearly past your shoulders in, what, ten hours?"

How did he…? I didn't reach up to my unexplainable locks. Their growth was random—some days almost normal, others I could pull a Lady Godiva if I liked horses. But I never let the office know.

"You can shrug off death. Your luxurious hair sprouts down to your ass in days. Only iron can stop you in your tracks."

No. He had used a cursed bullet. It wasn't just a piece of iron.

Zimmerman edged closer, his eyes glowing below the rim of his glasses as he tapped them. "You can see magic without these. What creature is capable of all of that, Agent?"

It isn't possible. This is a mind trick. He's fucking with me to keep me from freeing him. "I'm human. My parents' walls are plastered with pictures of my bare-naked ass on a rug. I am not a —"

Gray fur burst from the side. On instinct, I aimed my gun, about to open fire on the werewolf plowing into Zimmerman. His gun clattered to the stained altar and he fell. It'd take nothing for the wolf to bite his head off, but he only held the director down while the rest of the agents raced to help.

"I wouldn't if I were you," the sardonic demon's voice cried out before he slammed a fist into the cheek of one and bent the gun of another. Shots rang out, striking the immune demon, then aiming at the wolf.

Feathers tumbled and the angel stood before the werewolf, shielding him. His body was speckled with blood and harpy feathers, but he smiled wide while sticking his fists to his hips.

"This is going well," the angel shouted before looking out at us. "What happens next?"

"It's a lovely time of year for a barbecue," the demon crowed. He cast off his human illusion and whipped his tail into the knee of an advancing agent. I winced in sympathy, but focused on aligning the trigger in my hand.

"Ink, we're not killing them."

To my shock, the witch approached, one hand on her book, the other extended. The fire in her palm told a different story, but the demon at least bowed his horns to her. She slammed her palms tight, casting a line of sparks that sent the agents skittering away. But her biggest problem was the other witches.

"My bond, if I may...?" The demon wrapped his hands around one, then vanished.

"Layla, behind you!" the ghost shouted. She ducked, just missing a blade spell, and directed a powerful force that sent the witch flying.

God damn cheap piece of... The button finally slotted into place. I tugged at the bandana hidden below my shirt, when Zimmerman dug a blade into the werewolf. The fur shrugged off most, but the wolf whimpered and the director rolled out from under.

"You goddamn bastard!" Leeland shouted, but the director didn't look once at her.

"What do you think you're doing, Stone?" he shouted at me.

I raised the trigger. "Saving you."

Every bottle I'd painstakingly hidden burst, the mind-clearing gas exploding into the air. The angel grabbed the wolf and flew away from the rising yellow cloud. Zimmerman and the other agents panicked, reaching for masks they wouldn't find. I... *Oh shit, the witch!*

Not thinking, only doing, I grabbed her by the shoulders and clamped my mouth over hers. At first she melted, her sultry lips softening. As the gas plumed around us, we vanished in the yellow haze. She began to fight me, but it wasn't safe. I held her tight, staring into her enraged eyes. A hand landed flat on my belly. One that could possibly eviscerate me.

But I held tight, praying she had enough sense to not doom us both. One by one, the crumple-crash of bodies hitting the ground pierced through our sallow bubble.

Four, three, two... I broke the kiss.

She blinked at me, shock in her eyes. Tenderly, she grazed the edge of her puffed-up lips. Her wondering gaze sharpened. With a hard slap, she smacked me, then leaped away.

We were alone save the slumbering agents I'd freed from Conquest's grasp. "I did it to—"

"I know why. I'm not an idiot," she snarled back.

"I didn't want to give you the wrong impression."

She laughed and took a longer step away. "I never want to kiss, or touch or look at you ever again, witch hunter."

Ouch. I shouldn't have felt anything for that condemnation. She was as off limits as they came. Telling myself that sleeping with a witch would get me kicked out and mind wiped didn't stop my gaze from sweeping down her tight T-shirt. More than the memory of her breasts behind that thin camisole riled up my blood. I thought the taste of her lips had only been in my dreams, but as I pursed my mouth, more of her lightning tingle dripped down my throat.

"You think—"

I jerked at the voice and wiped my hand through the lingering fog. Zimmerman stared up at me from his knees. He dropped a gas mask to the ground. "You've won?"

He didn't breathe it in. His mind was still Conquest's. I raised the gun. "I'm sorry," I said, locking away every memory of my mentor. He was only a liability now.

My finger slipped into the trigger and I pulled. A force slammed into the back of my head, sending me flying forward. Zimmerman launched, snatching the gun away as my vision faded in and out. I slammed a hand to the ground and turned…to find River pointing his gun at me.

Chapter Thirteen

Layla

Winds crackled and steaming rain dripped upward as Stone scrambled to his feet. He wouldn't take his eyes off this agent, missing the damn leader snatching up a glass vial. A single drop of a dark green liquid rested in the exact middle.

"He's…" I began, but the vortex swirling around us picked up speed. It swallowed my voice and sent it careening out past the stones. The winds whipped so fast, no one could get through.

"River, man, you don't understand. Conquest—"

"I kept telling you"—this River aimed his gun square at Stone's temples—"he's no longer your concern."

"But…you're free. I freed you from the…" Stone looked to the director.

A disquieting giggle broke from the man. "There was nothing to free us from, my boy," he said and shattered the vial. The green liquid zipped straight into the heart of the blood sphere and crackles of light burst from its hardening surface.

"You're working with a Horseman?" Stone shouted above the rising winds.

The director tipped his head. "It's more he's working with us."

I cried out, "You're a fucking idiot if you —!" The winds caught my cloak, plastering the damn thing against one of the standing stones. It dug the brooch deep into my throat, cutting off my taunt. Though it did draw the director's attention.

"Keep an eye on her," he ordered River while calmly switching out the bullets in his gun. Zimmerman loaded a black shot into the chamber without looking up. The River guy waved his gun at me. I snarled back, too angry to feel fear.

"You were a good agent, Stone." He slammed the chamber shut and pulled back the hammer. "One of the best. It's a shame you had to break the seal."

"What seal? What are you…?"

They were going to kill him. The people he'd bled and nearly died for. They'd shoot him without question.

I could have stayed put. Waited for the winds to die down so my cavalcade of men would rip these guys to pieces. What did Stone mean to me beyond yet another asshole trying to kill or control me?

The director leveled his gun and I struck, swinging my fist into River's side. It sent him slamming into the broken rock. Racing, I flung myself in front of Stone. His hand landed around my waist and he gasped.

My lips moved, reciting the shield spell. Just as it was about to launch, the winds yanked on my cloak, snuffing out the last of the incantation. *No!* The director's finger moved, clenching on the trigger. I was the human shield who'd take the bullet with nothing to save me.

Suddenly, he twisted, firing the unstoppable bullet to my right. "Fuck!" he screamed. We barely had a chance to breathe, as the iron shot right into the floating sphere. A great crack shattered the surface and magic erupted like magma spurting from the ground. Tendrils flailed in the air, slashing at anything in their way. One touched a crate and it exploded into dust.

Stone's limp grip tightened around me. We both ducked as a tendril whipped over our heads. "We have to..." He tried to pull me for the stones, but the centripetal force fought back. The enraged magic ball began to suck like an inescapable vacuum. I got a foot down only for my body to crumple and slam into Stone.

Grunting, he held his ground while clinging to me. "If we can get outside the stones, we have a chance," he shouted directly in my ear. Even still, most of his words were muffled by the tornado of freight trains erupting from the blood ball.

The cracks shattered again, every splinter casting more tentacles that slammed into the rocks. They thundered into the ground, tearing straight through to bedrock and leaving behind floating dirt clods. The whole world thundered like missiles rained down from the heavens.

I needed to focus. Stone crashed to his knees, taking me with him. The extremely intimate position of both of us crawling while he had his hands around my waist would have made Ink either laugh or rage. I tried to focus on the idea of my irate incubus chewing me out while rocks and dirt pelted my face. *I'll see him again.*

We'll get out of this and they'll all say 'I told you so.' I'll happily let everyone get a jab in before…

A massive tendril as big as my thigh burst from the breaking orb. It strained up to the sky, then rolled down and smashed clean through a standing stone. The huge boulder tumbled for the ground, but as it struck, it bounced and rolled straight for us. Screaming, I turned and tucked to avoid the giant rock. Stone came with and, even as its rough surface scraped against my flesh, it passed on by.

I breathed deep, a laugh rising in my chest, as I turned back to check on Stone. It struck from the right, magic scissoring apart the fabric of reality. My entire body sizzled at the nearness of the oncoming tendril. I dodged, letting it harmlessly slap the ground. But as it buried into the dirt, everything we'd been holding on to dissolved away.

"No. No!" I shrieked, scrabbling for the floating dirt clods. My legs lifted into the air along with Stone. I tried to swim against the current, but the grip had me.

"Hold your—" Stone shouted as the enraged ball exploded. Screaming, I clawed thin air as the bursting magic of the universe sucked us into total darkness.

* * * *

Cal

"Layla!"

I shook off my fur and ran for the standing stones. A moon-damned hurricane rose inside of them. Splinters of wood and dirt pelted my naked body. Flinging a hand over my eyes, I wasn't going to let a few baseball bruises stop me. I could see Layla hovering in the air with the damn witch hunter clinging to her. Magic undulated between the dark stones, none of it reaching beyond the circle. *If I could just…*

Her scream burned me to my marrow. A massive burst of energy cast out a shockwave. It struck me in the chest, cracking a rib or two. I fell back hard, but as I was tumbling, I saw her between the gaps in the stones. One minute she was there, floating in the air, the next…the light consumed her.

In an instant, it sucked in and vanished. The pounding winds and pressure faded, taking the dark clouds with. To rub salt in the wound, a rosy sunset stretched across the forest and crickets sang. Pain. It hurt to breathe, it hurt for my heart to beat. It hurt to think. But I didn't have time to tend to my wounds. Layla needed me.

Fighting through the sharp stabbing of my own ribs trying to puncture my lungs, I managed to get a foot to the ground and rose. Blood dripped into my eyes, but I kept going, limping for whatever had taken Layla. The fucking bastards who had started this were beginning to stir. I couldn't do much as a naked man, but the wolf could slit open their throats.

Fur shivered down my spine first, the hackles already up. I took another step, barely noting the guns piled at their feet. All my concern was on getting her back and torturing the ones who did it. The balding one caught me. He raised his weapon at the half-man, half-wolf snarling at him. He'd get one shot in before I shredded his intestines. Good luck.

"Hold, wolf."

Ink slammed against me, placing a hand over my battered chest. I gasped in agony and the incubus rocked on his heels. Another two shots rang out, but he took them without blinking. "This is the tactical time to retreat."

Before I could respond, he hefted me over his damn shoulder. I slammed my claws into his back, but the incubus did his disappearing act. The last of the witch hunter bullets sailed harmlessly into a tree.

"But Layla..." I shouted as we appeared on a dirt road.

"Would tan my hide if I let anything happen to you." Ink hefted me back to my feet and I shook off the fur. He barely looked at me before glaring to the west. I followed him and heard the gunfire we'd just escaped from.

A shadow blanketed the sun. I didn't look, just waited for the loud *whoomph* as the angel landed behind us. "What has happened? Where is the lady witch?"

"I don't know. Ask the demon that ran away with his tail between his legs." I wanted to run back and slash until one of them explained, but just standing had me nearing blackout. And Ink could pluck me away again.

"The state of my tail and its functionality is of little help in this matter."

I didn't have time to deal with his sex nonsense. Snarling, I stared around and noticed we were down one. "Where's Daniel?"

"No doubt back at the site of his death, or in the drawer of random baubles."

"Ink, what the fuck happened?"

"I know only two things, Calvin. One, the realms were ripped apart and pulled Layla to another world entirely."

Fuck! The last time we had tried to make a portal, it'd taken all of us plus her mother and had barely worked.

How were we going to get her out, especially when we didn't know where she had gone?

"What's the other?" I asked, clamping my hand to his shoulder to keep from collapsing.

The incubus raised his arm and circled his wrist. "That if I am not in hell, she yet lives."

God, that was everything I needed to hear. In exhaustion and relief, I clasped my arms around Ink. He didn't return the hug, but he at least put up with it. Babbling, tears falling without end, I begged him to tell me, "What do we do now?"

"We wait," he said, casting his fiery gaze to the witch hunters. "And we plan."

Chapter Fourteen

Layla

I struck grass and tucked in tight, my stomach whirling after the trip. Pain ebbed from my fingers and toes that I refused to look at. Instead, I whispered a soft healing spell to myself while trying to keep from hurling all over the ground. For a beat, I risked opening my hands. The black and blue skin began to lighten, fading to my normal brown with a touch of enraged red. I flexed my fingers, wincing in anticipation of pain, and every tip danced against a swaying piece of purple grass. The lingering frostbite of the in-between fell by the wayside. Reaching out, I darted the tip of my pinkie over the wafting grass.

It wasn't just purple — this stuff was neon. It glowed like a black light at a haunted house. I darted the vibrant blades through my fingers, shocked at how soft it was. A shadow passed overhead and I craned up.

The sky...

Panicking, I fell to my ass, giving me a panoramic view of a broken sky. Pockets were bright blue with nary a cloud, others green and churning with storms. Tornadoes would hurl the clouds in the direction of the clear sky, where they'd strike some invisible barrier and vanish. It was a patchwork quilt of every possible weather above my head.

The shadow passed again, forming what looked like a normal goose shape across the ground. Then it stretched its wings and another four appeared behind. The arachna-goose bellowed as it burst above me. Its neck was easily as long as my body, the wings stretched clear across the haphazard sky.

I gulped and tried to make myself look as little like a bug as possible. In ducking down, I caught the horizon. The broken world didn't contain itself to the sky. Verdant grasslands of purples and blues sharply turned into black dune deserts with a single boulder separating them. Rain tumbled from one part of the sky, striking a jungle that circled a white-capped peak of unscalable mountains and screaming goats.

"What the hell is this?" I stuttered and took a step. Or I tried to. The world smeared as if I were about to faint and my body bowed back for the grass. A hand caught my arm, and I realized I hadn't fallen here alone.

It was comforting to not be facing this insanity alone, but infuriating that it had to be with Stone.

"I believe we're in another realm," he said in a tooth-gnashingly calm voice.

I dug my knuckles into the side of my head and it calmed the wooziness. "No shit," I said, fighting to stand up. I shrugged him away without looking back, not ready to deal with this mess. In doing so, my spell book smacked into my hip. Oh, thank god, I had that at least.

"Do you fall into other realms often?" Stone asked with a laugh. As if he thought I was too stupid to know when I wasn't in Kansas anymore.

"I opened a portal to hell," I bragged. Clamping my bag tighter to my side, I stood taller. That shut him up.

Of course, I had just told a witch hunter that I was behind the destruction of a crap-ton of their agents. And I was powerful enough to rip apart the realms...provided I had lots of help.

Damn it. Why did I say that? He's so fucking aggravating, it makes me want to stab him in his stupidly handsome face.

Not handsome. No.

Okay, fine, he's handsome. But so what? Lots of terrible people are hot.

I breathed deeper, pulling in the magic floating around us. It wasn't like back on earth where every breath was a sip. My entire body filled up, like my magic battery shot to a hundred percent in one second. What could I do with so much power?

Stone still wasn't talking. I could walk away, leave him to his evil, powerless hunter ways. Try to figure this out on my own with just my spell book and my magic. Fall in a bear trap. Die of an infection. Never see any of my guys again.

My rebellion ended in an instant. I planted my foot and turned my head to find Stone's back to me. His suit jacket was ripped to pieces and his hair had fallen, the long brown locks swaying against his ass.

"Listen. We don't have to like each other, but..." I began.

He chuckled and slowly pivoted his chin.

"Holy shit! You're green!"

Stone

The witch's jaw fell to the disquieting ground as she jabbed a finger at me. "You're green!" she said again, as if I'd missed it the first time.

"What are you...?" At first I glanced to my chest, expecting to find a large grass stain after I'd bellyflopped onto this strange dirt. I found nothing out of the ordinary — a bit of blood, but a bleach pen would get that out. I placed my hand to my shirt to untuck it.

At first, my eyes skipped over it, like I found it normal. Then I spotted the haze out of the corner of my periphery. Green. My skin radiated a vibrant neon green so bright I could barely make out the lines in my knuckles.

I clenched my hand, certain it couldn't be mine. But the fingers bent and my cuffs tugged back. It was mine. And it was green.

"It's not just that," the witch said. She raised a shivering finger up to my face. I patted the familiar features, my cheeks where they should be, my lips unchanged. It was as her finger rose and I traced the lobes of my ears that my mouth dropped open. Instead of stopping at the edge of my hairline, my ears kept going. Up and up, coming to a sharp steeple pointing toward the back of my head.

"No. This isn't..." I wrenched off my suit coat and, without thinking, yanked open my shirt. Buttons ripped off and I stared down at my bare chest. Every other morning it was svelte and tan, a normal human torso save the intricate scars carved from my collars to my thighs. Now it radiated a light green and the scars...

They glowed with such a dark green they looked like veins of poison running across the whole of my chest.

"What the hell am I?" I stuttered, first slapping my hands over the impossible sight, then yanking them away. What if I made it worse? What if it never came off? That spell, this was Conquest's doing. He'd convinced Zimmerman that I was a sleeper agent with it. I was getting too close. He had to turn me into a creature for his nefarious plans. There was no other logical explanation.

My bat-like ears picked up on a single quick gulp. I ignored my exposed chest to look over. Leeland stared at me with her lips parted and her eyes wide as pools. The wind blasted back my shirt, exposing all of me down to my low-slung trousers. I waited for her to cast a spell to pin the monster. Instead, she placed her finger between her teeth and bit down, her gaze taking its time over my trim waist and hips.

Pride tugged at my lips as she fought to get control of herself, her face pinking in embarrassment. Only a dead man wouldn't find her beautiful. Correction, dead men found her beautiful as well. It was no wonder she kept a packed stable of men at her beck and call. But I had no interest in being a witch's familiar, regardless of the perks.

Cursing myself for acting without thinking, I struggled to button my shirt. Gaps formed, exposing some of the scars glowing below the white linen. At least the witch had enough sense to look away.

"Where are we?" she asked, as if I had a clue. Then she darted her gaze over her shoulder and pinned me to the ground with a single look. "You don't know, do you?"

An urge to kiss that smart-ass look off her lips boiled my blood. I wrested control from my wayward dick and stared at the unfortunate landscape. "I'm a witch hunter, not a travel agent."

To my shock, she laughed. It was probably a pity chuckle, but I'd take what I could get.

"Oh shit, I forgot. Your fingers, your toes..." She turned and held her hands out to me expectantly. I don't know why, but I placed my hands on top of hers. Normally, my skin would be a touch lighter than hers. Instead, its glowing green played off her brown perfectly.

The witch clamped her hands over mine. I half expected her to leap into my arms, but she turned my palms upside down and stared at my fingers. "They're...fine? We just fell through a portal to god knows where, and you didn't suffer any damage?"

She was going to heal me without my asking? Damn, she'd have made a wonderful badged witch. "Afraid not," I said, growing uncomfortable with how comfortable her hands were. I pulled mine out and dropped them to the side. "Should I have?"

Nervously, she scratched her arm and flicked at her nail. "Yeah. I mean. Humans do. Well, I do. The in-between is...it's bad."

"You've been in the in-between?" I'd never heard of a human breaking into the creators' trash heap. Though, I'd never heard of a human that glowed green and could survive falling into another realm.

"That'd make three times now."

"How are you still alive?" I gasped. Demons could traverse it without question, being tied to the creators and destroyers of reality. But humans...never. It'd eat up a person in seconds.

She wrapped her arms around herself and shrugged. "Stubbornness."

Whatever it was, it'd served her well. I stared in awe at the witch. Covenless with no known line to her name and an incubus suckling at her power, yet she shrugged off death like a light tickle. I should be terrified of a witch like that. The ones with nothing to care about were dangerous. But the longer I stared at her, the winds brushing her curls against her dewy cheeks, the larger an ache formed in my chest. An ache that wanted to protect instead of prosecute her. It certainly helped that with her arms crossed under her breasts, she'd lifted them so high I feared I might fall through her cleavage.

She caught me. I jerked my head up and her big brown eyes were a tempestuous slide into sin. I was enthralled as they shifted from innocently gazing at me to narrowing at something behind me.

"Ho there!" a man's deep voice shouted from directly past my shoulder. I damn near snapped my vertebra for how fast I spun around.

That was a lot of pink. A very tall, Pepto-Bismol-pink man with a fur stole across his naked chest smiled at me. He extended a mystery basket with a checkered towel above the contents.

"Who are you?" I ordered, dipping back my hip as if I had a gun.

His lavender gaze dropped to my empty hand for a second before he smiled. "I'm Nym. Judging by the wild look in your eyes, and the confounding clothing you're wearing, this must be your first time in Terrabail."

So this place had a name. A name that sounded familiar. It scratched at the back of my neck like a burrowing tick, but I couldn't place it.

"Why are you here?" I ordered.

"Maybe play nice with the tall pink man," Leeland whispered. Cloth fluttered over my palm and I realized I'd extended mine out to protect her. A habit, of course. Not wanting to anger the witch, I dropped my hand and focused on the pink man.

"Nym? Yes. You are correct. We've never been to this terrabull."

"Terrabail," he corrected with a pursed lip. His face looked both human and feline at the same time. A tiny nose, wide cheeks, but massive cheekbones and a long chin. It was unnerving in the uncanny valley way, while also objectively beautiful. "Don't worry, you'll lose that vulgar accent in due time."

I sneered but the pink man's attentions drifted past me to Layla. She squirmed at the lavender gaze bearing down on her. "And you've brought a pet with you."

The witch scoffed. "No."

"A servant, then?"

"Try again."

"The most unruly sclab I've seen in an age. And that's saying something." Nym laughed and jabbed an elbow in my direction. When I didn't laugh along, he turned, sweeping a long train of red velvet outlined in furs behind him.

"What are you doing here, Nym?"

We were easy pickings. Two strangers clearly out of their depths in the middle of nowhere, and he showed up with a big smile and an offer of help? I didn't trust it.

"I'm the greeter. I greet people who travel to Terrabail. Be greeted."

No. "Why?"

He pursed his lips and stared longer at me. "Why is your skin that hue?"

"You can't just ask someone that," Leeland unhelpfully said.

I waved my palm to tell her I had this under control. She glared and crossed her arms hard. I half expected her to stick her tongue out, but she settled on tossing her head back instead. "I wondered the same myself."

"Oh, I see." Nym, the stranger who'd appeared out of nowhere, grabbed my shirt and yanked it open. The sunlight struck my green skin, turning the hue more yellow. Nym placed a fingernail to my scars and traced down them, starting at my shoulders, then down my abs, and finally heading for...

"Okay!" I leaped back as he started down treasure trove lane. Most girls didn't get that handsy with my scars.

"They didn't finish you. How are you here then?"

Didn't finish me? What? Was I supposed to be greener? Maybe three feet tall? Have giant black eyes? Mary and Joseph, I wasn't making any sense.

"No, they didn't," I thundered back, wanting to be as far from the touchy man as possible. But turning my back on him wouldn't get me any answers. I stared at my fist, the verdant hue unnerving me to my core. I wanted it gone. Now. "What were they supposed to do?"

"Oh, I have no idea. I'm only the greeter of Changelings."

"The greeter of..."

Changelings. Babies transmogrified to replace completely normal infants. Goblins did it on occasion. Sometimes trolls if they were forced from their mountaintops. But none of them were tortured by pure iron.

"Yes, Changelings. Which you are. Congrats on your ascension. Seems to be a few years late. Lots of treasure to be had in your realm. Anyway, here." Nym handed me the basket.

I couldn't be a Changeling. I had a middle name. Two of them. Parents. Annoying cousins who'd douse my washcloths in Tabasco. A typical, Catholic-boy childhood…until those monsters attacked. They did it. They must have changed me, tried to turn me into one of them. And Zimmerman had stopped it.

"What's in this?" Leeland picked up the edge of the towel and peeked into the basket.

"A welcome gift of elven breads, pixie jams and centaur cheeses."

"Centaur cheese? What animal does that come from?"

Nym cast a withering glare at her. "A centaur. If you'll excuse me, I have many more to greet. Nearly market day and all." With a jolly whistle, he took off down the hill.

"Wait!" I shouted, running for him. "What do I…?" I'd been trained to anticipate the strangest of situations. Finding a manticore in a high school library. Sitting down to tea with a banshee. Chasing a pack of wargs out of the McDonald's play place. But in all of that, no one had thought to teach me what to do if I was alone and far from home.

Heavy rains pelted down on Nym as he stopped in the storming rocky terrain. Even as his furs flattened to his body, he raised his chin and waited.

"Where do I go?"

"Find your clan. Surely they... No? Some fellowships these days. Can't bother with the bare minimum. If you walk that direction for a day, you'll come across a city. Ask around there."

Ask for what? I was opening my mouth when the sky crackled. The weather began to run backward, clouds retreating back to where they came, rains falling upward, and a man with blue skin plummeted to the ground. Nym shook his shoulders, and from nowhere plucked out another basket. "I hope this one brought spoils from the creator's realm." Giddy, he raced to the newest drop-in, leaving me lost.

Past the floating trees and upside-down mountains, I spotted a smattering of tiny buildings sticking out from the earth. Or it could be pillars of salt for all I knew in this crazy world. It wasn't until my hand clenched around the cold metal that I realized I'd been reaching into my pocket for the one thing to bring me balance.

The glint off the Animal Control badge revealed my face. Instead of a harried man with a long jaw, thin face and thick lips, a green stranger stared back at me. If my friends saw me now, they'd lock me up on sight.

Of course, they'd do that even if I was human. No. Conquest had gotten to Zimmerman and he...he had used his influence to talk River to his side. But not everyone would go along with Mr. White's mad plans. I had to get out of here and save them before they too were sacrificed in the name of Conquest.

The witch wandered over beside me. She dangled the basket off the crook of her arm and delicately nibbled on the edge of a piece of bread. "Kinda tastes like focaccia," she mused before looking at me. "What do we do now?"

A portal opened, casting yet another elf to the dirt of Terrabail. They'd keep falling around us, and eventually one wouldn't be as friendly as the furred Nym. I pointed a finger in the direction of the city. "We walk."

I reached out to take her arm and fire burst across my fingertips. It didn't touch my skin, but I got the warning and froze. Rabid eyes glared at me as she held her hands out. "Right now we're at a stalemate, but the second I don't need you and you don't need me…"

"I know." I sighed, accepting my fate. Oh, I could look. I could let myself dream. But when it came to witches and the people who kept them in line, the war never ended.

Chapter Fifteen

Layla

If I wasn't drenched to the bone by random *derechos* passing overhead, I might gaze in wonder at the impossible landscape. Floating forests, violet sunsets, some kind of flying fish with opal scales — everything impossible that only dug another layer of dread into my heart.

"Still back there?"

And I was trapped with my sworn enemy. Despite my shorter stride, I picked up speed and didn't just catch up to Stone but powerwalked past him. We'd been walking for what felt like hours. I'd tried to clock it by checking my phone, but the numbers kept jumping around. Either it was glitching again, or even time made no sense here. Another burst of snow fell on my shoulders, freezing the drenched cloak to my body.

Snarling, I hurled my shoulders back, cracking off the ice, and stomped into a desert biome. At least the heat would dry my clothes.

A deep chuckle broke from behind and I refused to look. "That explains the werewolf."

"What does?" I asked before realizing I talked myself into a trap. "Shut up, I do not need to hear your take on my... Just shut up." The last time I'd seen them, they'd been tossed outside of the stones. But what if the magic lightning got them? What if the hunters rebounded and attacked once we were blown here? What if Ink had slaughtered them all in a blood rage to get to me?

I pursed my lips. It bothered me that the idea wasn't a total deal-breaker. A girl could only take so many kidnappings before a little retribution was called for. Light rose off the darkening horizon. That was the city Stone was leading us to. Even after walking until my legs wobbled, it felt no closer.

Why couldn't anything be simple? I took a step, expecting my foot to sink into ankle-high sand. But the land shifted and mud sucked up to my calf. Panic and exhaustion caused a shriek to slip from my lips like I was trying out for a horror movie. I hefted at my stuck leg, my back one left in shifting sand.

"What the hell is wrong with this god...? Damn —!"

Hands cupped around my calf. Stone reached his fingers deep into the mud and clamped around my ankle. As he tugged, his eyes staring into mine, a squelching noise normally made when a well-lubed body part had some fun erupted. I didn't know why, but my eyes darted down to his crotch and a tiny part of my brain wondered if that was green too.

Fuck. I don't care.

"Calm down," he said with all the smugness of a man behind a badge. My foot dropped to the ground and I realized sand was coming up between my bare toes. Great. I wasn't getting that shoe back.

After digging my naked foot deeper, I tested to see if I could swing hard enough to kick his balls into his throat. "I am as fucking calm as I can be." Stone quirked up an eyebrow and I didn't care if I fell on my ass. Before I went for a penalty kick, I smiled. "Elf boy."

He shivered, a scowl wiping away that smug grin. "Not funny." Stone turned his back on me and trudged on through the bog.

I took more careful steps to avoid the calf sucking pits but wasn't going to let this go. "It's what you are, an elf. The whole time you were kidnapping witches and torturing creatures, you were one —"

"I am not an elf!" he screamed, bearing down on me.

Every battle-honed female instinct told me to shut up and keep the yelling man happy. But I wasn't a twelve-year-old girl getting cat-called by grown men. I had power, and in this place, the magic pulsed through my hair. "That's what the pink Viking elf said."

"He's wrong. I am...I was changed by the elves who captured me. Who tortured me." Stone slapped a hand to his chest, igniting the scars. Did he know he could do that?

They didn't just glow at once, but a pattern pulsed down them, trailing the swoops and whorls before they vanished under his pants. I tried to look away, but I was a moth on a crash course for the flame. Sure enough, a hint of green radiated from below the black belt.

What in the hell am I doing? I turned my head and placed a hand over my eyes as if one itched. "Is that how it works?"

"Yes," Stone insisted before he frowned and looked away. "I…if they can create Changelings of their young, why couldn't they do it to a human? It's the only thing that makes sense."

He sounded like he was about to blow and, as much as I loathed to admit it, we had to stick together. I didn't like that word Nym had called me. It made me think of a piece of luggage, and I had a sinking feeling other elves would think the same. For as deep as my hatred of Stone ran, at least he saw me as a person…a person who was also a weapon he wanted to control. *Why can't I be stuck here with Ink?* He'd have seduced the pink elf into getting us a ride. Or Cal? He could have sniffed out whatever was going on. Garavel could have flown us straight to the city while I nestled in his arms. And Daniel…

Numb, I placed my hand to my locket and lifted it. I hadn't even told him why I was mad. I had just ignored him. Hoped that my anger would cool and I'd get over it. *But what if he loses his already waning control? What if he goes full poltergeist before I can even get out of here? What if I lose him forever?*

"Witch, I think it's in our best interest to camp."

I dropped my locket and stomped to Stone. He perched on a hanging rock, staring across the horizon.

"Hell no. I'm not spending one more second with you than is necessary."

Darkness like I'd never seen plummeted across the valley. With no streetlights, no passing cars, not even a wayward lantern, the entire land was plunged into midnight. I could barely see six inches in front of my face. My foot faltered at the cry of a loud animal, invisible in the darkness.

No. My guys need me. I flung my head back and kept going.

"This isn't smart."

"Then you stay here, and I'll find us a way home. Isn't that what you do with witches—force them to do all your dirty work?"

Stone sighed. "No, we work in tandem with... For fuck's sake."

I took a confident step that quickly crumbled. The rocks under my bare foot only skittered a little. It was the rubber in my muscles that shook me up. I flailed a hand out to grab a tree, and smacked into a hard pec instead. My fingers clenched on their own, before I realized who I was touching. I tried to wrench my arm away, but Stone caught my wrist and held me.

"You're exhausted. If we keep this march up, we're liable to be eaten by animals, or you'll give yourself a concussion."

"I'm fine," I said, yanking my hand free. But I did it so fast, it caused my body to turn and my damn twenty-pounds-heavier cloak to furl out. I was yanked off my feet and my ass landed on a patch of dirt. The sound of breaking reeds caused me to wince. I rolled to the side to find the welcome basket partially crushed.

Stone stood above me, crossing his arms.

"Don't say it," I interrupted and turned my back on him.

"We can set up shelter here and continue on when there's some damn light out."

I didn't answer him and dug into my purse and laid my spell book on the ground. By the light of my cracked cellphone, I hunted for the right spell. While moving or fighting with Stone, it was easy to keep my mind focused, but struggling to read the old text, my thoughts hit. *What if there's no way back?*

Ink had spent four hundred years in hell and even he seemed surprised that he'd gotten out. What if there was no answer in the city? What if I was trapped here for the rest of my life without any of them? I clenched my hand, digging into the cold, alien ground. A thousand memories flashed at once. Cal blushing after he accidentally tickled me with his scruff. Ink dipping a banana into a jar of mayo and eating it in one bite. Daniel blowing a piece of hair out of my eyes. Garavel kissing the tears off my cheek after a sappy movie. There were supposed to be another hundred thousand more just like those. But…

A cacophony of tumbling wood jerked me up. Stone had his back turned as he bundled up the sticks. "This should work well enough…" he said, before trailing off and turning back to me. I quickly ducked my head and tried to focus on my book, but the spell was watering and falling out of focus.

"What are you doing?" he asked.

I smeared my tears on my shoulder and found the incantation. Without Daniel to help, I went over the words five times, making certain I had every one right. Stone finished the frame of his stick tent and began to lay giant leaves on the top. A shock of thunder caused me to tremble and rain began to pelt my already soaked head. Raising my palm, I cast the spell. An invisible shield formed above me, cutting off the rain.

It didn't protect Stone, who kept silently stacking the leaves while keeping an eye on me. "That's not going to hold all night."

"And you think your backyard foraging will?" I asked, crossing my arms. Without the rain sizzling on its angry pages, my spell book calmed as I pulled it into my lap. I crossed my legs and watched Stone while running a finger over my grimoire's spine. It wasn't much comfort, but it was something.

He must have finished whatever he was doing as he wiped off his hands and crawled into the dirt under a three-sided hut. Wet grass slapped against his legs but he was competing with Ink for the smug crown. "You should sleep under here," Stone said.

I eyed up his shelter already creaking in the rising storm winds. "I'd be better off crawling into the den of a lion."

He sighed. "Witch..." I glared at him and he shook his head. "Leeland, your magic will eventually expire, ripping away your shelter."

Roaring laughter of pure absurdity in the face of terror and loss broke from my lips. When it reached Stone, he frowned. "Please keep huntersplaining magic to me. That will go well for you." I turned my back on him and lay on my side. The magic kept seeping in, overfilling the hole before the barrier could drain it. I tucked my spell book back into my purse and curved around it. My stomach grumbled with hunger but I knew better than to eat what little rations we had. So much for that 'one bite of magic elf bread lasting for a week' idea. It had barely satiated me for ten minutes.

"You're going to freeze to death when a snowstorm passes overhead."

"If you want to fuck me..." I yawned and slumped my head onto my arm acting as a pillow. "You'll have to take a number."

Stone scoffed, but I ignored him. I tried to ignore the whole damn world. *Home in Cal's huge bed. He adjusts my bonnet then kisses the tip of my nose, only for Ink to pop in and yank it off. They both snuggle around me, I kiss Ink, then Cal, before I'm flipped to my back and take Garavel's lips as he floats above. Daniel leans down from the pillows, the chill off his skin touching mine and...*

A breath passed across my trembling lips. I parted them, expecting to feel the cold of a ghost's tongue in my mouth. Instead, a wet leaf wedged itself down my throat. Coughing, I sat up and a massive wind yanked my hair. It burst through the forests like a shot, skipping over my prone form and slammed into dickhead's branch tent.

It shattered to pieces. I smirked and rolled over, watching Stone half bent over as he struggled to catch the pieces. Rains picked up harder than ever. Tiny pieces of hail slammed into the ground and the witch hunter. I could lie here safe in my magic enclosure watching him get beaten and drenched. He'd do the same.

"Get over here," I said.

He stopped collecting the remaining leaves but kept his back to me. "No, thank you."

"I'm offering you shelter. If you're too fragile to take a handout from a witch..."

Lightning shredded apart the sky. As the sparks zapped through the lumbering clouds, I'd swear I spotted massive tentacles prying apart the horizon. Darkness descended before I could see if my nightmare was real. Stone yelped and dove, rolling under my magical shield. Another bolt slammed into the ground, obliterating what remained of his shelter.

I waved my hand, tugging the sides of my shield down and encompassing the both of us safely inside. The storm quieted like we were inside an old house watching it through the windows.

"You didn't need to do that."

"Can you survive a barbecuing?" I asked, before remembering how he had kept dying on my couch. Maybe he could. Maybe he was indestructible save for a scrap of iron. I didn't have the energy to find out. Flopping back to the ground, the storm shifted and snow blew back in. I shivered and reached for my cloak, only to land my hand in ice. This was no help.

I undid the clasp, finally breathing freely, and was about to fling the whole thing away. "Are you cold?" Stone asked.

I'm shivering and my lips are turning blue. Clearly I'm having the time of my life!

All my raging sarcasm bit in half when a stomach brushed against my lower back. I clenched my toes, waiting for his hand to fall across my waist or his crotch to press into my ass. But neither came. Instead, he draped the cloak over the both of us and settled in behind me.

"Trapped body heat helps."

I should have shrugged him off, rolled to the other side of the shield and kept him as far from me as possible. But, as exhaustion and pain wore down the last of my reserves, I let myself pretend it was one of my guys behind me.

Cal crushing me to him in a nightmare, Ink nibbling my ear in the morning, Garavel sweeping a palm up my belly, Daniel whispering how much he loved me. I cried out, crumpling tighter into a ball.

"I love you," I whimpered to the wind. "And I'm sorry."

Chapter Sixteen

Stone

The birds were being obnoxiously loud this morning. I tried to bury my head in the pillow and breathed in a perfume of jasmine and feminine mystique. My hand flexed in surprise, smoothing over a warm belly. She shifted, not pulling away, but leaning tighter. An ample ass brushed up my thighs and found my morning wood.

A moan slipped past my lips and I nearly ground back against those pillowy cheeks. But the birds didn't sound like the nest of robins outside my window and the sun was far too bright to be coming through glass. I opened an eye. Past the nest of curly black hair, I spotted a creature like a deer made of jelly. It wobbled on its four hooves, ripples shivering down to the ground, as it chewed on the grass mere inches from Layla's...

Damn it!

I tried to spring away, but she shifted and clung a hand to mine. Panic shivered down my body as I used every skill I had to ignore how warm and soft she was. The assuring beat of her heart marched in time with mine, and the gentle whistle of her breath combined with the breeze. I wasn't some starry-eyed virgin losing his shit over draping a hand under a girl's tits. But it'd been a long time since I'd woken beside one. Longer still since she'd wanted me to stay.

"Mm," Layla moaned, stretching her neck. Her hair fell to the side, leaving me to stare down the graceful curve of her throat. A handful of dark freckles twinkled like black stars. In her sleep shifting, my hand fell lower, slipping to just below her belly button.

It broke one of the most sacred laws in the agency, but I couldn't stop staring at her freckles crying out for a kiss while my fingers caressed down. This was a nuclear strike situation, the kind that'd get us both neutralized if anyone found out. But we were on another realm, far from anyone who'd care or know.

The tip of my pinkie brushed over the top of her thigh. She groaned and parted her legs. My tightening cock pressed against her ass cheek and I almost bit my groan into her clothed shoulder.

"What are you waiting for?" she asked, her voice so husky my dick pulsed.

She's a witch, I'm a witch hunter. My duty is to contain and control her. Preferably on my back while she digs her heels into me and runs her toes up my shaft.

Fuck. My raging libido combined with a dry streak and my lingering dreams. Somehow I knew exactly what her feet felt like in my hands, even though I hadn't touched them. And the idea drove me wild.

A coy giggle rose from her and she reached her hand back. "Come on, Cal."

I sprang away as fast as my erection tried to spring for her hand. Less than gracefully rolling in the dirt, I was safe to watch as she dropped a hand to empty grass. She patted it a few more times before turning over. Her deep brown eyes opened. For a brief moment, they were hazy with memories of a good dream. But as she looked up at me, anger snapped through them.

"Good," I said, taking control of my voice. "You're awake." I stood and dusted off my hands. "We should get moving."

"Can I have a minute to wake up?"

"Only if you wish to be eaten by the native wildlife," I said, directing her to the jelly deer staring at us. The grass it'd ripped up was still visible in its translucent body even as it slowly dissolved.

When the creature gave a loud honk, Leeland jerked. She was trapped below her cloak, struggling to find the edge of our makeshift blanket in order to get her legs free.

"Will you please take it?" I demanded, jerking my hand for her. We didn't have time for her to fumble around in the name of self-reliance.

The witch glared at my eyes, then to my offered palm. I waved it again, but her gaze drifted and she smirked. *What was she…?*

Oh, fuck. My pants tugged on the raging erection that was tenting the tight fabric straight up.

"No thanks," Leeland said, pressing her hands to the ground and rising on her own. She gathered up her cloak and put it back on. After slotting her bag onto her arm, she stared at me. "I've got better at home."

* * * *

As we approached the city, I expected to run into guards. The closer we drew, the more people began to appear. Often friendly, asking me my clan name and if the witch knew any tricks. She seemed to take that rather badly, and rather than risk an incident, I kept tugging her along. But for all the merchants and travelers, there was no sign of a police force. People came and went through the bronze gates without end.

The buildings that'd looked like white marble far in the distance close up bore far more colors than I had ever anticipated. If a rainbow could vomit all over giant trees and stone temples, it'd match this elven city. Seemed the fae didn't do anything by half measures. Wooden huts were placed next to towering stones carved with doors and windows. There was no rhyme or reason. One minute it was a line of trees and little houses in the top branches with giant strips of fabric run between them. The next, we walked into a world of stones that looked like giant coral with elves passing through the ten-foot gaps while chatting.

"Wow, that's... That's a big tree," the witch whispered. I doubted it could be that large. I followed her line of sight and found the entire block to be nothing but bark. Slowly, I tipped my head back, struggling to spot a single leaf. The branches had to be touching the ionosphere, defying all laws of physics.

To make matters stranger, there were small knots formed all across the world tree. Or they were small relative to the massive bark. Elves zipped up and down, climbing nearly vertical to run from one cutely decorated knot to the other. Smoke rolled out of two as if someone was cooking inside, and another had linens hanging off a line.

Leeland snickered. "It's elf apartments. I bet it's bigger than my first one."

"We should not be wasting our time gawking. We have a job to do."

She dropped her arms and glared at me. "My god, that stick up your ass has another, longer stick up its ass."

Her impression of me didn't matter. Once we fixed this minor problem, I'd be free of her...until it was time to capture and collar her for the agency. With my head raised high, I walked on. It seemed the elves dressed in fine silks and furs were heading up a road lined with gold cobblestones. That had to be our answer.

I was about to point it out, when the witch stomped next to me and muttered, "I'm starting to see why your partner turned on you."

My heart jerked. Ten years we'd worked side by side. I'd relied on him and him on me. We'd sat for hours on stakeouts. He'd give me the yogurt his wife always packed for him. I'd bring him tamales from my rare trips back home. He had put a gun to my head and would have pulled the trigger. I had seen it in his eyes.

"He's... He was my closest friend," I whispered, still in shock. I winced the moment the confession slipped. Why was I giving her more ammo to torture me?

To my surprise, the witch gasped. She held her hand out awkwardly, as if she wanted to reach over and comfort me. "I'm—" Her eyes darted away and she mumbled, "I'm sorry."

For my closest allies turning on me? Or because she had brought it up? Either way, I had never expected to hear an apology from her. "Forget it." I shrugged it off. "We go this way."

At least she didn't argue, though the back of my neck burned as we slipped into a crowd of elves. The personal space lessened with each foot until Leeland bounced into my elbow. Before she fell, she grabbed onto my biceps and I harmlessly dropped my palm to her hip. I expected another growl from the wolf-lover, but she was too busy trying to avoid losing her head to a massive fishhook dangling off an elf's back.

"They are not what I expected," she said, watching a pair of elves dressed in bronze chest plates and fur cloaks shoot the shit next to a fountain of cherubs.

"No?" I asked in surprise and there went that glare again. She was disturbingly hot when angry. Tearing myself from that fire-starter look, I glanced around the modest square. "All right, I wasn't expecting the array of skin tones." It wasn't just every color of the rainbow — browns, grays, blacks and literal whites were mixed in. "They didn't mention that in the manual."

"What do you know about elves?" she pressed.

This was the time for me to dazzle her with my vast array of information. I'd spent nearly two decades studying the occult. Reciting minotaur strengths and weaknesses were guaranteed to get any woman into bed.

I stopped next to the bubbling fountain with a gold chariot at the top. The chances this had once graced a Grecian temple seemed high. Staring into the blue mosaics at the bottom, I caught the ripples of my green face and winced. "Very little," I admitted.

"You're a huge help, thanks." She folded her arms and collapsed onto the fountain basin's wall. It was so high, her feet barely reached the ground. I watched them sway, aching to tug off her filthy socks and wash her feet in the fountain. Though there was a good chance she'd set me on fire if I tried.

The witch dug into her purse and excavated the crumpled basket. "There's one piece of bread left. Oh, and the cheese."

I shivered at the idea of eating centaur cheese and plopped down beside her. "Rock, paper, scissors for the bread?" I asked, holding out my fist.

She stared at me as if about to go for it, before breaking the last piece in half. To my surprise, she handed me the larger part and nibbled on hers while gazing at the towers piercing through the clouds. "It's so medieval, but shiny and vibrant. I guess I expected white marble and muted metal."

"Well, they wouldn't have any iron here."

"Right, the whole…only way to kill an elf."

"Be a bit like sleeping on a bed of daggers."

"Like someone hasn't done that before." She snorted and I laughed too. No doubt there was a man doing just that either for religious or clout reasons.

"So that explains all the brass, but the random-ass architecture, the clothing that looks like they fell into a theater's costume box?"

That was a fair assessment. "Elves are the highway bandits of the occult. They are the only ones capable of crossing the realms and use that to loot whatever catches their eye."

"Elf Vikings?"

I snickered. "I guess they are." The manual had described them as dangerous and greedy, but we had been handed a basket of goods upon arrival. And no one had charged us entry into the city, nor to sit and enjoy a rest.

"Is that all you know about them?"

I could recite pages upon pages about cockatrices, of which I'd only seen one in my entire life. But all I had was three sentences on elves. They were realm striders. They would loot every civilization they came upon. They could only be harmed by iron. Raising my hands, I stared at the sunlight skipping across my green flesh. Wherever the yellow landed, my skin glowed. Nothing in my literature had mentioned that, or how elves lived inside massive trees, or that they gave gift baskets to people and made centaur cheese.

It was my job to be an expert, and I was nearly as useless as the witch. "There hasn't been a sighting of an elf on earth in years. Thirty years, at least. I guess the assumption was that they'd grown tired of plundering our realm. Or..."

She turned to me, her damn eyes piercing through to my flesh.

I shook the idea off before it could even take hold. Despite the ears and the green, I was a red-blooded human. "I'm surprised you know nothing of them. Don't witches use various bits of creatures for potions?"

Her cheeks paled and she shook her head. "I don't do potions. At least, I leave that up to Ink and Dan... Uh, I mean." She gulped with fear wavering in her eyes.

It would take nothing for me to keep her on her toes. I could switch from good cop to bad cop in a heartbeat. But there was no point in hurting her now. "I am aware you have an incubus and ghost at your disposal. You haven't revealed anything to hurt them."

"Yeah, that's been bugging me. How is it you could see Daniel?"

I tapped the side of my head before remembering my glasses were long gone. "The agency provides us with special tech. The sunglasses use a combination of registering EM pulses and temperature changes along with a spell allows us to detect all manner of magic fluctuations."

She swayed her foot back and forth, the tip of her big toe tracing along the cobble. "Except when you stumbled into my house, you didn't have them on."

I blinked, struggling to remember that moment. My crawl through the sewers had taken forever, and I'd taken them off just as the sun set. But surely I had put them on. No chance would I risk entering the domain of a witch and her gaggle of monsters so unprepared.

"You're misremembering."

"I think I'd remember a weirdo wearing sunglasses at night—"

"You're wrong!" I thundered, my heart throbbing. If I didn't need the glasses, if I could see a ghost without the help of the agency, then why did they make me wear them? *What am I?*

Leeland pursed her lips. She slammed the basket back into her purse and leaped to her feet. With a rigid spine, she began to walk away. I dropped to my feet, prepared to follow, when she spun and jabbed a finger into my chest. "I know you're going to turn on me. That the second we're back home, you'll try to hurt them and chain me."

I blinked slowly. A cold fury radiated off of her. For the first time, I feared she might obliterate me and carry on alone. Taking a slow breath, I said, "Witches are—"

"Don't start this shit up again. I'm not a fucking weapon."

Again? A half dream bobbed up, fleeting moments of me losing my cool, her shouting back, then...

The touch of her body, the taste of her mouth and the smell of her skin all slammed into my mind at once as I watched her walk away. I'd chalked it up to a dream, my cock obsessed with a gorgeous but forbidden witch. Had it really happened and I'd forgotten?

The witch walked with confidence even as elves turned to gawp at her. I narrowed my eyes, watching her move through the world with cold confidence. What had she done to me and my memories?

Chapter Seventeen

Layla

I knew it wouldn't work, but I couldn't stop checking my phone and praying that somehow a Wi-Fi signal could pierce through the realms. My last text had come from Dana, who had said she'd bring another pair of comfortable shoes for our first day at clinicals. I stared at my sock, my pinkie toe slipping out of the hole. Sure would be nice to have those now.

In less than twenty-four hours, I was supposed to start the next stage of my new career. I rather doubted my program would accept "Sorry, I was stuck in another dimension," as an excuse. I kept toggling the messages, reading through Cal asking about dinner plans, and Daniel... My hand pressed to my chest, pushing the locket tighter as I tried to squeeze away the guilt. What if he went mad thinking I had abandoned him?

Tears teetered on the edge of my lash line. I blinked to shake them away, and spotted the witch hunter standing perfectly still in a dark corner. "What are you doing?" I shouted.

"Finding a way back home."

"Really? Cause it looks like you're hiding in the shadows like a creepy pervert."

He frowned, but come on. Dude in a tattered suit standing in a dark alley staring at everyone — it was no wonder the other elves were avoiding him. "I am gathering information and observing the local populace, not...perving on them."

"Right. Sure. Find any good feet?"

For a beat, his gaze drifted down, but he stopped before reaching past my knees and glared at me. "This requires finesse. I have to compile enough data before I act."

Jesus Christ. I turned away. The upscale market area was amping up. If we were back home, I'd expect everyone to be carrying Birkin bags and talking loudly about their Christmas in Naples. All Stone would learn here was how much the elves stiffed their servants.

"How long will that take?"

He tipped his head in thought. "Four or five days for a proper dossier."

Fuck that. I had a life to get back to. He could stand in the shadows watching everyone else live. I marched away from him even as he called out, "Leeland? Stop. What are you doing?"

"Excuse me?" I walked right up to the first elf carrying wicker baskets loaded with a fruit that seemed to hum.

He held out the food with scaled skin and smiled at me.

"Could you tell me how I can find a way across the realms?"

"You'll be wanting the Stone Keeper. Lives down this road, take a right, big building covered in runes. Can't miss it."

I smiled my thanks and stepped back, arms outstretched to show I had no coin for his singing fruit. Pausing beside the dark alley, I leaned against a tree and propped up a foot.

"We have to go see the Stone Keeper."

"That was highly dangerous. What if he was hostile?"

"Maybe you should try being nice for once instead of barreling in and making demands while bleeding all over people's floors."

I didn't expect an apology, but Stone high-vaulted over the low bar of begrudgingly agreeing with me to grumble, "You might have been kidnapped."

"Been there…" I stepped into the road, my loose ponytail swaying. Glancing over my shoulder, I met his eyes and snarled, "Stopped that."

It was surprisingly easy to find the Stone Keeper's tower. I had half expected it to be shadowed in mists or locked behind a portcullis with alligators in a moat. But the imposing tower was more like a cute cottage with five stories. It even had a trellis of overgrown flowers against a window and a series of centaur lawn gnomes leading up the path. I pushed on the wooden gate, half expecting to find a sign about a birthday party on it, and slipped inside.

A hand clamped onto my arm and I sighed. "What now?"

"This could be a trap."

I stared at Stone, then shifted my gaze to a porcelain bathtub crammed with plants. "The trap of overcharging you on homemade jams, maybe. Come on, the sooner we get out of here..."

Rather than finish the thought, I shrugged off his arm and jogged up the steps. I thought Cal got paranoid, but Stone didn't seem to trust anyone. Anyone but the men that had betrayed him. It wasn't until I stood on the quaint porch that I realized there was no door. Three colorful windows gave a peek into what existed inside, but no way to enter. I glanced around, wondering if maybe I needed to use the back.

Stone clamped a hand to my shoulder, banged on the wall and stepped back. "Are you in a hurry to return to them? Or is it because you're already tired of me?"

Says the guy that plans to capture me...again.

My mouth opened, ready to ream him out, but a lilt in his words paused me. Every word from him was like his namesake, solid and unbendable, but this time a touch of sadness lingered in his tone. "I want—"

The wall moved. No, the wall disappeared. An elf with dark violet skin dashed through the gaping hole. Her hair was stark white and done up in two puffs at the top of her head. She wore a series of aprons, the lowest and heaviest looking like a blacksmith's, then a chef's white over that and finally a frilly strawberry one embroidered with pink letters saying "I flip both ways."

"Hello. Come in. What are you here for? You're not selling any demon fruit, are you? I couldn't get the imps out of my teeth for days."

"Ah..." My jaw dropped and I struggled to think. Perched on the tip of her long nose were three sets of spectacles. One was like the old-fashioned pair that pinched, another had lenses shaped like octagons, but the third churned my stomach. If I stared through them, her eyes began to melt. They'd go all wobbly and leak down her face until I blinked and returned to normal.

Stone silently nudged himself in between us and took the brunt of her attention. "I require passage to another realm."

"Of course. Why else would anyone stop by to see the Stone Keeper? For my pleasant company? Ha! Name's Amara, by the way. But most people call me 'Hey, did I miss my excursion time?' Ha!"

My god, her energy was infectious. I couldn't stop smiling even as I walked behind Stone into the log cottage. The ceiling vanished high into the stratosphere. I gazed up the towering walls that shifted from quaint and kitschy-covered wood to impenetrable stone. Embedded into them were octagon alcoves making it look like a massive beehive. Soft lights of various hues glowed from deep inside. Staring at them made my stomach toss so I focused on the chatty elf instead.

She hustled for a lectern in the middle of the room. "Let me see…" As she touched it, a globe rose. My heart lurched, hoping to find the familiar lines of continents and seas, but I couldn't make heads or tails out of any of them. Did the different realms have different lands too?

Waving her hand wrapped in gold, Amara pursed her lips and touched the center of the globe. A thousand other tiny worlds burst into the air. They filled the room, hovering just above our heads. I ducked, trying to find Earth.

"Do you have an appointment?" Amara asked. "Whatever your name is."

"I'm Stone."

"Ha. Wait, really? Your clan leader needs a good talking to for letting that one pass. Let me see, I'd surely remember a Stone booking an excursion." She shoved her hand, sending the planets flinging to the side so even more appeared above our heads.

"Sorry, I'm afraid we just dropped in here," I said, trying to get her attention.

Amara dropped her hands and the planets vanished. She stared over her three pairs of spectacles at Stone. "No warrior piercings, clothing of strange origin." She reached over and ripped the last of his shirt. Stone reared back, but Amara dropped her finger to his chest and traced down the scars. "Ley lines barely activated. You're a Changeling, huh?"

A low growl burst from Stone. He yanked his shirt back into place and stepped away. "I am a —"

"Changeling," I interrupted. "He's a Changeling, and we need to get back to where we came from. As soon as possible."

Amara turned from studying Stone to me. "Got yourself an eager sclab, eh?"

I didn't need to know what that word meant to know I hated it. She stared through me and focused only on the other elf in the room. "Do you know your realm of Changeling?" A massive book slammed into the lectern. Amara pulled it open, licked her finger.

"Earth," Stone said.

"Hm… Is that the prison one? Home of the mages?"

"Humans," I interrupted, causing the elf to stare hard at me. "And witches."

She shrugged. "Let me see... Block seventeen!" She slammed the book closed and snapped her fingers. A ladder zipped from the far side of the room to stop by her side. Amara hooked a hand to it and the ladder took off for the wall.

I stumbled beside Stone, watching the old woman zip her way up to the honeycombs and keep going. It was Stone who wasn't paying attention. Instead, he kept stealing glances at the book.

"Leeland?" he whispered.

"What?"

"Your phone? Does it still work?"

I pulled it out to check. Ink wasn't here to drain the battery playing one of his stupid games. Stone reached a hand out as if I was going to give him my life line. When nothing landed in his palm he looked at me and frowned. "Take a picture."

"Why?" I asked even while lining up and taking a quick shot. Then two more.

"An opportunity to study how the elves manage realm travel is not one I'll waste."

He would give this information to the witch hunters, and they could use it to banish people, maybe even witches to hell or worse. My finger hovered over the delete button. But then again, maybe we could use this to stop Mr. White. I slipped my phone away, leaving the pictures intact.

"Excuse me, Miss Amara?" Stone called and I jerked at his voice. There was no gruff, demanding tone. Instead, he sounded pleasant with a surprising California accent.

"Oh, please, you'll make an old lady blush. It's Madam Amara, if you please."

"Of course," he said, slightly blushing.

If just the word 'madam' set Stone off, Ink would have a field day with him.

"Could you tell me how exactly the realm striding works?"

The keeper crawled into one of the alcoves. I didn't realize how large they were until her tall body slipped inside. "Oh, you know." She hummed under her breath, then sang, "And that's how you bend the light of life. Every elf knows."

Stone jerked at that, his shoulders back and head high. Damn it, if he told her he wasn't really an elf, she'd stop helping us. I tried to poke him so he wouldn't nuke our chances, when he paused and smiled at me. "Of course I understand. I was merely hoping a professional could explain it to my companion here."

"Companion, huh?" Amara scrambled back to the ladder, then kicked her way around the room. "Did no one ever tell you to not dip your hand into the spoils?"

Sweet beaded on Stone's brow and he slammed his hands behind his back looking like an errant schoolboy caught with cherry bombs in his pocket. The panicked gawping was oddly endearing as he did his best to not look at me. "If you'd be so kind as to share your expertise…?"

Ink would have had her eating out of his hand in two seconds, but Stone wasn't as smooth as he tried to pretend. The old keeper glared down at him before sighing. "Fine. Not that I expect the uninitiated to understand. See these…" Amara hoisted out one of the lights. As I stared at it, my eyes began to slide to the right. On the edge I could see colors, but every time I was certain I knew which one, it changed.

"Is that a touchstone?" I asked.

"Surprising you know of those, but wrong! It's a counterweight. If an elf doesn't keep one of these stored and guarded by yours truly, then they can't come home."

That didn't sound good. I glanced at Stone, but he was staring intently into the honeycombs that numbered in the thousands. How many more of these keepers existed?

"It's like a piece of their soul, but not really. They give me this, I say a spell, light up the touchstone and boom, they're off acquiring with their clan. All in all, a good day's work." Amara balanced the orb in her hand before stuffing it back. She kicked off again, circling the room and scurrying to the top. Whatever she was looking for seemed to be giving her grief.

I leaned closer to Stone to whisper, "So what we need to find is…"

"The earth touchstone." As he finished, his gaze darted up to mine. I blushed and found the cauldron with what looked like a bone sticking out of the… Oh, that was a bone. *Okay. Elves are creepy.*

"Excuse me, madam." Stone said. His cheeks brightened to a shinier green at that word and I bit my lip to keep from chuckling. "What exactly is a touchstone?"

Amara grunted from above us. The air shook with the angry stomp of her feet down the ladder. She hustled quickly to the ground. "You should know." When she landed, she dusted off her hands and faced him. "You're one."

Oh my god.

Of course. Why didn't I put that together? White said he'd make me into a touchstone. They weren't rocks or artifacts… They were people.

"Ha. Maybe that's why they called you that? Stone for touchstone."

He kept swallowing, his face paling to a mint green. A shiver trembled across his stooped shoulders. "You're wrong," Stone thundered.

"I'm sorry, who wears the bones of the fallen? Oh damn, where'd I put my hat?" She scuttled off to a cozy reading nook and put a giant skull on her head. It had one eye socket across the center of the cranium and the lower mandible was gone. *What is it with elves?*

"I am a...visitor who'd like to return to Earth. Can you or can you not make that happen?" Stone clenched his fists at his sides.

I placed my palm on his shoulder. "She's our only hope," I whispered, hoping he didn't go all witch hunter on her. Judging by the giant skull she wore as a bonnet, something told me she'd kick his ass before he got a chance to pull out his badge.

"Please," he spat out.

"What do you think I was doing up there? Checking for hydra eggs? Here's the problem, son. There's a mention of a touchstone on earth in the annals, but no link. I have a record of whoever last tried to connect with it, except their counterweights are missing."

I gulped. "What...what does that mean?"

"That this slug-brained touchstone forgot to leave a replacement before he joined his ancestors." Amara waved a staff at Stone as if to smack him upside the head, but he caught it and crushed the glass tip in his hand.

"I. Am not. A touchstone!" He opened his palm, casting the broken glass to the ground. I caught the glittering shards embedded in his skin before he stuck it in his pocket like a damn fool.

That caused Amara to growl. Not the fangless human version, not even the pants-wetting werewolf one. This was a bobcat snarl, a sharp and fast warning that knives were gonna cut throats before anyone blinked. I raised my hand, a shield spell forming on my tongue.

Before I could get the first syllable out, a dagger flew through the air and stuck right into Stone's chest. He didn't cry out, or even fall back. Instead, he stared down at the still vibrating handle. Amara rushed forward, pushing me to the side. I bounced against her armchair, fire spitting up my hands as she yanked the knife down and split open Stone's shirt.

There wasn't even a red mark. The knife had to have embedded deep into his skin but I couldn't spot a laceration, never mind gashes into his internal tissue. Amara tossed the knife, and smeared her finger down Stone's scars. He reared back, but didn't throw her off. Had she paralyzed him?

I caught the grit in his jaw as if he were grinding his teeth down just to move a pinkie. *Oh god.* Amara ignored it and pulled out a long sheet of paper. Okay? She laid it against Stone's chest, then tapped it again.

In an instant, his scars lit up, burning a trace into the fine paper. Stone scrunched up his eyes, but didn't say anything as Amara yanked the paper off of him. As she scuttled off to her lectern, he lunged forward. I leaped to catch him, wrapping my arms around his chest. His naked, warm, heaving chest.

Focus on the patient. His long hair fell into his eyes, obscuring half of his face as he panted against me. I willed my healing spell up out of habit, placing my hand to where the dagger had struck him. Suddenly,

Stone shoved me off and he stumbled back. "I don't like being touched there," he muttered, sounding in shock.

"I'm…" I dropped my hands and shook away the spell. He turned his back to me then stared down at his ripped shirt. There was no fixing what she had done.

"Ha! See." Amara pointed to the trace she made of Stone's scars. Lights danced from the lines and swirls, rising into the air. As they hovered above the lectern, another one appeared, then five more flanking it.

The keeper scratched her chin. "Seems you're a member of the Wayfarer clan. Haven't seen them in ages."

Stone turned his head and looked. As he stared, his pupils constricted and eyes widened. Suddenly, he flung himself back and screamed in agonizing pain.

"What's the matter? What…?"

He cried once more and shoved me aside. Running like the hounds of hell were on his heels, he dashed through the open door and into the streets. I looked up at the swirling lines that formed a galaxy of stars on the ceiling. Whatever he had seen in there had terrified him.

Chapter Eighteen

Raul

"*That's fucking awesome!*" *Instead of praying to Mother Mary for forgiveness while the principal glared at me, my flauco ass had wandered into the dense forests outside* mi familia's *apartment. It was where the* chaneque *would abduct naughty boys. At fifteen, I didn't believe in those stupid fairy stories until I was staring at a bright green man with a chest of glowing scars.*

He smiled at me with the same kindness of the Jesus painting on my mama's wall. Tossing back his jet-black hair, he turned to the other green people with huge ears. If these were chaneque, *the stories did them dirty. One by one, each hooded person tossed back their cloak to reveal bare chests exuding nearly the same glowing dark green scars.*

"*Verga!*" *It wasn't just men who were going all naked. The women were tatted up too, with barely a scrap of fabric scooped over the parts I got ten rosaries for drawing on my history book. My skin burned hotter the longer I tried to not stare. I hadn't even touched a girl's hand yet. And probably never would because they only went for the guys named Brock and Terry.*

"Little one," the first chaneque *said.*

I sneered. "I'm already five foot six, which is quite tall for someone..."

Every green creature clasped hands as one they tipped their heads back and their weird scars burst into the sky. It was like a laser show but without the old fogey music. My breath caught and a tingle reverberated down my chest. It wasn't the other one that was a sin on baby Jesus. I'd gotten to know that one quite well last summer. This one grew from my heart and spread out, as if tracing the same lines into my skin.

"Stone!"

I shivered at the sound tickling my ear, but kept staring.

"What do you think of them?" the guy who'd lured me into the woods asked.

"I've never seen anything like this," I said before shaking it off. "I mean, it could be cooler. There's not even any stars or demon heads."

He laughed uproariously and clasped a hand to my shoulder. My knees bent at the force as if he had no idea how strong he was. The chaneque *kept braying. "He's a true Wayfarer." The rest joined in, sharing in the joke.*

"Stone? Where are you?"

The green dude lowered to a knee. I thought they were supposed to be tiny, wrinkly old men but he towered above me and couldn't be any older than my cousin's weird college friend that stank of skunk all the time. "My mab, do you wish me to reveal your marks as well?" He pointed a long finger to my spindly chest.

"You mean, I can have those cool tats too?"

He brushed back my wayward hair behind my ears and smiled. "You already do."

"Raul?"

The voice penetrated my hazy fog. I clung white-knuckled to something wooden and stared at the face of the man who'd found me in the woods when I was fifteen. I'd blocked it as much as I could, to escape the trauma, to keep from waking up nights in a cold sweat. For years, I had worn shirts to hide the scars, to keep people from asking me to explain something I barely remembered. But when that woman had drawn all those lights in the sky, my decades of repression had shattered.

"Oh thank god, I thought I'd lost you."

Her voice sounded relieved but also uncertain. The wet woods faded from my mind, but I couldn't leave entirely. It was as if I had to relive that horrific day on the edges of my vision. I blinked and tried to shut it off, but the sounds reverberated in my ears.

My scream—a raw, brutal, unending shriek—cut apart my memories. In every nightmare, in every counseling session, I heard it when the creature placed a long claw to my chest. It was from the pain, it had to be. No one could get covered in these deep, permanent scars without writhing in agony.

"Raul?" Her hand landed on my shoulder, yanking me from almost piecing it all together.

I gasped in air, emerging from a decade of deep trauma. She didn't call me Stone, or witch hunter or even agent. "How do you know my real name?" We were trained to never tell them that. Witches could use names for curses. All of our real truths had to be hidden.

She gulped and her eyes wobbled. "You told me."

"When?" I scoffed. I was never so careless as to reveal a piece of myself to a witch. But she knew, and there was no way for her to unless...

"After I saved you from drowning."

"I would ne—" Flashes struck from the depths of my brain. A dark cistern, razors in the teeming water and warm hands cinched to my waist, plucking me free. It was supposed to be another nightmare, a rare one that ended happily. But if that really happened, then...

Her careful eyes drifted away, though she kept rubbing her palm over my shoulder. "What do we do now?"

I shook my head, trying to dislodge a memory or dream of her hands unbuckling my belt. It didn't help to get us out of here.

"If you're the, or were, the touchstone for earth, we don't have a way back."

"I am—!" I stormed, but as she swung her gaze to me, her eyes beading up in tears, I crumbled. "Maybe I am their touchstone, or was."

"Did they turn you into it or...?"

It was the 'or' that churned in my soul. I thought I'd been dragged to that strange stone circle in the woods. That they'd strapped me down, gagged and tortured me. But the memories tugging on my brain were full of laughter and excitement. I'd chosen this? Why?

"Matthew..." I clenched my hand, scraping my fingers over the burn in my palm from that iron coin. "Zimmerman told me that he, he killed all of my attackers. But if they were really elves, then, I don't see how."

"What do you mean?"

"You saw me come back to life repeatedly on your couch."

She laughed a minute and I stared hard at her. "Sorry, it just…it sounded like a euphemism for… Fuck. I mean, never mind."

Goddamn, why did she have to be so cute while blushing and stammering? I placed my hand to the wooden railing around a pond I'd run to instead of touching her burning cheek. It seemed a safer bet.

"What I'm driving at is, maybe whoever they were, they're here. Maybe we can find them and figure out a way back home."

"The crazy keeper lady couldn't find their counterweights," she said, almost excitedly.

More than a way home, I might finally have the answers I'd been running from. Did I go willingly? Did I turn my back on my humanity? On my family, my mom, just for the sake of some shiny tattoos?

I pushed off the fence and tried to balance myself. A warm breeze brushed against my exposed chest and I frowned. I tried to pull my ripped shirt together, but there was no fixing what she did. When people'd ask about my scars, I did my best to pretend they didn't bother me. But having them revealed to the whole world was terrifying and also oddly freeing. Everything I'd been hiding, including my name, was known.

She wasn't running away. Instead, she ran to me.

"Our first step is finding shelter. Real shelter. We can't keep relying on your magic." I tried to use standard operating procedures to put some distance between me and the witch.

Layla nodded her bowed head, then she lifted her eyes and the same fretful tears bubbled up. I wanted to reach out and wipe them away, assure her I had this under control. She raised her palm and I could see the magic thundering inside of it. "Your chest, she stabbed you."

"It feels fine," I said and breathed deep, surprised to find it so. How much punishment could this elven body take?

"Oh." She poofed out the spell and bunched her hands together.

"Thank you for offering. I've never had someone..." Fuck, why was this so awkward? Her cute little nose turned pink and she brushed her hair behind her ears. She was a witch with a stable of dangerous creatures in her bed. I should look upon her with pity or disgust, but my hand kept fumbling through the narrowing space between us. "Why did you chase after me? I thought you hated me?"

"I..." She raised up her chin, her wide soulful eyes brimming with unexplored emotion. "We're in this together." Her lips quivered and the once tight, angry pout softened.

"We are," I whispered and cupped her chin. At my touch, her eyes slipped closed. I guided her on her delicate little toes and kissed her pillowy lips.

Chapter Nineteen

Layla

His finger circled my chin and I raised my head. I expected an explanation, maybe a traumatic reveal of what he had discovered or an accusation about the memories I had stolen. What I didn't anticipate were the warm, soft lips pressing to mine. He didn't take, or even force me back, but caressed with a gentle brush of his mouth. The heat plunged down my throat, chasing away any sense I had.

He drew the back of his knuckles against my cheek and swept his fingers up to hold me. As his pinkie circled over my earlobe, a moan parted my lips. He drew his tongue inside, teasing the taste of him across my famished palate. Trees and grass by the summer sun—his body overwhelmed mine with a flavor of green life.

My hands reached up, wanting to wrap around the back of his neck and pull him in deeper. To drag both of us to the muddy ground without a thought and run my tongue down every swoop of his scars. The hand holding my chin fell and his lips faded off of mine.

A throbbing beat cascaded from my ribcage down to my toes. Hazy light cut through the sun, casting him in a white shadow. I blinked, struggling to focus, and my heart lurched. Stone stared at me, his lips glistening from mine.

"Why did you do that?" I asked both him and myself. I couldn't stand this bastard. If it weren't for him, I'd be home lying on Cal's lap while Garavel rubbed my feet, Daniel recited more of his lyrics and Ink kept stripping down for a fivesome.

The dreamy cast in his eyes hardened to flint. He ticked his lips up into a sneer. "Because you were about to lose it and needed a distraction."

"Excuse me?"

Stone stumbled back and swept a hand through his hair. "Last thing we need is you causing a scene."

"You're calling me hysterical after you fucking kiss me!" I hurled my palm out, fire crackling over the surface. He had taken a knife to the sternum — he could handle a few third-degree burns.

Stone didn't even blink, only folded his hands over his naked chest and stared at me. "This is why witches need to be contained. You're too unpredictable."

"I'll give you contained, you pig in a suit." Grumbling, I folded my hands together, calling forth the shield spell but casting four walls all around Stone. He stood tall, as smug as fucking ever, until the roof smacked into his head. Oh, he tried to fight it, keeping his head level, but the chin began to dip. Then I hit him again, surging the back wall forward. He jerked, and I crushed the next two together, pinning him in place.

All the while, he kept sinking, unable to fight against the invisible force. "Very funny," he muttered, his back bent into such a stoop his head was level with my chest. "Stop this."

I rolled my fists and shoved him harder until his legs buckled. Then I stopped and smirked.

"Do you think you've proven some point by doing this?"

"Other than that I can bring you to your knees whenever you piss me the fuck off? No." I broke the spell. He tumbled forward, almost face-planting into the mud. Good. I turned my back and focused on the rising sounds of a busy market day. It reminded me of some of the old small towns my mom would take us. Cute stalls that looked like they'd been passed down for generations, the most unimaginable goods dangling from poles and lines to get attention, people shoulder to shoulder as they haggled.

"Have you no sense of self control?" Stone sputtered. As he stood up, his pants made a horrifying squelching sound. Oh yeah, they were caked in mud. Served him right, the bastard.

"Are you dead?" I asked, casting a single glance back. He scowled and it made me smile. Certainly no heart skipping a beat with that face. A flush shivered down my spine as my memory overran with the angry kiss of his lips in the cistern. I shook it off, reminding myself that it wasn't real.

"If you can cease your childish games..." He stopped beside me and almost reached over to grab my shoulder. I ducked back, leaving his hand sailing on past. Stone knew better than to try again. "We need to find more information."

"On what?"

"Eventually the Wayfarer clan, but for now a place to sleep and food to eat. Do not leave my side."

"Why? You think I can't handle a few elves?"

He stared down at me like I wasn't a person. Like I wasn't even a tool. He looked at me like I was a stray cat clawing at his pants. "Because you are still under the command of the witch hunters."

That fucking son of a...

Stone took a step, then turned to look at me. I should stay in place, refuse to even meet his eye. But the crowd was growing larger, and if I kept playing this game, they'd either separate us or notice me and get ideas. Summoning all my dignity, I walked near the asshole. Elves bumped into us, offering quick apologies to him but paying me no attention. It sent me tumbling for Stone's side, but I managed to swerve, slamming my socked foot to the squishy ground.

"Ugh. Hey, jailor? Any chance I can get some damn shoes?"

He frowned at me calling him what he was, and glanced to me balanced on one foot while trying to rub life into the other. I knew that fire in his eyes and half expected to find them staring down my bowing shirt collar. But no, they were burning straight to my foot.

"Or would you rather make me walk around barefoot for your pleasure?"

Stone jerked as if I'd shouted a litany of his kinks in front of a church. Which was probably something Ink had done. I should ask him once I... The if floated in my mind, taunting me, nearly pressing me to tears. I chewed it into little bits, swallowing it like glass. There was no if, only when.

"Shoes are not a priority, food first. Then shelter. Have you no survival tactics?"

"Sorry, I didn't get my 'camping in another realm' badge. Maybe next year."

He didn't answer, instead pushing through two elves to reach a stand I'd guess had a bunch of carpets for sale. This was my chance. I could turn and run, fade into the crowd. Let him figure his own way back. Surely something in my spell book could tell me how to make a touchstone without slitting throats.

"Leeland?"

I froze, nearly free. Stone pierced through the crowd and reached out to me. Run. Dash off into the night. I could haggle as good as any Romanian farm wife on her last *leu*.

Why I took his hand and let him pull me close to the stand, I couldn't guess. I still woke in cold sweats after the witch hunters stole away my magic. The next time, I might not survive.

Stone led me to a quaint stand with a whole lot of leather. It'd make some dominatrixes giddy with envy. Black, brown, red, even pink and green—the leather hung in strips and flat squares from the overarching sign. More finished pieces like belts...or whips lay across the flat of the stand. But of course, the owner was a wrinkled old man shorter than me. He had skin a pale blue and his eyes were so sunken in I could barely see them below his fluffy white brows.

"What do you be needing, young squire?" he asked. Jesus, if he said he had snuck into Ren Faires in his youth, I wouldn't be surprised.

"She needs shoes," Stone said and pushed me closer.

I blinked, my jaw dropping. "But I thought they..."

"We don't need you dying from some weird elven parasite. So, go on, pick something."

"Ah, I'm a size seven. Sometimes eight in a sneaker. Like, this big." I held out my hands for the kindly shop owner. Stone reached over, gripped my wrists and slightly pushed my palms closer.

"More like that," he said.

How much did he stare at my feet? The shy, awkward guy who'd blushed at getting called out was gone. Cold confidence stared back at me, and my knees wobbled.

The shopkeep shoved a long black box across the counter. "Put your foot in that, dearie."

I dropped it to the ground and was about to do just that. "Er, with or without the sock?"

"What's a sock?" he asked.

Probably without. *Okay, going to put my bare, naked foot into a strange elven artifact. No big deal.* I pressed the tip of my big toe against the black surface.

"Real nice of you!" the shopkeep shouted. He slapped Stone on the back, causing the man to leap from where he'd been staring at my bare foot.

I smiled to myself and took my time, easing the ball of my foot onto the box. As I added my heel, my foot sank into the black box. A soft foam formed around it, molding my foot's exact shape.

"Now the other one," the shopkeep said.

I tugged my foot out and the box returned to what it was. Prying off my remaining shoe, which I put in my purse for safe keeping, I pressed my second foot inside. This time, Stone was looking everywhere but at my pink nails digging into the soft black foam. "There," I said, slipping out and handing him back the box.

Taking it, the shopkeep shuffled to his leather working station. "Not every master gets his sclab a new pair of boots. You're real lucky."

Master? Darkness descended between us. Stone didn't look at me but at the shopkeep happily stitching together a pair of boots. I burned harder, trying to awkwardly dig myself a hole like I did every time someone had to remind me I didn't look right. I didn't talk right. And I didn't belong.

"How long will this take?" Stone pressed.

"About a one-eighth pass of the sun."

He nodded in response and took my arm. Guiding me around the gathered throngs, we moved to a small bench carved from the trunk of a tree. "I have no idea how long that is, but it seems smarter to wait away from people."

"You mean creatures to be corralled?"

"It'd take a lot of rope to get all of them," he said and, damn it, I laughed. More at the idea of Stone in full cowboy getup trying to lasso an elf petulantly standing there.

He didn't chuckle back, but sat up taller.

Every pry of my foot left something stickier on the sole. I picked up both of them and placed the tips of my toes on a flower basin across from me. Stone stared, then darted away fast.

"There's nothing wrong with it."

"I know," he said too fast, then swallowed. "With what?"

"Tons of people are into them." Okay, no one I'd ever been with, unless Daniel was keeping it way on the down low and Garavel hadn't discovered it yet. Ink would worship every inch of my body if I wanted him to, but it wasn't the same as an obsessive foot fetish.

"Do you think I'm...bothered by it? I...I don't care. Go barefoot. Don't go barefoot. You can do whatever you want."

Except cast magic and live as I want to.

"Is it weird?" he sputtered, the pompous twat replaced by a perturbed man begging for assurance.

Okay, I may enjoy him on his knees more than I want to admit. "There's nothing wrong with admiring nice body parts. I mean, assuming the...feet are okay with it." *Fuck, why is this so weird?*

He did laugh at that, and rubbed his chin. "Are they...okay with it?"

I glared at my toes. I'd never thought them special, though I liked the occasional pedicure done at home because I was made of Spam and ramen instead of money. I should tell him no. Stuff my feet into the clomping boots and never take them out.

"Yeah," I said, stretching out. It felt too good to have the sun on my skin and toes in the air to care what Stone thought of them.

"They're... They are nice feet."

It wasn't the bragging snicker from when he had insisted he'd kissed me to stop me from being hysterical. Instead, his voice dropped to a gentle whisper and he placed his hand next to me on the bench. Stone kept raising a digit in the air, almost placing it on top of mine. He wiggled it once more, rubbed his chin, and swept his finger between mine.

"Fresh face?"

Stone jerked to his feet at the bellow of the shop keep. I was more careful, dropping my bare toes to the cool ground.

"Yes?" he asked the man before scowling. "What did you call me?"

The leather-worker lifted up his goggles. "Nearly done with this pair. Nothing too fancy, they should keep her feet warm at least. How about one sixtieth of your latest pillage?"

We both glanced to each other, then darted away. Technically, one sixtieth of zero would be zero, but I doubted the man would accept that. Stone shook his head and commanded, "That is not a possibility."

"Why? Already pledged it all? Youths, they can't keep a single gold piece in their pocket before the end of market day. What else have you got?"

I didn't even think of this. Stone patted his pockets with that 'end of the date, here comes the check' energy. I glared at him but pulled open my purse, only for the brooch to burrow into my throat. Gasping, I turned to find an elf standing on the hem of my cloak.

"What about this cursed, I mean beautiful, cloak?" I yanked the clasp off, finally taking in a breath, and laid it across my arm.

Stone fingered the material and smiled. "It's sturdy and warm during the coolest of nights."

I frowned. This was a gift from Ink. Even though I hated it and was tired of nearly choking to death with every step, I couldn't give it up on a whim.

The shopkeep barely glanced at it before turning away. "No."

"What do you mean no? It's got…okay, no pockets. But it's a solid cloak."

He sighed and gestured far above our heads. Hundreds of wool, leather and velvet cloaks wafted in the breeze. "This market is jampacked with 'em. Some damn fool made a huge plunder with the weaving spiders and we're drowning in cloaks. Anything else?"

I took the cloak back and tugged open my purse. There wasn't anything too exciting. A handful of old mints from restaurants Cal had taken me to. My phone, my spell book. "Do you think he'd take a tampon?" I asked Stone, waving the pink wrapper around.

It seemed to perk up the shopkeep's eye, but Stone shoved my hand back in and growled. I snorted. "Men. It's just a little blood and organ tissue. Grow up." I kept digging and hit something metal. What in the...?

My fingers clenched around a hard object shaped like a U. Was that what Ink had put in there? I began to tug it out, when a noise shattered through the market.

I didn't realize how loud the shopping elves were until their voices died. They staggered apart as a woman in very little clothing rode atop a giant cage. It was hard to see inside, the slats tiny, but massive bangs erupted from inside. At the dry fountain, she stopped and blew a horn. "Your beloved beast keeper has returned. Feast your eyes upon..." She yanked on a rope and the door flew open.

Hooves sparked on the road as a deer-like creature dashed out of the box. Its coat was a sienna red with white lines forming a pattern of intricate designs across its back and down its snout. But what stood out was the horn. Instead of a pair of antlers on its head, a single horn with a multitude of branches towered off of its forehead. As the creature swung its bearded chin, a haunting melody whistled from the holes in its horn.

"A shadhavar," Stone said.

"A what?"

"Think of it like a unicorn, but for Djinn."

"Who's stupid enough to steal from Djinn?"

He snickered and pointed to the woman pulling out a saddle. She leaped off the cage and began to approach the shadhavar. "What will I get for this rare and haunting—?"

Lighting quick, the shadhavar spun and gored its horn straight though the woman's stomach. She cried out as it pinned her to its cage, then yanked the horn back. The squelching sound of her pureed organs rang out and the elves panicked. Blood spurted from the holes of the shadhavar's horn. It swung its head, pipping a flute-like song of rage.

This is bad.

I grabbed Stone's hand to pull him back. Luckily, he seemed to have the same idea. This was an elf problem. I might have a bad habit of stepping into shit, but they had brought this one on themselves. He wrapped an arm around my waist and I fell in beside him, the both of us trying to blend in with the panicking elves. They put as much distance as they could between themselves and the raging shadhavar.

A sound, the sharp cry of a baby, cut above the trampling. I froze in my tracks, and peered around the slamming shoulders. Someone had dropped a wicker basket in their escape. It was probably full of apples. *No reason to…*

The blankets shifted, and a tiny blue fist waved in the air. Oh no. The sharp cry of fear caught the attention of the murder-music-corn. It swung its head around, a demented lullaby bursting from its horn. It slammed another hoof to the cobbles, setting off more sparks.

"Stone!" I shouted, weaving my way closer.

"Leeland… Don't even think about —"

The shadhavar charged. Its horn dropped to skewer the baby and I flung up my shield. It smashed into my magic, sending me shuddering back. My feet burned but I held my stance.

Enraged, it whipped its head back and forth, smashing into the shield while the child kept screaming for their mother. I gritted my teeth, letting the magic flow.

"What are you doing?" Stone demanded.

"I can't just let it kill the kid."

"I know that. But this is making it more deranged. The angrier, the stronger they get. Use a sleep spell."

Oh. Holding my shield out, I dipped into the vast well. I weaved my fingers together, repeating the incantation. It was gonna have to be strong to stop this thing. "Can you get the baby?"

"Why?" Stone shouted.

"I have to drop the shield in order to put it to sleep."

"Very well." He dove forward and scooped his arms around the basket. In doing so, the blanket fell away revealing a tiny blue face scrunched up in tears. The baby was not happy with Stone and began to pummel him. He winced and struggled to turn.

Which was when the shadhavar swung so hard the shield shattered. "No!"

It raised its horn up, prepared to smash both Stone and the baby with the flat side. I rammed my hand out, casting the sleep spell. It rocketed through the air, striking the shadhavar's nostrils. At that moment, the woman who'd trapped the creature stood and she got the blowback. Her eyes rolled back and she crumpled to the ground. The shadhavar stumbled. It shook its head, a mournful dirge playing from its horn. Taking one step closer to Stone, it snorted, then collapsed.

"Whew." I moved to wipe my forehead studded with sweat, and the hairs on the back of my neck prickled. Numb, I turned to find every elf staring not at the murder creature, or even the woman that caused this. No, they were focused only on me.

"Is that…?"

"She's a witch!"

Fuck.

"Here." Stone shoved the baby at a random elf and ran to my side. He curled me tight to his body as I tried to shrink away. The elves screamed 'witch' and 'magic' and they surged toward us. I yelped, tucking in my arms. Hands tried to pry them away, to pull me from Stone's side even as he waved a hand at them.

"It is. This sclab's a witch."

"How much for her?"

"I'll give you a quarter, no, a half of my next pillage!"

"You can have the entire thing!"

"I'll trade you my first born for her!"

Holy fuck. Their mouths snapped at me like cages, screaming out offers to buy me. Hands and fingers snaked out to rip at my skin, pinching and tugging like they were measuring me for the pot. My ears bled from the voices shrieking to own me. I tried to reach up to cover them, when Stone grabbed my hand. He clamped his fingers and I froze.

They were offering him the world. And all he had to do was get rid of me. I tried to tug my hand out, but I was trapped.

Then, he raised his chin and shouted, "She's not for sale!"

Of course, he wasn't going to sell me. *Why did I even think...?* Because he still wanted to own me in the name of the witch hunters.

"We have to get out of here," Stone shouted.

I brought my palms together, pulling his with. Whispering the spell, I looked up into the rabid eyes of the elves who weren't even looking at the person they wanted to own. A small amount of glee tugged my lips up as I threw my hands open. The spell crushed them to the ground, hurling the elves away like bowling pins. Before they had a chance to shake off their concussions, we were gone.

Chapter Twenty

Stone

"This place is fucking insane." I groaned, stumbling to a halt in a tiny alleyway that looked like it had been stolen from Victorian London. To my surprise, the witch they were all hounding for began to laugh.

Doubled over, with her hands on her knees, it was impossible for me to see if it was a panicked laugh or a genuine one. A flurry of commotion dashed past and I inched closer between the two brick buildings. Was that an advertisement for a haberdashery up there? In staring at the aging image of a top hat, I completely missed when I walked not just near but into Layla.

She jerked up, and I instinctively swept a hand out. It was supposed to catch hers before she tumbled into a dry well behind. But my palm cupped clear up to her elbow and I tugged. She skidded across the gap nearly into my arms. My breath fled at her panting chest pressing against mine. Only the fabric of her T-shirt kept us from being skin to skin, a fact I was growing more and more aware of the longer she stood there chuckling. Each laugh jiggled her gorgeous tits and I had nowhere to pull back my hips.

"Why are you laughing?" I asked, needing her to stop before this awkwardness hit Defcon level two.

She dashed up on her tiptoes and slapped a hand over my mouth.

The elves that'd been chasing us turned and ran back the way they came, just missing the two people crammed in the alleyway. Her raised body began to teeter so I drew a hand around her waist. Damn... I knew she was curvy, but the sweep of her ass down my palm was a rollercoaster.

She shifted to stare out into the open road. Curious myself, I leaned down to look and she turned back. Her nose nearly pressed to mine, her eyes widened in surprise and her damn lips quivered with a suppressed sigh. Heat burned up my bare side as I realized her palm rested on my waist. She wobbled again, but wouldn't lower to the ground. I clung tighter to the small of her back, pressing her hips into mine.

Fuck. These pants were awful at keeping my cock at bay. The silk lining cupped right around my rocketing erection as it chased the heat of her belly. *Do not think about that thin camisole and her nipples...*

Damn it. Layla shifted again. No chance she missed my cock nearly impaling her belly button. I girded myself for a biting comment, but a cute blush swept over her cheeks igniting her freckles.

"You were laughing," I said, my brain losing too much blood to think straight. A mob of very determined capitalists were ready to rip me limb from limb to get at her, but all I could think about was taking her against the brick wall.

She bit down on her bottom lip and another giggle slipped free. "I was. Sorry."

"Gonna tell me why?"

Her laughter wasn't the flints under my nails I expected. Instead, it left a flutter running down my spine. She tipped her head back to stare into my eyes. My gaze darted to her lips bunching up as if she didn't want to reveal a secret. "It was you. You're so pompous all the time. When you let loose a fuck, it's…reassuring."

She was laughing at me, of course. "Reassuring how?"

Layla lifted her hot palm from my waist up my lats and swerved toward my chest. God, why hadn't I hit the gym in weeks? At my sternum, she paused and stared up at me. "That under all the pretentious agent bullshit, you're human."

Am I?

My eyes dropped to her palm, a normal skin tone, against my unearthly green. I shuddered out a breath, afraid to admit to myself what I was coming to fear. *What if this is permanent? What if I can't go back to being Stone?*

A finger curled to my cheek. I blinked as Layla brushed away a tear. She stopped, and held my face in her hand. I bent low and she slid up taller to meet me.

"Excuse me?"

Fuck! I jerked away and slammed the back of my head into the brick wall. "*Cabrón de mierda!*" I shouted, hunting for whoever did that through the stars in my eyes. When I realized the red wasn't the brick but a face,

I clasped onto Layla and pushed her away. An elf strode out of what I thought was a deserted alley.

"What do you want? Do not try anything. I have more skills than you can ever know."

He wasn't dressed like the marketplace denizens, who'd had a varying mix of wool and furs. This one wore a sheer fabric that to my eye was silk, but judging by the shifting colors, was probably something alien. His entire chest was exposed, the scars more blocky than mine. And…a tiny loincloth was all that separated him from an indecent exposure charge.

I darted my eyes to his right ear while trying to protect Layla.

"Uh, Stone?"

"You're with the Wayfarer clan aren't you?"

"I am of no one," I said, standing taller.

He chuckled and drew a finger across his top lip. "Your chest says otherwise."

Damn it. I needed to find a shirt to cover up before we found ourselves in deeper shit.

The stranger glanced over my shoulder and I shifted, trying to hide Layla. "A bit foolish of you to bring a witch to market. They'll eat her alive before you get through the gates."

"Stone…"

"If you try to take her —"

He raised a hand. "I have no need for a witch. But I do have something for you." From his pocket, he plucked out a small brass knob. Etched into the top was a thicket of thorns. He extended it as if I should be excited. This had to be a trap.

"What is that?"

"What...?" He scoffed and shook his long blond hair. "You must be one of the lesser cousins, perhaps from a shorter branch of the family tree?"

"Tell me before I disembowel you."

The laugh cut through me like tinfoil on teeth. "You know, if your witch there casts a single spell, it'll send the whole marketplace down on you. And they're rabid for a magic user."

"Get to the fucking point." I girded myself for another chuckle from Layla but she'd gone silent.

The elf reached out for my hand. I jerked away, but at his glare, I held mine out. He slammed the strange knob into my palm. "Your family's estate key. I thought it might serve as a place for you to lay low, or at least hide away your witch sclab for whatever it is you do with them."

From behind me broke a growl so feral, I feared a giant wolf had been sent to track us down. When an arm slashed through the air trying to gut the elf, I caught Layla's hand. For as much as I agreed, he was right. If she cast a spell, we'd be found out and fast.

The elf smirked and turned.

"What do I do with this?"

He lifted an eyebrow and stared as if sizing me up to see if I was joking. After a beleaguered sigh, he said, "You know the estate alcove on... No, of course you don't. To the east, which is the direction I am pointing, you will find a huge stack of doors. Put that into the slot."

My thumb fell into the thorny pattern etched into the polished brass. "And then what?" I asked, but as I looked up, he was gone.

"Well, I hate him," Layla said. "So that's a trap, right?"

As I held the knob, the weight of it pressed not just on my palm but the back of my mind. It wasn't a memory, but an instinct. I knew this pattern the same way I knew my name. It always was and always would be.

Suddenly, she yelped, and skittered across the ground to hide behind me. The hunting party was making another sweep. We didn't have a choice. Either this was our salvation and a way to regroup, or it was a trap. Better to spring it now when we were on our guard than wait for another to strike.

"Damn it." She winced and hobbled against the wall to look at her foot. Tiny gravel had embedded into her light skin. "I nearly had those stupid shoes, and…"

"Here." From out of my pocket, I handed her the pair of folded-up leather shoes. They'd compressed down like slippers, but Layla's eyes lit up as she snatched them away.

She stuffed one delicate foot inside before looking at me. "You stole them? When? How?"

While I was sad to lose the sight of her toes pressing against the top of my shoes, she seemed to sigh in relief while touching the ground. "I'm not as straitlaced as you think," I said.

"Pretty sure I said pompous, but…thank you. So I don't get gangrene of the foot."

A witch's gratitude meant little, but I still nodded. Weighing the brass knob, I gazed in the direction the elf had pointed. It was our only option.

Due to all of our backtracking, the sun had dipped behind the horizon by the time we approached the estate alcove. The elves seemed hellbent on getting their hands on Layla. I'd anticipated climbing over a high magical gate and jogging down gardens outside gigantic mansions.

"That's it?" she asked, coming to a stop beside me next to a gap in the dying hedges. A massive wall stood before us, stretching so high it blotted out the stars and moon. Sorry, moons. Embedded into the pale gray brick were hundreds of doors. Fifteen stretched across the bottom and another twenty or so towered above. Tiny, one-person ladders led up to the doors scaling into the clouds.

The doors had, at most, a two-foot gap from their neighbors. I tried to peer to the side, but the wall vanished into a hazy fog. Maybe it was like a row house — a row house three feet wide. I weighed the knob in my palm and a hazy flicker rose on the thorn etching. The light caught as I held it out, growing stronger while I drew it to the right.

A pull tugged me on, guiding me past the nondescript doors. They were varying colors — reds, yellows, blues — passing me by. The witch took a minute to stare up at the ladders before asking, "Do we just pick one?"

"I think the knob knows what hole it wants."

She snickered and I looked back at her. It wasn't until she bit her lip and darted her eyes away that I realized what I had said. "That wasn't..." I stammered, and she whistled softly under her breath.

The knob jerked in my hand. The brass one, not my... *Ugh.* It shivered again as I walked closer to a door in pale green. The wood was a splintery nightmare with gaps between the boards, but I couldn't see inside. As I approached it, the knob shivered, then leaped into the dead center hole. When it locked in, the thorn etching glowed bright white.

I placed my hand over it and electricity jolted through me. "I believe this is it."

"So we thinking trap?"

"Possibly."

She held both hands out, palms up. On one a spark of fire looked ready to burst into an inferno. On the other, a terrifying chill crackled into an ice storm. I stared, not at the door lighting up with glowing runes, but her. I knew her to be a witch and powerful enough to catch the attention of the agency, but I'd never seen one wield two types of elemental damage at once.

"You know, even if it's not a trap, we're gonna be stacked on top of each other all night."

I snorted and looked back. Her cheeks turned bright pink. "Not like that!"

"As you say. Turning the knob..." I cranked it to the right and the door fell open. Holding my breath, I took a step into total darkness. "Hello?" I called out, my voice echoing like a cavern.

The witch's heels bounced into mine causing me to jerk forward. My hand landed on a cool wall. As it did, light rose along the brick and marble. It trickled at first, a small stream of green dancing in waves across the wall. It kept going, vanishing deep into the darkness. I held my breath until it struck a farther wall and the entire place lit up.

"Holy—"

"—shit," Layla whispered, both of us in awe as we strolled into a palace that'd make Roman emperors green with envy. White brick and marble strained a good three unimpeded stories above our heads. I had to strain my neck back to spot the ceiling that flickered with small lights mimicking stars. Columns held up a second level deeper into the grand foyer, all of them painted to mimic a tree trunk while branches sprouted at the top to form the banisters and railings.

Statues not of people but nature—leaves, cherries, leaping fish and more—filled the alcoves nestled into the walls. I paused beside one with a strange four-legged creature I'd never seen and, as I looked, a pattern of lights rose above it like a plaque. If the dashes formed words, I couldn't read it.

"This is a bit nicer than expected," Layla said. She clenched her hands, closing off the fire and ice, and walked up to the massive fireplace.

It was big enough ten men could sit inside. Every brick was etched so a vine and thorn pattern circled around the fireplace. A massive spit stretched across the fireplace and a pot dangled off of it, both of them made of gold. A show of wealth or the only option for people who were injured by iron? Judging by the size of this estate, it could be both. I approached the fireplace cautiously, my gaze drawn to the space above the mantle. Something was clearly there, but it hung in darkness as if the house were trying to obscure it.

"What the…?" Layla darted away, running through a small archway. There seemed to be no other doors aside from the one we had come through. Strange. Lifting my head, I stared harder into the impenetrable shadows. A pulse shivered from my chest. Clamping a hand to my sternum, I tried to shake off the chill when the darkness glowed. Lines danced above the fireplace, sweeping and curling like a laser light show set to calm music. I'd never seen this place, had no idea what any of it meant, but my mind and soul fluttered with a feeling of…home.

"Stone! You've got to see this!"

I wrenched away and the mantle darkened. The witch stuck her head out and she waved me on. I took one last look at the fireplace, but there was no hint anything had appeared. "What is it?"

"Well, it was dark as night out." She shuffled away from me and dashed through a room holding a stone desk and honeycomb shelves crammed with scrolls. "And now." The witch pointed out a glassless window to a serene pasture. A blue brook wound between trees bulging with fruit and strange birds hopping from branch to branch.

I didn't understand, the setting was picturesque. "What of it?"

"The sun." She jabbed a finger to the sky where the sun sat just below a ring of mountains in the distance.

Yes, a beautiful sunset with a beautiful...

"How did it go from being set to being up there? Did we time travel?" Her eyes were wide and she stepped away as I peered out. The sweet green scent of hay and baking river rocks struck me. If this was an illusion, it was a thorough one.

"Time travel isn't real," I said.

"You sure about that?"

I wasn't certain of anything anymore. "Elves, they are capable of instant travel. Perhaps..." I glanced over my shoulder to where we'd entered. The door was still open, but only darkness lingered in the threshold. "Perhaps we're somewhere else on the planet. Or another realm entirely."

She shook her head hard at that. "No. I'd know if that happened."

"Really? You're an expert in realm travel now?"

"I know I get super fucking queasy whenever it happens. Since I don't want to puke on your shoes, I'd guess we're still in elf land, just...far away from where we were."

"That knob must be a powerful relic," I mused. My skin burned and I glanced over to catch the witch staring intently at me. "What?"

"Just thinking... Never mind. This place is massive. I'm gonna go look around, see if there's a kitchen or pantry." She took a step for the archway, then paused and curled a finger in her hair. "Are we safe here?"

"Safer than where we were," I said, unable to fully reassure her. She accepted that at least and took off, calling out what she found as she went. Her voice echoed off the tiles that glittered in emerald and gold. I returned to the door and plucked the knob off. The door slammed shut and shifted from plain wood to a twelve-foot-tall intricately carved image of elves striding across various orbs. They all stretched their hands to the middle where the hole for the knob waited for another trip.

Deep in my mind, all of this nonsense made perfect sense. The knob was a way to the family estate from anywhere across the world. No one could gain entrance without my say-so. Very powerful, indeed. Why'd that strange man have it in the first place or give it up so easily?

A fluttering rose in my chest and my scars lit up. The door mimicked them. Every swoop and tattoo on the carved elves glowed, just like mine. Whatever secrets this place had held for the elves that'd tortured me, I'd find them out. And I'd find a way to get rid of this elven curse once and for all.

C h a p t e r   T w e n t y - O n e

Layla

I stirred around the innards of a goopy but delicious fruit, my hunger vanishing. Stone seemed to be of the same mind. We'd both torn into the armful I'd found. They were the size of small watermelons but red as pomegranates and twice as juicy. A part of me was still famished. I'd been literally living off of water and elf bread for the past day.

But as the fire crackled an ominous purple and I'd swear the statues moved whenever my eyes darted away, the situation sank my spirits. Tomorrow morning, I was supposed to be all nerves heading to the hospital. *I'll meet with Dana before for coffee to make us even more jittery, then we'll get assigned our nurses and be one more step to graduating as RNs.*

Something told me the program wouldn't accept 'trapped in another dimension' as an excuse.

"What's your plan?" I asked, dropping my spoon. I hadn't been able to find any hint of a fork, but there were drawers and drawers of knives. "What do we have to do to get home? Tonight?" I dug out my spell book and placed it on the leaf-shaped table.

Stone stopped mopping up the fruit juice and stared at me. The glare of the witch hunter unnerved me to my core. I almost scooped my book into my arms and fled. But no. Even if it meant revealing my spells, I needed to get home. I'd do whatever it took...within reason.

"You're in quite the hurry," he said and dropped his chin into his propped-up hand. "Worried your wolf is sniffing around someone else?"

"Are you serious?"

"They are known to have the attention span of the last female in heat to stroll past."

I slammed my fist to the table and launched to my feet. "You don't know a fucking thing about him."

"Calvin Rollin, age twenty-nine, two-point-seven GPA. Took a series of random but steady jobs before returning to the town of his birth. Lives beyond his means in a house practically gifted to him. Am I getting close?"

How the shit does he know all of that? "You've been spying on him?"

Stone chuckled and languidly placed a hunk of metal on the table. I caught the glimmer off the pentagram on the goddamn witch hunter badge. "We spy on everyone. Well, everyone with fangs and claws and wings. I have to ask, isn't the werewolf a little too...pedestrian for you? An incubus for bondage, an angel for punishment and a ghost for, I don't know, light cleaning? But the werewolf? He recycles."

I loved him. I was hanging on by a thread telling myself I'd hold his face and kiss him stupid soon. I loved all of my damn idiots who were probably tearing apart heaven and hell to get to me. If this banishment lasted much longer, they might do White's job for him.

A thousand thoughts roiled in my brain, of how Cal was resilient in the face of unimaginable abuse. But he was on a knife's edge already. How Ink was so much more than a fuck buddy. But he needed to feed. How Garavel was a ray of sunshine. But he also hated Cal with a passion that could only ignite without me there. How Daniel meant the world to me. But if he lost control, he could be lost forever. Pain and love tumbled into one, until all I could think to do was slam my hand and shout, "Stay out of his garbage!"

Stone blinked, looking as surprised as I was at what came out of my mouth. I scowled, angry at myself for not being able to tell this fucking witch hunter off. Shoving my book back into my bag, I stepped away from the table. "If you won't help, then…then I'll figure it out myself."

I stomped off, not looking back once. Where I was heading was anyone's guess. The place was a damn maze, but I had a hunch the bedrooms were on the top mezzanine, so I aimed for the stairs.

"Leeland?" Stone called out. He drifted through the archway, the light catching on his green face.

Maybe he'd actually apologize? Maybe he'd realize we had to work together to get home.

"He wears New Balance."

Fuck him! I dashed up the stairs, paying no attention until I found myself panting in a random room. Flinging a spark at a fat candle, I dashed for the desk and slumped down in the chair. I couldn't think of them. I forced myself to stare at my book, begging for anything about touchstones or realm travel. The pages quivered, but seemed uncertain where to go.

If I thought about them, I'd fall apart, then I'd be trapped here in the disorienting elf maze house with the world's biggest asshole.

I had no idea how long I sat hunched over, reading and re-reading the same words. The candle was no help. Every time the wax burned down, the drip would travel back to the top. All I knew was that my back ached from bending over and my fingers throbbed from how hard I clenched them. What I needed was to clear my head and...

My jeans stuck to the chair. Gritting my jaw, I yanked my leg. The rip of denim and bog mud sundered the air. I should get cleaned up, then hit the book again. God, what I wouldn't give for Daniel to read me what he found. Or for Ink to tell me all he knew about elves.

It wasn't until my hand hit empty air that I realized I'd expected my incubus to take it. To feel his hot lips on the back of my neck, and his hand prying away my filthy clothing. Every other time I thought of him, he was there. Making some smart-ass remark that'd cause me to groan or gasp, but he was there. Now, there was no one.

This isn't helping, Leeland. Focus on the problem. Stare at the damn words until your eyes bleed and get it right.

My coping mechanism for my dyslexia was to hate myself a lot. It at least got me through high school. Feeling ten inches tall and like my chest was caved in, I wandered past an archway, certain I imagined what I saw.

There was no kitchen in this place, no fridge, no stove, not even a couch. But as I stepped back and turned, my jaw dropped. A huge, claw-footed porcelain bathtub sat below a chandelier. Okay, there still weren't any doors in this place, but I'd spent the past night and day tramping through an elf swamp. I deserved a pampering in a hot, Olympian-sized tub.

To my shock, there was a tap. It was a single spigot of, what else, gold. When I turned it, crystal-clear water burbled out, but it was cool to the touch. Well, I knew how to fix that. I undressed, doing my best to ignore the demoralizing thud from all that mud and grease hitting the mosaic tiles. Naked, I waited until the tub was three-quarters full, then I plunged both my arms into the cool waters and whispered my spell.

It took a moment before bubbles of heat and steam burst to the surface. I kept going, wanting the hottest and steamiest damn bath the world had ever known. "Ouch!" Too much. I yanked my red arms out and shook them off. After letting more of the cool water in to even things out, I dipped a toe in then took the plunge.

"Sweet baby ribs," I whispered, losing my damn mind at the luxury of hot water on my skin. Maybe there was soap somewhere, maybe even a washcloth— I didn't care. I closed my eyes and let myself dream.

Ink would find me first. Shit, Ink would draw the bath with exotic salts and rose petals. Then Cal'd spot us and stand behind rubbing my naked shoulders while Ink perched on the edge of the tub fully clothed, running his hand over my leg. Daniel would blow on the petals, claiming that they weren't even a tenth as soft as my skin. And, just as Cal's massage was moving to my breasts, Ink's touch caressing my inner thigh, Garavel would leap into the tub, splashing everyone.

A laugh escaped from me at the idea. But the foreign echo in the strange bathroom ripped me from my fantasy.

I will see them again. I will hold them, all of them, and cry big fat tears. They could laugh at my sappiness, insist that they always knew I'd be back and had no doubt I'd find them again.

"Er..."

"Stone?" I leaped up in the tub, spotted a shadow in the open archway and dove deep underwater. "What the fuck are you doing here?"

"I heard dripping water and feared there might be a leak. I guess there's a tub."

"Yes, there is. One that I'm inside, right now." Completely naked. I slapped a hand over my breasts, squishing them tight to my chest, and crossed my legs. I left my other hand free. If he did storm in like the asshole I knew, he'd get a punch to the nose.

"That...makes sense. Tubs are where people go to get, um..." He coughed and sounded nervous as hell.

What the shit? One second he's mocking me and the next he's awkwardly stammering?

"You didn't tell me why you're so hellbent on getting back now."

"Probably because you picked on me for it." God damn, this sounded like some stupid schoolyard fight where he dumped gravel down my shirt because he... *He does not like me.*

"If I said I'm sorry, would you believe me?"

"I don't know. You haven't tried it yet." *Not to mention I'm in here naked while you could peek in without a second thought.*

Stone laughed but kept his ass outside the archway. I kept peering out, just my eyes above the lip of the bath like an angry crocodile. If he saw me, hopefully he'd think a witch was about to bite his hand off. "Given the situation, it is wrong of me to question who you do and do not take to bed. I'm sorry."

There was that pompous speech. He seemed to fall into it whenever he was in witch hunter mode. Like

Ellen Mint

kidnapping and torturing people was fine as long as you sounded pretentious while doing it. "Fine. Apology humored. Now what did you want?"

"An explanation. We are safe for the moment. It seems a good time to regroup and recuperate, but you are determined to get home. Why?"

"Because..." I didn't owe him a damn thing. I should lie. Say I had a huge orgy with all my guys, and they were gonna invite friends. Send him into a judgmental tizzy. "Because my clinicals start tomorrow."

"Your what?"

"It's a nursing thing. Kinda like an internship. And if I'm not there then I'll have wasted two years of my life. I could get expelled."

"I don't understand. You're a witch who's trying to be a nurse? To hold down a normal job?"

What the hell is he on about? "Yeah. I'm a witch, who also needs to eat, and, ya know, likes to not sleep in the rain." Or with a witch hunter curled behind me.

I frowned at that. I'd known he was there. I could have shoved him off at any moment, but I hadn't. It'd been nice to keep warm that way.

"Why don't you use your magic?"

"I haven't found the fat stacks spell yet. But I'll keep looking." The fact it wasn't on page one in bright red letters told me it probably didn't exist.

"Witches don't hold down jobs. They use their spells and potions to provide a modest income."

He said it like it was an immutable fact. *The heart is a cardiac muscle. Veins pump deoxygenated blood back to the heart. Witches can't be nurses.* I dug my hand tighter to the porcelain tub, wanting to wring his neck. "I'm getting real fucking tired of people telling me what I'm supposed to be doing with my life."

"It does seem rather foolish to waste so much time and energy on a job that can't get you a tenth of what selling snake oil will."

"Maybe I want to be a goddamn nurse and fucking help people. Not because a witch hunter forced me to do it, but because I choose to." My entire life was a chaotic mess of blood, and fangs, and demons and pain. I'd scraped and worked so hard to get into school. Even if it killed me, I was going to be a nurse and damn all those who told me I couldn't.

"You sound angry," he said, causing me to growl.

"What gave it away?"

"Well, there was a bit more cursing than I'm used to. But you haven't hurled me over the landing and snapped my neck, so I'm guessing it's not all aimed at me."

I was trapped here from my guys, my life, my... "I wouldn't be here if it wasn't for you."

"I don't remember asking you to follow me. You and your sex demon took it upon yourselves to interfere. This is as much your doing."

"You said you'd get me unicorn skin, then fucked off."

The voice outside the bathroom went silent. Only the glug of sloshing water filled the air as I shifted in the tub. I reached a hand over the lip about to look, when the shadow outside shifted. Yelping, I dove back, but Stone didn't enter. "Did you really think I wouldn't honor my word?"

Yes. No. "You kidnapped me," I said. "And you're going to do it again. Aren't you?"

He didn't answer because he didn't have to. Even with all of his old pals turning on him, he still believed he had to control my magic. That he had the right to tell me what to do with my body. Just like my damn mother

216

telling me I had to find some random man to knock me up.

I turned my back on him and curled my knees to my bare chest. It caused the locket to bunch up at the top of my cleavage. Inside of it was a piece of a man I loved, but the heart was from my father. A man my mother would never tell me about.

"Do you have any idea how much it hurts to have magic taken from me? This void slowly sucking my life away until the pain becomes impossible to bear. Of course not. If you did, you wouldn't be able to do it to another woman."

Stone coughed and I heard his feet shuffle outside the bathroom. "I found some fresh clothing while exploring. I don't know if any will fit, but I'll leave them out here for you."

I closed my eyes and listened to his heavy footsteps as he walked away. Even as they vanished, I waited a few more minutes while my skin pruned to make sure he was gone before blindly reaching for the clothing. The fabric was buttery soft while also impressively sturdy. Rather than put any of it on, I slipped back into my muddy shirt and jeans. I folded up Ink's cloak with the silver brooch and placed it on top of Stone's offering.

A part of me said I should return to my book, to finding a way home. But I couldn't look away from the silver pin. He'd been so damn insistent on it. I don't know why. Most of the time, he had acted like he could handle anything that came for me — my sex bodyguard.

Everything had changed that Halloween night when he'd popped into my living room, barely dressed and smirking. For as infuriating as he got, I wanted him here. To pull back my hair, swear vengeance on Stone, take me home, take me to bed. Just be here.

Tears bubbled in my eyes. I heard footsteps somewhere down the long hallway. Not wanting to face his judgmental gaze, I ducked into the first room I found and stumbled upon a bed. It looked more or less normal. Tall—the mattress came up to my waist—it had four posts made of dark wood surrounding it and a leafy canopy. I placed the clothing on the chest below a mirror that cast no reflection and my heart jerked.

Daniel's in trouble. I almost saved him, brought him back to life, to me. But if I can't get back in time, if I can't cast the spell... What if I make it back, and he's gone?

What if I never get back to them?

My legs collapsed, sending me spiraling onto the bed. I clung to the mattress, clawing over it and sobbing uncontrollably. A void opened in the depths of my heart and I curled up on my side. Memories danced in my mind, what should have been happy moments now tinged with the terror that they could be the last. Without me, Cal could lose to Eric and the pack. Ink would starve. Daniel would go mad and vanish. Garavel might return to the stone.

I'm going to lose them all.

* * * *

Stone

What did I know of the void of death? Nothing, except for the dread I'd suffered for two days while crawling out of the sewers below our office, my chest refusing to heal. I'd drunk every healing draught and slapped on every poultice I knew of. Scars from decades back had vanished into baby-smooth skin, but the hole straight to the heart had remained. Sleep had been impossible, my mind darting between fearing death and losing what I'd spent my entire adult life becoming.

Without the agency, I was... *I am nothing*.

There were other witches I could have called upon. Most wouldn't have put up the fight she and her companions had. They wouldn't have even struck a bargain, just done it for fear of reprisal. But after two days of my chest leaking cold blood, I'd limped my way to her door.

Because the agency couldn't have gotten to her. That's all there is to it.

Why else would I call on a witch?

Why else would I want to see her?

A cry echoed off the stone walls. I jerked in surprise and my badge dropped to the ground with a loud plunk. Turning my head, I listened closer, and a round of gasping sobs broke. *She's in trouble!*

Without pause, I dashed through the massive number of rooms. Bathrooms, bedrooms, studies, one that just had a big orb in it to figure out later. After peering inside and not finding her, I came to skidding halt at a loud shriek just to the right.

Only the moons hanging outside the window cast a touch of light across the black room. I peered in, readying myself for an attack from anything. My eyes skipped past the bed, then rebounded back. A curled-up bundle shook on the high mattress.

I dropped my arm and eased in. Sure enough, another screaming cry broke. She wailed, then crumpled up, muffling herself in a pillow or the blanket.

Damn it. I eased my way in. Her wailing pummeled my heart into a million pieces. No man wanted to hear a woman cry, doubly so when he thought he might have caused it.

I could leave her to it. Let her work through this and come back to her biting tongue in the morning.

After shrugging off my suit coat, I slipped onto the edge of the bed behind her. She didn't stiffen or worm away, but seemed so trapped in her despair she didn't notice me. Tenderly, I brushed my palm over her hair.

"It's okay," I whispered, curling my body around hers. She gulped in air, her sobs becoming silent. Burying my nose to the nape of her neck, I swore, "It's going to be okay."

Chapter Twenty-Two

Cal

I hate this.

"What have you found?" My voice carried across the field, the wind dying once the sun dropped. I lifted the flashlight close to my face and beamed it at the stone.

Garavel pointed to the standing stone laying on the ground. "It's broken."

"I know it's... We're looking for runes. Anything to give us a hint of where Layla's gone. Dan?" I whipped around for the ghost and he appeared directly behind me. In the light of my kitchen, I didn't care. In the woods at night with Layla missing, it scared the crap out of me.

He narrowed his eyes. "Daniel."

Is this really the fucking time? "Sorry, Daniel." I knocked around the change purse holding his spare bone. Ink kept threatening to toss it away. "How do we get her back?"

"Without her spell book," he grumbled to himself, but I was glad she had it. Wherever she was, she'd need all the protection it could give her. "I'm afraid I don't have a lot to go off. Not many books make mention of the realms, never mind a way to pierce them."

"Keep looking," I ordered, before marching to our base.

"What do you think I'm doing?" he muttered under his breath before jerking in the air and appearing next to our base of operations. It wasn't much. The cooler from my truck held a handful of scratched-out theories and my phone. I picked it up and scrolled through the pictures of the runes before the light vanished. As the sun dropped, they'd faded away, leaving us in both the literal and figurative dark.

"Wolf, I require more," the angel shouted. I shifted my phone to my left hand and held out my right. Garavel clamped onto my wrist and sliced my palm open.

"Damn it. I thought you were gonna take a few drops from my fingers."

He looked up from the handkerchief welling with my blood. "This way I don't have to ask again."

It'd been a pure accident discovering that blood revealed secrets in the stones. I'd only wanted the damn witch hunter to tell me what was happening. But that one had freaked out so much, he had tripped on the altar and slammed his head into the rock. The others had peeled out, dragging him with, but the blood had seeped into once hidden crags.

"What'd you find?" I shouted.

"It seems to have been a moth."

Just like the last three times. If I hadn't known any better, I would have thought he was cutting me for fun. I kept shifting the images back and forth, hoping for an answer to appear. *Damn it.* Werewolves didn't do magic. The closest we got was getting drunk on sixth moon and dancing naked outside while howling. I had no idea what I was looking at, only that it had taken her from me, and I had to get her back.

My finger hovered above the messaging button. *There's nothing from her. She's in another dimension. I shouldn't get my hopes up.*

I pressed it, reading our last texts about nothing important. I should have told her I loved her. That I'd love her until the day they put my bones in the earth. But no, all I'd cared about back then was pizza.

"Your tail is drooping."

I turned my back on him and wiped at my eyes. "Where the hell have you been?"

"Here." Ink thrust a huge cup of coffee into my hands. I blinked in confusion and took it. "We do not need you wearing yourself to the nub. She would not want it."

I drank it. Even knowing it'd be a sugar bomb, I guzzled the caffeine to feed my waning systems. "Thanks," I said, putting the half-finished cup on the table and focusing on Daniel's notes. Most were worthless, just like we were in saving her.

Ink suddenly raised his head and I turned to him. "She's still...?"

"Alive," he assured me before frowning. "Unreachable, but alive."

"Small miracles. It's all we can hope for now. Damn it, how do we open a portal to another realm?"

The demon bunched his hands behind his back and gazed up at the stars. "We have done it once before."

"Yeah, Layla did, with her mother. And..."

"A sacrifice," Ink summed up.

"She'd never allow that," I said. Layla'd curse us a blue streak and probably vow to never see us again if we killed someone to save her.

Ink didn't answer, only grazed his claw across my palm. I gulped and stared at my bleeding hand. I'd been cutting it without thought, trying anything to find a way to her. When I clenched it closed, the pain was nothing to the agony in my heart. How far would I go to save her?

"We still need a witch."

I'd been hoping to ask her to marry me, now I was debating slitting my own throat just to bring her home. Love was a hell of a mind trip.

"It may take some time to find her, but she'd have as much reason to find our beloved as we do."

I ignored him and focused on the information. If I stopped to think about this for two seconds, my ears buzzed and vision went hazy. "So far it's our only plan."

"Calvin." Ink clasped a hand to my shoulder. "Do you have any concept of how enraged she would be if you were to sacrifice yourself?"

Biting my lip hard, I glanced over at him.

"The sun would explode," he said and, moon help me, I laughed. Yeah, it would. But she'd also be safe, just…not in my arms. "It is an option, not a plan."

"Then what do you suggest?"

"Witch hunters, Conquest, they both seem to know how to open a portal, or whatever they were attempting here. I suggest we capture and bleed them dry for a change of pace."

Fuck, how I wanted to. Chain that Zimmerman bastard to the tallest stone and let Ink get out all of his anger. He seemed to be dealing with it by being one part helpful to two parts smug bastard. I could deal with smug. I doubted even I could stop an enraged incubus.

"That would take time," I said.

"I have faith in her survival skills. She can be quite persistent even in the darkest of nights."

I shook my head and stared longer at the incubus. "What about you? Don't you need to feed or else you... I don't know. I mean, you eat but don't die. How's that work?"

He cast a single flaming eye at me. "Trying to suss out my weaknesses? You're more cunning than I give you credit for, mutt."

"More concerned. We need you at your fighting weight and if you're drained... Can you eat off of someone else?"

Ink laughed, placed a fist to his hip and swept the pad of his thumb against my chin. "Are you offering yourself upon the altar of the incubus, Calvin?"

"What?" I yanked my head back and shook him away. "No."

"I have enjoyed the sight of your vigorous body in action."

"Yeah, I know about the pictures. Which is weird, dude."

Instead of scowling, Ink winked at me and my damn cheeks burned. Being naked around him didn't bother me, having him watch me fuck Layla didn't bother me. But him just sitting there thinking of eating me was...confusing.

"While I am grateful for the offer, and a bit intrigued—" Ink swerved his gaze down me before he popped back up. "I am bound to Layla. No one else can sustain me."

"You could break the bond," I said. He stared at me as if I grew a second head. "Just while she's gone. To feed. Then, you know, put it back once she's returned."

Ink swept his fingers around his wrist, circling it like a cuff. My idea seemed to have unnerved him, but it made sense. Okay, Layla might be a bit annoyed, but it was for practical reasons. And he didn't kill people. Ink dropped his hand and stared long at me. "You wish me to cut off our only way of knowing if she yet lives?"

Fuck, I didn't think of that. "Stupid idea."

"You seem to be rampant with them this eve."

Offing myself, setting Ink loose on the public — my brain was gone. I couldn't stop thinking about the empty bed waiting for me and it was driving me mad.

"None of your plans will matter until we can determine where she was sent," Daniel said. He dropped a book to the cooler, then staggered back.

"Aren't you working on that?" I asked.

"I'm trying. There's not much to go on. What wasn't exploded or tossed in the wind storm, the witch hunters destroyed." He cast a glare over the rubble we'd been struggling to piece together.

Garavel pumped his fist. "I believe I found a... Oh, that's a caterpillar. Carry on."

Tugging over one of Daniel's books, I tried to read by torchlight. It was damn near Greek to me, and in some cases Latin, but I had to keep trying.

In my madness, I almost missed the slow chuckle of a demon. Putting my hand in as a bookmark, I stared up at Ink who was holding his sides as he doubled over in laughter.

"What the shit's your problem?" Daniel fumed.

"For all your bluster and bravado, and an ego of unearned girth, you've missed the obvious."

The ghost crossed his arms. "I mapped almost all of the runes. They're to open a portal, nothing more."

Ink chuckled and skipped over to the altar. "Of course they are, that was what they were intending to do. Or perhaps some other perverse plan, it's difficult to say."

"They may have been trying to pull something out instead of throw it in, but that doesn't tell us where."

Raising his arms, Ink said, "The runes don't but the location does."

I glanced up at the stars and Daniel to the ground. "A field?"

Ink scowled. "You waste of an orgasm, no. The stones. A portal rune cast in the middle of a ring of standing stones can only lead to one destination. Our beloved is with the elves."

I sighed in relief. Elves, that didn't sound so bad. "Thank fuck it's not hell or..." I caught the dour look rising on everyone else's faces. Garavel jerked up at the word elf and grabbed his sword. "What's wrong with elves?"

"They are a parasite! Split from the mages of old, they can weave minor spells but remember when they had access to all." The angel drove his sword into the ground. "For this reason, they hunger for a witch in order to bleed her magic dry."

"Layla...?"

No more waiting. We had to get to her before the elves did. Ink sighed and slipped in beside me. "I suppose sacrifice is back on the menu. I'll get the ceremonial blade."

Before he wandered off, I grabbed his hand. "Ink." I dropped the box into his hand. "Tell her... Just, make sure she's happy. Okay?"

He closed his claws around the ring box. No smart-ass remark came. With a slow nod, he declared, "I swear it."

Chapter Twenty-Three

Raul

"Need anything else, bright eyes?"

I smiled to myself at the compliment, more out of discomfort than interest. The woman tending to her stall had been eyeballing me since I had walked into the market. Whether for herself or to be promised to a daughter as many had tried, I couldn't guess. Luckily, I had years of dodging matchmaker *tias* under my belts.

The week's worth of food, mostly salted meats and herbs, lay bundled on the stall's counter. "Any chance you have some of that red fruit?"

Her razor-thin eyebrows dropped. "Red? Ah, you mean the firefall. Happen to have three right here."

"Excellent." She loved those and I'd feared I wouldn't find any on this side of the planet. "I'll take all of them."

The woman smiled and wrapped it up without taking her eyes off of me. An oppressive awkwardness rose in my bare chest. No matter how hard I searched from closet to stall, not a single elf had a shirt that covered my scars. It was a society of nothing but vests for men and even less for women.

"Now how will you be paying for that?" she asked. "Pillage or barter?"

"Barter." I dug into my satchel for a handful of trinkets I'd found in the house. If they were the people who'd scarred me, I'd say I deserved it for recompense. "What about this?"

She frowned and prodded at a candlestick made of pure gold. It weighed a damn ton and I couldn't wait to be rid of it. With a shrug, the woman shoved away what could have bought me an entire grocery store back home. Furs were nothing, jewels were pretty baubles they used to entertain children. And gold damn near ran down the streets. *What would make her…?*

My hand slammed into a metal piece deep in my pocket. Slowly, I pulled out the badge.

"Ooh, what's that?" The foreign trinket caught her attention instantly. That was what these people cared about—anything that wasn't elven.

Brushing my finger over the bottom, I wiped dirt from the motto. "To Control Magic & Protect the Weak." I hadn't even been seventeen when I had stood in that empty room and sworn to uphold these duties. Every day I woke up believing I was doing a good. Signed away my name, given up a normal life and the potential of a family for this small piece of pewter.

When Director Zimmerman had handed it to me, this badge had been worth more than its weight in gold.

"Here." I tossed the scrap of metal to her. She happily scooped it up and polished the back until it gleamed. Now it was worth a week of food. I scooped the bundles of preserved meat and fruit up into my bag.

My work wasn't done. I still had to find the local stone keeper and probe her for information. But as I turned to move, a massive horn like the arrival of a Viking ship blared through the quaint square.

"What the hell is that?" I stuttered.

The old woman glared at me. "Don't you know?"

"I'm a Changeling," I said quickly. It was an easy excuse for every common elven occurrence I didn't understand.

Her once greedy eyes slipped off of me and she mumbled, "Thank you for your service."

I didn't know how to respond to what everyone said after. What service they meant, I had no idea, and wasn't in the mood to learn more. As soon as I got home, I was finding a witch or other magical creature to remove this curse. Then I'd never have to think of it again.

In the distance, I heard a squeal as the brass gates were flung open. The shop keep leaned over and pointed. "The Bramble clan's returned."

"Bramble?" They sounded adorable. I bet they spent their time making jams and jellies to sell at county fairs.

The very cobbles shook. Rolling through the gates came a monstrous wagon from the end of the world. Every side was covered in thick gold or brass plates. Fire belched from two tail pipes curved up off the back and the front came to a razor-sharp point. An elf wearing the skinned head of a minotaur stood at the top, waving a giant axe. The murder wagon slammed to a halt just before piercing the town fountain. Steam hissed through every rivet and the gaps in the plates, blanketing the ground and people below.

Hefting his axe higher, the elf screamed incoherently. The once calm shoppers all responded with the same and the axe-man dug into a bag at his side. He showed off a heart glistening in the sun and, without a second's pause, bit it in half. Blood squirted from the ventricles, drenching his face, but he only laughed.

"Must have been a good raid," the old woman said as she cleaned off her counter.

"Can you tell me about the Bramble clan?" I asked while the axe-man roared so hard, his minotaur skull fell off revealing a shock of red hair. His scars burned white-hot against his blue skin. A strange familiarity tickled the back of my head, as if I'd seen them in a book. They were blockier, like a dull blade or spear point to my thin waves.

"What's there to say?" she said, waving to the man leaping off his wagon. With his bare hands, he pried off the panel, revealing a treasure trove of what looked like Minoan artifacts. "They're raiders. The best, no doubt. Wise to get on their good side because you don't want to run afoul of any of them. Especially the quiet ones."

Loud, bombastic ones to entertain crowds and flay skulls, quiet, cunning ones to plot and scheme behind the curtains. I nodded grimly.

"The only ones who ever kept them in check were the Wayfarers, seeds guide them."

"The Wayfarers?" I spun on a dime and pressed on the woman. "What do you know of them?"

Her green cheeks paled and her chattering jaw slammed shut. "Nothing. I don't know anything about them, or anyone else for that matter. Changeling, if you're quite finished, I need you to move on."

I did as she asked, but only more questions thundered in my mind. Every stone keeper I asked about the Wayfarers would play dumb, or try to lead me in a verbal goose chase. No one wanted to say what they were, or what had happened to them. But everyone seemed frightened of talking about them. I'd assumed it due to their cruel nature and habit of kidnapping children.

But as I watched the woman dart her eyes to the Bramble man paying her no attention, I began to wonder. Had I walked into the middle of a clan war unaware? Best to steer clear of asking them directly.

My watch beeped and I turned it around. Damn, it had already been three hours?

Sighing, I bundled the food over my shoulder and trekked for the gateway block. It'd taken me a few tries to figure out how to get the knob to work. The trick was in the turning. One click meant one town away, two was two and so on. But from every town and city square, the doors led right back to the mansion.

As I approached, a man asked me, "Did I hear the horn?"

"Yes, the Brambles are back."

"At last, I've been waiting for…" He darted his gaze down to my chest and clammed up. "Uh, what clan are you with?"

"Changeling," I said with a sigh.

"Thank you for your service," he mumbled while sidling away.

As I walked up the steps, the air split with a massive crack of thunder despite there being no clouds in the sky. I craned my head back to see lightning spitting off of the bronze wagon. Did they even know what they had or were they stealing anything they could and killing their people by mistake?

My watch beeped a second warning and I turned my back on the morons. Slotting the knob into place, I raised my chin and returned to her.

* * * *

Layla

When my eyes started to water, I pitched back in the surprisingly comfy chair and stretched. My book sat beside a dozen scrolls that I'd pinned down with various trinkets and rocks from around the estate. It looked hot as sin outside, but a cool breeze smelling of warm seas broke apart the sun. This place was a temperate paradise, with a hint of a huge body of water just beyond the horizon. I stared out of the window in the study across the gardens I'd paced around for hours. Light shimmered off the water past the trees.

It'd be fun to take a boat across it. Lay on deck soaking up the sun, or feeling the twin moonlight on my bare skin.

The candle flickered, drawing my eyes to my notes. They were a scattered mess of half ideas, but I skipped past all of them to the ten hatch marks. I'd be adding another to it tomorrow, and again and again. All while my guys were trapped at home, probably threatening witch hunters and picking on each other to death.

An image of Ink shaking a witch hunter upside down by the ankles crossed my mind. Of course Cal would tell him to put him down while Daniel encouraged it. Garavel would have to be the voice of reason, much to Ink's dismay. He had a strange soft spot for the angel.

Damn it. I clenched my fist around my locket, pressing my knuckles so tight to my sternum, my chest ached. My heart thumped a sluggish beat slowing with every lost day. If I didn't get to them soon then... I didn't know, but every cell in my body told me it'd be bad.

In a flash, all the lights in the house snuffed out. Small puffs of smoke lingered in the darkened room. It had already been three hours? Sighing, I pulled out my phone and turned on my flashlight. It lit the papers as I gathered them up and stuffed them into my book. I left the scrolls behind and made my way to the stairs.

He had to be coming home soon.

Here. He had to be getting here soon. I paused and stared down the winding marble steps waiting. *Any second now. Come on, Stone. You know better than to...*

"Fuck!" I jerked just as a ten-foot-long blade sliced out of the wall. It went for my neck, but I managed to dodge. Oh, the house didn't like that.

A handful of the candles lit up blood red and an alarm like a keening elf burst from every wall. I couldn't cover my ears and had to take the blast. My hands were too busy calling up a shield spell. Another attack, this one a series of knee-high blades splintering out like a murder snowflake, plunged for me. I slammed my hand down, bursting the gold into a thousand pieces on the marble.

Okay, next is the...

"Whoa." My body remembered to move in time for the ten-foot pendulum swinging to hurl me down the stairs. I darted to the side and lined up a pressure shot for the fulcrum. That damn physics class we'd had to take was finally paying off.

Gripping my hand, I fired it off, when a metal beam slammed into my side. "Ooof!" was all I managed, my hands flying to catch the railing. My head almost bashed into the hard wall. Instead, my shoulder took the brunt. I threw myself away just as a series of spikes burst from the stones.

"I hate this goddamn place!" I shouted to a house that felt the same about me. The whine increased dramatically and I dug my bare feet in. "You want me? You're going to have try a hell of a lot harder!"

Did it hear that? The statues lining the hallway turned. Okay, they'd never done that before. One by one, small holes opened in their mouths. *Oh god, it's gonna be deadly poison wasps.* Gritting my teeth, I urged the power through me to reinforce my shield. Fire burst from every gaping mouth and I clenched for the attack.

The whine stopped, every candle lit and the murder blades retracted into their holes. Panting and exhausted, with my legs spread wide and arms stretched, I watched as the front door opened and he stepped inside.

"Took you long enough!" I shouted.

"Oh, I'm sorry. I thought I still had time," Stone called from the foyer that greeted him like a loyal dog.

Clenching my fists, I broke off the shield spell and eased my way down the stairs. But as I reached for the banister, my shoulder flared in pain and I hissed. He looked up to me in concern. "Did it get you?"

"No," I said, then rubbed my palm over the wound while healing the aches away.

Instead of heading off to our makeshift pantry, he climbed the stairs and stopped two below me. It was a bit strange to loom over him. "Then why are you healing yourself?" Stone asked. Damn bastard caught on fast.

"The murder house didn't get me, I hit my shoulder while dodging. Which wouldn't have happened if you were on time."

"There was a surprise at the market that caught me off guard." He pursed his lips and looked away, a sure sign it wasn't anything good.

"Learn anything helpful?"

"I'm not sure. I'll need to look into those scrolls you found. Are you sure you're not injured?"

I raised my arm to show it was still attached, not that the house didn't try. That'd been an awful first day, when he'd headed out for supplies and information. It hadn't taken us long to realize that without Stone here, the house went berserk. I'd managed to fight my way to the garden and had hidden until he'd returned. Since then we had a hard rule—no more than three hours— which he kept skirting around every time.

The damn thing was making me glad to see him when he returned which I wasn't happy about. "There has to be some way to turn this thing off," I said, glaring at the statue that'd tried to murder me. "I mean, it couldn't have killed all the servants every time they left for a raid."

"You think there were servants?"

I stuck my hand on my hip and stared down at him. "People who live in a place this fancy don't clean their own toilets."

Stone began to laugh and I joined in. "True." He held his hand out to me and I took it, needing to get off the stairs before they flung me away. As we walked toward the kitchen, he said, "They'd rather sit in their own shit than scrub a toilet seat."

"Here I assumed you were some trust-fund baby. You telling me you've cleaned toilets?"

He chuckled and shook out his long hair. It was already past his ass by now. "Walking into my apartment would require level-five clearance. I don't see any cleaners willing to suffer the gauntlet of unending horrors for that. Alas, I'm on my own."

What the hell kind of life did he live? Asked the witch who had an angel in the attic, a werewolf in the bed, a ghost in the dining room and an incubus wherever he wanted to go. I lost my nerve for asking a follow-up question. As we slipped past the huge fireplace, the mantle lit up in the same light show it did whenever he came home. Something told me that was important. I just didn't know what.

"I'm surprised you know which way the toilet brush goes."

Stone paused at the archway and stared at me. "I used to help my mom out. She had to take a cleaning job after the economy cratered."

"Really? You?" I put my hand on my hip and stared at him. "I'm struggling to picture you in that fancy suit on your knees scrubbing a toilet."

His eyes flared in the dark and his voice dropped low. "Is that where you want me?"

"What?"

Stone leaned on his hip, his warm breath brushing against my cheek. "On my knees?"

I swallowed and failed to pull the image from my mind. He took his time sweeping his gaze down my elven-hoisted breasts, my bare ribs and stomach, my hips and the low-hung skirt, before finally reaching my naked toes. "The suit is optional."

His chest glowed, the tattoos lighting up brighter in this dark corner of the house. The fire drew this moth right in. He'd been walking around half-naked for ten days. I'd ignored it to the best of my ability, but, damn it, a girl had to eat. He was infuriating and dangerous, but also a five-course meal in those tight elfy pants. My hand lifted on its own. Where it was going, I couldn't guess.

Stone didn't even look at it, all his focus on my burning cheeks. I skirted up his long jaw to find his lips slipping from a smile to a soft pout. They, and the rest of his face, dipped down for me. My eyes slipped closed, my head tipped up and I parted my mouth ever so slightly. He reached for my cheek, his pinkie twirling in my hair.

My hand landed on a warm hill of soft skin. Stone jerked back and my eyes flew open. He glared down where my palm was caressing his pec. *Oh, god. What am I doing?* I yanked it back and shook my hand as if to teach it a lesson. *No, we don't fondle witch hunters!*

"I should...put the groceries away," Stone said, his forehead a swamp of sweat. He stumbled into our makeshift pantry and I dumbly trailed behind, having nowhere else to go.

What the hell is wrong with me? Okay, so I haven't had any in ten days. Big deal! I went years without so much as a handy before Ink appeared.

Did having four hot men at my beck and call ruin me for life?

He placed the meat in a frosted box I'd whipped up — the chilled part, not the box — his back to me. *Totally fucked that one up. Which was good. I should have fucked up, not fucked him. Just fucked the situation. Why is this so hard?*

"Ah." He reached into the bag and pulled out a red oblong.

"Is that...?" I dashed for the heavenly fruit, the perfect mix of spicy and sweet. It was like chili honey to my tongue.

I cradled the holy melon to my chest like a baby. There was so much I could do with this thing. At least season some of the bland elven food. Everything was either salt, pepper or nothing. This bad boy was my only hope to keeping my tongue from dying of boredom. I paused in foolishly rocking it and looked to Stone. "Thank you. What'd you have to trade for this?"

He curled his hand under the melon and I let go. While hefting it up, Stone turned to look at me. "Not much."

"Well, there's a ton of gold pieces up on the top of the stairs now. I wish I knew how the house kept making them."

The conversation fell quiet as Stone finished putting the last of the food away. It'd have to last us for a while. Luckily, I was an expert on stretching out ramen. This wouldn't be too hard. "We should talk about what I—"

"There's something I wanted to show you," he interrupted, his green eyes flashing. The light carried down his scars until they vanished below his trousers.

"Um..."

"Trust me." He caught my hand and smiled. "You'll love it."

Chapter Twenty-Four

Layla

I placed my hand on that weird orb in its own room. Stone sidled up next to me and did the same. My heart lurched and stomach churned. I closed my eyes to steady myself and breathed in a scent unlike anything I'd ever known. Crisp without being cold, electric without the ozone, it shivered down my veins, giving me a burst of energy. I blinked and found the orb glowing in a blue grotto.

Instead of the dark, marble room, we stood in an indigo paradise. Small lights of yellow and white hung in the trees like personal stars. The branches wound together, forming a braid that enclosed us from even a passing bird. Leaves of silver dripped off the branches. As a breeze rustled the radiating flowers, a scent of lilac and amber washed over me.

"What do you think?" Stone asked, a huge smile on his face.

"Wh…" The trees themselves pulsed with a glow that'd travel from the roots up across the dark blue horizon. I stumbled away trying to peer up through the woven branches. My hand slipped off the orb and I froze, certain I was about to be left behind.

Stone chuckled after watching me, like he'd done the same, and dropped his hand. We were still in this exceedingly private and breathtaking grotto. "Here, this is the best part."

He held out his hand like we were on a walking tour of an English garden. I stared at it, my mind churning with a thousand thoughts. We'd put the mortal enemies fighting to the death issue on hold until we got home. But that didn't mean I was supposed to follow him like a lovesick puppy either.

Nervously, I reached up to scratch my neck when Stone dipped his head. The pale blue light caught on his emerald-green eyes and a smile of cozy warmth rose. I swung my hand over into his, trying to not feel his heartbeat up through his ensnaring palm.

"Is this an illusion? Magic?" I asked, wafting my other hand through the heavy air. Small swirls of opalescent silver floated from my wrist up into the sky. As I drew my fingers against them, they shifted. Twirling in my finger-created vortex, they created an explosion of small sparkles raining down onto the cottony grass below.

"I don't know what's causing it," Stone said. He tugged me onward, away from the center stand to the edge of the trees. The darkness deepened until all I could see were the sparks of light dancing in our hair and Stone's tattoos. They glowed in a pattern that flowed across his pecs and swooped down to his clothed hips.

"Here." He slipped to the side and placed my hand on the woven branches.

I stared at him, then the wood. "What do I...?"

Stone hooked a hand to other side and pulled. A gap formed in the foliage weave and I gasped. Set against a blanket of eternal black hung a huge blue and green marble. I blinked, certain my eyes were playing tricks, but the orb remained, barely drifting past and so close I feared I could touch it.

"Is that...? Are we...?"

"We're on the moon." He beamed. "Not certain which one. It's hard to tell."

"How? Why? What?" My brain shattered into a million pieces. *If we're on the moon, then how are we breathing? Oh, god, are we breathing?* I filled my lungs and they inflated. But what if it all vanished?

"This realm is thick with magic. I suppose anyone could use it to create a spot of paradise even in the desolate cold of space."

Right, I should be freezing to death. I held my arms out, expecting to see huge goosebumps just before they turned blue. But I felt good, my barely covered chest almost warm. Instead of the subzero temps, it was like a perfect May afternoon.

"How did you find this?" I asked, staring at Stone, then back out to the planet just below. It looked so much like earth with blue waters, green land and white clouds circling above. But the continents were all wrong, like someone had taken a puzzle of the earth and hammered the pieces wherever they wanted. Homesickness rampaged in my heart. I placed my hand over my chest, terrified and awe-inspired at the same time.

"I wondered, if the knob allowed me transport to the cities, did the orb do the same?" he said before staring through the hole. "Not quite."

"When did you...?" I stuttered, unable to break the shock of being on the moon. "Why didn't you tell me?"

He snickered and stepped back. I gave one last look to the fragile marble below. "I did my first test last night and...you looked so peaceful asleep, I didn't want to wake you."

"That's stupid," I said. He blinked in surprise. "Who knows what an evil elf ball could do. It might have trapped you in a volcano. Or dropped you into a lion's den. Maybe even outright killed you."

"You...you're saying I should have waited for you, as backup?"

"Duh." *I can't believe I have to explain this to a professional.* Walking back to the teleport orb, I passed him and said over my shoulder, "That's what partners do."

My ears barely registered a soft gasp as I stared harder at the orb. It could teleport, and unlike the knob it could do it a long distance. Thousands of miles. What about to other realms?

"Stone!" I shouted, turning to find him jerking upright. "This could be our answer."

"What?"

"The orb, or crystal ball, whatever elfy thing it is. It's a transporter, it's made of distance-piercing magic. I read a bit about it in my book, theories anyway. And there'd been a hint of it in the scrolls, but my head was aching after casting too many translate spells and..." My babble fell away as I dug out my phone. Holding it up, I snapped a picture of the orb and the pedestal it sat on. The gashes into the stone could be from random moon damage, or elven text. It was hard to guess.

"How is your phone still working?"

"Oh, I made a charging spell. It's basically an updated version of a spell to get an exhausted horse to travel one more league. Took me a while to get it right. I blew up like, three toasters."

"How does it work?" he asked, slipping in behind me.

I waggled the tip of my finger above the screen and whispered the words, "*Move tuum culum asine.*" The battery bar zipped from twenty-five percent to ninety-eight. I couldn't get it to a full one hundred or it'd catch on fire.

A protective hand brushed against my shoulder. I turned and found myself adrift in Stone's eyes. "Do you know what you said?"

"Oh mighty spirits, please enliven this device of cellular?"

He laughed hard, amplifying his dangerous cheekbones. "It's Latin for 'move your ass, ass.'"

"I guess whatever works," I said before staring at him. "You speak Latin? Oh right, the agency, probably made you learn all kinds of ancient tongues."

"No, that would be a strict Catholic schooling."

What I knew about Catholics amounted to crackers and the scene from *The Exorcist*. I wanted to press him if they really drank wine when kids, and if every church had a bell ringer. No. I had to focus on getting out of here and not his mysterious past.

"With this, and maybe a few more, I think I could build a portal," I said, jerking my head to the orb.

"To where?"

"Earth. Where else would we go?"

"The stone keepers have been pushing hell every time I visit. I guess Beelzebub throws a rocking yacht party this time of year."

I walked to the stone and reached for it, before remembering that might zap me back. Taking a breath, I placed a fingertip to the edge. Nothing happened. Probably needed an elf like every stupid thing in the house. As I looked closer, very faint lines were etched into the shiny surface. I traced one, having to bend to follow it.

"I'd read something in my book about elf sightings. They'd sometimes leave these balls behind and witches would..." I gulped and stared back at him.

I expected to find him glaring, arms crossed. Instead, his jaw dangled and he stared in awe at my... Oh, right, the short skirt. Elven seamstresses must not have expected to account for a big ass and thighs. I stood up, trying to hide the crescent moons rising from below the high hemline.

Stone jerked as if he'd broken from a trance. He wiped at his forehead. "Witches would steal them to strip for magic. Yes. It's happened often."

"They'd do that instead of needing a sacrifice to open a portal. If we get enough and put them in a ward, I might be able to send us home." Ready to risk it all, I reached out and pressed my arms around the ball. It cooled to a freezing touch but I wasn't about to give up. Gripping tighter, I tugged, but the damn thing was stuck.

"A little help."

Stone slipped his palm over the surface, then shoved at the top. My arms dropped off, fleeing from the chill while I stared at him. "What are you doing?"

"This was supposed to be a gift. So you didn't have to feel trapped in the house."

"Yes, thank you. Lovely thought. But it can get us home."

I expected him to leap for joy, or at least give me a smug nod. Anything but the tic of his lips as he strolled away to stare into the impenetrable trees. I breathed in the strange air and remembered where I was. Stepping back, I rubbed my arms to get heat into them. "Okay, so we don't steal the moon one, but we can find others. Just three, maybe even two. And we already have one back at the house."

"This is unsanctioned magic," he thundered, the asshole firmly in place.

"Excuse me?"

"Dangerous, untested. I cannot allow you—"

"It will get us home!" I screamed, my heart thundering. Stone turned, his face washed with a weary sadness. "Or…do you not want to get home?"

Ten days I'd worked myself ragged, forgoing food, facing off against murder statues, fighting off migraines as the translation spell wore off. And this whole time he'd been out doing what? "You said you were gathering intel."

"I was. I am."

"But you haven't found a solution. You haven't found anything."

A flicker of anger caught in his stoic eyes. "No one wants to talk to me. To tell me who the Wayfarers are."

"That doesn't fucking matter. We don't need them. We can get home with this!" I jabbed to the orb that he'd discovered and Stone scowled.

"It's too danger—"

"Fuck you! I've interrogated Djinn, I've sent a demon to hell. I can do this."

He ran forward and grabbed my arm before I could touch the orb. "No, you can't. Not until…"

"Not until what?" I screamed in his face. They'd been waiting for ten days, suffering in silence, not even knowing if I was alive. And the whole time he'd been fucking around at the market. "Is this a goddamn vacation for you?"

Stone growled, his shoulders shaking as he glared down at me, but I wasn't scared. I'd taken down scarier and I'd fuck him up, too. Maybe he saw my fists bunching up, maybe he realized he was being an ass, but Stone sighed and let go of me. Turning away, he whispered, "You don't know anything about me."

"I know you're running, you're refusing to admit that—"

He whipped around so fast I gulped and dropped both my spells to the ground. Fire and ice plunged near my feet, sending me scampering…straight into his arms. Stone caught me around the waist. Barely surpassing his rage, he hefted me into the air until I met him eye to eye. "You are the most infuriating woman I've ever suffered."

I lunged for him. Maybe it was to bite him, maybe to headbutt him. I didn't know. But his lips pressed to mine and a heat we'd been simmering for ten days exploded. I clamped onto his hair, tugging the long locks back until he broke off the kiss.

"You're an asshole," I snarled against his open mouth, then kissed him hard. "A judgmental." I bit his jaw, causing him to groan. "Pompous." He clamped a hand over my ass, wrenching the skirt down to reveal half a cheek. "Power-tripping, control hound…"

I scraped my nails down his chest with all the force I could manage while screaming out, "Asshole."

Stone snarled and ripped my arm away, his fingers clamped around my wrist. I hit the ground hard, my feet breaking apart the ice on the grass. He panted wildly, his long elven hair scattered down his bare chest as he stared at me. A smirk crested on his flushed lips, his jawline pulsing red from my teeth. "If you hate me so much, why did you kiss me?"

"I don't fucking hate you," I shouted, as shocked as he was when the words left me. "I want to hate-fuck you!" It'd been ten days of unending torture trapped in that house with only Stone to talk to. Not because he was an infuriating bore, but because he wasn't. And the longer I had to pretend I had no interest in the hot, half-naked elf staring at me from across the table, the angrier I got.

"You are beyond a doubt the most uncontrolled witch I've ever met." He drew the tips of his fingers down the inside of my arm, setting off a cascade of trembles. With his other hand, he cupped my chin, lifting my eyes. I burned and shivered at once, trapped by the wanton thirst in his gaze.

"Dangerous." He reached the halter of my shirt and pulled on the tie behind my neck. "Flippant." Stone pulled my hips to his, letting his fingers trace over my naked curves. "With no regard to the rules." He had me by the nape. With his fingers digging into my hair, he pulled my head back.

Even if I tried, I couldn't ignore the hard shaft pressing his thin silk pants against my exposed belly. A low growl rumbled and his chest lit up, the light tracing down his scars and beneath the waistband of his trousers. I didn't bother to hide looking, taking my time to inspect every swoop and whorl on his body. Stone's stance hardened as if he were about to throw me onto the ground or over his shoulder.

Raising my eyes, I met his. "Fuck your rules," I declared and cupped my hand around his pulsing cock. Stone groaned at the touch that was practically skin to skin. It pressed against his trousers so tight I could make out the vein and his retracting foreskin.

"You...woman!" he cried out, bucking his hips so my hand slipped down to take in more. Roaring, he ripped at the halter knot, tearing the two pieces of cloth. As the boob holster fell, Stone traced his fingers across my clavicles. The silver air chilled my exposed nipples, hardening them to their full length. "You...god."

I panted as he brushed his thumb across the top of my breast. "Damn."

He kept going, curling his palms to the sides of both. Stone shifted his stance as he stared down at me, his hands cupping beneath my breasts. Gulping, I met his gaze and he snarled, "Witch." Before I could curse back, he slipped two fingers to either side of my nipples and pulled.

"Son of a...!" I cried, thrusting my chest out and clenching tighter to his cock. The pressure abated and I glared at him. "Don't stop, you pretentious twat!"

He grinned maniacally and tugged harder, nearly bringing me to tears and a cascading mess of pleasure-pain. A panting whimper rose in my shivering chest. Stone lowered himself to a knee. At first, he traced the lightest of kisses from my ribcage up the side of my breast. Then, he skipped over the throbbing nerve endings and licked his way down.

I stared down at his head trapped between my cleavage. He must have sensed it, as he planted his chin right on my sternum. I gasped at the pressure. With his eyes pinning me in place, he yanked on both my nipples.

"Fuck me!" I cried out.

"Have I?" he asked. He smoothed his hands down my exposed waist, caring nothing for the extra twenty-some pounds waif elves didn't have. As Stone cupped along my hips, he sucked on my nipple. When he added his teeth, I gripped to the back of his head, struggling to hold on.

"What?" I stuttered, my brain blank as the pleasure kept spiking across my neurons.

Tugging on my skirt, he exposed most of my pelvis and the start of my bare mound to the magical air. "Have we fucked before? Why do I know the taste of your skin before I kiss it? How can I anticipate what your wet, hot pussy feels like if I've never shoved my cock in it?"

Oh god. He remembered. I gulped and Stone stopped yanking my skirt to the ground. He rose and towered above me with far more menace than I remembered.

"We didn't," I said, then winced. "And we kinda did." He crossed his arms over his chest. I dropped my gaze, but in doing so zeroed in on his cock practically popping out of his waistband. "There was a siren and—"

"A siren? Of course. One went missing and you...you used it to erase yourself from our memories." He sneered at me and shook his head. "Clever. Dangerous. What else would I expect from you?"

"You kidnapped me!" I shouted.

"Because you're a threat to people," he snarled back in my face. "I'm so furious with your disregard to the threat you pose, it makes me want to..." He curled his hand just next to my jaw.

I raised it. "To what?"

"To slap your ass, bite your toes and fuck your pussy so hard you forget your own goddamn name."

I snickered at his threat. "I'd like to see you try."

Stone lunged for me and I met him. He ripped at my skirt, leaving it in a pile at my feet. Kissing, then biting my lips, he hefted me up in his arms. The head of his cock swept across my soaked vulva through his pants. I parted my thighs, straining my legs to circle his waist. He jerked his hips, slicking his hard cock up to press my clit.

I cried out so hard, he broke from chewing on my lip. Taking a breath, I leaned back and stared into his wild eyes. "How are you going to cause vagina amnesia with your pants on?"

His lips twisted to the side. "You'll see," he said, and my ass slammed into a hard stone. Not that hard Stone—this one was granite. Though, that one could be too for all I knew.

A chill radiated up my buttocks and I squirmed, only for Stone to drill his fists beside my hips and keep me in place. I arched my spine and cold metal shivered up my back. The pedestal. Of course.

Stone bit my lip, sucking it into his mouth and dragging his tongue over mine. He was fast and wily, taking what he wanted and moving down my raised chin, my throat, and swerving over my nipples. He pressed a hand to the small of my back and hauled me closer without stopping. His tongue kept going down my trembling belly where he fell to a knee and spread my thighs apart.

The chill shivering over the heat of my soaked vulva caused me to gasp. I waited on pins and needles, but he kept licking over my thigh, while rubbing the other with his hand. He didn't blanch at the stubble that was basically leg hair at this point, but sucked on my weary muscle. It wasn't until his palm curved under my heel, that I realized what he was going for.

Stone practically pressed his face to the grass as he drew the tip of his tongue over the top of my foot. He curled both hands under it and raised my foot.

"You know I've been walking everywhere on those."

He guided my other foot to rest on his shoulder and reached behind himself to swing around a canteen. "I always come prepared."

"Or you're always prepared to come," I babbled, uncertain about this new venture but willing to see where it led.

Stone actually chuckled and uncorked the bladder. Picking up my foot, he drenched my toes in warm water. A great sigh broke from him and he wiggled his fingers between my toes, working off the last of the grass and dirt. He didn't do it by any half measures, taking his time massaging across the whole of my sole and working out the knots.

I leaned farther back, my spine molding with the teleportation ball. When he pressed in one spot, my shoulders drooped and at least ten days of stress fell off me. "Holy shit," I cried out. There were serious perks to this kink.

A tiny heat pressed to the tip of my big toe. Opening my eyes, I found Stone on his hands and knees pressing a delicate kiss to my foot. He looked transfixed, like the prince finding his princess by sucking on her toes. I couldn't say I was getting a sexual thrill from the act, but the absolute delight and devotion in his face had me panting.

After finishing with lefty, he moved to my right foot, showing it the same care and attention. At my pinkie, he chuckled. "There's still a bit of polish on this toe."

"Don't tell me you're one of those guys who hates when women do anything to their bodies."

Stone gazed up at me, pulled my foot to his mouth and sucked on the polished pinkie. As he did, he reached under his waistband, never breaking eye contact while jerking on his cock. I squirmed in place, wanting to grind my thighs together, but also keep my legs apart. Instead, I swept my fingers straight down to press on my clit.

Holy shit was I soaked. Drenched. A typhoon of arousal not only slicked my finger, but had left a wet spot down his pants. Stone watched me finger myself with a low moan. He jerked faster, then stopped.

Gripping to my ankles, he dove right for my vulva. Heat burst across the enflamed flesh, then the transcendent sucking as he licked his way over my lips. I kept flicking my clit, ramping up fast, when Stone's tongue traced up and down my finger.

"You taste better than the siren dreamed," he moaned against me. I began to retract my finger when he gripped onto my wrist and kept me in place. "Make yourself come just how you like."

He groaned against my clit, then clamped his mouth over it and my finger. In the wet heat between his lips, I tried to get any motion going, but it was a slippery ride. Stone backed off and, with just the tip of his tongue, traced over my clit's hood. I'd follow it up with my finger, bringing myself nearly to the brink before pulling back. Then he'd slowly ramp me up, tracing his tongue and lips across everywhere he could, pressing his cheek against my inner thigh and tugging on his cock.

I wiggled my clean toes against his shoulder and got a wicked idea. As Stone dove back to sucking on my clit, I made my move.

Chapter Twenty-Five

Stone

She clenched her thighs, cutting off all sound save the rabid pounding of my heart. Saints save me, it'd been too long since I had a woman melt in my mouth. I chased her finger, trying to make a game of that to keep from focusing on the scent and taste of her arousal smeared from my mustache to my chin.

She was beyond the most maddening woman I'd had to deal with, and every glance of her skin pulled me deeper into this mania. Throwing her head back, she propped up on her elbows and I risked looking up. Fuck. At this angle, she was nothing but curves I wanted to wring my hands around and knead until she screamed. Her *tetas* bounced with her every panting breath, the jiggle entrancing me.

My cock jerked, swiping across the wet spot from her dripping pussy and I moaned against her *concha*. She whimpered in response and I wound my arms under her ass. Torturing her was fun, but it was time to go in for the kill.

Her thighs parted, giving me ample opportunity to…

Something wily tapped against my balls and traversed outside the silk pants up my cock. Four tiny nubs bounced one after the other over the crown and I knew. She was jacking me off with her foot.

"¡Halaaa!" I cried out, risking a peek at her dainty toes and the delicate ball of her foot sweeping down *mi bicho*. My trousers tugged with her impudence and I gasped just as Layla sat up.

"Do I have to get down there and take them off myself?" she asked, her lips twisted in wry amusement.

At the back of my head, a small voice blared a warning. Letting a witch take control of me could spell my doom. She flourished her toes out, showing a level of control that made me yank my trousers clean down to my knees. The strange silver air danced around my cock as it sprang into the light.

Sure enough, the witch peered over with curiosity. I cupped under my balls, trying to raise it to her line of sight. She didn't cry out or kick me away, so that was good. No, instead she laughed once and said, "I knew it."

I frowned, wondering if it was that obvious how green it was, when the tip of her big toe graced my shaft. *Fuck me*. My head lolled back, my throat working overtime to swallow, while my heart pounded faster than a cheetah. All the while she smiled impishly, like she knew exactly what she was doing to me and loved every second.

This isn't right. I torture the witch, not the other way around.

Time to pull out the big guns.

Locking my arms under her ass, I pulled her onto my face. She slipped clean off the pedestal, her one foot landing in the ground beside my knee. The other, I propped up on my shoulder and dove tongue deep. With a burning fury to feel her come apart around me, I sucked hard on her clit.

She yelped, then ground onto my tongue. *This one likes a bit of pain.* Smirking against her clit, I traced my nails over the curvy swell of her hips. She kept swaying, struggling to keep her balance on one leg. Her ankle flipped and she dug her heel into my back.

Groaning, my hand clenched around my cock. I meant to tame it back, but she somehow flattened her foot, all five of her toes digging in. I jerked hard on the shaft, then swerved my thumb over the head. A droplet of pre-cum warned me I was playing with fire.

Dropping myself for later, I reached my hands around and spread her ass. She cried out as I dipped lower, my tongue traveling from the pearly gates down to the forbidden cliffs. Surprised moans and anticipatory gasps rose from her. Fingers dug into my hair, at first combing then yanking it. I delved deeper into her ass, teasing the bundle of nerves out of curiosity and need.

Her body jerked at my first touch. I was about to slip away and play it off as an accident, when she pressed her ass against me. A groan of regret fell from her as I pulled my finger away, then shoved it deep into her piping hot *concha*. Layla cried out, her nails scraping up my back.

I licked around her clit, teasing the throbbing nub. She began to rock her hips in time with me just missing the motherlode. "Yes," she cried out. "Right there. Don't you fucking stop, Stone."

Or what?

What if I left her hanging on this edge unable to come as I held her hands behind her back? What if she drew her toes up my cock, teasing the tip until I nearly burst?

Fuck! I plunged my lubed-up finger into her ass. Barely farther than the tip, but she hurled her head back, cried out and dug her nails deep into my skin. The flash of pain sent me sucking over her clit. I rolled every 'r' in my arsenal against the head of it while thrusting my finger deeper into her ass. She spasmed on top of me, incoherent words and half-spells falling from her lips.

Then her mouth opened and the last word I expected to hear slipped from her honeyed lips. "Raul," she moaned.

Her orgasm clenched around my finger and trembled against my lips. Still, I kept going, waiting for her to call me off. She ground back, pressing tighter as if to draw forth a hundred more orgasms. The way she needed me, ached for me, made my cock tighten so hard it ached up to my teeth. It was liable to blow and take my heart out with at this rate. I should stop, but she wasn't, all sense gone as she rode my exhausted tongue.

Suddenly, she shivered down to her toes and paused. My ears were ringing and I'd lost all saliva, but I stared up at her in a happy stupor. She roughed her hand over my chin and said, "Layla."

"What?"

Lowering her foot off my shoulder, she stood before me. Her thighs glistened with my work, but her face was ascendant. "You said you were going to fuck me so hard I forgot my name. It's Layla."

I growled, enraged and intrigued at the same time. Standing, I kicked off my trousers and clenched a hand around my cock. "I'm not finished yet."

"I don't think you've got the stones," she said with a laugh.

Oh, that's it. Grabbing her arm, I pulled her against me. My cock burrowed into the curve of her belly, nearly causing me to scream in blissful agony. I buried it against her mouth, kissing hard while I wound her hair up in my fist. I tugged it back, pulling her panting lips off of me.

"You'd dare to challenge me?"

She smiled and waggled her hips. "With all I've got."

I hefted her up in my arms. The heat of her soaked pussy screamed for my cock. I could plunge her right onto me, thrust her back into the stone until she was scraped and pleading for more. The idea burned through my mind while I kissed her. I reached a hand out to do just that, and her ass struck the edge of the pedestal. Precariously balanced, she had to rely on me.

Taking her legs, I swept both around my waist, doing my best to ignore her feet clenching to me. Oh, she was toying with me. Well, I'd teach her. Gripping my cock, I growled deep and took a step closer. Her heavy eyes burned with desire. She raised her hand to crook a finger at me, when suddenly her come hither smile flatlined.

"We…we can't do this."

My brain crashed into a brick wall and I froze, cock still in hand as she crumbled in on herself.

"I'm fertile, like super fertile. If you even come near me with that…" She shivered as if the idea of carrying a witch hunter's half-elven baby was such a bad idea.

Okay, she had a point. I traipsed my fingers down to cup my empty balls and laughed. "It's a good thing I'm sterile."

She raised an eyebrow and stared in total condescension. "The kind of sterile a man claims once the condoms come out?"

"The kind where a doctor snipped into my balls," I said.

Her wary guard dropped and she muttered an, "Oh."

"But for the love of god, do not tell my mother. She still thinks she's getting grandbabies."

To my surprise, she laughed. Drawing her hand out, Layla glanced the edges of her fingers against my chest. I held my breath, waiting to see a look of disgust or perverse interest on her face. She didn't even look at my myriad of scars, only stared up into my eyes as she traced over them.

"Why don't we go tit for tat?"

"Tit?" My eyes found their way to hers heaving and bouncing as she slipped to her feet, then kept dropping. Oh. She meant…

My brain caught up just as she opened her hot mouth. Her hand wound its way across my pelvis to dance against the base of my cock. Layla rolled her eyes up to me as she pressed her lips to the crown. I groaned, digging into her hair while lost in her infuriatingly entrancing eyes. She worked my balls, kneaded a knuckle against my taint and sucked my cock deep into her throat.

I locked my knees in, knowing that if I thrust even once, I was a goner. But the way she twinkled at me, the idea of her pussy soaking the grass, the feel of her nipples brushing against my thighs was sending me crashing. Then she had the audacity to lick her tongue from my base to the head, pull me in and moan around my cock. "Raul."

I lost. Clenching to her shoulder, I could barely get out the warning I was coming before a pound of sperm-less semen burst down her throat. She swallowed it all with a pleased smirk and it made me want to kiss and fuck her all at once. All the wound-up energy burned up into smoke. I pulled out, watching the last drops of my cum bead up and streak down my cock, and fell. Not far. My knees hit the grass, leaving me staring eye to eye with her.

"I don't hate you," I said.

Her flushed lips parted with a pant. Layla swallowed and shrew eyes stared back. "But you want to control me. It's all you've wanted since you kidnapped me."

Is it?

I'd been following protocol to the letter, perhaps painstakingly slow, but better to be cautious than dead. Even knowing she was so powerful she'd already slipped our grasp once before, I didn't make the call. I waited, and I watched because...

"You are aware I'm not the only witch hunter in existence?"

The glittering silver air that'd swept into stars and whirlpools by our thrusting bodies turned cold. Darkness became impenetrable shadows as she tumbled back. I expected her to dash for her clothing, but she sat cross-legged in the grass gazing up to the handful of stars peeking through the branches. "I'd ask if you intend to turn me in when we get back, but I know the answer."

Home. Facing Zimmerman and the rest of them not under White's control but working beside him. Having to take down the entire agency just to save them.

She snorted, a feral gut-wrenching laugh, and turned her burning eyes to me. "I guess you're all for getting back now that you got what you wanted."

I frowned. "That wasn't what I wanted." Her eyes went wide and I panicked. "I mean, I...I quite enjoyed." Scrambling, I turned and planted my bare ass on the ground just behind hers. I tipped back, the warm curves of her skin warping against mine. Her hair spread across my shoulders as I rested the nape of my neck at the top of her head.

"It's against witch hunter regulations to get close to a witch."

"You're not supposed to fuck your captives," she said with a wry chuckle. "I'm surprised you hunters don't violate every human right."

"We do not treat you as captives. You'd be paid a stipend. You are an employee."

"An employee who can never quit. What do they call those again?"

I shivered, the heat of her skin fighting against the chill of more than this terraformed moon garden. My past wasn't clean. I knew that. I accepted it, but I woke every morning knowing I was doing what was right. Witches would fight us, of course. No one wanted to put on the shackles themselves, but in time, most came to accept it was the best solution for an unsolvable problem.

Not her. She would let herself die before serving anyone.

It was infuriating and arousing. I either wanted to own her, or her to own me. Every time a witch challenged us, the hunter won. For all her teeth, statistically she didn't stand a chance. In the dead of the night, when I'd read through her file and enjoyed the bikini shots more than I should, a part of me wondered if she'd be the first to get me to submit.

"I can't go back," I said. Her spine stiffened against me, and I could sense her preparing, if not an attack spell, an argument that'd sting even worse.

"Not yet," I interrupted. "Not until I know what happened to the elves that changed me. I have to find them."

"Or what?" she asked. "We play house in a creepy elf murder mansion for months without learning a damn thing? Meanwhile Conquest and your old coworkers are trying to destroy our world, and this world and every other fucking world. Does finding someone to answer for your past matter that much?"

Digging my hand into the dirt, I watched the tendons flex below green skin. But as I pulled back, my mind turned it back to the proper brown. I wanted it back. I wanted to be me and not this abomination the elves had forced on me. And yet...

"I don't remember that day. Just moments here and there. The creatures, the elves in long robes hiding what they were. Me screaming bloody murder. I've lived with that unending nightmare for decades." Planting my green hand to the grass I turned. Layla shifted as well and she caught my eye. "Would you give up on finally silencing the nightmares?"

Her pretty lips drooped. "I should say yes."

I laughed at her answer. "I'm afraid I've watched you too long to know that's a lie."

"Creepy," she said, but there was a smile in her words. "Are you saying you remember some of the ritual?"

"Yes. It's not as if it's been erased, only blocked. Much like what happened with the siren."

She turned a quarter and I did the same. We sat shoulder to shoulder. Layla clenched her hand around her locket, which she often did when distressed. I wanted to reach over and wrap my arm around her. Instead, I kept both clinging to my verdant thighs.

What she was thinking was beyond my guess. Only the catch of a gold loop clinking against the chain broke through the silent garden. The silver dust fell into her hair, turning the dark, curly locks into a field of stars. Sure, her *tetas* were amazing, her ass fine and feet perfect, but a light shone from inside of her. I feared staring too long. Without my sunglasses, it could burn me for life.

"I think"—she sighed and looked up at me—"I can help you."

My burst of laughter brought her hopeful eyebrows to a death glare. "I'm afraid some recollection tea won't help with this block."

"Not that. Whatever that is. I have a, it's not even a spell. A skill. That can open up people's memories. I think it'll work for you."

I'd never heard of such a thing. She held her hands up, power surging between them. But I'd never worked with a battle witch before either. They were said to have the ability to tap into magics only meant for the Celestials.

"May as well try, right?" she said, easing across the grass with one hand out.

Finally rip open that door and see what lurked in my past. Find the culprits that scarred and set me on the inescapable path of collaring witches.

"Will it hurt?" I asked, sounding pathetic.

"Physically, no. Emotionally..."

Stop being pathetic. This was my only chance. She'd found a way home, one I'd be a fool to ignore. And if I wanted vengeance on these people, I'd have to learn what had happened now. Extending my hand, I raised my head. "Do it."

Layla swept her fingers against my forearm, then traveled down. "Think about that day. Remember what you were doing just before the elves took you."

I closed my eyes, feeling the itchy uniform clasped around my neck, my body boiling in hormones and rage. I'd just fled from detention when the sister's back was turned. Instead of heading to the abandoned convenience store to throw rocks at the windows, I...

Her fingers clenched around mine and the world burst to white.

Chapter Twenty-Six

Raul – Age Thirteen

My fingers released, sending a chunk of concrete hurtling for the window. I expected it to shatter, but the damn thing bounced back straight at me. Instead of ducking, I watched the missile come shooting *subió a la cabeza*. A hand shot out in front of me, not only catching the concrete but crushing it to dust.

"*¡Mierda!*" The hand was greener than my priest when I caught him smoking behind the school. It snaked back into a black robe and the hairs on the back of my neck prickled. No one had been behind me. I knew it. I always knew. Nobody, not even Julio, could get the jump on me.

But as I stared at the reflection in the unsheltered window, a dozen people in creepy robes stood in a circle. "What the hell?"

The one who had saved me tugged down his hood to reveal a face as green as leaves with ears twice as pointy. I jabbed a finger at him, incoherent noises falling from my lips. One by one, the others lowered their hoods, most green, some other colors, but all with pointy ears and weird tattoos over their faces. "*Chaneque!*"

What the shit? *Chaneques* were gross old men who lived in forests. These people were…beautiful. Not the dudes, though. I mean, they were fine. Long hair, longer than anything I'd seen on a man. Mine could get nearly that long in the summer before my *mamá* made me cut it off for school.

The leader pursed his curved lips, then smiled. "Yes, we are *chaneques*."

"What are you doing here?"

"We have come for you, my *mab*. Follow us to the gate and all will be revealed."

With that, he glanced to others who tugged back up their hoods and took off into the stand of trees past the abandoned highway. *Follow them? Oh right, 'cause I'm some stupid brown kid who's gonna just do whatever the weird green people tell me to.*

What the…? My feet moved without me telling 'em to. They took off trailing after the *chaneques*. "No!" I ordered, clinging to my knees. My march stopped, but I couldn't look away. The strangers made their way to the trees and, one by one, walked into the darkness.

I was gonna lose them. I might never see them again.

Panic thumped inside my chest, ordering me to rush headlong into the forest. It was irrational, sending me running headlong across the street. A horn blared, but even that couldn't shake the spell. As I stepped into the dark shadows of an old tree, the ground lit up. The footprints of the *chaneques* glowed a soft white, beckoning me.

The fact they were green should have been freaking me out. That they could leave radioactive footprints behind ought to have made me run home. But what should have really punctured through this fog and made me call the cops was the circle of freaky stones they stood inside. Especially the one in the center that screamed, "Here's where we bleed little boys for fun."

Yet, deep in my soul, this seemed normal. Like I expected it and was almost glad to see them. If this is Jesus and the twelve apostles, them crucifixes need a paint job.

"You've arrived," the leader said.

"Who are you?" my brain had enough sense to ask while I kept smiling like a jackass.

"I am Vulere," he said placing a hand to his heart. "And this is why you're here." He ripped open his cloak, tossing it to the ground. I gritted my teeth, stranger danger playing in the back of my head, when the passing clouds shifted and his bare chest lit up with a million glorious tattoos.

"That's fucking awesome!" And not just because they glowed. I was in awe of the lines and swirls covering him from neck to pants. They looked like the same random whorls I'd doodle on my homework that'd get me a few whacks across the knuckles.

One by one, the others shed their cloaks, revealing the same kinds of but not exact tattoos.

"*Verga!*" I shouted. The women were tatted up too, with barely a scrap of fabric over their *tetas*. My skin burned hotter the longer I tried to not stare.

"Little one," the first *chaneque* said.

I sneered. "I'm already five foot six, which is quite tall for someone…"

"What do you think of them?" Vulere asked me.

"I've never seen anything like this," I said before shaking it off. "I mean, it could be cooler. There's not even any stars or demon heads."

He laughed uproariously and clasped a hand to my shoulder. My knees bent at the force as if he had no idea how strong he was. "He's a true Wayfarer." The rest joined in, sharing in the joke. "My *mab*, do you wish me to reveal your marks as well?" He pointed a long finger to my spindly chest.

"You mean, I can have those cool tats too?"

He brushed my wayward hair back behind my ear and smiled. "You already do." Vulere reached into his pocket and held out a stone with a bunch of thorns carved into it. Reminded me of my *abuelo*'s garden.

I didn't know why, but I reached for it. The second my finger brushed over the cool surface, energy flooded through me. My hair flew back and a little itch crossed over my chest. Without thinking, I pulled my hand away and scratched it, only for a small shaft of light to beam up from under my uniform.

"No way." I yanked off the tie and unbuttoned the shirt. Sure enough, there was a sick line from my collar to my shoulder. *Holy shit, a real tattoo. My mama's gonna beat me senseless for this.*

Vulere stared at me with weird concern. He held the weird rock in one hand, while brushing hair off my forehead. "Do you wish for all to be revealed?"

"There's more?" I gulped. I could pass this one off as a scar, maybe invent a cool story about some *pendejos* terrorizing a girl I saved. Placing my finger to the line, an understanding pulsed through me. I couldn't put words to it, but I felt what I was missing. "Yes. I need them all."

Smiling, Vulere glanced behind at the others. As he did, I spotted a streak of white in his dark black locks. "Come, family, gather for the reveal. My child, if you would please recline on the slab and remove your shirt. It is easier on you."

I eased my butt onto the altar, then froze. "I'm keeping my pants on. And if you try anything, I can kick your ass." I was a scraggly thing, but Vulere held up his hand, surrendering to my threat. Watching them all gather in a circle smiling, I tugged off my shirt.

"Recline as I reveal what has been hidden from you, and what truths shall be restored."

Okay, bit weird, but holy hell, Maria would lose her shit if she saw me covered in these awesome tattoos. She'd have to be my girlfriend then. Taking a breath, I pressed my shoulder blades into the cool stone. Vulere waved the weird stone over my chest, and the altar wrapped around me.

Tentacles of rock just rose from the surface to envelop me and pull me down. I opened my mouth to scream, but my head submerged into darkness. Panting, I started to fight it off, but nothing clung to me. Alone in the black, I began to cry out.

"Welcome, son of the Wayfarer."

I jerked at the voice coming from everywhere. Why'd it sound like my history teacher? "What are you doing in here, Father Domingo?" It was impossible to see anything, the place darker than...

Light. It streaked before me, cutting through the darkness like a single blade. I reached out to find the source, and in doing so obscured it. *Esperar un momento.* This light was coming from me. I stared down as the lines drew across my chest. One circled down my impressive pec. I puffed it out as it crisscrossed with another appearing on the other side. They both entwined and kept going…down under my pants. Were they heading to—?

"Your time on this world is about to change forever, young one," the voice boomed. "Or not. The choice is up to you."

"What choice?"

The light grew along with the lines, beaming out into the darkness. As I stared it began to move, at first forming letters. They weren't like none of the alphabet I knew, but I knew they were letters and words. I began to read them, only for the symbols to speed up and create an image.

A grand home with fancy columns and statues appeared. Gathered outside the gates were the same people watching over me. In the middle was Vulere holding out the stone and smiling. "You were chosen to be a great gift for our people. A touchstone to this land from ours. But to do so, we had to give you up and change you to fit into this world."

The image shifted like sand into Vulere standing outside a doctor's room with a bundle in his hand. I didn't get it. He waved his fingers and the blanket fell away. The baby's green head became tan and the ears sucked down to normal.

"What are you saying?" I cried out.

A tingle shuddered through my chest, and I opened my eyes. The darkness was gone. Instead, I stared up at Vulere holding out the stone. The others stood around him, all smiling wide. One of the women with gray in her hair was openly weeping.

"A choice lies before you, my *mab*. Remain here as a touchstone, a focal point for my people to travel to your world and back."

I had no idea what any of that meant, but last thing I was gonna do was admit it. "Or?"

He smiled deeply, as if he wanted me to pick this choice before I even heard it. "Or complete the ritual and return with us. Become who you were born to be, a prince of the Wayfarers."

"I'm a prince?" I gasped, wanting to laugh at him, but the old man looked deadly serious. "What do I do?"

"Take this stone and choose. Either return to the human we left you as, or embrace your elven heritage." He held it out to me and I froze.

Flat out, my arms wouldn't work, my jaw hung open and my brain crashed. Become an elven prince? Like in robes and long blond hair with a bow and arrow? Or stay here and pretend none of this happened? Be that touch thing he mentioned? Ugh, I didn't want any elves touching me. Unless there were cute elven princesses. They could touch me all they wanted.

"What is your decision?" Vulere asked.

I stared at the stone reflecting the light from my chest. The tattoos were beautiful, more vibrant than the moon. I needed to know more. I had to see this through to the end. Stretching my fingers out, I cried, "I want to—"

Vulere jerked and a loud popping sound ripped apart the air. He clenched his fist around the stone and swallowed hard. Blood splattered from his chest, splashing me across the face.

I opened my mouth and a scream was all that came out. Vulere's body pitched forward, pinning me down. I kept screaming, shrieking with all my lungs while his hot sticky blood beat out across my naked chest. I couldn't see anything but the old man's green face. He'd landed with his forehead on mine, trapping me right into his panicking eyes. Twelve more pops burst around me, gunshots. I knew the sound. Maybe the others were screaming in terror or pain. I couldn't tell. My unending shriek deafened me.

I tried to close my eyes, willing away the sticky blood oozing down my chest, the sounds of death raining upon me. A cool hand pressed to my cheek and I stared into Vulere's darkening gaze. "My..." He coughed, his lips turning white. Paleness crept across his skin, shifting the vibrant green to a dull gray. A cold burrowed under my skin from his dying body stiffening above me.

"Help!" I shouted. "Help me, please!"

Vulere crashed, his lips stilling as a single word slipped out in a dying gasp. "Sun." I watched in horror as the life crawled out of his eyes and his cold cheek planted against my mouth. I wanted to scream, but opening my mouth would push his corpse flesh against my tongue. I froze, certain I was going to die under him. Whoever did this was out there, walking around. Maybe if I stayed still, they wouldn't see me.

I tried to leave my body, to go back to the darkness that'd welcomed me. The light shifted, and the heaviness crushing my ribs yanked back. Vulere's body flew back and landed with a thud on the ground. Still, I remained frozen, praying they thought his blood was mine.

"Well, what have we got here?"

I shouldn't have looked, but I opened my eyes to find a human hand holding the stone. He stared at it in the sunlight, not noticing me. If I just stayed quiet, he wouldn't...

The hand dropped, and he leaned in. A smile slowly rose on his lips. "Hello, son."

Screaming, I sat up, wrenching my hand away from Layla. I kept screaming, the same way I had while Vulere died on top of me. The man who'd killed them all, who'd debated killing me, was Matthew Zimmerman.

Chapter Twenty-Seven

Raul

"He killed them?"

I grazed my lips, certain the words had to come from me. But they remained still, trapped in my terror scream. If it wasn't me, then…? I spun in the grass and glared at the naked witch rising to her legs. She'd skittered back, as if prepared to launch a spell at me. Or was it pity? Her hand drifted not with the palm out to attack, but extended for me.

"You worked for the man that killed your —"

"What did you do?" I screamed. "How did you see that? You put that in my head."

My bare toes dug into the ground, girding myself for a cackle. But as her eyes softened and her hand remained out, my heart sank. It had to be her, an evil witch's plot. Zimmerman would never… The screams rattled in my head. Not just mine, but every elf cut down with the same nonchalant SOP I'd followed hundreds of times. He'd bled across my body, the red seeping into my scars that would never heal because...because they were mine. They'd always been mine. I was a...

"Stone?" she asked, easing closer.

My entire life had been devoted to the wall. No one could understand what I had gone through in that forest. No one should know. No one could know what I did for a living. No one would know. But this witch had shattered every brick I'd laid with blood and sweat, leaving me naked before her.

Had he stolen my memories? We had ways not to alter them, but remove parts that were inconvenient. Did he chop apart each second until he looked like the hero swooping in to save me? Training me to be the best agent while hiding what I was?

"He named me that," I said. I'd stood in that hidden bunker accepting my badge with pride. The first agent to graduate training at seventeen. Zimmerman had clasped my hand in his and called me Detective Stone. "I thought it meant I was solid, dependable. Immovable. But he was mocking what I was to them. Their touchstone."

I understood now. The elves couldn't travel to other realms at a whim. They needed a life, so they'd place their children in the care of a loving local family. With that 'sacrifice,' the elves could raid at will. No wonder earth was out of reach. I wasn't there.

Layla's dark eyes drifted down. Her offer of compassion was left unanswered. Instead, she wrapped her arms around her naked chest in a self-hug. "That was...a lot."

It's a lie. She did it. She faked it with a spell we'd never seen. They were always inventing new ones, evolving.

God, I want to believe that. I stared at my hand, begging for the light to shift and an assuring brown to replace the green. Instead, the silver settled into my pores, causing them to glow. It wasn't just the memories of that day... My head filled with a genetic memory that'd been locked away. I could hear the voice droning on in the back of my head. It was too quiet to make out, but if I closed my eyes and listened...

"So he used you."

I jerked, losing the train of thought. She finished slipping on her skirt and reached for the abandoned halter. "He took you from your family and forced you to work for him." She tugged her hair out of the loop and adjusted her breasts. Fully dressed, she glared at me like I was the dangerous animal. "You had your choice ripped away from you, and he used you without your consent."

"That is not what... You dare to compare our work with witches to him ripping away my memories."

"You ripped away my magic," she snarled.

"To protect you," I countered with the common excuse.

It went over worse than I had expected. She scoffed, her eyes blazing. "Because I can't be trusted. Because it's better to kill me than believe I know how to handle my own power."

"What are you implying?"

She crossed her arms and raised her head high. "You're awful at playing dumb."

Witches were dangerous. We'd hunted them for centuries, risking ourselves to stop women mad with power. It had nothing to do with their gender. It was just that all witches were female by the decree of the

Celestials. The fact most hunters were male didn't mean anything. "We're protecting people," I shouted.

"Bet he thought the same thing," she said and jerked her chin closer.

No, it's not! "He lied to me, kept my truth from me."

"Been there, done that. Got the incubus to show for it."

Every day, with a smile on his face, he'd lied to me. He had kept me from learning the truth by hiding my powers, by denying any nonhuman ability I tapped into by mistake. He had used me. He couldn't trust me to choose and had taken that choice away.

A warm hand landed on my arm and I turned to find her staring at me.

Exhausted, I mumbled, "Maybe he was right to do it."

She dug her nails in, the rage igniting. "What kind of brainwashed, kiss-ass, brown-nosing bullshit is this?" She swung her hand around. I caught it before it could cast a spell.

Clenching around her wrist, I pulled her close. "Witches cannot be trusted."

Layla jerked once before accepting my stronger hold. She raised up onto her tiptoes and glared me in the eye. "Neither can witch hunters."

Our enraged panting smashed against each other. I wanted to chain her up in a cell, to force her to listen to every recorded atrocity committed by a witch. To throw her over my shoulder and hurl her onto the bed. To fuck her senseless while screaming that no man controlled me.

She yanked her arm, causing me to press my chest against hers. I hooked my leg outside of hers, pinning her in place. It also caused my rising cock to traipse down the curve of her waist. Still she glared, looking ready to bite my throat out...and it was hot.

"You fucking bastard," she sneered.

"You said you didn't hate me."

Her laugh turned almost playful. Suddenly a jolt of electricity shot down my arm, opening my hand. Layla broke free. I didn't even have time to protect myself. She grabbed the back of my head and yanked me down until my forehead smashed into hers. "I lie," she declared and kissed me hard.

Fuck, I hated how hard I was. How every beat of my heart wanted me to slap her ass, pull on her hair, and make her come a thousand times with Raul on her lips. Not Stone. He was beyond all of this. Trained to put away any desires for an infuriating witch that made my cock twitch every time she walked past.

"If you keep this up, I'm going to fuck you so hard you'll be trapped in bed."

She wrenched her lips away and stared at me. "You're such a goddamn liar."

That's it. I slapped my palm over her ass, savoring the hard strike and her jerk of shock then low moan. Hauling her up, I dug my hand under her shirt and reached for her soft tit.

The traveling orb burst into the air.

I caught the movement out of the corner of my eye and yanked her down just as a wave of shimmering glass burst above us. Our threats were forgotten as Layla turned to stare at our only way home. "What the shit was that?"

Given how the rest of my life had been going, it had surely exploded and we had no way back to... "Oh." The ball was fine, but the once calm surface trembled with red pocks of clouds.

"Your ball looks angry," she said, jerking a thumb to it. Then she cast her gaze to my crotch. "Those too."

Not about to give her the satisfaction of knowing how painful they were from the promise and loss, I picked up my clothing. "Whatever it was, we should get back and investigate." I focused on my pants, struggling to bite back a moan as I stuffed my raging erection behind the waistband. All the while she watched, making it ten times harder.

When I nodded to her, we placed our hands at the same time and left the moon oasis behind. It took a moment for my eyes to adjust while Layla clutched at her stomach and bobbed like a seasick sailor. I watched her to make certain she was okay, when the sound struck my ears.

"The alarms." The entire place screamed in rage. "Are they always this loud?" I shouted, running out into the hallway.

"Sometimes worse if you're late." She screamed back to be heard.

A nub of guilt grew in me. I had thought she could handle herself, but I had no idea how dangerous this place was.

"How do we shut this off?" I asked.

"Well, it usually shuts up when you come through the front door, so...?"

Along the way to the door, we spotted blades embedded into walls. She picked out one of the darts that'd stuck straight through rock and stared at the tip. The floorboards had shifted, opening up to reveal a pit of spikes below. I took her hand at first to jump across, then pulled her tight to my hip as the floor kept shaking.

I dug out the magic knob and shoved it into its hole. A tingle shivered across my palm, and for the first time I noticed the lines hidden below my skin. They only glowed for a second before vanishing back to green, but the alarm system silenced itself.

"Thank god. What do you think happened?" Layla asked. "Stupid alarm went off by mistake? Ghost?"

Staring around the carnage, I spotted a blade embedded into the wall. Another three were beside it, but as I pulled it out, a piece of cloth fell to the ground. I raised the bloodied edge to the light, and she gasped. "I don't think so."

What's that?

Layla took the blade from me. "Great. I can't even get banished to another dimension without someone trying to kill me."

I placed my hand on the wall. All this time it'd been solid stone below the staircase. The splattered blood wasn't smeared against the flat rocks. It'd dripped into a straight line. I drew my finger down it, tracing the path, and the rest of the line lit up. It kept going, forming a rectangle before the entire doorway vanished.

"Was that always there?" she asked.

I looked back to shrug. This place held secrets I'd been avoiding. I didn't want to learn that I wasn't Raul S—born to doting and occasionally demanding parents. That everything in my life was a lie. But I couldn't scoop that lube back into the bottle. Holding my hand out to her, I asked, "Shall we?"

She didn't drop the blade but slipped it into the back of her waistband. Prudent, and alarmingly hot. Layla placed her palm on mine. I clenched my fingers over hers and we descended into the darkness.

It was a very short climb, at most ten stairs into the basement. A part of me hoped we'd find the missing elven larder, maybe rows of jams and jellies they'd put up for a lost winter. But as it opened up onto a hallway, my hopes for a secret elven cottage vanished. Candelabra shaped like knots of thorns lit up as we walked past. They cast haunting shadows of the thorns crawling across the ceiling like poisonous vines.

I didn't know when she walked faster, only that my hand cupped around her waist and held her close. "I feel like I should have a torch and be wearing a fedora."

She snickered. "Whips, chains and feet. You must have quite the FetLife profile."

My mouth dropped as I stared back at her. She caught my gobsmacked look. "Should I guess your username? Is it Stone Throb-body?"

"Funny."

"Rock Dickswagger?"

A flicker of light caught my eye. The same lines and whorls that'd crawl across the walls had followed us down here. Before, they'd been nothing but pretty and abstract lines. Now, a letter began to form. No, not a letter, a feeling. It wasn't a word but an idea—honor. This place meant something.

"Oh, I know. Cock and Boulder."

My foot missed the next step and I stumbled in shock at how close she had come to guessing right. Unfortunately, I still had a protective arm draped around her waist, so I sent the both of us crashing into the inky darkness. "Fuck!" I flailed an arm out to stop myself. Layla's sharp intake of breath told me if I fell she was landing on top, which, in any other situation might be nice but down here was potentially flammable. Swinging my leg out, I jammed my heel into a slab of wood. The sprain snapped all the way up my calf and thigh. I gritted through it and kept going.

Whatever was in the way swung open. One by one, lights rose inside small alcoves. These weren't like the magic fire in the rest of the house — they pulsed in varying hues around the dark rocks set inside.

"Wow." She slipped away and stared at the alcoves that stretched to at least the second floor. "This is just like that stone keeper's place."

Except much smaller in comparison. There were at most a hundred or so counterweights here to the thousands they protected. A similar lectern sat before the alcoves. I approached it, hoping for a book.

"Why aren't they glowing?" she asked.

There was nothing but a small indent in the center of the wood. It looked like there'd been a carving once but all of it was worn away. *Wait.* I pressed the same knob that'd given us entrance to this house into the hole.

"Holy —" Layla leaped back as the mysterious lines burst before us. It wasn't the walls that drew the tracing lines, but the air itself.

My eyes couldn't understand, but my mind knew what I saw. "This is the greatest treasure of the Wayfarers."

"A bunch of dead counterweights? When something that's supposed to glow doesn't, it usually means…" She drew her finger across her throat and stuck out her tongue.

She wasn't wrong. I knew they belonged to the dead, or not dead but not revealed either. Elves like me who were trapped in their Changeling form and had no idea what they meant to the family. Devotion bubbled in my mind, but it couldn't touch my heart. I shivered at the alien emotion being fed to my brain and kept going.

"They are the ones who created the system of Changelings. They'd leave their own children behind, trusting them to help guide the people." I flinched and mentally swiped the lines back to read again. "*Mierda*. These elves are parasites. They don't create. Their entire civilization is built on stealing and it's all thanks to…them."

"So what's with the stones?"

"These are the children who chose to remain, remembered and honored for their sacrifice." That would have been me if I'd had the chance to turn them down.

I closed my eyes, certain I'd have said no. When I was thirteen, directionless, angry at everything thanks to a fresh dose of puberty? Would I?

"I found yours," Layla said, jerking me awake.

"What?"

"See, it's glowing, sort of." She held out a rock that pulsed a green light but intermittently, like a dying firefly. "It's almost like you weren't finished. Fully baked?"

Left raw on purpose so I'd be easier to control. I reached out to take the counterweight, but my hand recoiled. A warning deep in my heart told me to not touch it. "Put it back."

"Are you sure? Isn't it part of your soul?"

"Put it back now!"

She glared at me for yelling and I felt a right ass. Still, she returned it to an alcove on the bottom. I noticed there were no more stones after it.

Instead of explaining the unexplainable, I returned to studying the lines. They were looping, displaying the glorious rise of the Wayfarers. "This makes them sound like an elven Bezos and Buffet combined."

"Super-rich elves die far away, no one wants to talk about them and someone's breaking into their guarded house once the missing son returns. Any of that sound really bad?" she asked.

All of it. I gritted my jaw and kept going. "We have to get out of here."

She turned and crossed her arms over her chest. "So all you need is a few angry armed elves to get out of Dodge?"

"I'd rather like to skip the duel at the OK Corral if it's all the same."

"Forget the fedora, you need a ten-gallon hat, boots and assless chaps."

The lines kept trailing off, lauding the greatness of the Wayfarer clan as they raided and pillaged every realm via their cunning and tenacity. It read like straight-up banditry to me, but pirates got rich as hell as long as they were sanctioned by the crown. Was this any different?

"*Un minuto.*" I scrolled back and read it again. "You said we needed more of those teleportation orbs?"

"Yeah. I'd have taken the one from the moon if it wouldn't leave us stranded, but…"

Waving my hand, I followed the lines etching their way to the wall. They stopped next to the alcoves. I walked over to press my hand to the thorn-shaped hole. "How many do you think you'll need?"

"Three at the very least, five to be safe," she said walking over to see what I was doing.

A magic door formed. One by one, tiny lights reflected on two dozen transportation orbs ready for planting. Layla clapped her hands. "Oh my god, holy shit, we're going home!" She leaped in place, barely getting an inch of air, when suddenly she flung her hands behind my neck. "We're going home. We're..."

Her nose landed a millimeter from mine. I held my lips flat, fighting to keep from kissing her exuberant mouth. We were returning home, where she was the wicked witch and I the hunter sworn to collar her.

"I, uh..." Layla slipped back. "I should get my book, read over the spell again. You can bring the orbs up?"

I could only nod, my heart waring with my head. *Magic is dangerous, any fool can see that. I am sworn to protect the innocent from creatures that go bump in the night, including witches.* But my heart burned with betrayal, a sickening agony from someone I'd trusted taking away my identity, my choice, and acting as if everything was right with the world.

Chapter Twenty-Eight

Layla

For the first time, I greeted the fractured sky with a smile. We had a path home.

After dressing as quickly as I could, I gathered up my book and headed down the stairs. Most mornings I'd find Raul either mashing fruit into a glass or doing lunges down the hallway. This time, the whole level was dark.

I took a peek at the main door, but the knob was still in place. He couldn't have gone anywhere. Then I heard a sound from the large feasting table. "I think that was the best night of sleep I've had since we got here. The second my head hit the stone indent thingie, I was..."

Easing around the archway couldn't prepare me for the utter chaos before me. A hundred or so scrolls were rolled across the surface, some still moving. Hunched over, dead center, was Stone. His head was placed in his hands, elbows spiked into the table, as he glared down at long piece of paper in front of him.

"Did you get any sleep?" I asked.

My question caused him to jerk up. That green complexion did nothing to help the dark bags building under his eyes. He blinked madly a few times, then wiped at his face. "What time is it?" Raul asked before turning back to stare through the open window. A pair of silver birds chirped from a nest on the sill. "Morning? Already?"

"What were you working on?" I reached for one of the scrolls, but Raul leaped up.

Like a greedy miser, he scooped all the scrolls into a pile, tearing some of them in the process. "Nothing. It doesn't concern you."

Crossing my arms, I tilted my head and stared at him.

He looked like shit. The urge to point out the knots in his hair, the hunch in his shoulders and the nervous bounce of his knee all died on my tongue. We still needed each other, and picking on him wouldn't help when I was so close to getting back.

It wasn't until he clamped his hands to the table for dear life and stared down at the mess of elven words that it hit me. His entire life had just been rewritten under him. "Is this about you being a — ?"

He spun away and stared out at the brightening morning. "It looks nice out. Why don't we get out of here? Go for a stroll?"

"A stroll?"

"Or I could leave you alone if you'd prefer?" He rolled up two of the scrolls then tucked them into a bag on his hip. While his tone was curt and distant, his eyes crackled with pain.

Accepting that we'd be discussing the logistics for our return home later, I placed my spell book on the table. "A stroll before breakfast would be nice."

Raul stuck out his arm, then he winced. "Oh yes, food. ¿*Tienes hambre?*" He looked ready to dash for the kitchen to whip up a stack of pancakes.

The elephant in the room tapped its trunk for attention. I blushed, ignoring the glaring implications of the morning-after dance and shook my head. "No. I'm good. We can…stroll." Instead of taking his hand, I pushed open one of the two doors in the whole place and walked into the backyard.

Though calling it the backyard sold it short. It was less a field of grass and a few trees and more a strange, pink-tinted forest behind the house. A cool breeze wafted off the river that ran just beyond the stands of purple and silver bushes. Without thinking, I headed toward the stone path where I'd discovered fruit on the first day. He walked behind me, not saying a word.

High above, two birds with long tails like ribbons flew without a care. They kept weaving back and forth with each other, swerving at just the last second to not collide. It was enchanting. I pointed to the tails where a weird trail of colored smoke followed behind. "Do you know what those are?" I asked, trying and failing to trace the birds as they picked up speed.

Raul leaned in closer, his head nearly on my shoulder while he too attempted to follow. "No idea. I'm afraid…"

I glanced over to him, and he gulped. His gaze burned hotter than fire, and he licked his lips. My skin prickled. I hadn't a clue if it was because he was almost touching me or because he wasn't. A cloud passed overhead and he dipped his head back.

"I'm afraid there are too many unknowns in this world for me to understand them all."

"They are beautiful, though," I said, no longer looking at the birds.

"Yes, they are." His voice dropped to a tumbling gravel.

That damn elephant was stomping its foot and glaring at us. Raul opened his mouth and I beat him to it. "Did you have anywhere in particular, or are we just walking?"

"Walking. Away from the house. It's..." He rubbed his temples and frowned.

"What is it?" I asked, touching the back of his hand.

His arms fell and he stared past me. "Nothing." Striding ahead without a care, he shoved aside a mess of overgrown ivy to reveal not only the river, but a wooden boat resting on the shore. "How about a boat ride?"

"Does it have a paddle?" I asked. Raul reached in to hoist one up. Gold was inlaid into braids across the flat end and up the handle. Curious about the river, I pulled off the overgrowth with my bare hands and eased for the boat.

It took some tugging and carrying before the wooden hull hit water, but it floated. That was a good sign. As it bobbed on the waves, silver runes shimmered to life along the sides and up to the prow. Instead of anything impressive like a deer head or a minotaur, it was a curved line—a lot like the ones covering Raul's chest.

"Do you think it's seaworthy?" I asked, watching for any leaks, but it looked sound.

"As we won't be heading into the sea, I don't think it's a problem."

"Ass." I called out his pedantry, and he chuckled.

"Here." He extended his hand, and I took it. With a gentle touch, he guided me into the boat. It barely moved as I stepped inside despite the choppy waters. Magic flowed from the boat's center out across the river's surface.

"I think the runes are keeping it steady." Getting my balance quickly, I sat on the bench to the aft.

"Excellent." He climbed in and stood before the seat at the prow.

"Did you know they could do that?" I asked.

Raul dug the oar into the shoreline and pushed off. We floated away to where the current caught and pushed us down river. "No," he said, taking the seat so he'd stare at me. "But at least the elves are using their magic to help for once."

He paddled, dipping the oar from one side to the other with ease. I draped my arms across the sides of the boat, soaking in the warmth of the sun without the usual biting heat of summer, and breathed deep. Rather than go with the current, Raul turned the boat so we fought it, but he didn't show an ounce of exertion.

"Have you done this before?" I asked.

"Battled the rapids of an elven river in a wooden boat?"

"You're surprisingly natural with that paddle," I said.

He smiled. "Some of us use them for what they're intended. Not that your demon would understand."

Oh, Ink would understand perfectly. He'd paddle all day if that was what I desired. The ache in my heart wasn't gone, but it stung less in the calm glug of waves and flower-scented morning. Tipping my head back, I closed my eyes tight, and faced the rising sun. "You're saying the agency didn't train you as a gondolier? All part of a wine-and-dine a witch program?"

The splash of the paddle retracting from the water wasn't met by a slap and I sat up. He'd pulled the oar to his lap and was staring ahead at nothing. The current took hold of the boat, pushing it back to where we had begun. Raul kept gliding his hands up and down the handle, his lips parting with unasked questions.

I hadn't a clue what was going through his mind, but if it was guilt for us fucking on the moon, I didn't want to hear it. The only shame hanging over my head was feeling no shame for what happened. It sure as shit wasn't love-making, that much I knew. But a little rage-slash-celebration sex never hurt anyone. Probably.

"It was house documents."

Okay, I hadn't expected that.

Raul focused on me before he cranked his head away. "I spent the night poring over documents about the Wayfarers. About my...family." He spat that word, his shoulders tight. He clenched his fists around the oar.

Elves didn't have super strength, right? I peered at the wood, hoping he wouldn't leave us literally up the creek without a paddle. When he wrung his hands tighter, I placed my palm on the handle. Raul looked up at me and gave in.

Holding it safe, I sat back on my seat and tried my hands at paddling. It wasn't too bad, if I ignored the water that kept splashing me in the face and lap as I switched sides. When the boat's prow steered back toward dry land, I broke the silence. "Let me guess, you're angry and confused. How could this part of you, a cornerstone of your existence, have been hidden from you for your whole life? You're enraged at the people that kept it from you, but also yourself for not figuring it out."

"I'm a witch hunter. I should have..." He clenched his green fist, then dropped it to his lap. Raul swiveled and stared at me. "You're doing well."

"Thanks," I said, sweeping my arms to the other side. *Whew, this is harder than it looks.* "All I wanted was answers, but when I got them, well..." My mother hadn't exactly swept back into my life begging for forgiveness. She'd just assumed I'd be that obedient nine-year-old with braided pigtails who'd nod and do whatever I was told. Getting her to explain anything was harder than getting Ink to do the laundry. That man could turn weaponized incompetence nuclear.

The boat smacked into the shore. Raul reached a hand out and grabbed a tree branch hanging just above his head. Even as he fought against the waves, he stared at me. "If I do not hunt for answers, then I'm a terrible agent."

"Are you?"

He snickered to himself. "I've been shot by my director, tricked by elves, banished by a Horseman and..." His green cheeks shifted petal pink. "...been with a witch. What of that screams competent agent bulwarking against magical chaos?"

With a great heave, Raul twisted the boat around until it lined parallel with the shore. He held onto the branches above while I eased my foot onto steady land. Once I was certain I wouldn't fall flat on my ass, I held my hand out to him. He stared up at me, his body bobbing with the tossing waves. Sighing, he clasped his palm to mine, and I helped pull him up to join me.

The momentum caused me to skitter on my slick-soled elven shoes. When Raul slipped his hand behind my back and held me steady, my heart stilled to a strange calmness. After the moon, I had thought we'd burned through our confounding tension, but the heat simmered to a threatening boil all over again. "I..."

He licked his lips, damn near daring me to take a taste.

A hard wave slammed the boat into the shoreline. Then the water scooped back, taking the boat with. We both lurched after, as if we could catch the wild boat sent off on a journey of its own.

"Damn it. I didn't think to tie it up," I said, cursing myself.

Raul watched it swerve with the currents until it vanished around a bend. "It doesn't matter. None of this does. We belong elsewhere. Have you finalized the spell to return to Earth?"

"Ah, nearly. I'll need to brew up a potion and that requires ingredients."

He walked back toward the house, his head up and shoulders back. I skipped a bit to catch up with him.

"Draw up a list, and I will plan a trip to the markets," Raul said. He paused in his long strides to look back at me struggling to keep up. Then he extended his elbow.

I wrapped my arm around his and he patted my hand. "Any chance you'll get back before the house tries to murder me?"

"Of course," he said, his voice distant. "I wouldn't want anything to happen to you."

"Good?" That was all I asked, but my stomach dropped at the tone. While cold confidence could be hot, this near-on flip from the weary and concerned man from five minutes before was confusing.

I shook my head. It had to be nerves. I was on my way home and back to my guys...who'd probably try to kill the elf on my arm. Before we approached the house and dove back into work, I said, "Raul, when this is over, do you think you'll fall right back into being a witch hunter?"

He let go of my arm and stopped before the doors. "I suppose we'll have to see," he said, before vanishing into the darkness of the elven mansion.

Chapter Twenty-Nine

Layla

I wrote down what I could read of the spell and mindlessly bit into the bread. "Oh, damn." A moan slipped out at the perfect blend of sweet and spicy sizzling on my tongue. "I won't miss much, but it's gonna be hard going without this." The last of the magic red fruit lay on the table, its innards scooped down to the rind by me and Raul. Mostly me.

"Perhaps we could grab an armful from the market."

We'd damn near stripped the place down for parts in trying to trade for the supplies to cast this spell. Magic was plentiful here, but ingredients were harder to come by. Elves didn't get much into distilling, or anything else beyond robbing.

Raul plucked my bare foot off the chair beside him. "You provide the distraction—" He dug the sides of his thumbs into my weary sole and I almost cried out in relief. "While I nick the goods."

I finished jotting down the spell and slid it over to him. "How's this look?"

He didn't pause in rubbing my foot while pulling the sheet close. "This should be an 'a', and I believe that word is wrong, but I'm not certain how."

I bit my lip, trying to keep from screaming at myself. This would be so much easier if Daniel were here. He'd read over the book, take my hand and correct what I kept getting wrong. A pang thumped inside my heart like barbed wire. It'd taken longer than I had hoped, another five days to find the supplies needed to open a portal by myself. Even still, the witch who had created it seemed skeptical of the spell, as if it was just a concept. Over two weeks since I'd been gone.

Cal had to be losing his shit by now. Hopefully Ink was keeping him in line with assurances I wasn't dead. Though would Garavel be pressuring him and the two fall to bickering?

I worried about my guys, but none more than Daniel. Why was I so cold? He didn't know how much I hated being called stupid. I should have talked to him. I should have told him that he had to remember he was a ghost or else…

"Hey." A finger pressed to my cheek and I jerked, startled at the touch of warm skin. I half expected to look up into soft brown eyes, but I found vibrant green instead. "We're getting there. Don't worry."

My frown fumbled to a smile. Stone… Raul had been my damn cheerleader as of late, and I didn't know why. Sure, we had to get back and my magic was the only way home. But that'd been the case since we had landed here. What had changed?

Okay, we had fucked on the moon. That could be a small part. Or was he finally feeling a shred of guilt for how he'd treated witches for decades?

"What about this?" I scratched out the word my dyslexia had inverted and passed it over.

Adjusting the full spell in front of himself, Raul stared down while he pulled my foot closer. I slid in my chair, his massage somehow working out knots all the way up my spine. Moaning, I flexed my foot and my toes brushed up against his cock—half hard and quickly on its way to full.

Raul stiffened from the neck down. He let go of my foot and placed both his hands to the table. I should have pulled my leg back, played it off as little more than an accident. We hadn't so much as kissed since the night of the break-in. *I have four hot, sweet, often infuriating men waiting for me. I don't need another.*

"I think you've done it," he said. "Good job." His smile warmed my heart. Garavel was the only who'd compliment me on my spells. Now the dangerous witch hunter was encouraging me too.

"Do you think we're ready?" I asked and playfully thrummed my toes against the head of his cock.

Raul gulped, his forehead beading up as he struggled to focus on the plans. The table was covered in them, and they in turn were covered in red fruit stains. "I think…" He swallowed again as I twisted to cup my toes around his cock and teasingly caress them up and down the shaft.

"You think?" I prompted when he went silent, his head rolled back. He'd clenched his fingers into the wood, fighting tooth and nail to keep from pulling himself out.

I let him take a breather by slipping my foot off his cock. Raul sighed and wiped at his forehead. "We've bottled the boiled imp hearts, the traveling orbs are refreshed and—"

He full-on jerked when my big toe brushed against his balls. Straining in my chair, I reached out to run my foot back and forth below them. Raul rocked his head, his nails reaching the edge of the table.

The way he fought to keep from tugging his cock out was tantalizing. Cal liked to be controlled and collared, but the idea of grinding my foot into Stone's face while he pleaded for it drenched my panties.

"And?" I prompted again. I wrapped my foot around his cock and tugged harder. His silk trousers glided over his shaft and the tip of his crown poked up from the falling waistband. With precision, I circled my little pinkie toe across the warm flesh.

"Yes!" he cried out, reaching for his pants.

I paused in toying with him and quirked my head. Raul froze in tugging his waistband down. "Yes what?"

He shuddered from his eyebrows down to his trapped cock. The shaft momentarily knocked into my foot and he absently wrenched back his hair. "Tonight. Tonight we go home."

Finally. I could hold them again. Have them fuss over me. Worry about where I'd been. And face off against the witch hunter turned elf who could still hunt me. We needed night so no one would spot the magic, which meant we had a few hours to kill.

"Can I take off my pants?" Raul cried out.

I tapped my finger to my chin in thought. "What's the magic word?"

"For fuck's sake, I need you."

Close enough. With a smug look, I decreed, "Yes."

He yanked them down in record time and his cock slapped into my foot. Tenting my fingers together, I leaned forward in my chair and watched the evil witch hunter whimper and pant from my foot until his elven tattoos were drenched in cum.

* * * *

Raul

Far more than the transportation orbs had been kept in the secret room. Whenever she was fast asleep, I'd sneak down to read through a giant book. The pages were blank, but when the candlelight caught on my chest, my scars would light up to reveal the hidden words. "Fascinating," I whispered to myself, with only the glow of my tattoos keeping me company.

"Are you down here?"

I wished I could take it with, but the book was carved into the marble lectern. Even with her footsteps echoing down the secret hallway, I kept reading, scribbling notes in a mix of English and Spanish. More than wealth, the Wayfarers had power and I wasn't about to let it go to waste in this dead house.

"Stone?"

My shoulders jerked. I wrenched my gaze off of the family secrets. "Please don't use that name."

"Sorry." She poked her head in through the small doorway and struggled to blink in the low light. I deftly put out the lamp before she could read anything, then hefted up my bag. "Are you...?" Layla stumbled back as I joined her. "Are we ready?"

"I believe so. The stones are in place."

"Where no one can find them?" She'd been pressing on me to explain exactly where we'd do this. It couldn't be the house. There was a great chance of this going wrong and causing either fire or an implosion. My family's grandeur could never be tarnished in such a way.

"The area was completely abandoned," I assured her and held out my hand.

The witch pushed back her hair, and stared at me. This was almost over. For as nice as spending another night pacing about the study, gazing across the lake and watching her leave wet footprints out of the bath might be, duty called to me. I'd thought I was certain before, but now it clanged in my every vein, directing me to do what I was meant to. Be who I should have always been.

Her fingers crested over my palm. I expected her to rebuff it, but as she slid closer, a little smile pinked her cheeks. I clung to her hand and for a single heartbeat, my duty vanished.

Pull her into your arms. Kiss her, taste her tongue with yours. Run your palms across her bare belly, tug down her skirt and finally fuck her until she screams your name.

The thought vanished as quickly as it formed. "It's time," I said.

She pursed her lips and stared back to the alcove. Hundreds of dead Changelings rested in memorial. Only one glowed, waiting for the return of the Wayfarer clan.

"Are you sure we shouldn't take it along? Maybe it'll matter."

"No." I shook my head. The texts were clear — the counterweights had to remain. They were the lynchpin. "Let's go before we lose the light."

Arm in arm we ascended up the stairs. Instead of frowning at the signs greeting me like a long-lost friend, I tipped my head to them. This house hadn't been dead without the others. It was merely sleeping. My appearance had woken it and many long-dead ghosts.

"Why do I feel like I'm forgetting something? This happens every time I take a trip. Not that this was a trip." She frowned and stared at her phone. It seemed like she was having to charge it more. Any longer and it might not even operate despite her spell.

The pale light of her screen washed out her cheeks. I pushed a curl behind her ear. She absently reached up to touch her skin and found my hand instead. I almost pulled it back, but she pressed my hand tighter.

"I keep going over the spells. We have the potions, the incantations, the orbs for power. This should be everything."

"Is that really what's bothering you?" I asked, tracing the curve of her jaw. Her exhausted mouth parted and I swept my thumb across her cupid's bow. "Or does a tiny part of you wish to stay?"

She gasped and I flicked my thumbnail against her bottom lip, waiting for her tongue to follow. But she stepped back, her eyes wary. "I need to get back. We need... I get why you're not in a huge hurry to run back and confront your boss slash cult leader. But my life is there. My guys are waiting for me."

Assuming they had waited at all. Incubi were creatures of whim and hunger. Wolves needed their packs like fish did the water. I hadn't a clue with demi-angels, but the ghost had been close to his end time. Any minor stress had probably sent him poofing out of existence. I should tell her. I wanted to tell her that she'd pinned her hope on the hopeless.

"You presume that…"

It does not matter.

I need her helpful and a kind lie would serve better than the harsh truth.

The pang of jealousy washed away and duty stampeded over every emotion. "That they are not already attempting to find you," I said.

She didn't leap for joy, but tugged on her locket. "That's what worries me most of all." Slipping her hand into her purse, Layla raised up her chest. Her breasts nearly spilled out of her shirt. I zeroed in on her nipples, the dark circles evident below the thin white silk.

My palms cried out to caress them, my hips to press her ass against the wall and my cock to burrow inside her soaking *cochina*.

What am I doing?

I flinched, a pain throbbing at the back of my neck. But as I reached behind for it, all my worries fled.

"Raul?" she asked. My name on her tongue almost punctured through. The last shreds of my selfishness faded away, only duty remaining.

"Let's go home."

Chapter Thirty

Cal

The last of the sunlight ducked behind the oncoming clouds. A storm brewed on the horizon, winds picking up and tugging on the scraps of paper. I held them down for Daniel, who'd groan every time I tried to check my phone.

"For the... Hold that still. I need to check something."

I slammed my hand to the altar and pain shocked up my arm, but I gritted through it. "This good enough?"

"Yes." He'd been a barbed-wire fence ever since Layla had vanished. Even I was getting sick of it. Ink had threatened to hurl his backup bone down a random toilet and let the tides decide his fate.

I clung to our only piece of Daniel, buried deep in my pocket where Ink couldn't get it. Both of them could be infuriating in different ways. Both were smart asses who thought they were above everyone. And I needed both to keep her safe.

"I need to talk to you."

"I'm reading. If we don't get this right—"

I tugged the paper away and his eyes followed until he glared at me. "What? What do you want?"

We didn't get on great. Not for want of trying on my part. He just seemed to only care about Layla and suffered the rest of us to be by her side. His icy glare darkened the longer I kept the page from him, and Daniel folded his arms over his chest.

"Look," I began. I knew I had to have this talk, but the words began to flee. "If I...if this works, you have to be there for her."

Daniel's scowl opened to surprise. He dropped an arm and almost reached out to comfort me. His hand sailed right on through. "We haven't exhausted all our resources yet—"

"Yeah, we have." It'd been a constant refrain of 'you can't do that,' 'we'll find another way,' 'look through the books we have' and winding up back on sacrifice. Ink had been insisting we pick someone at random, Daniel refused to even acknowledge the option and Garavel... It unnerved me how the angel had nothing to say either for or against.

Whatever happened, he wouldn't be the one to do it.

"This is stupid," Daniel said. He slammed both his hands to the altar. The slap echoed against the rising storm winds and I winced. He was growing strong again.

"Think of it as one less man to compete with."

He shivered. "I know what it means to be dead. You have no idea what you're signing up for."

I rather doubted I'd become a ghost after this. Ink mumbled something about all my energy needed for the spell, which I assumed included my soul. "She's trapped and if I...if I can bring her home, then I have to try."

"By any means necessary?"

I gritted my jaw and nodded.

Daniel threw his hands up and stomped to the computer set-up. "Out of your fucking mind. All of you." He hunched over and glared, seemingly cutting off our conversation. I tugged out my phone and absently swiped for my messages.

"She'll hate us."

His soft plea drew my attention.

"She will never forgive us for this. For letting you kill yourself to save her? We may as well all cut our throats."

It can't be Ink, he can't die. It can't be Garavel, the same reason. And it can't be Daniel, he's already dead. I'm the only option left.

"What happened to forever? To you getting down on one knee and..." He wiped at his nose as if he was crying and stared at me. "And making all of her dreams come true."

I closed my eyes tight and swallowed the lump. In the back of my mind, a fleeting image of Layla in white faded away. "It's up to you now. The others. Ink's good at distractions but he'll want her to get over it fast. Garavel... I don't think he can understand his own emotions yet, never mind someone else's."

Walking closer, I held my hand out as if I could shake his. "Please. Just promise me that no matter how much she screams she hates you, that she wants to be left alone, that you'll be there for her. And...make her happy."

He stared at my peace offering and began to reach out with his palm. I couldn't shake it, but I could pretend to. At the last second, Daniel swerved and slammed his hands to the laptop keys. "There's another way. I know it."

The air shifted and the scent on the wind changed from hay and ozone to brimstone and magic. Ahead of Ink walked Layla's mom Isabel. Goosebumps ran the length of my spine at the grit in her jaw. She both looked nothing and exactly like Layla in the shifting light, opening the ache in my heart.

"Took you long enough," Daniel grumbled. It felt like months had passed before Ink was able to track her down.

"This one has something against charming incubi," Ink said, pointing to the only witch we knew.

"Demons lie," Isabel said. She yanked out her spell book and walked to the altar.

"We are in fact renowned to not...oh, why bother?" Ink waved her off and in doing so, his body rocked back and forth. It was looking reedier below his clothing, the shirt and pants hanging looser than I remembered. "Have you unlocked the secrets of the universe yet, ghost?"

Daniel answered with a slow growl.

"Pity me for hoping that a miracle had occurred and you at last proved useful. I suppose I shall go and collect the angel. Big man, the hour is nigh!" Ink shouted to the heavens. The storm clouds parted and a black shadow plunged through.

With a small barrel roll, Garavel dove to the ground. Ink gestured him closer from his job of watching for any hunters. "When this business is done, we deserve a treat. Ice cream perhaps, consumed in a large tub. With all of us naked," Ink said.

"I'm afraid I'll have to skip the party."

He shivered and turned to me. His face was drawn and eyes shadowed. I'd expected a laugh at my gallows joke, maybe for him to work off of it. Instead, the sarcastic demon tipped his head down. I almost looked to see if my shoes were untied before I realized he was bowing to me.

"Calvin, I wish you to know that out of all the flea-bitten mongrels I've had the misfortune to meet, you're the least offensive."

I wrapped my arm around him and pulled Ink to me for a half hug. He less than enthusiastically returned the affection. But as my mouth landed near the side of his face, I whispered, "Swear to me —"

"I will protect her, on my life."

It was all I could hope for. I began to break off the hug when huge arms crushed me tighter to Ink. Air burst from my crushed lungs as Garavel embraced us both. My body fought to get away, my wolf growling at the man who'd marked us as the enemy. But he too was Layla's only hope. Instead of fighting, I reached my arm around Garavel's back and held him. We were all hurting, knowing how badly we had to hurt her.

"We must begin." Thunder ripped through the clouds as Isabel ordered us. She snapped her book open and glared at me. "Now."

"It was nice knowing you," Ink said. "Let me guess, stand on the —"

"On the rune," she said, pointing to a ward in the grass.

Daniel didn't look at me, only hustled over to read behind her shoulder. Garavel reached behind to unsheathe his sword, and a little black head popped out. He plucked Fiona free from her napping spot and held her out to me. As I scratched her head and cheek, she rumbled like an unbalanced dryer. "She will miss you, werewolf."

"I know."

Nodding, Garavel returned Fiona and ordered her to stay inside where it was safe. As she was a cat, I highly doubted she'd listen. A lot like Layla in that way.

They prepared the circle for my sacrifice and my heart froze. I pulled out my phone and checked.

Be there for mom. I chose this.

The text to Mark remained unread. I just wanted to talk to him again, to explain why. First Eli, now me. Mark would be the last of us, and the only hope for the pack to survive Eric's reign. I swiped over my keyboard, spilling my guts as fast as the typos would allow.

"Wolf?"

I stopped, my autocorrect filling in 'love her' for me. Isabel held a dagger, handle out, to me. "We cannot wait any longer, or we may lose her forever."

Shutting off my phone, I left the text unsent. The leather wrap of the dagger chilled my palm. I clenched my fingers tighter, willing it to warm up. *Should I warm up the blade too?*

I shook the silly thought away and leaped up onto the altar. I refused to die on my back. The three men who'd have to piece Layla back together stood around me. Blinking away the tears, I thought of Layla in a tiny bikini on a tropical island. With no one around for miles, we'd have the beach to ourselves for the whole honeymoon.

Raising my chin, I shouted to the whole world, "I'm ready."

* * * *

Layla

The last of the imp potion dribbled to the ground. I wrenched away and breathed. At first the air was as clear as the spring water circling this hideaway. But as I turned to face the ward, the inescapable stench of rotting garbage on a hot summer day struck me. "God. Why does that smell so awful?"

"You are what you eat," Raul said. He wiped off his hands and stood in the middle of the huge ward. It wasn't as clean as the beach, but the runes stood out enough in the dirt. Probably enough. "Is it ready?"

Streaks of the fading sun cut across the flat trees. Their pink berry leaves shifted to a haunting purple in the light, shadows straining across the strange oasis in a rock desert. Bending over, I inspected my book one last time. A shiver climbed up my spine as impenetrable cold chased away the heat.

"Here." Heavy fabric landed on my shoulders. I reached to touch it and recognized the velvet from Ink's insistent cloak. Fifteen days had passed since he had given it to me. If this went right... *This will go right and I'll see them all soon.*

"Thank you," I said, pinning the cloak into place. "That should be all we need."

Nodding, Raul approached the first traveling orb. He placed his hand to the top and the metal surface shifted to a turbulent play of purple and blue clouds. One by one, he walked to the rest, lighting up each placed equidistant in the circle. I turned in place and held up my hand. "I think that one needs to be two inches to the left."

He looked, peered around me, then nudged the dangerous magical artifact with his foot. "Here?"

"A little bit. There. That's...or was it too much?"

"It's good enough. The sun is dropping. If we wait any longer..."

He didn't explain, just leaped into the center and crossed his arms. *Or what?* The question lingered on my tongue. *Or we have to wait another day and that isn't happening. He wants to get home as badly as I do, that's all.*

"Shall we?" Raul held out his palm.

I placed my hand to my neck and grazed both Ink's brooch and Daniel's locket. *I'm coming home, I swear.*

"Ready," I declared and clasped my hand to his.

The spell was simple, little more than a conduit really. It was the trauma and exhaustion of transferring power from the air through my body into the ward. On the beach, my mom had handled it. I didn't realize how painful it was, the magic burning then freezing my fingers and toes. It struck like lightning, building from the ground up to my brain and out into the world.

Directing it was like commanding lightning, the magic never happy about being told what to do. *Maybe that's where Ink gets it.*

"It's working," Raul shouted.

I risked opening my eye to find his body was glowing. Not just his scars, though they were brighter than the sun against his luminous chest. A wind I couldn't feel tugged back his long hair and he smiled at me. "Keep going. Don't stop no matter what happens."

No matter what happens? I had to be careful. The magic could overwhelm me, a fate my mother had mentioned but hadn't gone into details of. Take too much and suffer the consequence was the end of my lesson. But as the ground shook inside the ward and the runes started to spin, I risked taking a deeper drink of the well.

The transportation orbs lifted off the ground. They hovered above their spot in the makeshift pentagram, humming like an old microwave. Cold seized up my shins and my fingers fell numb. I had to back off. But as I did, the orbs lowered.

"What's wrong?"

"I can't feel my hands," I shouted, my blood pounding so loud in my ears I couldn't hear my own voice.

Warmth rubbed over my blisteringly frozen palms. "You can't stop. Not now. We're so close to breaking through. I know you can do this, Leeland."

Leeland? He hadn't called me that since we had landed in the mansion. I cracked an eye to peer at him, when the air shattered. Power thundered from the heavens to smash straight into the ward. As it drew back, a hole formed and grew.

"Yes!" We both cried at once, almost jumping for joy. He took control faster, rubbing my hands while ordering me to keep going.

I can soak in the warm tub while all four of my guys watch. Suffer now to hold them then. Gritting my teeth, I dug in. The power seared through me, every muscle in my body locking up. My head snapped back and eyelids popped open. Helpless, I stared into the endless vast of space. The elven skies had ripped apart, revealing the stars of creation itself, the dust of Celestials.

"Almost," he shouted, abandoning my hands to touch the orbs. They rotated to face him like a pack of dogs watching someone with cheese.

I only needed to grasp the power built into the creation of the realms and with it tear through to the other side. The stars danced in the swirling void, beckoning me to touch them. My muscles relaxed, letting me lift my hand to the sky...

"The touchstone."

In an instant, the piece I'd been missing slammed into my mind.

"What?" he called.

"The touchstone. The only way this works is if we have a touchstone. What is it?"

Raul raised his head, his face falling into darkness as the shadows fought with the light. "I am the touchstone."

"Back home you were, but here... Here, you're..."

Why isn't he freaking out? We couldn't do any of this without the touchstone. That was the entire basis of their weird-ass travel scheme. And he knew that. He told me he'd found a solution in the Wayfarer's texts, an unclaimed Changeling. *Except...*

"Raul?"

"Keep. Going."

"If I open this portal, it could go anywhere. We might be stuck in a worse place than this."

My heart plummeted as he crossed his arms, cutting off his radiating chest. "I know."

He knew? He used me? Again! *Is this all a trick by the witch hunters from the start? Is he working with Conquest to take control of all the realms before the apocalypse?*

I clenched my hand and wrenched it away. The power flow stilled, then sputtered out. "No!"

Stone lunged forward and clamped onto my wrist. I reared back to punch him, but he easily dodged. His eyes! There was always a touch of burning desire, but now they glowed with the glassy fervency of a cultist.

"You will finish the spell," he ordered, his voice devoid of all emotion. Devoid of his humanity.

"Or what?" I argued back.

He chuckled and bent my arm back, dragging my palm to the rising flames of the still burning magic. "Your spunk was entertaining before, but now it's a nuisance. Finish the spell, or do it with third-degree burns."

I went limp and he dragged me toward it without any resistance. Stone didn't even blink, just kept pulling my hand for the fire. Leaping up, I screamed in his ear and kicked as hard as I could for his crotch. I missed his balls by an inch, but my foot caught his thigh and sent him spinning away.

Before he could recover, I ran to leap out of the ward. If I got my book, I could turn it into his prison, then figure it out from there.

"Lay...la," he groaned, reaching out to catch the cloak.

The flames would only hurt for a second. Wrapping my cloak up so he couldn't pull me back in, I dug my foot into the rapidly disappearing dirt and prepared to jump free.

An arrow shot straight past where my hand had been. *Is that bastard shooting at me?*

With what?

"I wouldn't if I were you, witch."

My stomach dropped to my knees. Dumbstruck, I turned. Seven elves armed to teeth stood just outside the fires. They were dressed in barbarian furs and leather, all save one. The man in silk and lace, carrying nothing but a small walking cane, stepped forward. The man who'd given us the thorn knob in the first place.

"You're under the claim of the Bramble clan. Serve or die."

Chapter Thirty-One

Layla

He didn't looked surprised. He didn't even look annoyed. Stone raised his hand and greeted the people advancing on us with a, "Good evening."

"Your pathetic plan has failed," the red guy in the fancy pajamas said.

"Is that so?" Stone asked, an eyebrow quirked.

With a sneer, the Bramble man ripped a crossbow from the arms of one of his goons and fired right at Stone. I cast without thinking, raising a shield up to protect not only me, but the traitor beside me. The arrow pinged off of the thick air, harmlessly tumbling to the ground.

"The witch shows some promise. She'll be an excellent addition to our spoils."

"Fuck you and your Hugh Hefner cosplay!" I shouted at him. Stone shifted closer to me and placed a hand on my shoulder. For a brief second, I thought he might back me up. Then his fingers tightened to a hold of ownership. I spun and zapped him, sending electricity pinging off my protection bubble and lancing into him. It didn't do much, but at least it got him off of me.

"If any one of you tries to touch me, I'll boil your eyeballs in your sockets. Got it?" Power flowed up my hands, a spell that wasn't as gruesome as my threat forming on my lips.

Both men had the incendiary nerve to ignore me.

"Be careful, Gored Bramble, she'll fight to her last breath."

Gored — my god, did his parents hate him? — approached us without toeing apart the ward. "Even the wildest of steeds can be broken."

"You keep comparing me to animals and I'll rip your intestines out through your belly button. Assuming elves even have one!" A handful of the elves behind him began to chuckle. Sneering, I stomped my foot. The ground splintered under me, catching two of the unaware elves by the ankle. They stumbled, almost slamming into their fellow thugs. One snapped up and aimed a spear.

"Hold your actions. We need her in one or two pieces. As for you, I see you've finally learned your place in the world, Changeling."

"To your detriment, Bramble," Stone taunted.

"Who is the one in the cage, and who is the one outside?" the second pompous twat asked.

I struggled to keep my eyes on every elf. They ranged in color across the red and blue spectrum and, as I kept turning, I caught a familiar face in the mix.

"Nym?" Gored called him over. The elf who'd greeted us, given us snacks and sent us on our way approached with a massive war axe strung across his shoulders. He smiled wide. The tattoos on his cheeks and forehead were all painted up in blood.

Taking a scroll from Nym, Gored began to read it before he even unrolled the thing. "By order of rights of discovery, I as patriarch of the Bramble clan take ownership of all your valuables and the witch." He reached for the staff.

"Not on your life, oath breaker," Stone growled.

Gored paused and sighed. "I was attempting to be civilized. To avoid the bloodshed in honor of your fallen clan."

A terrifying chuckle rumbled from Stone and I froze. "They are not fallen."

"Their house is in disarray. They have lost control of the stones and their fortunes. None have seen their like, nor their mark, for years unending. They are carrion for the picking."

Stone crossed his arms as if we had all the time in the world. But the elves were drawing closer, and more importantly, drawing their weapons. Despite looking barbaric, power flowed from the stabby ends. They'd harnessed magic in their own clumsy way and could use it to break through my defenses.

"Why should I believe a word from your mouth, filthy oath breaker?" Stone spat at him.

"I let you misspeak once out of love for my lost friends, but not again." Gored looked like he was about to cleave Stone's head off with a bitch slap.

"Your body will rot as it dangles from the Beithir tree, and your soul be devoured by the fiery breath of the Brécaire cat."

I snapped my fingers, casting a burst of flames in both Stone's and Gored's faces. "What the fuck are you talking about?"

"It became clear in time," Stone said, making no sense. "My family created the wonders of the touchstones and shared that bounty with their sister clan."

His family? He hadn't even believed he was an elf until a few days ago.

Stone darkened and glared at Gored. "Until their great betrayal."

"Give me the names!" Gored suddenly shouted and plunged his spear straight through my bubble. I twisted my hand to burn his arm, but Stone shifted out of the way and clasped his palms around the metal.

"Traitor," he thundered and the dirt exploded. Hundreds of massive vines studded with thorns whipped out of the ground. They slashed at the elves, slicing apart hands and their weirdly exposed chests. Panicked screams echoed against my less-than-helpful barrier.

"Miserly bastards." Gored yanked his spear back, the bronze edges coated in blood.

Stone didn't even wince as he held out his wounded palms. "As long as I draw breath, you will never see a single name."

"That can be quickly rectified!" Gored yanked on the middle of his spear and out popped a second metal tip. Dual-armed, he spun both spears around, getting into what had to be a prime murder position. Stone, in his smug stupidity, was still unarmed, and the elves were starting to hack through his vines. One by one, they fell to pieces, leaving the rest of the elves free to attack from behind Gored.

"Kill him. We can use his body to find the names ourselves." With that, Gored swung straight for Stone's shoulder. I should leave him to face it alone. He'd betrayed me too. For all of his sudden giving a shit about oaths, he seemed unable to keep them. But as tips sliced through the sputtering magic, I raised up the flames, then hurled a slice of ice. The bronze heated, then cooled in a flash.

With one quick punch, Stone shattered both to pieces. He stood higher and grabbed Gored by the head. The man dug his nails into Stone's wrists, drawing blood but not loosening his grip an inch. "You betrayed my family. You tried to steal from them to enrich your coffers."

"The Wayfarers are dead."

"No. The Wayfarers will live again, and I will lead them to victory over all the realms!" He threw his head back and laughed, sounding every bit like a megalomaniac bent on world domination. For as infuriating as Stone could get, he'd never seemed power mad. What the hell had happened down in that room? What had he read? Or what read him?

"My lord?" Nym shouted. On cue, Gored twitched out of the way and a smaller axe flew. Stone had enough self-preservation to dodge, but it gave Gored the opening to break away.

"The touchstones are ours. By rights of conquest," Gored shouted and pulled a dagger from his boot. "Kill the Changeling, grab the witch."

Every elf advanced. Arrows aimed for Stone, but he was on his own. They'd turned on me. One weapon I blocked with fire. I shook the owner of another deeper into the ground, but there were too many. The attacks became blurs. I had to trust in my magic to catch them, the shield doing nothing. They pressed me back to the edge of the ward.

A bronze sword came slicing for my neck. I leaned over too far to avoid it, and in my haste, I almost smashed my palm over the ward. Fuck. If I smudged it, we'd have no way home. And right now that looked like our only way to keep our heads intact.

"I said capture, not kill!" Gored slammed a bloody fist into the elf that had almost decapitated me. He caught the sword while the other elves descended upon Stone. Feet flew everywhere, dancing just on the edges of the ward while I struggled to find my footing.

Gored tossed the sword from one hand to the other as he advanced. "You're rather powerful for an angel's pet. No wonder he kept you."

"Stay back or I'll burn your head off!" I threatened, one palm up.

"Witches don't need both hands," he said and swung for my wrist.

I slammed my foot back, then remembered the ward. The split second of shifting completely threw off my weight. As I moved to adjust, a hand clamped on my arm. Blue fingers squeezed so tight bruises formed and I crashed to my feet. Still, the arm wouldn't give up.

"I've got her," Nym cried.

"Excellent work, my son," Gored crowed. "Now take her to the orb and chain her arms and legs up."

No! Nym nodded enthusiastically about the idea of witch bondage. I scraped my nails down his arm, digging into the glowing scars, but he kept pulling.

"The rest of you, cut off the Wayfarer's head. And quickly."

I had to fight him. At first I thought to lie down and force him to drag me, but that'd ruin the ward. Popping to my feet, I pulled back. It'd probably have done something against a human who didn't have a hundred pounds on me. The elf barely blinked and reached a hand over to grab my other arm and bind it.

Something. Anything. My spell book? I groped into my purse, fighting against the drag and also trying to keep from smudging the ward. "Stop squirming and give in to Bramble's will!" Nym whined like I was the bad guy.

He reached in to wrap his arms around my waist. My feet left the ground and I had one shot. My fingers clenched around something hard in my bag and I swung. A low metal toll echoed from me slamming it into the back of Nym's head. He opened his arms like I expected, no doubt nursing one hell of a goose egg.

I landed on my feet and prepared a spell, but Nym was frozen. He glared at his hands and started to shake. His body shivered between the magical fire and, with a great roar, he raised his head up and screamed bloody murder. As he did, the back of his face peeled open. Horrified by his skin flapping off his skull, I stared at what was in my hand.

A horseshoe? Ink gave me a horseshoe?

Because they're made of iron. Grinning madly, I leaped for the other elves, swinging my little weapon. They saw what I had done to Nym and scattered back. Only Gored made one more play for Stone, which was when I pressed the tip of the horseshoe to his skin. It blistered in an instant, creating a burn that cut to the bone.

He tried to fight it, his forehead beading in sweat, but he couldn't. Screaming, he tumbled back.

"That's for trying to take my hand, you fucking asshole!" I shouted. "Anyone else want some shoe to the face?"

I waved the threat gleefully, ready to take them all down, when an unbreakable hand wrapped around my wrist. It locked my arm to my side, rendering my horseshoe useless. Stone didn't stare at me. No, he gazed out at the other elves regrouping just beyond the ward.

"You think so small," he jeered at them. "That was the Bramble's downfall. Slaughter, take, grow fat on the spoils. Leave the ingenuity to your betters. But you became greedy, you didn't want to share any longer."

"Stone. You're hurting me." I tried to wiggle free, but he'd clamped down, bruises popping up under his fingers.

"With this witch, and my legacy, I will do so much more than the Wayfarers ever accomplished. I shall rip apart the realms of the guardians and plant touchstones in the heart of the Celestials' kingdom!"

What the fuck? The others stared as if terrified, impressed and envious. One licked his chops at the idea of raiding from the coffers of the beings that created, well, creation.

"What do you mean with this witch? I'm going home."

He didn't answer.

"Stone? I can't open a portal on my own. It'll kill me."

"You have before, you shall again." He wasn't even listening, just chortling to himself about reviving the grandeur of a family he had never known, a family he didn't give a shit about two days ago. None of this made any sense. *And that's exactly what he needs knocked into him.*

"I want to go home. Please." Carefully, I transferred the horseshoe to my other hand. "Don't do this. I'm begging you." Stone kept staring at the Brambles, paying me no attention. With a whimper, I cried out my last chance, "Raul?"

He blinked, his cheeks falling slack. *Did I reach him?* The mad cloud over his eyes faded as he turned to me.

Smiling patiently, I smacked him with the iron.

Chapter Thirty-Two

Raul

In a flash, the dedication to my ancestors that'd fused into my marrow faded away. I blinked and pain shattered my jaw. The scream started in the bottom of my lungs, but by the time it reached my teeth, the sheer agony froze me in place. Numb, I raised my hand, terrified to find my entire lower jaw dangling by a strip.

Her palm came flying out of nowhere. I clenched my body, prepared for a slap to tear off what remained of my mandible. But as she settled a touch above, a cooling sensation froze then blew away the pain. "Don't move," she said.

"How bad is it?" I asked, surprised to find my jaw worked and it only stung a little to speak. Her magic worked fast.

Layla shrugged and cast a look at the other elves. "Not as bad as theirs. This thing can seriously fuck them up." She raised the horseshoe closer and I jerked back, terror clawing up my legs.

"What did I say about moving?" She locked her hand behind the back of my head and pinned me in place. The deadly piece of iron sat on the ground, no elf daring enough to draw near. I glared at it, certain it would fly up and tear me to pieces.

"How's that?" Her hand slipped off my cheek while she rustled her fingers against the nape of my neck. I tensed my jaw, prepared to tell her it was fine, when I looked into her eyes. They'd slipped from shrewd and enraged to flushed with concern. *For me? The man who almost...*

The idea chased around in my brain like someone else's thoughts, someone else's memories. I was going to chain her up the same as the Brambles, use her magic to grow an empire for people I didn't know, in a realm that meant nothing to me. If not for her, I'd have been lost to whatever spell this elven blood had put me under.

I reacted without thought. Cupping her chin, I tipped her head back and kissed her. Magical fire surged around us, the ward pulsing with the power of realms. As her tight lips softened, the fire grew, shifting from purple to red. The light danced between my shut eyelids while I drew my tongue across her parting mouth for one last taste.

"Thank you," I said, pulling back.

It took her a moment to open her eyes, her cheeks adorably flushed. She absently patted her hair and nodded. "Well, I did hit you. Only seemed fair I fix...you."

The sound of sharpened blades drew us back to the elves. Not about to be put down by a horseshoe, the

Bramble clan were regrouping for one last attack. Though Nym didn't look like he'd be frolicking in a forest anytime soon.

I balanced my weight, wishing I had a weapon on me. "I meant for hitting me."

"Well, if it'd all been an act, I was gonna hit you again." It oddly charmed me to know the witch wouldn't have hesitated to beat that brainwashed version of me to a pulp. Layla bent down and clenched the horseshoe in her fist like the world's strangest brass knuckles. "You got any idea what we do now?"

"Take down the enemy, then reassess our situation?"

The Bramble clan circled around the ward, each wiping their own blood on the tip of their weapons. As they did, the metal glowed a terrifying red-white color. The fading voice warned me it'd be twice as hot as it looked.

"Okay, question about the first part of that plan. How?"

A screaming elf leaped for us, twin daggers drawn. Without thought, I snapped my hand out for him and a massive pile of thorns ripped up from the ground. They clenched around his body, capturing him outside the ward. I stared at my fingers, shocked I could do that, when I heard a clang. Layla was swinging wildly, bashing into the swords and pikes. The elves knew better than to get close to her, but they didn't have to. All she had to shield herself was a bent piece of iron.

"Keep fighting, Wayfarer, keep exhausting yourself. There are hundreds of my clan waiting to tear you to pieces. And many more clans that your family cut out of the deal spotted your obvious call."

"You set this up on purpose?" Layla shouted at me.

"It was the only way to lure them out. It wasn't me doing the thinking," I shouted, not wanting to explain the insane voice in my head.

Set this up...?

"Can you put up your shield again? And raise the fire?" I threw the elves back and slammed my hand down. A wall of thorns burst through the ground giving us a second to breathe.

"Yeah, but—"

A spear pierced through the thicket. I latched an arm around Layla's stomach and yanked her down. We fell so hard, I landed on my back and she on top. Scrambling quickly, she rolled until her chest was against mine. My hands piled at the small of her back and she clenched her fists. The waves of magic pulsed out, forming the protective dome twice as strong as before.

For a moment, she wavered and I cupped her cheek. Layla shook off her swoon before it took and stared at me. "Done. But they'll hack through it again."

In the commotion, her cloak had fallen to the side, leaving my hands caressing her naked back. Her legs fell astride mine and her hips pressed just above my crotch, a fact I did not have the time to focus on.

"What we need to do is get out of here."

"Brilliant plan. How?"

"We're in the ward, the magic's working through it."

Her lip curled and she dragged the horseshoe through the grass and raised it. "So help me if you start cackling and talking about raiding other realms..."

"No, it's still... It's me. I want to go home, to earth, as badly as you."

She put the horseshoe down, but pushed off of me. "Small problem, we still don't have a touchstone. A fact you didn't seem to care about before."

Joder! She's right.

The sound of shattered rice cakes broke through the air. They were shredding my thorns, which meant we didn't have much time.

"Without the connection to someone on earth, I don't know what will happen, or where we'll go, but right now anywhere's better than here."

"We'll be back to square one!" she argued even while tightening her shoulders and facing them. Bloody hands pierced through the wall of thorns to drag sections back. Layla raised one fist with a spell and the horseshoe in the other.

"It's preferable to being torn to shreds here," I said.

"They only want to kill you." She frowned at that, her gaze darting to me then away.

They wanted to imprison and use her for her magic. The same torture I'd done hundreds of times to hundreds of witches before. It'd been part of the job... I was saving lives. Consequences were washed down the drain along with the blood.

"I'm sor—"

"Holy shit!" Layla slapped my bare arm. She cupped her locket of all things and stared down at the golden heart. "This might work. If not, we could end up fuck knows where and have no way home. So, maybe not."

"What? What won't work?"

A spear pierced straight through the flames and shield. It cut between us, causing Layla to yelp. I grabbed the wood on the way out. Instead of yanking back, I shoved it forward and heard an oof. Hopefully that hit a solar plexus.

Shaking off her near skewering, Layla ripped off her necklace and stood in the middle of the ward. "I'm gonna try it."

"Try what? You still haven't explained —" The edge of a sword swiped at me. "*Por amor de dios!* I am talking *aqui!*"

The air thickened to soup. I struggled to swallow then breathe as my lungs flattened in my chest. "What?" was all I could cry out before I crumbled to a knee. Suddenly, a lifeboat appeared. Her hand cupped mine and the pressure vanished. I took in crystal-clear air and found Layla caught in a personal whirlpool. Her hair swerved above her head like soft-serve ice cream. She smiled at me and held out her locket as if that'd explain anything.

"What are you doing?" I asked.

"Sending us home." Her skin glowed more than usual. More than was typical for a creature of magic. I tried to squint, but even closing my eyes couldn't cut off the immense power flowing through her. The ward picked up the same pulse, the two of them working in tangent.

Far in the distance, I could make out the impotent screams of Gored. He banged his fists against the solid shield, rendered unbreakable by the spell within.

"I will kill you, Wayfarer. You will die the last of your claAAAA!" His threat turned into a panicked squeal as all of the elves were plucked off their feet and hurled away.

I clung tighter to Layla's hand and stepped beside her. My stomach plummeted like I was on a roller coaster, but the ground remained steady. The fall was inside of me and growing larger.

"If this doesn't work—" Layla's voice was both beside and in me. I shivered at her touch reaching through to hold me from my nape to my navel. "I want to go home," she cried out like a prayer.

I bent my head and slipped back to the boy I'd lost in that forest a lifetime ago. "*Dios te salve, María. Llena eras de gracias, el Señor es contigo…*"

The pulse of the spell rose around us, my prayer to Mary eclipsing Layla's for home. An energy rose from her little locket, the tendrils waving in the air.

"*Salve, María.*"

"I want home."

"*Llena eras de gracias.*"

"I want Ink, Cal, Garavel and Daniel!"

"*Lo Siento…*"

The tendrils lashed to our wrists and before I could breathe, we were pulled inside ourselves while our final words floated on the wind.

Home.

I'm sorry.

* * * *

Cal

"This doesn't seem right!" I shouted. My words splattered against the storming winds and spat back at me with the slanted rain. Layla's mother stood outside the ward, her eyes trained on me but vacant, like she was staring through space. Making up the other points were Ink, Daniel and Garavel. They didn't seem to be doing much to open this portal, though Ink kept flicking his nails as if he were about to rush in and shove me away.

Another wind, this time from the south, slammed into my back. My hand jerked, almost flinging the dagger free. I clamped tighter to it with both hands. "At the beach it was a bit calmer. And less, um, that."

Low mooing circled the micro-hurricane around me as a herd of cattle flew. Not too high, their hooves at best a few inches off the ground, but it was hard to look away from hovering cows. "The spell is working according to plan," Isabel declared.

A dark thought entered my mind. What if she wasn't trying to get her daughter back? What if this was another spell, a spell for her, using my blood to power it?

"Ink?" I glanced at him.

He turned so he couldn't face me. "The runes are correct, at least for a summoning."

For a brief flicker, I'd hoped I was right. That she was screwing us over, and we'd find another answer. Ink finally caught my eye. He bowed his head and clasped his hands together. A demon praying for me? Or praying for her? Either way, that was a bad omen.

"Wolf, the wards are lit with all the power I can give them," the witch shouted. "Spill your blood before it's lost."

I didn't want to die. I wanted to hold her again, to press my chest so tight to her back I could feel her heartbeat. To comb oil through her hair as she explained the intricacies of a twenty-year-running anime.

But I couldn't have any of that, no one could, if I lived.

There were no tears. Enveloped in the eye of the raging storm, calm flooded my mind. I loved her. *I love her, and I will love her.* Thinking of Layla, I placed the tip of the dagger to my chest between the ribs. Slowly, I shifted that arm, needing the strength of the wolf to finish it off. Half human-half monster, I'd die for the woman I wanted so badly to deserve.

"Don't!" Daniel's plea made it through the pounding in my ears. "This isn't right." He walked through the wards, touching nothing, feeling nothing. "She wouldn't want this."

"She's not here to get a say."

"You sound like the fucking incubus," he snarled at me.

I laughed and steadied my shoulders. "He's not so bad, once you get to know him."

Daniel reached out to take the knife from me. His hand passed right through. "Son of a... Think, you damn idiot!" He tried again, this time aiming to take control of my hand clutching the knife, but he couldn't possess a werewolf. "Something feels —"

He jerked to the side as if someone had shoved him. Daniel jerked again, this time to the right. "Cal, for the love of god..."

"The ghost is throwing off the ward." Isabel waved her hand and the flames that'd ignored him before wrapped around Daniel's ankles. They raised him up, as if to hurl him away, when his arms suddenly flung straight out. "The magic is breaking down. We will not have another chance. Wolf!"

I love her.

I'll see her again. One day.

With Layla's smile in my mind, I pulled the dagger back. A thud slammed into my back, hurling me forward. The storm roared as I collapsed. Every fire raging in the field, every light burning in the sky, every twinkle in this life went black.

Chapter Thirty-Three

Layla

Cold cut through the bitter darkness, freezing my eyelids shut. My fingers could barely move as I tumbled faster and faster to god only knew where. It felt like a lifetime and also a blink. A voice echoed in waves, one word catching on another and reverberating in my head. I couldn't understand it, but I chased the sound and dove.

"Sonofa…!" I landed hard on the ground, the wind knocked clear out of my lungs. Heat ripped away the cold and light pierced through the shadow. A light that was just like the wards I'd left behind.

No. It hadn't worked. We were trapped in Terrabail and about to be ripped to pieces by those fucking elves.

A frozen tear pierced its way out of my duct and clung to my cheek. There it froze in place as the pain of the in-between clamped onto my fingers and toes. I whispered the healing spell to myself without looking up. It was our last chance, Hail Mary, and I had guessed wrong. As the healing magic worked its way through my system, my fingers unclenched and the light of the runes glinted on the golden heart.

I'm sorry. I tried to get back to you.

"Layla?" Brown eyes brimming with shock stared at me. Not green ones clouded with Machiavellian madness. I choked and raised my chin as Daniel... It was Daniel! The coolness of his hand caressed under my head and I cried out.

Arms scooped me up off the ground. They pulled me away from him. I reared back to fight them off, when familiar black claws brushed down my cheek. "Ink?" He loosened his hold enough I could turn in place. Holy shit, his smirk!

"Hello, my bond," he said as if we'd only been separated for an hour.

Clasping my hands around the back of his neck, I buried my face against his shoulder and cried. He rubbed a soothing hand over my back. I snorted out a bubble of snot on his nice shirt. "I'm afraid I'll need a few before the orgy."

I expected a crass joke, maybe about how he'd been trying to talk the others into a sausage party with him. But Ink only held me tight and whispered in my ear, "Take all the time you require. You are here, as are we."

He had to be starving, but he didn't even push for a kiss. I tried to wipe my blurry eyes on his shirt, but Ink's hand caught my attention.

A strip of cloth covered in black ichor was knotted around his palm. "You're still bleeding?" I asked.

"Concern yourself not, my bond. I feel no pain—" He cupped my cheeks and pushed back my hair before clasping me to his chest. "No longer," he whispered against my ear before looking up. "Garavel? Could you be so kind?" He passed me off to my angel.

Beaming, Garavel scooped me up like I was a bride. A little meow echoed from behind his wings. He leaned closer to press his forehead to mine. "I knew you'd find a way back."

It had been touch and go so many times. I couldn't stop shaking, my heart pounding fast. I wasn't just home, I was in their arms. They were here. Except...

"Where's Cal?" I turned to finally take in the scene. We'd popped out exactly where we had left, the standing stones still up. The magical fires doused on the ward dug into the wet mud. They must have reached out to a witch. I gritted my teeth, knowing who it had to be, but my mother wasn't my priority.

As I tipped my head to the side, I spotted a pair of dark jeans lying behind the altar. "Cal?" I cried out, dropping to the ground. Garavel let me go while Ink stood nearby.

"Lady witch, perhaps it would be best for you to sit," Garavel called but I waved him off.

I can walk, I can get to him. Whoa! The wooziness struck again, twisting my stomach into a knot. "Sweetheart? Are you okay?" My knee gave out, and I crashed to the ground. Crawling on hands and knees, I approached Cal, who was face down in the dirt. Had their spell worn him out that badly? I reached out, calling to him.

"Ink!" Daniel shouted. That was the first time I'd ever heard him use Ink's name?.

Why were they all standing around staring at me? No, not at me, at Cal? *What the hell's...?*

"Babe?"

Relief I couldn't explain flooded through me. Cal propped himself up on his elbow. He reached a shaking hand to me. When I took it, he hissed in pain. "You're hurt!" I cried out as if that was the greatest injustice in the world. Something had sliced along his palm.

Cal didn't even notice. He struggled to sit up while I whispered the healing spell.

"I hate it when you get hurt," I muttered.

He pulled his hand from me in order to place both to my cheeks. I watched the wound seal up as he drew both his thumbs over my cheeks. Tears rained in his brightening eyes. "I never thought I'd…"

I flew to his chest, Cal hugging me as tight as possible. His heartbeat was always steady as a drum, but tonight it fluttered in a racing panic.

Ink slipped by quietly, as if I wasn't supposed to notice him picking up a knife with a dash of blood on the edge. "Is that what did it?" I asked, relieved and angry at the same time.

Shame crashed Cal's face as he turned to Ink awkwardly holding the blade.

"For fuck's sake—" I lightly smacked his arm, then pulled him back to me. "Leave the knives to Garavel. Okay?"

Cal began to shake, his sobs buried against my shoulder. In the middle of it I heard him say, "Okay." One by one, all of my guys took a knee and wrapped their arms around me. Even Daniel reached through the pile of limbs to caress his cool palm over my cheek. *They're here, alive. I swear, I'm never losing them again.*

"Your elf is escaping." My mother's cold tone jerked all of us out of our love fest. Ink was the first to leap into action. He lashed a hand around Raul's wrists and pinned both arms behind his back.

"Let go, demon, before I make your existence a living hell."

Ink didn't even glance at him, but looked to me. With one hand pinning Raul, he raised the dagger. "Shall I dispose of him here or down the road?"

"No!" I scrambled to get my feet under me, tearing apart the wet ground. Garavel took one arm, and Cal the other. They helped me up and I dashed to Raul's side. "Ink, let him go."

He raised his chin and laughed once. "Unless you have a pair of shoes requiring cobbling, that seems unwise."

"That's leprechauns, you horn-headed, cloven-hoofed *cabrón!*"

"Those are saved for party tricks and Saturday Dom nights," Ink said without a care, but Raul froze and stared right at me.

A single knock of guilt stabbed me, but what did I have to feel shame for? *Oh wow, I fuck my incubus. Who could have guessed?*

It was when the guilt crossed Raul's face that Ink leaned close and…sniffed him? As he pulled back, he glared at me and his flesh turned demonic.

"Ink. I can explain—"

"I'm confused. Why is there an elf?" Cal asked.

Staring into my eyes, my demon clamped a hand to Raul's jaw and tensed his arms as if he was about to snap his neck. I threw out a spell without thinking and shouted, "He helped me!" Ink's arm was trapped in place, but I knew he could shake it off in a second. He'd done it before. "Please, let him go."

I had to trust he'd listen and shook off my magic. With a snicker, Ink released him and shoved Raul. He skidded on his feet and I reached out to catch him, only for the elf to turn back on the demon. "I will banish you to the fiery pits of Tartarus."

"Tartarus is a land of smoke. The doomed souls enjoy a barbecue of the damned for all of eternity." Ink shifted on his hooves and he embraced his full demon look while squaring off with Raul.

"So you know a few tricks," Raul said. "*Yo también.*" He raised his hands and thorns shuddered from the ground. They lashed for Ink, who swiped at the first round with his tail, but another struck from behind.

"For fuck's sake, don't you hurt him either!" I shouted and cast fire, burning the thorns to cinders. As the flames licked across Ink's body, his clothing turned to ash and he slotted back to his human form. His completely naked human form. I tried to focus my ire on Raul, but my eyes drifted down the man I hadn't seen in two weeks.

Ink winked when he caught me.

"Are demons at war with elves?" Cal asked Garavel. The angel shrugged.

"Look closer, Calvin. Take in his withered chest, his flaccid arms and his gnarled face."

Oh my god…

"This is the witch hunter in his true form."

"That's Stone?"

Raul shuddered and I stepped in. "He doesn't want to be called that anymore. And he's not a witch hunter."

"You heard that from those wrinkled and desiccated lips?"

Jesus, Ink would not let up. He dug a fist into his hip and jutted it out, causing his cock to sway like a metronome. I did my best to ignore his distraction. "There's a lot more going on, okay. And…"

I'd been so focused on the 'if' that I hadn't stopped to think what would happen when we got home. He was my enemy. He'd tried to chain me up and use me not even five minutes ago. But the witch hunters would kill him if they saw him like this. He had nowhere to go.

"My bond, your heart is lying to you," Ink interrupted before I even spoke. He caught my arm and tried to pull me to him, but I refused to move. Instead, Ink came to me and made certain to press his cock against my back for good measure.

Scoffing, Raul stared up at the naked man. "A jealous incubus. I didn't think it possible. She's got you completely wrapped around her finger."

What the hell?

Ink leaned closer, his fingers catching on the bruises left by all the other murderous elves. "If you believe I will not kill you because she says, then sleep with both eyes closed. I'm not one for a challenge."

"Pride goeth before a fall," Raul taunted, and Ink leaned so close I feared he'd either punch or kiss him.

"I've found the lack of a ground is also a necessity. Shall we see if elves can fly, witch hunter?" Fires burned in Ink's eyes and I wrapped a hand around him, trying to tug him back, but he was rooted to the ground. To my exhaustion, Raul raised his hand and there was a god damn demon-pinning ward in it. Where had he been keeping that? They both squared off, ready to tear each other to pieces, and all I wanted was a warm bath and warmer bed.

"Ink...please? Don't do this."

"Why do you not ask the elf to disarm himself?"

Curling my body around the side of his, I whispered in his ear, "Because I don't think he'll listen."

"And you believe a demon will?" Raul scoffed.

"I have faith."

Ink closed his eyes and smoke puffed from his lashes. The fires were gone, and he pulled his man illusion back on. "I do not have to beat you—" He slapped a hand to my ass and hauled me onto my tiptoes. As his lips crashed to mine, Ink traced his tongue between my parting heat and danced inside my mouth. After I had gone without for two weeks, the desire burst inside of me like a volcano. I could barely keep my body upright as my mind melted down my spine and my skin screamed for his touch.

With a quick pop, Ink broke the kiss. He released my ass and let me fall to my flat feet. Throwing on his douchiest smirk, he glanced to Raul. "...To win." I grumbled at him using me to score a point against a witch hunter, but Ink kept rubbing my back in a comforting instead of possessive way.

Raul glared from Ink to me. Then he laughed and shook his head. "Never bet against the house when playing cards, or an incubus when playing hearts." Turning, he began to walk away.

"Are we just gonna let him leave?" Cal asked. "Ain't he dangerous? Babe, they know about you. He knows about you."

Yes, and I had questions he needed to answer.

Pushing off of Ink, I dashed for the stalwart elf wandering alone in the field. "Where are you going?" I asked.

"That's not your concern. I doubt your werewolf's house will try to kill you."

My guys asked a chorus of what, but I ignored it and took another step closer. "You can't do this alone. You're...you're still green." With an exasperated sigh,

Raul lifted his hand and stared at the verdant skin tone. "You'll stick out. They'll find you."

"Concern for my wellbeing, witch?"

"I didn't hit you with that horseshoe just so I could escape."

He blinked, his cocky smile falling to a frown. "Perhaps it'd be better for the both of us if you had."

Probably, but if this past year had taught me anything pretending my feelings away only made shit worse. I was too tired to fight them, no matter the storm it'd cause. "There's a couch. You can at least get a good night's sleep. We can work together to take down Conquest and Zimmerman."

Raul rubbed his shoulder and rotated his arm. With his eyebrows perched, he pointed behind me. "I do not suspect I will last the night under the roof with them."

Seriously? I only looked quick, but for a brief second, I caught the glares from everyone, even Garavel. Had they been stewing, thinking Raul had pulled me into the elf world? They did have a long time to worry.

"Your concern is touching and…surprising."

Ink snorted. "He knows Layla as well as he does the risk to a solitary elf in a world of iron."

That was a good point I had forgotten about, but Raul didn't even look at Ink. He only focused on me. "Zimmerman is my concern, not yours. I shall handle him in due course."

"What about Conquest?" That threat was growing and for all the times we had stumbled in and mucked up one of his plans, god knew how many had succeeded. Time was not on our side.

He couldn't answer that. None of us had a plan to stop the apocalypse. There were surprisingly no prophecies, no ancient scrolls, not even a note scribbled on the back of a Burger King receipt to tell me how to save the world. We had to make it up as we went.

Raul tipped his head and turned to walk away. "Conquest is a problem for all who breathe. If we are to fight together, the fates will have a say." He faded into the darkness, his green skin blending in with the summer fields doused with fresh rain. I tried to follow, but even the shift of grass vanished.

"You sound like a pompous twat," I shouted to what could be empty air.

A single laugh struck from the shadows. "*La próxima vez que nos veamos, te follaré tan fuerte que olvidarás todos sus nombres.*"

"I and the wolf would be quite entertained in seeing you try, witch hunter," Ink shouted. If Raul heard, he didn't give a response.

"Er? What did he say?" Cal asked me, who shrugged, then Ink.

"I shall explain it—" He stopped glaring in Raul's direction as if planning to abduct him and looked to Cal. A strange energy passed between them, Ink's armor chipping away. "—when you've sprouted gray hair upon your chest."

What the hell was that all about?

"Laylee?" My mom closed her book. The wind swept back her braid and my legs wobbled.

The nine-year-old girl ran for her mother's arms. It wasn't until my head landed on her shoulder that my heart remembered what she'd done. "You're here? I thought you hated them."

"Baby." She patted my back and whispered in my ear, "I will do anything to save you."

An unexplainable shiver trembled up my spine and I slipped out of her hold. My mom let me go without argument. For a beat, her gaze darted to the men walking closer and she said solemnly, "Walk carefully, Laylee. Magic cannot shield your heart."

Cal reached me first and curled his arms around me. The steady pulse of his heartbeat against my back pulled all the exhaustion up my body. I wanted to collapse into his arms, or Ink's or Garavel's, and sleep for a hundred years.

"We should get you to bed."

"I might need a bath first," I muttered, liking the sound of that.

"To remove the stench of elf from you. It is as if you ran bare-naked through an onion patch." Ink groaned and raised his nose. I lifted my arm to take a sniff, when my bag slapped into my hip.

My phone. I had to ignore the pleasing hands of my guys to pick it up.

"Layla? Babe? What are you doing?"

"Maybe if I call my professors, or the school, I can explain where I've been." Oh blessing from on high, a satellite signal and Wi-Fi. I searched up my college's contact number, when Cal dropped a hand over the screen.

"Why are you calling the school?"

"Or should I contact Dana first? She's got to be threatening to tear the realms to pieces over this."

"My bond...?" Ink draped a hand over my shoulder. Rather than remove it, Cal took my phone.

"Hey!"

"My lady witch, how long do you believe yourself lost?"

"Well, it wasn't easy to keep track when I was trapped in the elfy manor, but fifteen, maybe sixteen days?"

Cal's lips twitched and his eyes opened in horror. He wrapped his hands around my cheeks and pulled me close. "Babe, it's Sunday."

"Which Sunday? Is it August?"

Garavel circled a hand around my ear and clung to my shoulder. "From our perspective, you were trapped for the rise and fall of the sun."

"Time has a way of warping in the other realms. One year here can be a century there, and vice versa," Ink said.

"One...? I was so worried about all of you." I looked past Ink to catch Daniel's eye. He'd been quiet, as if he'd had no part to play in this, but if it wasn't for him, I wouldn't have made it back home.

"I'm so sorry you had to go through that," Cal said.

Tears fell but I smiled through them. "You only had one day, thank god. I mean, without me..."

"Yes, we'd likely fall to barbarism and tear each other to pieces within a matter of days," Ink said.

I locked both my arms around Ink's neck and Garavel's, pulling the angel and demon to me for a hug. Cal swept his arms around my waist and he pressed his forehead to mine. "Let's get you home."

Raising my head, I looked for my mom, my heart aching for her hug. But she'd vanished again.

Holding my men tight, I whispered, "That's all I've wanted to hear for weeks."

Chapter Thirty-Four

Layla

I walked out of my first day at the hospital, dead certain I could only dig ditches for the rest of my life. My assigned nurse seemed to feel the same. Absolutely nothing had gone right and, after twelve hours on my feet, all I wanted was to crawl back under the covers.

"Layla?"

Even as my ears figured out who it was, I glanced at the family carrying a balloon bouquet instead of the shadow lurking by the cars.

"There are a lot of people around here, Daniel," I said. *It's my first day and I don't need them seeing me talking to thin air. There's probably a mark on the forms for crazy nurses, right next to incompetent.*

"You're angry with me."

Forgetting the sick and worried moving in and out of the parking garage, I shouted, "No!" Okay, that was more forceful than I'd meant. Daniel winced, his head hanging lower.

We hadn't had time to talk since I got back. Shit, I hadn't had time to talk to any of them. I'd gotten one warm bath, one hot meal then I had fallen asleep on the couch. Someone had taken me to bed. When I had woken up at five for my job, I had found them all sitting in the kitchen whispering together. No doubt they had plans on how to deal with Raul, but that was a problem for later.

This one I could finally face head on.

Reaching into my scrubs pocket, I approached Daniel. "I was angry with you...maybe not angry. Hurt by what you said."

"What? I wasn't threatening to rip your elf toy to shreds like the demon." He looked up as the light from the exit sign glittered off the locket's chain. Daniel graced his fingers over it and I sighed.

"You called me stupid. Said that I was an idiot. I...I know, you probably didn't meant it. Lots of people throw it around, sometimes as a joke. I just... I heard it a lot growing up and you saying it..." I refused to cry. Those tears should have been long since shed—but when a cool breeze touched my cheek, I looked up into his mortified eyes and they fell.

"I'm the idiot. With your... It's not your fault. I never should have called you that. I will never call you that again."

In order to dab my tears away, I had to reach through his hand, my fingers chilling to the bone. Daniel clenched his, as if trying to take my hand, but they couldn't catch. "I don't want you to die."

"I'm not a big fan of the idea either."

"You don't understand. This purgatory, this hell between life and death is... It's beyond torture. I see your lips smile and I can't kiss them. I watch your hair blow and I can't caress it. I hear you laugh, sob, scream and I can't hold you. It's agony. I can't ask you to forgive me for what I said."

Bouncing the necklace in my hand, I looked into his eyes. "No, you can't. Because I did weeks ago." I clasped the necklace around my neck and positioned the heart above mine. "I love you, you fool."

"How? How can you love a man who died years before you were born?"

"It's easy when he looks like you."

His jaw-dropping cheekbones didn't burn because his heart no longer beat, but his eyes gleamed with the blush. "You've risked your life three times now for me. If you do it once more, I don't know if I can take it."

He bunched his hands into fists and the lights began to flash overhead. *Fuck!* "Hey." I reached out, almost touching his shoulder, but if I did it might push him deeper into ghost dementia. Holding my palm above, I said, "We're going to get your body back."

"How can you be so certain?"

So Raul had vanished without the unicorn skin, but I had to have faith so blindingly stubborn that Daniel did too. "Because I still need to hear my song."

He chuckled and dipped his head, causing his blue streak to tumble. If he lived, it'd have caressed my forehead instead of freezing my skin, but I enjoyed the chill I'd almost lost.

A vibration in my bag caused me to jump. "Oh, it's my phone," I said out loud and fished it out. "A text from Cal. No doubt he's worrying himself mad. I'm surprised you didn't all text me today. Or I'd have walked in on Ink with some fake rectal injury. Perhaps a 'doctor, my penis is too swollen, it requires first aid stat.'" I couldn't stop babbling to myself, needing a reminder that I was home, and they were a phone call away.

Babe. To celebrate your first day, meet me at Grizzly's.

The idea of coffee sent a jolt of electricity through my sagging muscles. Though, we had caffeine at home. I started to type to ask him for a raincheck, when Cal beat me to it.

I sent you a ride.

He did...? A great whoomph shoved back my hair and I looked up as Garavel glided into the parking garage. He banked to avoid the cement pylons and landed before me on his knee.

"My lady." He held out a hand like he was proposing, and I giggled at the silly idea.

This was a lot. But maybe they had a right to be overprotective for a few days. I turned to tell Daniel to meet us at Grizzly's, but he'd vanished. We could talk later.

Smiling, I took Garavel's large hand. In one fell swoop, he scooped me into his arms. I nuzzled my cheek against his chest as he walked to the edge of the parking lot. It was hard to feel safer than in the embrace of an indestructible man. As we approached the metal barriers, Garavel flared his wings out. He glanced down at me, partially asleep from his strange heartbeat, and smiled.

We rocketed up over the metal barrier. Then, he tipped us parallel to the ground and we shot out into the dark night. The unforgiving summer blasted away as we rocketed over the roofs of buildings. It was hard to tell at night, but I knew Grizzly's direction by feel like some caffeine sense.

"I think the coffee shop is back that way," I said.

"You're correct," Garavel bellowed. *Please don't tell me they're fighting. They'd seemed to be getting on and...* "I wished to show you something first."

His gentle wings picked up speed, causing me to buck in his arms. I clung tighter as we rose away from the crowded downtown. The lights faded to nothing more than a twinkle below the clouds. I shivered, the heat of summer eclipsed by the chill up here. Garavel thumped his wings hard one last time.

We crested through the last tuft of fluffy clouds and I gasped. The moon hung in the sky looking so near, I felt I could reach out and hold it. Wrap my arms around the beautiful orb and let it float me away like a balloon.

"I thought you might have missed this sight in your exile," he said. I strained in his arms to catch his eye. Was this what he'd do after his angel let him out of the dungeon? Garavel gazed at the view, a hint of a tear catching on his ebony cheek.

"Thank you." I caught the drop before it could fall and pulled him down. Garavel kissed with a tenderness I'd expected, and a wanton hunger that surprised me. I shivered, not from the cold, and his hands slipped up to caress my butt. He moaned as he found my panty line and toyed with the edge below my scrubs.

"Whatever the future shall bring, my lady, I will remain at your side."

Bit cryptic, but we were all spooked as of late. He looked at me as if I was supposed to answer him. After cupping his cheek, I wrapped my hands back behind his neck. "I wouldn't have it any other way."

With a little laugh, Garavel dove, and flew both of us to the heart of the city. I didn't expect many people to be at Grizzly's, but when we landed, there wasn't a single car in the parking lot. Good thing for keeping my angel undercover, less so for the business. Garavel didn't release my legs. Instead, he dropped to a knee, then to both while I got my feet under me.

Garavel smiled wide as he held my hands. "Whatever may come, all I want is your happiness."

"Okay?"

He traced his thumb over my lips, then kissed the tip.

A familiar jangle caught my attention and I turned around to find a silhouette standing in Grizzly's open door. "My bond?"

"Ink?" My hair blew back and the hands holding mine let go. I looked up as Garavel took to the air. "Wait? You can get a hot cocoa here. I think they have donuts too."

"He has played his part." Ink swept an arm around my shoulder and held my hand.

"What part? What's going on?"

My incubus, who couldn't tell a lie, but knew every way around one, pursed his lips and shrugged. "You'll learn soon enough."

"Is this about Raul?"

His hazy expression sharpened to anger. The hot, human skin shuddered momentarily, revealing the demon flesh below—which was also hot in its way.

"We use his personal nomenclature instead of the one bestowed upon him now?"

"It's—"

"Complicated. You humans do seem to enjoy throwing that word around for situations that can easily be remedied, yet you refuse to take your medicine."

"We were...scared. And we fought a lot. He's. He's gone, okay. I mean, it's not like I'm gonna ask you to be his friend."

"Because you've never, say, required an angel and werewolf to share the same roof."

He wasn't going to let this go. Demons had a stubborn streak as wide as the grand canyon. "You're safe from having to grow as a person," I promised. "I don't even like him."

Ink stared at me, the fires in his eyes sizzling. "But you care for him. You understand a piece of him in a way no one else has. That is far more treacherous than any liking."

My chin collapsed to my chest, my arms heavy and legs wanting to give out. "I can't fight with you on an empty tank. Let me get coffee, then we can bicker about human philosophy before you inevitably rip my pants off. Okay?"

For a beat, he smirked as if impressed I knew the endgame. But as I took a step for the darkened café, Ink caught me in his arms and spun me around to face him instead. "What are you...?"

"There is a matter I have yet to discuss with you. That is not about the witch hunter," he interrupted me before I could argue. "Your life. For the past year, you've slapped it together like a knight building his armor from broken plates and discarded food trays."

Rude. But…also kinda accurate.

Ink took my hands in his and he leaned away. At first, he gazed down at where he held me. "Do you consider this arrangement sustainable? If your future plans were to change…" Slowly, he lifted his eyes to mine. "What would change?"

He knew about the damn baby. My mom hadn't contacted me after her vanishing act. But what if she'd told all of them about witches being walking incubators? Did Ink fear I was already carrying the spawn of an elf slash ex-witch hunter?

"Don't worry," I said with relief.

His chuckle was oddly forced. "Demons do not worry."

"Well, you're not a demon," I countered, and he frowned. "But regardless of witch shit, you're good. We're all good." I slapped my stomach with great glee. "This thing is staying empty, at least for now. Nothing's changing, aside from the world maybe ending."

Ink stared at me like I'd gone mad. Did he not know about the baby-rule? "So you are saying that should your world shift? Your future's path diverge, you would keep all of us in your arms?"

I hadn't thought of that. If I did give in to my mother's demands and do as all the witches were required to, at least I'd have four guys of varying degrees of responsibility help out. That soothed the anxiety building in my heart more than I had ever imagined. I wouldn't be alone, no matter what happened with this witch fertility.

Maybe Ink read my desires, maybe he could see it in my face. But before I could form an answer, he enveloped me in his arms and pulled me to him for a kiss. I expected the rush to drown my panties, for his tongue to tussle with mine and his hands to roam. But he closed his eyes tight and his lips softened until his touch was as gentle as the kiss of a rose.

"Ink?" I touched my lips in shock as he pulled away.

"Come, my bond. Your destiny awaits." He took my arm in his and guided me for the café's door. As he pulled it open, I walked into a fairytale.

Tiny twinkling lights and curtains of tulle dangled from the ceiling. Romantic music played instead of the usual indie folk rock. Hundreds of candles danced on the tables pushed to the sides save one directly in the middle. Two mugs sat on the table, both of them filled with coffee.

The lack of people here, or Frank, meant nothing once I saw the promised caffeine. I instinctively dove for the source, when the curtains parted.

"Holy shi—!"

My mind fully blanked at the sight of Calvin Rollin in a tuxedo. The poor fabric was having trouble reaching across his shoulders, reining in his biceps or not ripping at his thighs. But fuck, he was that ridiculously hot groomsman, secret agent and naughty CEO rolled into one.

Cal laughed, his cheeks turning hot pink. He had his palms slapped together to hide something inside. "You made it."

"I did. Thanks for the ride." The coffee was completely forgotten as Cal walked toward me.

"Do you...um, do you remember the first time we met?"

"I remember Dana pointing you out during orientation and whistling so loud the TA stopped talking," I said with a laugh. I'd blushed and tried to hide in my shirt. But the first time we had actually said hello was…? "Here."

"The whole time I kept thinking, 'she'll have a boyfriend.' Though, I'm used to that now."

I laughed at my pile of boyfriends when Cal reached over and took my hand. "I don't know how I found the courage to ask you to sit at my table. How I didn't stupidly slop coffee down my shirt, or shove my foot in my mouth."

"You mean me. I'm the one who almost did that. For months after we met, come to think of it."

Cal chuckled. "Layla, my… Oh, moon, what was I going to say?"

"I don't know." This was so sweet I wanted to pluck him into my arms and kiss him. I tried to tug back, hoping he'd take the hint.

But Cal threw me for a loop as he dipped down to one knee. I laughed at his joke when he held out what he'd been hiding on his palm. "Holy—!" I gasped, covering my mouth.

"I love you. I've never loved anyone that fit me the way you do. Every morning, I can't wait for you to wake up. Every night, I'm going mad until I can cuddle beside you. I didn't think it was possible for me to ache to my soul if I think of my life without you. Layla…" Cal opened the box. Light struck on a burst of purple inside a silver art deco band.

"Will you marry me?"

Chapter Thirty-Five

Layla

Marry?

But his brother hates me. Werewolves in general despise witches. His whole family will probably disown him for it.

Even when I want to, we can't have kids together. Can I force him to live without having any of his own?

What about the others? How will all of this work?

I shouldn't. It wouldn't be fair to him, to all of them.

Cal's smile strained, his balance tipping on the one knee while he held out the ring.

It'll break his heart. It'll break mine.

What do I know about being a wife? Or marriage? I'm going to fuck it all up.

"Layla?"

A thousand reasons why I should say no pounded in my mind. *I don't deserve him. He's in pain. When he heals, he'll want someone else. It'll end in tragedy.*

Everyone I'd loved had eventually abandoned me. I hadn't realized I'd been expecting the same until he got down on one knee and begged me to stay forever. I should call it off, call all of this off. Protect him from the horrors stalking my every step.

"Yes," I squeaked, tears falling from my eyes.

"Really?" Cal jerked in shock. I cupped his cheeks and bent down to kiss him.

"Yes!" I cried again, sealing my pledge against his lips.

He yelped with joy before softening enough to kiss me. I wrapped my arms around the back of his neck.

I love him. Every self-sacrificing excuse was obliterated to dust by that simple truth. *I want him, and I never want to lose him again.*

"Babe!" Cal leaped to his feet, sweeping me into his arms. I clamped on to the back of his neck as my toes left the ground. There wasn't room for him to spin me in a circle, so he settled on swaying back and forth before crashing his forehead to mine. "I had a speech, it was pretty good."

"Yeah? What was in it?"

"That there's no one in this world I've felt so safe with. For the first time, I feel like I can take off the mask and be me, claws and all."

The tears hit me hard. I tried to laugh them off, but they wouldn't stop.

"Oh, shit, I forgot." Cal set me down and glided the ring onto my finger. The round amethyst stone was surrounded by a circle of small diamonds. They glittered like a beautiful purple flower. The band itself was carved to mimic old art deco in white gold.

"What do you think?" he asked.

"It's perfect." I lifted it up to the light and the ring tipped inward. "A little loose, but..." Holding his face, I lost myself in his tearing eyes. "It's the second most beautiful gem here."

Cal groaned. "You stole my line." He kissed me, his hands pooling at the back of my waist, his hips swaying in time with mine. Our lips pressed and caressed as if we had centuries to kiss.

Alas, all good things had to end, and we both needed oxygen. The sight of his pink lips turning red from my touch reminded me how long I'd had to go without him. Without any of them. "Sweetheart?"

"Hm?"

"Is this one of those proposals where all my friends leap out to celebrate?" I asked while drawing my hand down his white shirt. I stopped at the cummerbund and curled my palm around it.

"No," Cal laughed. "It's just us here."

"Good." Leaping to my tiptoes, I kissed him so hard that Cal stumbled into a chair. It hit loudly, but I kept going. I cupped my palm down the front of his pants. When I brushed over the bulge I'd missed for two weeks, we both groaned. Cal worked his hands under my scrub top, tracing his warm fingers across my skin before he delved below my pants. At the swell of my ass, he dug in while I popped open his fly and tugged on the zipper.

I pulled on his waistband, kissing him hard, needing him to my marrow. Cal skirted a finger straight down my asscrack, before he tipped his head back. His Adam's apple nearly landed in my mouth, and I wanted to take a bite.

"Are you sure you want to...now?" He asked that even with his eyes wild and his cock peeking through the shirt curtains. "Shouldn't we do romantic stuff first?"

I nipped the side of his neck. Cal bent his knees so I could bite along his jaw and circle my tongue inside his ear. "I haven't touched you in sixteen days," I whispered, sweeping my fingers up and down his thigh. "Do you have any idea what that does to a woman?"

Cal turned so I could gaze into his eyes. The adorable sweetheart that'd gotten down on one knee shifted to an insatiable animal. His chest rumbled against mine in a growl, stimulating my nipples. He lunged, hefting me off my feet by my ass. I locked my legs around his waist as he dropped me to the table. The cold coffee went flying, but the shattered sounds only made both of us wilder.

Enough of the man remained for him to carefully pull off my scrub top. Oh, I had forgotten I was wearing my graying beige bra, the least sexy one of them all. Cal glanced down at me barely balanced on the table. He caught my wrists and pinned them to the wood. Just as I moved to sit up, he plunged his teeth to the top of my breast.

"Fuck!" The pressure struck fast, pain racing from how hard he'd bitten. But as I squirmed, giving in to his teeth clamped onto me, my body burned. I locked my thighs in, pulling his washboard abs close so I could grind against them. God, my panties were soaked and getting wetter. They had to go.

I tried to slip my hands free to pull my pants off, but at the movement, Cal clenched tighter. His hot breath washed over my cheek as he whispered, "One day without you was torture. I'd die if it was any more. Don't you agree?"

He raised his head to look behind me. I struggled to do that too, unable to see anything but a hint of crimson. A hand reached over me, and the olive skin ripped away to reveal the red and black demon below.

"Indeed," Ink said. He curled his palms under my bra and kneaded my breasts. "Without you in our lives, my bond, we'd lose what little remains of our minds."

Holy damn it all! While Ink teased my nipples by bouncing my breasts and causing them to sweep against my bra, Cal thrust his hips. He'd lost his pants and was slowly undoing the tie. With a coy smile, he slid it off his neck while taunting me with his naked cock. Only my damn scrubs and panties came between me and paradise.

"She enjoys the sight of you stripping yourself of all artifices," Ink declared.

Cal stopped his maddening thrusting. He dug a fist into the table and leaned over me. "Is that so?" With one hand, he undid a button. "Why don't you finish it?"

Why are my hands trembling? The way they watched, the way they hungered made me shiver as I clutched Cal's shirt and popped the next button. He leaned back and I came with. A single claw swept from the back of my neck down my spine before it snapped open every bra hook. Cal darted his gaze to my breasts and drew his tongue across his lips, when Ink nuzzled my neck.

"Oh, god, I need you," I moaned, clinging to his soft waves.

"Which one?" Ink asked. His voice was teasing, but I could sense the fear in his question.

I worked off the last button and tugged Cal's shirt out of his pants. Latched onto his lapels, I pulled my future husband and personal incubus to me. "All of you," I declared before kissing Cal, then turning to bite

Ink's lip. As my teeth sank in with all the force in my jaw, Ink moaned and his human illusion shuddered. I wanted to rake my nails over his demon skin, to grip his horns while he ate me out.

Cal tugged off my pants and underwear in one quick go. When the cool air struck my soaking vulva, I cried against Ink's lips and he smiled.

Gripping the base of his huge cock, Cal circled the tip around my pulsing labia. He glided the shaft back and forth, drenching it in my arousal and stimulating my clit. With a little laugh, Ink plucked off my bra and — from behind — dove tongue first to my nipple. He playfully toyed with my nub while my body cried out for more. I moaned, trying to thrust my chest out for Ink and grind back on Cal. Then Ink pulled a huge power play — he split his tongue in two, and circled the forked tips around my nipple.

"You son of bitch!" I shouted. "Why are you hiding shit?"

"To keep you guessing," Ink said as he switched to my other breast. I was gone. I could fight off the orgasm for a few seconds, half a minute at the most. But they had me in their clutches and I'd never been happier.

That was, until the bell rang.

I reached a hand back, expecting to find this was all a dream, but I smacked into the naked thigh of my incubus. A flash of white caught the corner of my eye. Both Ink and Cal paused as I looked back at the intruder.

"Garavel," Cal greeted him.

"You've come to join in, I pray," Ink said to him, extending a hand.

"My lady." Garavel's breath was hitched as he walked over. I staggered up onto my elbows, prepared to smooth this mess over, when I caught the unmistakable tent in his angelic trousers. He threaded his fingers through my hair and pulled me to his forehead.

"I ache for you," Garavel whispered before kissing me.

"Don't we all," Ink said with a laugh. "Calvin? Shall you sit back and enjoy the show?"

Werewolf and angel in the same room fucking me? Were they going to kill each other? I bit my lip, knowing if they made me choose for tonight, I'd have to pick Cal. But he wrapped a hand around his cock, and a sly smile rose on his flushed lips. "You have no idea how much I will."

Disrobing at lightning speed, Garavel only broke eye contact as his shirt flew off. I strained my leg out, trying to trace my foot up his bare skin. He caught my ankle and drew his palm up my calf for my inner thigh. Ink claimed the other side, using his damn tongue to flick over my nipple.

"Come along, angel. The feast is flushed and nearly fit to burst."

Garavel ignored Ink's invitation and kissed me instead. As his soft lips fluttered against mine, bliss slipped down my spine. I leaned back as Garavel kissed the top of my breast. Ink slipped below, then on cue, both men sucked on my nipples. Garavel's was soft and tender while Ink practically bit down, the edge of his fangs drawing along my throbbing flesh. I fisted my hand in his hair, and rubbed my other palm over Garavel's smooth head.

"Only a fool would turn down the ripest of melons," Ink whispered against my skin. He teased his fingers up the sides and lapped more into his mouth. I squirmed, rocking the table on its wonky leg. It pitched under me, sending my nipple deeper into Ink's mouth, then Garavel's while hooded werewolf eyes watched from the side.

Angel and demon pushed their hands under my back, arching my spine as one gave a final tender kiss and the other flicked then bit my nipple. I cried, my heart pounding. If it'd just been Ink, I'd have lost control. But the combination kept me on the edge, my skin humming and blood throbbing to my core.

Lazily, Ink turned and lay his chin against my ribs. He peered up at me and said, "But it'd take a man of madness to forgo the nectar of nature's sweetest peach. My unassailable compatriot?"

A blush burned across Garavel's glowing skin. Together, the two of them kissed down my stomach. Meanwhile they drew their hands across my back, lifting my lower half up so they could caress the top of my ass.

Garavel swerved to the left, and Ink the right, both kissing around my hips. Their hands swept out from under me, taking my thighs. I pointed my toes in expectation, but they ignored the offer and each man placed my leg on their shoulder.

A yelp slipped from me as angel and demon hauled my ass off the table. My head went flying for the Formica, but warm palms caught me. Blinking, I looked up to find Cal staring down at me. His eyes were dark with desire and he bent over to kiss me. I tousled his hair through my fingers, pulling him for that last reach.

Just as I was about to touch his lips, one tongue slicked up my taint while another circled over my clit. "Fuck!" I gasped against Cal's mouth. Instead of pulling away, he kissed me hard, plying my mouth with his tongue while Ink and Garavel licked every inch of my splayed pussy.

Cal locked onto my wrists, pinning them back behind my head. It broke our kiss and he stared not only at me struggling to maintain my sanity but the two men between my legs. "Are you close?" he thundered, his voice panting with every syllable.

No. Yes. Fuck, yes!

Garavel's lips pressed against my vulva, pulling me from the lustful fires to heavenly serenity. Then Ink would shiver his forked tongue against my clit and I'd plunge straight back to hell. They were too much, it was maddening, my heart pounding so fast it'd pop. I couldn't think, my mind focused on the men switching so Garavel tenderly kissed my clit, while Ink tongue-fucked me as hard as his cock.

It was bliss and torture in one. I clenched my fists in Cal's tight hold, trying to grind on both their faces. *I'm close, so fucking close. It just needs one more. One more lick, one more suck.* I tried to thrust, but my ass dangled above the floor.

Then teeth bit into my breast, hard and deep. They shifted from flat to sharpening fangs, nearly puncturing my skin. A steamroller wouldn't have hit me as hard as my orgasm. I tensed up, my legs locked around both Garavel and Ink, dragging them together as they pressed their tongues to my clit. And Cal, he licked his tongue over my bite, gently kissing the wound.

It felt like his teeth pierced all the way to my heart, but in a good way. Cal let go of my arms and I snaked one back to hold him by the hair. Pressing his mouth tighter to my throbbing breast, I hissed in his ear, "Do you have any fucking idea how hot that was?"

He chuckled. "I may have missed it. Would you mind doing it a —!" Cal jerked as I managed to cup his cock. Around was impossible, but I corkscrewed my palm, my thumb straining to close off his huge girth.

"My turn," I said, flushed with power. Cal struggled to keep his hips frozen. He had to clamp both his fists to get them to stop, but he didn't go for my hand.

"My lady, I'm nearing the apocalypse." Garavel moaned.

Ink swung out from below my leg. "Please, angels first." He took his spot at the side, his cock rod-straight while he watched with wicked curiosity. Garavel didn't even glance at Ink, all his focus on me.

"My lady, my heart," Garavel cried out as he thrust inside of me. Heat pooled in my spine and washed down my thighs. I tried to grind back on Garavel when he pulled me further off the table. My hand slipped off Cal, who groaned at the loss. I looked up at him, his cock slick with pre-cum and the tip dangling just beyond my head.

As Garavel started moving faster, I strained to lock onto Cal's thighs. He stumbled forward and I sucked the tip of him into my mouth. "Fuck, Layla." He shivered, his pale skin burning up his chest as he tugged on my nipples. I rolled his balls in my palm while Garavel kept pounding into me.

"Lady, there is none more deserving of us than you!" Garavel cried out. He locked his hands around my crossed ankles, pulling and pushing me so I kept sucking more of Cal down my throat. God, my jaw was aching. I'd almost forgotten how huge my werewolf was.

I have this. Breathe through my nose, don't think about choking. Then Ink had to go and finger my clit. A gasp ricocheted through me, nearly sending Cal's cock to my stomach. At the last second, Garavel yanked me clean off the table. He held me in his arms, bouncing the both of us as he screamed incoherently with his orgasm. As the tremors of pleasure passed, he buried his face against my neck and kissed me.

My cheek pressed to his smooth head, my heart slowing from matching his thrusts. Buried so deep in his embrace, Garavel whispered and only I could hear, "I love you, my lady."

I gulped, but before I could respond, Ink picked me off of him. "An excellent showing, but please take a break to compose yourself. Allow a master to work."

Ink kissed me and raised my leg up by my thigh. I strained, my calf nearly resting flat to his chest. He stared into my face and kept teasing me with his cock. The tip would sweep against my flushed pussy before wandering away. "Fifteen unending nights without knowing these lips, this tongue, these instrumental fingers and this intoxicating, overwhelming, highly mountable—"

"Would you just fuck me already!"

He smirked. "With all the pleasure at your disposal, my bond."

I bit my lip, my toes curling in anticipation for him to thrust inside. But Ink lowered my leg to the ground. He drew his hands around my hips and spun me. With unassailable strength, he planted my hands to the table and stood behind me.

"So you may also enjoy the girthy fruit of the wolf," Ink explained as he swept a hand down my spine.

I stared up into Cal's eyes. He'd clenched a hand around his cock. It glistened from the tip nearly down to the base from my tongue. My mouth opened, aching for another taste and Cal gasped. He scrambled closer, pressing his muscular thighs so tight to the table, it almost sent it flying across the room.

He slammed his hands down, pinning the table in place, and guided his tip closer. Suddenly, palms slapped my ass. I jerked, crying out, and two fingers brushed over my clit. "If you think you shall get off easy for forgiving the witch hunter—" He forced my thighs apart, then plunged balls deep into me.

Ink pulled out and slammed into me. I rocked against the table, his slick fingers slipping over my clit in the process. Moaning, he cried out for the whole café to hear, "You don't know your own desires." Leaning over, Ink clenched his palm over my left hand, digging the new ring band into my skin. I whimpered, the pain turning into a jolt of surprising pleasure while he kept thrusting harder than he ever had before.

When cool fingers caressed my cheek, I was surprised to find my eyes had closed. I glanced up into Cal's concerned face. He looked about to throw Ink off me, but he wasn't seeing the whole picture. I needed this. I'd been craving it every night in that lonely mansion. To be punished for giving in to the loneliness, to Stone.

Taking his cock, I sucked it into my mouth. "Holy moon maiden!" Cal shouted. Ink's thrusting sent more of him deeper until Cal was tickling the back of my throat. Tears burned in my eyes from fighting off choking and the flush of desire transformed to a tornado—wild and vengeful.

I screamed for more around Cal's cock, my words garbled while Ink slapped my ass harder. Cal reached for my breasts, but Ink beat him to it. He yanked on my nipples, setting my entire body aflame as my heart twisted inside my chest.

I'm a selfish asshole. I want them all to myself. And I don't care if that makes me a monster. I deserve it!

Ink stopped. Pain flared down my legs and across my stomach from where it'd been beaten into the table's edge. He bent over, draping his chest against my back and slowly cinched his arms around my waist. "My bond." His voice was ragged, as if all the smirking artifice had been washed away. "*S'agapao*," he whispered and kissed my back before pulling out.

Heart pounding, I turned to face him, but Ink was staring at Cal. "I believe she is more than ready for you, bridegroom."

"Babe?" Cal looked to me, and I blushed. Smiling, Cal swept a hand over mine. He caressed the ring, then wrapped our fingers together. I was flushed from two other men's touches, their tongues and their cocks. He held my chin and raised it up. "You are so beautiful while being eaten out, it hurts," Cal said, and he kissed me.

Moving around the table, Cal's eyes didn't waver for a second, and he held my hand tight. "Are you tired?" he asked, gliding a palm down my thigh.

"Of spending fifteen nights without you?" I bit my lip to keep my voice steady. Cal's tender caress paused and he gulped. My eyes drifted to Ink, and Garavel, before returning to him. Pushing up onto my elbows, I curved my legs around his waist and pulled him to me. "You know I am."

"You can make a guy blush," Cal said. He let go of my hand in order to cup his cock.

"I can do a lot more than that."

Holy...! Stars burst in my vision as he lined up the thick crown and pushed in. Even wetter than a swamp in July, my body burned from the waist down.

"Babe?" Cal froze, worry etched on his face.

"She aches for you," Ink declared. He swept his palm up my inner thigh and pulled my leg wider. Oh, blessed relief, the fire faded.

Garavel then stepped up, lifting my leg and opening me wider than the gates of heaven. "Does she not deserve you?" he asked point blank.

Whatever he was talking about flew over my head. I looked to both angel and demon, but it was the werewolf who kept ensnaring my attention. His forehead was beaded in sweat, his jaw clenched as he fought himself for my sake.

Moaning, Cal began to glide his hips back. "I don't want to hurt you."

"Too late."

Daniel?

I'd feared he'd stay away, but he leaned close, resting his chin by my shoulder. The chill chased off the flush on my cheeks, freezing my sweat droplets in place.

"For all the pain we cause without care—" Daniel reached his hands down above mine, cooling my skin. "The pleasure is twice as sweet." He assumed control of my arms up to my elbows. Using my fingers, Daniel teased my already throbbing clit.

My head fell back as my hips moved, trailing the touch. It pulled Cal in deeper. He worked his ass, clenching it to slowly bore through me. Ink and Garavel both swept their hands up my thighs, holding me open for them.

"Fucking hell!" I shouted as Cal worked his shaft all the way to the base. Just thinking about clenching down on it make me ache to my toenails, but also ignited the flame I'd been tending alone for too long.

"Layla?" Cal asked, holding in place.

Daniel parted my fingers, spreading my lips and rubbing the V against my clit. At the same time, Ink's hand kept carrying higher, curving under my ass until his impish pinkie caressed my taint. Garavel unfurled his wings. With great care, he spread his feathers over my breasts.

Wild-eyed, I stared up at Cal. I'd have grabbed him and kissed him if Daniel didn't have my hands. "I fucking love you," I shouted.

Cal laughed and started to thrust. They weren't much at first, maybe a half inch, but as he grew confident, his mega-cock would expel then pound my life back into my body. "I love fucking you too." His thrusting picked up speed, Cal moaning as he jerked harder.

Ink's exploring finger became two circling my ass and toying with the pucker. I fought to keep my eyes open, my body wanting to revel in the pleasure pulsing through it. When I caught his eye, Ink winked. Garavel shook his wing down my nipples, hardening them to the point I wanted to scream for a tongue or finger. And he kept massaging my calf, tending to me in every way he could.

"Oh, *mierda*!" I moaned. "You're setting me on fire."

Cool lips caressed just next to my ear. I shivered at not the touch but the words. "I love you," Daniel declared as he pinched my nipple and flicked my clit hard.

White wings flew up, caressing my face. Cal dug his fingers into my hips, pulling me to him, and Ink... With a cheeky smile, he blew me a kiss, then bit my thigh.

Everything went white. My body burned from my hair to my toes. I opened my mouth to scream, but all the panting had turned me mute. A power surged through me, sending me into shaking, uncontrolled spasms. I clenched hard on Cal's cock, my vagina ravenous for every dollop of pleasure racing through it. He cried out, thrust as deep as possible, then went rigid.

Despite the hot burn, the orgasm lingered. It hummed in my chest, it trembled in my legs, it caressed my face and dripped down to my fingers. I'd never felt so alive, so beautiful, so loved. One by one, each of them let go of me. Cold rushed to fill its place, taunting me that, in the end, everyone was alone.

Sitting up, I caught Cal's cheek. "I love you," I whispered to him, "future husband."

His smile was infectious. "Not as much as I do you, future wife."

"I love you," I said to Garavel, "my guardian angel."

He took my hand and I pulled him close for a kiss. "Your heart is mine, my lady."

"And you?"

Ink smiled and laughed. "Yes, you love the talent in my body from my wiggly fingers to my" — he swayed his ass and a familiar sight waved back — "teasing tail."

Before he could fade behind Cal, I caught Ink and pulled him close. "I do, and lots more," I whispered. His eyes opened, but I kissed him before he could make another smart-ass remark.

Ink tried to heat it up, but my energy was spent, and the retreat of the chill caused me to turn to look. Daniel was drifting away.

"You needn't pretend for now, Layla. I know that I hurt you and it takes time to —"

I hopped off the table. Holding my palm above his cheek, I gazed into his deep eyes. "I love you, Daniel." Leaning forward, I pursed my lips and pressed them to where his would be. The chill didn't frustrate but invigorated me.

No matter what, I was bringing him back. I could marry the werewolf, fuck the incubus, adore the angel and love the man who was no longer dead. God save anyone who got in my way.

Epilogue

Raul

The stones were long gone, but the earth hadn't forgotten. I sifted the dirt through my fingers, feeling the energy that lingered. It tickled my mind, drawing forth the memories that'd haunted my every night since Layla had pulled them free. Death, rebirth — they were one and the same in this place and the trees remembered.

My long ears twitched at the sound, but I didn't react until he pulled back the hammer.

"He said you'd be here."

I dusted my hands off and rose from my crouch.

"But I didn't think you were stupid enough to make it this easy." River's aim of the gun shifted from my brain to my heart.

"Are you here to kill or capture me?"

"Depends on you, Stone."

I cringed at the name. Stone. Because that's what I was to him, to them — a tool to be used to cause pain, to inspire terror, to grow fat with wealth.

"Get on the ground, and I won't have to put a bullet in your heart."

"Be careful. It didn't work so well the last time."

River steadied his aim. He always had been a better marksman. No doubt he'd embed that pure iron directly into my cardiac tissue. Not even a witch could save me. Ten years we'd worked together. He'd seen me take down impossible creatures thousands of times. Yet he had come here with just his pistol in play.

Scratching my nose, I looked into his sunglasses. "River? Don't you think I'd know you'd find me here?"

His mouth dropped open and he turned, but far too late. I unleashed the spell. Thorns erupted from the ground and plummeted from the trees. They clamped around his body, digging tight to his skin.

"Did you know that elves can also use magic? Albeit in small quantities, but a little's all one needs for brewing."

"What...?" River gasped, falling to his knees. "What are you going to do to me?"

The thorns slammed his hands to his chest, causing the gun to fall. I slipped on my wool gloves and picked it up. The aim landed on his skull. It'd be so easy to pull the trigger. To do to him what he had come here to do to me. I tossed the gun deep into the forest and bent down.

Staring him in the eye, I said, "We're going to talk. About Zimmerman, and the hunters and Conquest." He stared defiantly at me, his blue eyes flashing as the thorns crushed his sunglasses. With a sigh, I shoved the needle into his throat and injected the serum.

River gasped until the last of it hit his blood stream, then he became very compliant.

"But first—" I emptied his pockets and frowned at the last call on his phone. Director Zimmerman. Redialing the number, I pressed the phone to River's head and ordered, "You're going to get me a chunk of unicorn skin."

Want to see more from this author?
Here's a taster for you to enjoy!

Happily Ever Austen: Ember
Ellen Mint

Coming October 2023

Excerpt

"I'm Ember Woodhouse, and I've been blessed with beauty, intelligence and a blissful life." Ember leaped in her chair, her arm extended so the gold and diamond bangles nearly snagged the mike. Steadying her chair, she looked to the shadow behind the massive lights. "How was that?"

"Good. Do you want to mention your father?"

"Oh, how could I forget?" Ember flicked her freshly tipped nails against her forehead, doing her best to not smear the makeup. "The Woodhouse name isn't traffic stopping. I mean, we don't have a yacht and there's only the one summer home. We're not *rich*, merely well off."

"Uh-huh." The producer—who'd taken Ember under her wing—rolled her hand for more.

Narrowing her eyes, Ember could just make out the producer with a hand pressed to the side of her headphones while staring at a tablet. "Why don't you tell us why you tried out for this show?"

Again?

The second she felt her smile dipping, she cranked it back up to eleven, then lowered it to an eight. The last thing she wanted was to come across as insincere. "Well, I'm pleased as a punch to be on *Constructing Love*, the only DIY and romance show."

"Yeah, that's...that's fine." Producer Sam scooted forward in her chair, knocking into the three-hundred-watt light that'd been beaming directly into Ember's eyes for the last twenty minutes. "But why pick this show? Is it because your family made their money in lumber? And please answer by including the question."

Smiling to show off her new veneers, Ember straightened her back. "While my daddy's lumber has gone into some of the most famous buildings, that isn't why I signed up."

She'd thought her family connections would be a detriment. Actual construction workers were cut within the first three episodes over seventy-eight percent of the time. The last thing Ember wanted to come off as was a ringer — they got the villain cut every time.

Sloping her shoulder down, she let her gaze wander past the hanging screens keeping her penned in. Behind the camera, a tree branch shook. The red and yellow leaves danced, threatening to tumble right in front of the shot.

"I'm here for love," Ember said in a soft voice.

The producer sighed and jabbed a stylus at her tablet. "Isn't everyone?"

"Not for me," Ember interrupted, causing the woman to look up in surprise.

"Why not?"

Sweat beaded on Ember's brow and she nipped her lip. "Under the tutelage of Miss Shandy — a respected life coach — I am on a sabbatical from sex."

The cameraman behind the black lens snickered. "What the shit's that mean?"

Smiling without a care, Ember declared, "Instead of falling in love, I intend to be this season's matchmaker."

Sam leaned back. "That's a lofty claim. We've only had one successful matchmaker reach the final two."

"I can do it. I recently returned from the beautiful wedding of my sorority sister Anne whom I set up with her future beau. Their love was destined in the stars, but they would have never met were it not for me."

Producer Sam twitched her lip as if she were about to laugh, but Ember was dead serious. "Excellent. Well, why don't you close this interview out by saying, oh, I don't know. I'll craft buildings and make matches on *Constructing Love*."

Were they going to give her the first bumper? Ember raised her shoulders and steadied her back. Lifting her chin, she opened her mouth while still smiling. "I'll cra —"

A massive beam swung from behind, knocking out the PVC pipe holding up the background screen. The entire structure collapsed, revealing the parking lot of an abandoned Home Depot behind them. Ember's heart leaped into her throat. She jerked in the chair, narrowly avoiding the metal beam smacking her in the forehead.

"Damn it!" Producer Sam berated the two guys who were staring at the destruction as if it was some else's problem. "Will you watch where the fuck you're going? We don't have time to reset all of this for the rest of the day. If we don't get them into the woods tonight, she'll have my head. You hear me?"

Two burly men in sagging construction belts bent over and delicately picked up the fallen purple silk. "Sorry," the largest muttered while slipping it into place.

"Okay." The producer ran her hands back through her hair, tugging down the ponytail as she slammed her butt into her chair. "Do the line again."

* * * *

"What's the point?"

The producer below the ball cap splashed with the logo for *Constructing Love* flashed his teeth. No doubt he thought it a soothing smile but the fact only his top lip moved gave him away. He glanced behind to another gaggle of harried but silent watchers, then focused on the man in the hot seat.

"Mr. Knightley... Can I call you Booker?"

He answered by shrugging, his long legs bent wide to fit in the short chair.

"We need you to introduce yourself to the cameras, so America can get to know and love you."

Booker dropped his hard cross and glared directly into the dark, uncaring eye of the camera. "I suspect much of America formed an opinion of me the moment I sat down." He stopped and looked behind him to the paler screen glowing like a nuclear explosion from the massive lights. "Assuming they can even see me."

"Of course they can," his producer said before leaning back in the chair. No doubt he wasn't supposed to overhear him whisper, "Gary, check the exposure. What? Well, get a few lights over there. Sorry about that. We've had a few setbacks as of late."

The scattered gaffers hustled over a huge light, its legs snagging on a cord. They kept pulling, dragging the set of monitors and the producer watching it with. His producer, a far too friendly man named Ash reached over as if to pat Booker on the knee.

Booker shifted his legs before he could touch him. "When will we be arriving at the construction site?" he asked.

"Excited to get to work?" Ash didn't answer. "Ah, says here you've done some work. Anything official?"

Booker glanced to the tablet crammed full of white lies just sparkling enough to be true. "No," he said and the producer kept staring as if he needed more. "I helped my grandmother build a shed once."

"That's so kind of you. Why don't you tell me about her?"

"She's dead." Mr. Knightley's tone dropped to the parking lot cement.

"Oh, well, that... We don't have that down here. Why don't we have that here?" Ash leaned back, furiously whispering with what looked like a fifteen-year-old girl holding ten clipboards. She squirmed at the attention and kept offering up excuses Ash wouldn't take. He looked about to fire her on the spot.

"It happened recently," Mr. Knightly interrupted, drawing the producer's attention and forced smile. "And I'd prefer to not discuss it."

"Of course, of course. We'll be nothing but respectful of your wishes."

Indeed.

Ash fiddled with his tablet for so long Booker began to wonder if this waste of time was over. He slid forward in the chair and reached for the mike they'd wired up under his Henley.

"You're the oldest person we've had on the show."

Booker froze, his fingers wound in the cord, and he stared at the producer, who then tapped a cardboard circle above the camera. Sighing, Booker looked to that instead. "I find that surprising."

"The closest was Mac from season five at thirty-two. You've got him beat by four years. Are you at all concerned how that will affect your showing in the competition?"

"Most people can swing a hammer well into their forties. I'll be fine."

"Ah, but what about — ?"

"Wrap this up!" a voice shouted from beyond the camera lights. Booker raised a hand over his eyes to try to see, when the assistant tapped him on the shoulder and told him to keep his face visible.

His producer complained to what was probably the lead on this farce, "But I haven't gotten anything useable."

A woman with that LA-standard pinched face that looked both thirty and fifty at the same time clamped a hand onto Ash's shoulder and glared over at Booker. "We don't have time, the sun's dropping. We've got to get to the next location."

"He hasn't even introduced himself," Ash sounded panicky, as if the lack of a cheesy line from Booker would spell the end of his career.

The woman glanced once more at Mr. Knightley sitting primly in his seat and turned away. "He's a premiere. Don't worry about it. Mr...Kingly?" She finally looked at Booker like he was a person and not a piece of the set.

"Knightley."

"Sure. Could you please get in the limo? We have a schedule to keep. And you, get your ass to the site. Sam's riding with the contestants and I need a producer before arrival."

Nodding madly, Ash sprinted to his feet, only for his head to jerk back. The headphones pinned to his ears were still plugged in. The woman in charge watched with minor interest as Ash swung backward and crashed into his foldable chair. "Mr. Knightley?" she said, pointing behind him.

Booker got to his feet and tugged on the mike, ready to be rid of the tether. The assistant once again caught his hands and pleaded in a whisper for him to keep it on. If not, then he'd be going home early.

Sighing, he let go, leaving the cursed thing on. Not that it was going to get much from him. In the distance of the parking lot idled a stretch white limo that glinted in the fading sunlight from a recent wash. He didn't care about the glitz or the fame. Nothing mattered to Booker except the work. Stick it out until he could get to the site, put up with this stupid competition and all of this trouble would be over at last.

Play the damn game.

His brother's parting words rang in his head. Casting a glance over his shoulder, Booker glared at the camera and said, "I'm Booker Knightley, and I'm here to win. There? Happy?"

"Uh, we weren't rolling, so... Do you want to do it again?" the assistant asked.

"No."

About the Author

Ellen Mint adores the adorkable heroes who charm with their shy smiles and heroines that pack a punch. She has a needy black lab named after Granny Weatherwax from Discworld. Sadly, her dog is more of a Magrat.

When she's not writing imposing incubi or saucy aliens, she does silly things like make a tiny library full of her books. Her background is in genetics and she married a food scientist so the two of them nerd out over things like gut bacteria. She also loves gaming, particularly some of the bigger RPG titles. If you want to get her talking for hours, just bring up Dragon Age.

Ellen loves to hear from readers. You can find her contact information, website details and author profile page at https://www.totallybound.com

Home of Erotic Romance

Sign up for our newsletter and find out about all our romance book releases, eBook sales and promotions, sneak peeks and FREE romance books!